DEEP CREEK

DEEP CREEK

Dana Hand

HOUGHTON MIFFLIN HARCOURT

BOSTON   NEW YORK

2010

For information about permission to reproduce selections from this book,
write to Permissions, Houghton Mifflin Harcourt Publishing Company,
215 Park Avenue South, New York, New York 10003.

www.hmhbooks.com

Library of Congress Cataloging-in-Publication Data
Hand, Dana.
Deep Creek / Dana Hand.
p. cm.
ISBN 978-0-547-23748-0
1. Snake River Massacre, 1887 — Fiction. 2. Gold miners — Crimes against —
Fiction. 3. Chinese — Crimes against — Fiction. 4. United States marshals —
Fiction. 5. Mountaineering guides (Persons) — Fiction. 6. Métis — Fiction.
7. Murder — Investigation — Fiction. 8. Hells Canyon (Idaho and Or.) —
Race relations — History — 19th century — Fiction. I. Title.
PS3608.A69845D44 2010
813'.6 — dc22   2009015395

Book design by Brian Moore
Map by Jeffrey Ward

Printed in the United States of America

DOC 10 9 8 7 6 5 4 3 2 1

For the two Marys

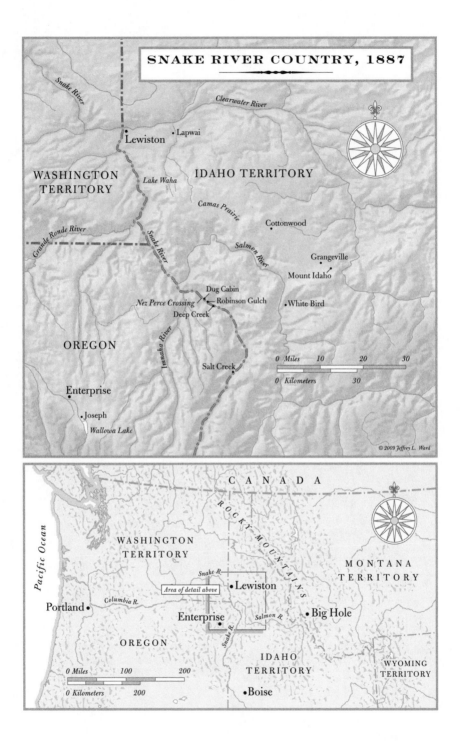

BASED ON
ACTUAL EVENTS

PART I

FLOOD

MAYBE I'LL CATCH a sturgeon," Nell Vincent told her father. "Maybe two."

"Using what?"

Nell held up a twist of frayed red yarn.

"Good choice," said Joe. After five days of rain, the Snake River was running fast and high. The white sturgeon that trolled its depths grew eighteen feet long and could weigh a ton.

Well, nothing beat experience. Nell was small for twelve but hardy, with straight brown braids that fell nearly to her sash and freckles no buttermilk wash could dim.

"Or maybe I'll start with some trout, and work up."

They smiled at each other. Half-dried mud covered the Vincents' best picnic spot, and over on the Washington shore, piles of brush and fencing clogged sandbar and cove. But Nell loved to fish, and Joe figured his youngest deserved a treat, even a medal. Her older brother Lon had spent the week of rainstorm sleeping, her sister Letty, sulking. Nell wanted to collect salt and turtle eggs and homestead in a cave, like the Swiss Family Robinson; she had it all planned.

Beside a young cottonwood, his daughter spread their smuggled feast: six ham biscuits and a jar of lukewarm lemonade. Joe did his best, then stretched out in the patchy shade to recover. A pity he had not brought along some bismuth powder.

3

Nell watched her father sleep. He was a neat, durable man with a shock of coarse gray-brown hair and a lined, clean-shaven face. At the moment he was snoring lightly. He would turn fifty-seven this year and needed his rest. Nell saw no reason to wake him and no reason to wait. She scrambled down the bank and threw out the silk line, swinging it toward open water. To the west, morning sun warmed the low dun hills to copper and gold.

Joe lay on the carriage rug, keeping an eye on her out of habit, but Nell was old enough to cast unsupervised. He went back to sleep, for real this time. Tethered beside the buggy, his bay saddle mare, Trim, nosed at a stand of red willow.

Ten minutes later, Nell felt the hook catch and tug. The rod bent low, then lower.

"Pa, bring the net! I got a big one!"

"Take your time," Joe said, watching a jay stalk the last biscuit. Nell's estimates ran high. Then he heard her agonized whisper.

"Pa!"

He sat up and stared at her catch: an arm rising in the water. He floundered into the shallows to seize the small, bloated body at shoulder and thigh. Long black hair, unbound, trailed over his hands like river weed. *Poor lady, poor lady.* He turned the corpse over, then saw a gunshot wound in the upper chest, the face chopped like cabbage, the genitals hacked away. Nell had thrown in a line and caught a man.

Joe's best fishing rod floated nearby, still hooked to one ear. Upstream he glimpsed another figure lodged in driftwood, pale among pale logs, and ten yards beyond, a third dark head. That victim might never come to shore. Joe saw the north-running current find and take it. Behind him, Nell moaned.

"Get back to the rig, Nellie. *Now.*"

Two hours later, Lewiston deputies had dragged ashore six flayed and battered corpses, all male, all Chinese. Joe looked away as Marshal Harry Akers bent over, hands braced on thighs, breathing hard.

The deputies were country-bred, and Joe a Union veteran, but Akers was a town man.

"Judge, can you take this over? I got a lot to do. A lot."

Joe nodded. He was police judge now, and the Chinese case would land with him anyway. He left a silent Nell at her grandparents' tall brick house on Main Street, then sent a deputy to find the local doctor who doubled as town coroner. Decades ago Henry Stanton, an ex–Royal Navy surgeon, came inland from Vancouver to practice in Idaho's gold country. His neat full beard was gray now, the genial face grim. Joe held open the leather satchel as his friend laid forceps and tenon saw beside the first victim.

"Throat cut," said Henry. "Very slowly. It's butchery."

"Massacre," said Joe.

Three of the Chinese dead were naked and bound hand and foot, faces ripped by animal bites. Maybe canine, maybe feline; the wilder reaches of the Snake River above Lewiston still harbored puma and wolf. All the men pulled from the Snake were shot, though some backs and skulls also bore deep ax wounds. One victim was beheaded, the ghastly cranium wrapped in a ragged blue coat and tied to the waist. The rest were castrated. Two were gutted like deer. A skillful job, said Henry, when pressed.

"Poor devils, poor sad bastards," Joe murmured as he walked the line of shrouded bodies. He knew a crew of Chinese gold miners had wintered up the Snake. He'd even talked to a couple, the morning they left. September of '86? October? His town logs would say. Twelve clothbound ledgers still sat on Joe's desk, one for each year spent as Lewiston's marshal. He should have given the whole set to Akers back in November, as a post-election courtesy, but Joe wasn't that sure his successor could read.

My fault, Joe thought. A river full of dead men. *My mistake.* He pulled the vinegar-soaked bandana back over nose and mouth, then turned a notebook page, slapping away flies. The battlefield stink was getting worse. Beside him the doctor probed and measured, his bare arms dark to the elbow with river mud and human rot.

5

Once they tried to sit beside the Snake and rest, but moments later Henry was wading out again. The deputies had missed one. Joe gave the doctor a hand back to shore, then hauled the dead man halfway up the slope. Maggots, pale and writhing, webbed the nostrils and open mouth.

"Corneas slit," said Henry.

"Before death or after?" Joe asked.

"Before, I suspect."

Together they heaved the sodden weight toward their riverbank morgue.

At sunset Joe crossed Tammany Creek and turned his mare toward the big shingled and turreted house on the hill. He sat on the stable mounting block to pull off his boots, which smelled of corpse. Likely they always would. He glanced up and saw lamplight in Nell's room. His father-in-law, Alonzo Leland, the town newspaper publisher, must have brought her home.

The front door was locked, so Joe went around to the kitchen. The Vincents had lived in this new house only since Christmas. A dozen packing crates still sat in the parlor, leaking straw, and once again the whole downstairs smelled of fresh paint. Lib and the man from Hale & Cooper were deadlocked over the merits of ivory versus cream.

Alonzo waylaid him in the hallway, hungry for a *Teller* exclusive. "What's this about dead Chinks in the Snake?"

Joe put one hand on the banister. "Can't tell you anything, Lon."

"I've got a deadline, J. K.," said Alonzo behind him.

Trousers soaked, back aching, Joe Vincent climbed on.

6

WITNESS

A S JOE RODE PAST the brick storefronts of downtown Lewiston, he saw the glint of standing water, block after block. He could put a name and history to each drowned yard and lot. Telegraph and gasworks were still out, cordwood littered every boardwalk, and at the crossroads near the Unitarian church horses splashed knee-deep. The Sparbers' big chicken coop was gone, swept away. Old Mr. Sparber waved down Joe to complain, forgetting that he was no longer marshal.

In town the daily round had resumed: Joe saw the cart from Alleman's Dairy cut past a line of hay wagons, while at riverside, dockworkers unloaded the Portland overnight, the first steamer in days to brave the swollen Snake. Akers was indeed behind on every one of his duties: getting medicine to outlying families, feed to cut-off stock, notices to the *Teller,* cats out of trees. Pleas for aid were still coming in from all over Nez Perce County.

Not my worry. Joe turned onto a deserted, muddy A Street and hitched Trim to the porch rail of the one-story Beuk Aie Temple, listening to the nasal clatter of Cantonese within. The caretaker led him down the dim, narrow room. Along the gilded altar stood incense burners and porcelain wine cups, plus five sets of chopsticks, one for each temple deity. A dozen thin, tired, wary Chinese watched Joe approach. Nearby stood a C Street grain merchant, ready to translate, but the lead miner spoke fair English.

Lee She, Joe wrote. *Occupation: junior boss, gold-mining crew. Born: Canton.* Probably in his early twenties, if that; manner composed, eyes lightless.

"How big was your group?" Joe asked.

"Forty-four, sir."

The merchant flinched, just a hair. Joe wondered why.

"All from around here?"

"Yes, sir."

The mining-camp survivors waited near Lee She, taking care to look away from the *da bidze* judge. Young, slight, and wiry, most of them. So foreign, with those long rattail queues and shaved foreheads, but tough enough to take eight bad months up the Snake.

"Where was your camp?" Joe asked Lee She.

"Deep Creek, for sleeping, sir. Robinson Gulch, for the work."

Six weeks ago the Chinese expedition leader had sent this smaller party to prospect farther south. *Chea Po,* Joe wrote. *Senior boss. Home: Canton.* On returning to Deep Creek, Lee She and his men found only burned wreckage and murdered compatriots, too mutilated to recognize. The miners' largest craft lay stranded on the rocky shore, oars broken, bottom chopped out. A half-mile away, Robinson Gulch was a charnel house. Fourteen miners lay buried upriver, Lee She told Joe. Hacked, bludgeoned, castrated, faceless. The missing: probably thrown into the Snake.

Joe added a row of stars to his notebook page. That timing fitted the flood dates and condition of bodies recovered at Lewiston all too well. He did recall that the Deep Creek crew included two boys, unusual in an over-winter camp, and asked about them.

"Gone."

Joe looked at the young man's clenched and callused hands and changed the subject. Their venture's backer was . . . ?

"The Sam Yup Company. In San Francisco," the translator told him. Joe knew it, dimly, as one of several big Chinese labor exchanges there.

"A benevolent society," said the translator, not elaborating.

Lewiston barbershop and tavern talk about the Snake River dead

8

seesawed daily, and the favored line was, *Well, at least they ain't from around here.* But Chea Po's mining crew *was* local. Joe was stuck and he knew it. As police judge he could rule on civil and criminal cases within his jurisdiction, which in practice meant all of Nez Perce County. A few years back the territorial legislature in Boise trimmed down Nez Perce; it was still larger than Rhode Island.

The big river marked the border between Idaho Territory and the State of Oregon, and both Robinson Gulch and Deep Creek lay on the Snake's western bank. Maybe he could hand off these killings to Oregon authorities. But around four in the afternoon Henry Stanton came in, nodded to the Beuk Aie elders, and opened his hand to show Joe evidence from the final autopsies. In the rainbow light of a lantern hung with colored beads, Joe saw the lead gleam. Two dozen bullet rounds, more than enough to force an inquest.

"That's it?"

Henry shook his head. "That's one man."

Three days later, Dr. Henry Stanton, coroner, and the Honorable Joseph Kimball Vincent, police judge, issued their ruling: mass murder. Joe still had no idea how to solve the legal puzzle of aliens residing in a territory yet killed in a state by persons unknown. A day spent reading case law showed only the extent of the maze. As a Lewiston magistrate, he seemed to have as much jurisdiction as anyone.

The Beuk Aie elders wanted him to keep local Chinese safe. That much was clear. Yet when Joe went to tell Lee She that a court proceeding was under way, the Deep Creek miners had vanished, every one. Halfway to Canada, Joe figured. He ran over the count in his head. Lee She's burials upriver. Seven bodies recovered near Lewiston. Two washed ashore at the Almota steamboat landing; a frightened farmer rode in yesterday with the news. Marshal Akers sent him straight to Judge Vincent. The sheriff at Pen-a-wa-wa, forty miles off, reported four more. Joe began composing his telegram to the Sam Yup's head office.

• • •

9

The reply was swift. A Company representative had left San Francisco to take a full report; please afford every assistance. The Imperial Chinese government planned to protest this outrage in the strongest terms and demand reparation from American authorities.

At his office desk Joe turned the telegram over, then peered into the envelope. No follow-up, no softening addendum, no mention of paying expenses. *Wonderful.*

Lewiston was no town for secrets. Lake's jewelry store housed a Bell telephone exchange, where service was so erratic that its twenty-eight subscribers usually sent a child down the street with a note, like everyone else. The Western Union clerk was a gossip, never more than when a silver dollar lay on the counter. Joe knew the man gave Alonzo Leland first crack at the juicier wire stories. Confidential public business was a lost cause. He opened the latest *Teller,* expecting a furious editorial on heathen meddling.

The news columns yielded only one paragraph, a masterpiece of misdirection squeezed between an ad for John Carey's pack train and a report of amateur theatricals over at Pomeroy.

> A boatload of Chinamen came down Snake River on Saturday last and brought the news that another boat load of Chinese had been murdered about 150 miles above here by some unknown parties; they claim that the Chinamen, some ten in number, who were murdered had upward of $3000 on them, having been mining on the river this past year. They found their boat with blankets and provisions in, but three of the Chinamen have been found, and three in the river, two of whom were shot and the third could not be captured. Some think the Chinamen murdered them, while others think Indians or whites, but the mystery may never be solved.

One hundred fifty miles? Sixty was more like it. And three thousand in gold dust? No survivor mentioned any such amount, nor would, not to a foreign devil judge. As usual, the *Teller* was best appreciated as fiction. One fact would not change: between Canton and Lewiston lay nine thousand miles. A long way to come to die.

Henry Stanton stood in the doorway, waiting for a decision.

"Flood or no flood, some evidence must survive," Joe said after a while. "I guess I could charter a boat and go see."

Chatter. Under pressure, his Massachusetts accent turned more pronounced. The doctor had not heard it this strong in years.

"No one rows *up* the Snake," Stanton said.

Joe slung the broadsheet into his kindling box.

"It's a drought year. At least we'll see the rocks we hit. Hand-line past the big rapids, chance the rest. Two, three weeks round-trip. I need a close-in look at whoever did it. I doubt they've gone far. It takes a fair-sized crew to slaughter so many. All else aside, murder on this scale is hard work."

"Didn't stop your lot at Antietam," said Stanton. "Or mine ever, really." He paused. "Didn't stop *you* at Big Hole. So I hear."

Joe was on his feet, not knowing how he got there.

"Christ almighty, Henry, sometimes I don't understand you. You bring this up now, after ten years?"

Stanton waited, arms folded, watching.

"I sent my shots high," said Joe Vincent. He turned away.

FROST MOON

OCTOBER 1886

UNDER A FULL FROST MOON, two boys ran. At thirteen and eleven they often worked shirttail and barefoot, but Elder Boss wanted every crewman outfitted for cold weather, so now Lim Dow and Chu Yap wore denim pants, blue padded coats, and stiff new boots, all a size too large.

Ahead, a train of ox carts filled the road, bound for the Clearwater diggings. Dow pulled his cousin into the ditch just in time. Two Chinese out so late, even young ones, could easily get shot. Dow lay in the weeds, face in his arms, rabbit-still. Yap peered up nonetheless and saw by swinging lantern light a pale curved horn as long as his arm, and an inquiring dark eye.

An hour later, the boys silently studied the narrow river town of Lewiston, nestled below a line of bluffs where the placid Clearwater met the larger, faster Snake. Moonlight picked out a switchback road down to the sleeping port. Yap pointed to the distant docks. Lanterns, moving. They ran on.

In the shadow of riverside warehouses, Chea Po surveyed the six big boats, careful as always to school his broad, mild face into sternness. His young underboss, Lee She, was on hands and knees in the lead vessel, checking waterproof tarpaulins lashed over tents and bedrolls. Chea Po urged three last miners down the boarding ladders.

Almost the last. Each river craft, broad and sturdy as a dory, held seven men. A crew of forty-two was a good roster, two desirable even numbers that together made six, signifying smooth and easy. Chea Po liked the symmetry of having four groups of eleven miners each, if he added in the two boys hired at the last minute. Wherever they were. Possibly two boys counted as one man, bringing the crew total to forty-three, whose sum was seven, the number of anger and desolation. No. Try again.

(When Lee She first heard about Chea Po's extra recruits, he put a quick hand to the lucky fish amulet at his throat. In Cantonese the word *four* sounds very like the word *death.* Yes, forty-two men plus two boys made forty-four, Chea Po conceded, but two fours were eight, *baat,* which rhymes with *faat,* wealth. Eight, the most fortunate number of all, would rule their winter venture.)

The faces of his crewmen lay in shadow, but Chea Po caught traded glances, tiny shrugs. The moon was setting. Up in Lewiston he could see a scatter of lamplight. Past time to be gone. As the two bosses bent to work the last boat ropes free, they heard the clatter of feet on planking. Lee She reached out and caught both boys as they slid to a stop.

"Marshal Vincent saw us, Elder Boss," Dow whispered, bowing. "He asked where we were going so early."

"And what did you tell him?"

"Up Snake River for gold," Yap said proudly. "He was very impressed."

Lee She swore; now a *da bidze* lawman might come visit the mining camp. Chea Po knew they had to get under way before Vincent arrived at the docks. At least the boys' boast of good English seemed no lie. Lee She had said they were fluent, but Chea Po was no judge.

"Get in," he said, aiming a cuff at Dow's ear, to satisfy the watching eyes.

TRACKERS

O N MONDAY MORNING Joe sat in his office, reading police
logs. A runaway four-horse team on Main Street, no damage. A dog barking at night near the lumberyard, owner unknown.
Boys throwing pebbles at churches during service; complainant not
close enough to take names. Sabbath disturbance in Lewiston used
to mean a dozen drunks galloping down Main Street, firing as they
rode. He yawned and walked out to the side yard to check on Trim.

"Why, ma'am, I remember back in '71 . . . ," he told her, using
his best old-codger voice. Trim laid her ears flat and kept grazing.
Christ. Not even appreciated by his own horse.

Back to the log. Aha—a case of assault. A pig bit the finger of
a Spokane visitor. Joe knew both pig and visitor and was not surprised. One large panther seen crossing the yard up at John Shutte's
place. Maybe Shutte could use the barking dog.

Joe turned the page. His town office was a converted barn on a
corner lot. Ten years back he filled the stalls with bookcases (glass-
fronted, to thwart the mice), brought in a roll-top desk and a black
potbelly stove, then stood an army cot under the old hayloft. The
wide plank floor stayed bare. When thinking over cases, Joe needed
to sweep. He had the cleanest floor in Lewiston.

A stranger leaned over the barn's half-door: a young Chinese.

"Judge Vincent? I'm Lee Loi, from the Sam Yup Company."

He was about twenty-three, wearing a dark suit with a silver watch

14

chain slung across the brocade vest. Under a roll-brim derby his black hair was cut short. Joe stared a second longer than he should have. He'd expected a white man.

"Good to meet you, Mr. Lee."

The Sam Yup emissary looked gratified.

"I usually get called Loi, so I'm glad of the correct form."

"I was a Forty-Niner," Joe told him, by way of explanation. "Pull up a chair, sir."

Lee Loi stuck out his hand. Joe felt cornered but took it. He had never shaken with a Chinese before, not as an equal. And how in hell was he going to house the fellow? The Sam Yup man would have to take meals — specially catered, no doubt — in the private parlor at Raymond House. And sleep in Joe's own rooms there. Joe foresaw a long week on the army cot.

He soon discovered that Lee Loi ate anything, often, and chewed as much gum as Lonny and Letty put together. The Company representative was also a fast, careful worker, easy to deal with as they certified descriptions of the dead miners. He arrived too late to examine any bodies; Dr. Stanton tried to preserve a few with formaldehyde and arsenic, but putrefaction was too advanced. Any bone man sent upriver to boil and smoke remains for shipment back to China would have a tough job. Joe decided to issue the most comprehensive John Doe complaint and arrest warrant he could construct. He low-balled the number of victims, knowing a higher count might frighten off someone with a useful lead. He could revise upward later.

... Lee Loi, first being duly sworn, complains and accuses Richard Doe, John Doe and others, names unknown, of the crime of murder by feloniously, willfully and with malice aforethought cut with an axe and shot with a gun or pistol loaded with powder and ball, which they, and others, names unknown, did hold in their hands, kill and murder ten Chinamen, belonging to what is known as the Sam Yup Co. Said murders having been committed on Snake River in the State of Oregon, Wallowa County, and Nez Perce County, Idaho Territory, on or about May 25th 1887 to the best of his knowledge and belief ...

Now young Mr. Lee sat at Joe's desk, double-copying documents in English and Chinese, one set bound for the Sam Yup, the other for San Francisco's Imperial Consulate. Joe watched his visitor look around for a pen-wiper. Lee Loi proved to be China-born, sent to the States in childhood for schooling, although at Yale College he apparently specialized in the study of baseball, the New York Metropolitans in particular.

Joe could tell Mr. Lee was used to getting his own way, Chinaman or not. The voice, the stance, were not Oriental, as Joe understood it, nor Western, in the Idaho sense. In his own New England youth Joe had waited on drawling, well-born East Coast boys, and Lee Loi had all of their cocky, slouching ease.

Joe wondered how Lee would get on with Lewiston's Chinese. Most lived bachelor-style, crowded in meager lodgings along C Street, where small dark shops sold them secondhand blankets, sieves, pick handles, and the soft hot dumplings called *won ton:* swallowing clouds. Either they were miners, hard-bitten as Lee She's lot, or else they worked in town as cooks, houseboys, and laundrymen. In the land they called Gam Saan, Golden Mountain, their only goals seemed to be getting rich and going home.

Meanwhile they flocked to the Hip Sip hall adjoining the temple. Our fraternal lodge, the Chinese told white Lewiston. Like your Masons. A public scribe, a bowl of slow-cooked soup, a loan for the needy: the Hip Sip offered it all. Customers arrived from dawn to midnight, drawn by a triangle of yellow cloth flying over the door. As marshal, Joe had walked through the public rooms, smelled the hot cooking oil and cheap tobacco, heard the roar of talk and the wail of the caller at the fan-tan tables. Once he'd asked the owner for a translation. *Buy the corner, buy a twist, buy and make money, buy, buy, buy.*

Lee Loi asked if Joe had local suspects for the Deep Creek murders. Joe dug around, then handed over a *Teller* clipping from April, headed "A Little Mystery." Out of habit he still cut items from the region's papers, then let them compost in a bottom drawer.

16

There are reports of a band of horse thieves over in Oregon, 25–30 of them, well armed and energetic. Their range is the little grass valleys nestled between high, precipitous and ragged cliffs and mountains. These valleys have lots of bunch grass for stock. Hundreds of cattle and horses are run across the Snake and disposed of to unsuspecting buyers in our region. Men of Lewiston should get up a party and break up this gang.

Rustlers were a staple of Territory journalism, the sure sign of a slow week.

"It's a start," Joe said. Lee began taking notes. Joe could usually read upside down, but not this time; the Sam Yup man had small, quick handwriting, and all his entries were in Chinese.

The two investigators began searching for anyone who knew the Snake River dead: dry-goods merchants, moneylenders, crewmates from past jobs. Beuk Aie officials produced a dozen candidates to interview, but Lee Loi said he was getting nowhere.

The more time Joe spent in the Chinese district, the less he understood it. He liked some of what he saw in warehouse and counting room, and always had — the graceful blue-and-white jars of preserved ginger, the ducks baked to succulent redness, the iron courtesies. The endless hawking and spitting did not bother him much; every bank and church in white Lewiston kept cuspidors for tuberculars and tobacco chewers. But he did not linger by any Chinese market garden on fertilizing day, not when the proprietor moved from row to row with a hoe and a bucket of fresh human dung.

Two days of trailing Lee through low, dark rooms made Joe's head ache. Talk, talk, a river of noise. Sometimes he thought he caught the mining bosses' names: *Chew Po, Lee Shiu.* Though Joe was no great size, among so many small, anxious strangers he felt enormous, nose and feet especially. Lee Loi, gabbing at his elbow, was big for a Celestial and in bounding health; Joe chalked it up to a schoolboy diet of codfish and baked beans. Mostly Lee seemed to issue orders, then expect locals to jump. Joe guessed the Sam Yup man was high-caste.

Also highhanded. Once Lee pushed a miner against a wall and

shouted in his face like a young demon, until the man hunched to the ground, whispering replies. A few steps down the street and Lee was all sunshine, discoursing on the stellar pitching of the Detroit Wolverines. Joe saw the bullied miner stand up and make a gesture at Lee's back that even a *da bidze* knew was obscene. The Company did not seem beloved by its rank and file.

Back at Joe's barn, Lee said he didn't much care that the Deep Creek underboss and his men had fled. The Sam Yup was spared arguing over lost wages in cases of disappearing to start over. All that mattered now was the murder investigation.

Again Joe explained the Idaho-Oregon jurisdictional tangle, the wilderness conditions on the upper Snake, the undoubted destruction of evidence by the May flood, and Lewiston's limited appetite for solving an all-Chinese crime. Bury and move on, that was the local sentiment.

Lee Loi leaned forward. He looked anxious.

"I want to hire you to lead the case, sir, on a private basis. I don't see any conflict. My Company and my government would like this resolved, and I expect you would too."

"You need someone younger," Joe told him. "By about thirty years. I have dyspepsia and a bad foot. Try the federal marshals out in Portland. Or else get the Pinkertons."

"Please, sir," Lee said. "Please. You were recommended in the highest of terms. You've been marshal twice, I understand, and probate judge, and justice of the peace, and federal commissioner, and territorial representative. A most distinguished record. Which is why the Sam Yup Company would be honored to offer a thousand dollars for your time and trouble."

Joe tipped back his chair. This two-year appointment as police judge was a face-saver. Arraignments, bail hearings, misdemeanors. Small beer. He'd never lost an election before, never. Well, fifty-six was nothing. He could still ride all day and read all night. The sooner he closed out this Chinese matter, the better. And the money was astounding.

"I run an auction business, you know, and a hotel. This is a busy time for me. I'm sorry."

"I'm authorized to go a little higher, sir. Fifteen hundred?"

Lee would never make an auctioneer.

"Who did this recommending?"

"I'm not at liberty to say, Judge. My apologies. But your reputation for square dealing precedes you. Do you need . . . to consult your wife, perhaps?"

"No," said Joe. "Have *you* ever heard of long pig?"

Lee Loi shook his head.

"It's a term for roasted human flesh, or so Dr. Stanton alleges. Understand me, Mr. Lee. Whoever killed your countrymen put them through the tortures of hell. You never saw the bodies. I did, and my youngest girl as well. Some of those men were not just mutilated, they were slaughtered. Skin peeled off like an apple. Faces chewed to shreds. Even if we do make it up the Snake and find anyone responsible, a clean arrest and a fair trial are long shots. Why not let the dead bury the dead?"

Lee Loi sat silent. Joe hoped he was starting to think of the Deep Creek killings as more than a career boost. But then:

"If *we* find them, sir?"

"The river's low this year. A small, light boat should make good time."

"I'm a decent rower. You could use me."

Joe hesitated. By *we* he'd meant the professional help he planned to hire. On the Sam Yup's dime, of course. Georges was not cheap. But their search party would need a third man, for safety, and anyone was better than Akers.

He took another look at the Company emissary. Civilians often made trouble on field jobs, and Lee Loi would be conspicuous upriver. But leaving him alone in Lewiston was out of the question: too many Chinese lynchings of late. And he did have the guts to volunteer, even after swearing out that grisly warrant. If Georges agreed, maybe they could pass off Mr. Collegiate as Nez Perce. Or something. He wasn't much older than Joe Vincent, Jr., the *Teller*'s best (and only) ad salesman.

"I could use you, indeed. If the killers are still around, they'll expect a posse on horses, not a water approach. The problem is, I know that reach, but not well. We'll do better with a river guide, preferably a tracker."

"Where can you get one?"

"The best is over in Oregon, a fellow named Georges Sundown. I don't know if he's free."

"Send a wire, please. If he comes at once, I'll add a bonus."

Joe met Henry Stanton on the street that noon and explained about taking on the Chinese murders as a private job. Still in the public interest, of course.

"You're not out of your jurisdiction?"

Nettled, Joe said, "Deep Creek and Robinson Gulch are just across the river from Nez Perce County. A stone's throw. Literally."

The doctor said only, "Forgive me, but do you recall the last time a persuasive stranger offered you a large sum of money?"

"Repaid," said Joe. "And paid, and paid. Once more into the breach, all right? I'm not drooling yet."

A small but definite crack in a two-decade silence. Stanton said, "I agree, barring the part about the English dead. You'll use a tracker, surely?"

"I wired Georges."

Stanton walked him back to Lewiston's courthouse, still housed in the old Luna Hotel, a broad white frame building in need of fresh paint. Joe disappeared inside, but Henry sat thinking on the front steps for a good ten minutes, then went to send his own telegram.

By morning Joe Vincent and Lee Loi had a reply:

Offer accepted arrive Lewiston Friday noon – G.S.

As they walked to the docks on June 17, Lee Loi kept stopping: first to fan his face with his straw skimmer, then to read store-window placards, each a riot of screamer type. Joe towed him past Simpson's barbershop (*Hot & Cold Baths*) and then the untidy aisles of Libby's nemesis, Hale & Cooper (*Vendors of Crockery, Picture Frames, Moldings, Gilding, Paint and Wallpaper, Parasols and Fans*). They crossed the street near the Vollmer furniture emporium (*Determined to undersell all competitors! Gold cash coin only!*), and as the Boss meat-market door swung open, Joe could smell new sawdust on the floor and the copper odor of fresh blood (*Beef, veal, chops, sausage, poultry! Catarrh cured, health and sweet breath restored, by novel effect of Shiloh's Catarrh Remedy!*).

Customers and clerks craned necks without shame, but Lee's breezy chat never faltered. Lewiston was home to fifteen hundred whites and five hundred Celestials. A Chinese this Americanized was a decided novelty. Everyone knew the Sam Yup man had posted a thousand-dollar reward for information leading to conviction. Henry kept Joe abreast of town whispers about the big murder payment. *Tong money, you know.* Chinese urban crime rings — drugs, prostitution, gambling — were all over the headlines.

As they waited for the *Portland* to unload, Lee Loi leaned over.

"What's Sundown look like?"

"Like a man you want in your boat on a rough river," Joe said.

The last passenger off was straight-backed and slight, wearing a tailored traveling dress of dark serge and a dashing veiled hat. She walked directly to them, set down her carpetbag, and with both gloved hands folded back the dotted netting.

An Indian's tip-tilted eyes, the aplomb of a Parisienne. Lee glanced at Vincent for guidance but saw only a first-class poker face. The newcomer matched him and more. Clearly she knew to look for them. Perhaps she had a message from Mr. Sundown? Perhaps she had not met many judges, or many Chinese. To reassure her, he offered his best New Haven bow.

"Lee Loi, from the Sam Yup Company. Your servant, ma'am."

She turned and smiled and he felt himself grin like a freshman. The duelists' tension between her and Vincent vanished so fast that Lee decided he'd imagined it. Anyone could see she was a lady. Nor did

21

he mind the fine lines around her eyes and the stray silver threads in the dark upswept hair. Older women rather intrigued him. Suddenly he wanted to make her smile like that always. He could not place her looks at all. The curve of tan cheek told him nothing. Some kind of Spanish? Creole? *Métis*? He was no good at reading non-Chinese features; fifteen years in the States and he could barely tell an Italian from a Swede.

"I'm Grace Sundown. So glad to meet you, Mr. Lee."

Her alto voice was charming and clear, her accent American and educated.

"Judge Vincent." A brief, correct inclination of the head. No offered hand. No smile.

"Miss Sundown." Then Vincent said softly, "Where is Georges?"

"Detained," said Miss Sundown. "Gentlemen, shall we?"

Vincent took one long step and blocked her way. "I repeat — *where is Georges?*"

"You have your tracker, Judge. I know the Snake better than Georges ever did."

"Damn that Henry," Vincent said.

She replaced her veil and turned toward the two-block commercial street leading up into Lewiston. Hoping to earn another smile, Lee Loi seized the carpetbag. Victory. He decided they must all dine at Raymond House before sending her packing. He glanced at Vincent, eager to learn when the real river guide might arrive.

Vincent hadn't moved. "Where do you think you're going?"

"Home," she said.

"You know each other?" asked Lee Loi, too fascinated for manners.

"In a way," said Miss Sundown, walking off.

Judge Vincent said, watching her, "Not any more."

BRIGHTNESS

OCTOBER 1886

THE MINERS MADE CAMP on a wide sandbar, ate cold rice, washed their feet, and slept for the first time in twenty hours. Only Lee She lay awake, searching the canyon skies for constellations he knew — the Ox, the Willow, the Cowherd — but finding none. Up on the rimrock, a coyote howled. Lee She tried pulling his share of blanket away from Lim Ah. No good. The mapper was the tallest man on the crew. Lee She had known him since they were both six. Their families still shared a greenmarket stall in Panyu. No wild dogs there. No money, either. Lee She left at fourteen, lying about his age to get a steerage berth to Gam Saan. Almost no one cared, except the Sam Yup accountants. By the time he paid off his Company debts he would be forty, an old done man, like Elder Boss.

Lee She woke to river fog and went to check on the boats, picking his way through long grass bent and beaded with moisture. He was desperate for a smoke, but his tobacco pouch was soaked. Yesterday the boats tackled a run of rapids at a bad angle; he fell in twice. Through the grayness he saw Chea Po rousing the mining crew, nudging shoulders, making jokes, applying a foot to some sluggard's rear.

"Move over," said a voice in his ear. Lim Ah handed him a tin mug of steaming tea.

"Respect your underboss," Lee She growled. "Or learn to swim." Neither of them knew how. Miners rarely did.

23

The expedition cook, Hong Lee, thin and intent, began shouting for more firewood. The big kettles of rice congee were on their last boil. Crewmen streamed past the two friends, heading for the hot food, crowding, jostling, pushing. Lining up was not the Chinese way. Many had been on other Sam Yup backcountry jobs. Chea Po kept a lookout for sound workers from reliable clans. Lee She wandered the shore, slurping porridge as the fog broke up and streamed away.

Hong Lee came by with a bucket of fried fish. With his back to the others, he gave young Yap a double helping. The cook offered the same to Younger Boss, who pointed with his chin at Dow, knowing the older boy would not ask of his own accord. As the nine Christians among the miners finished morning prayers beneath the cottonwoods, they could look up through rattling golden leaves at a sapphire sky. Lee She touched the little clay fish at his neck. *Let the weather stay fair, let the luck keep on.*

For twelve days the Chinese rowed steadily up the Snake, bound south against the current. In the lead boat Lim Ah counted off the steep-running streams that rushed in from both banks. The miners lined every rapids, hauling the heavy craft upstream with long pull ropes, the river rising four feet each mile. Like climbing a giant flooded staircase, thought Dow. Two men stayed in each boat, one to row, one to steer, while the rest clambered along rock falls and half-submerged ledges, the vessels pitching sideways in every olive-green cascade. Younger Boss told both boys to bail the supply boat, which carried half a year of food.

"Speed it up!" Dow yelled. The roaring stream ate Yap's furious answer. Dow could guess. They had both picked up some new expressions. Everyone was turning foul-tempered, even the cook and Elder Boss. Dow had never been so wet for so long. He could tell Yap was sick at his stomach but too stubborn to admit it. The boat smashed into an underwater rock, hard, then harder. Dow threw both arms around the rough plank seat as a wave sent his bucket tumbling. He scrambled after it.

Quiet current again, and a steady creak of oarlocks lulled the travelers to near-silence. From the lead boat, Chea Po signaled to pick up the pace. Almost there. As a red sun retreated behind the western ridge tops, Lim Ah scanned the banks. They were passing the rocky strand of Dug Bar, a sand-and-gravel delta thrusting out from the Oregon side of the Snake.

Americans spelled this place name as Dug Bar and Doug Bar. Lim Ah neither knew nor cared; he spoke no English and was using a sketch of the river supplied by a C Street merchant. Dug Bar was a longtime Nez Perce crossing, the only safe ford for miles either way. A white miner named Thomas Douglas panned nearby for years, then added a new line of work: holding up travelers. He did good business until the summer of 1883, when someone blew open his head with a well-placed rifle shot.

Three years on, the cabin was a shepherds' outpost, and the tale of Douglas fading. Still, the old robber died badly, and when the Chinese rowed past his cabin of sun-bleached logs, in boat after boat heads turned to check young Mole's reaction.

Everyone called An Duk Big Mole, because he was round, brown, and blinked in the sunlight. A good geomancer could tell a neutral spot from a treacherous one by reading the intricate flows of wind and water, and Mole's metaphysical estimates would guide all their labors. Only a fool—or a big-nose—disturbed the unseen world. As the flotilla passed the ramshackle cabin, An Duk's fingers flickered in a strong sign against evil. A dozen miners followed his lead.

Lee She saw, and his worry redoubled. An Duk was watching the cliff tops again, but he felt Lee She's fears, looked over, and smiled. Duk always knew. Lee She drummed his fingers on his knee in respectful salute, though the geomancer was a full two years younger.

Beyond the Douglas cabin lay Robinson Gulch, a narrow gorge edged in black-streaked sand, caught in the slanting late light. Half a mile more, and the miners put ashore on the Oregon side of the Snake, dragging the boats up a stony beach beneath a steep grassy ridge.

"There," said Lim Ah.

Chea Po turned. A swift narrow stream, clear and cold, tumbled down into the Snake, washing a gap between gray outcrop boulders. The American name for the little cascade was Deep Creek. Its headwaters were ten miles off, high on the ridge that *da bidze* miners called Somers Point. The Lewiston merchant's map marked it another way, with a small quick drawing of the sun and moon. Lim Ah knew that combining the characters for each heavenly body made the word *brightness*. Any civilized person, reader or no, could find the spot and guess its meaning, however veiled by the mapper's ingenuity. Gold, immortal gold.

UPRIVER

JUNE 18, 1887

A NIGHT GUARD sat in the dockmaster's shed. Lewiston merchants insisted. Floods, dead bodies – the times were so unsettled that warehouse looting might be next. The watchman shoved a logbook across the counter, nodded to Joe, and went back to dozing, fingers laced across his paunch.

Lee Loi waited at wharfside, shivering. The sky's eastern rim flared blue and gold, like gaslight. A June dawn in Idaho felt Arctic, despite his new fringed buckskin jacket. A worker in a broad-brimmed hat brushed past, then dropped down the ladder to their hired boat. Some local youth on the early shift, Lee supposed. Vincent began passing knapsacks for stowage.

Five minutes later, Lee Loi realized their silent aide was Miss Sundown. Loose canvas jacket, denim trousers, hair tucked under hat; in childhood he had seen Chinese women in neat dark pants and tunic coats, but this was freakish, beyond boldness. He had dined with New Haven faculty daughters and patronized New York *da bidze* prostitutes without ever seeing more than a flash of female ankle. Lee was so agitated that he reclaimed the log, intending to add his name in characters – the hell with local feeling – and saw she had signed in as James McCormick, the best pitcher in baseball, which upset him more.

As they headed south up the Snake, the two men rowed and Miss Sundown steered, watching the river at their backs. Both lawman and guide invited Lee Loi to use first names ("It's a small boat and a long trip," Vincent observed), but he kept, uneasily, to "Judge" and "Miss Sundown." Evidently she had decided to call him Lee, in American prep-school fashion, and he found he did not mind; amid all the strangeness, it was a touch of the known.

Yesterday she had not dined with them, only upended all of Vincent's careful packing, reduced it by five sixths, doubled the fishhooks, tripled the ammunition, confiscated Lee's entire valise – "You only need one set of clothes" – then vanished toward the residential streets beyond downtown.

Lee heard Vincent sigh, but the judge agreed they had no time to spare. Every hour now could mean evidence lost. Sorry. The Sam Yup would have to make do with the other G. Sundown.

"Who is she, anyway? His sister?"

"Cousin," said Vincent, half out the door.

"But is it safe, having a woman along?"

"We'll protect her," Vincent said. His poker face was back. "Get some sleep, Mr. Lee."

Rowing hard, Lee Loi watched morning warm the lunar vistas along the Snake, creek and wash, fissure and gorge. The windswept heights, the changing light that painted the river rose and gold, all excited his photographer's eye. He'd left his new portable camera in San Francisco. A mistake.

Miss Sundown made sure he knew it. Lee soon learned that the Snake River canyon was deeper than the Grand Canyon of the Colorado; that the Snake's thousand-mile watercourse rose in Yellowstone country to become one of four great rivers in the West, longer than the Columbia, swifter than the Missouri; that Lewis and Clark, the Nez Perce, and the mountain men all called the Snake by other names: Shoshone, Yam-pah-pa, Mad.

He might go mad, if this kept up. Her navigation was better than expected – she had not yet run them into anything substantial, like a cliff – but Lee did not much want to know that Lewiston lay 470 miles from saltwater yet commanded a fast road to the Pacific, or that river steamers brought its merchants English ales and Japan tea. Local lore bored him rigid. Apparently once Idaho joined the Union, the Territory might split in half, as Dakota planned to do, or even join with eastern Washington to make a new state, with Lewiston its crown jewel.

"First gold fever, now inland-empire fever," said Vincent, shipping his oar for a rest.

"Inland fantasy," said Miss Sundown, studying the current. No train or bridge crossed the next two hundred miles of river, she told Lee. Likely they never would.

"Oh. Well. Why is that, ma'am?"

"It's cursed," she said, as if commenting on the weather. "Take the water bottle. You need to drink more in this heat. Not that much. And try to aim your oar at a tighter angle. No—yes. That's better."

Joe said, "Slow down, son," and went back to thinking on what lay upriver. While he would never publicly agree, she might be right about the curse. A few sheep ranchers and gold miners inhabited the bleak upper Snake, but also far more than the usual run of rustlers, desperadoes, and fugitives. At best it was chancy country, at worst . . . well, even he, a professional rationalist, had to admit its persistent strangeness. Some were starting to call that lonely stretch Hells Canyon.

Miss Sundown led them steadily upriver, as cloud shadow raced over gray heights and cobalt flowage alike. With oars cutting smoothly against current, side canyons and crags unfurled behind them like a panorama. Lee thought it the starkest country he had ever seen, and the steepest. Judge Vincent pointed out a herd of elk crossing a bare slope to higher summer ground; Miss Sundown showed him an osprey's nest, and a mare's-tail waterfall tumbling down a cliff of black marble.

By late afternoon Lee knew he was flagging but thought he hid it well. At Yale he had tried single scull on the Housatonic and enjoyed it. Surely he could out-row any aging rural lawman. Vincent called this a record dry year; if so, Lee could barely imagine the Snake in normal flow.

The mouth of the Grande Ronde went by, and then Cache Creek, a curtain of folded pale gray limestone soon rising along one shore. Then came a hard traverse over slick ledges, scrambling and wading before lining the boat along a cliff face beside a triple run of boiling rapids. Miss Sundown went in waist-deep to steady the bucking craft while the men heaved at pull ropes. A hot dry wind swept down-canyon, parching lips and eyes.

The river narrowed, bluff turned to cliff, and a long flat stretch took the rowers into full shadow, except for one slanting mile-long shaft of sun that fell onto the Snake. The little boat drove toward it, through and out again, inches from a granite outcrop where glittering spume left all three travelers soaked. Salmon leaped past, twisting and swimming in the air.

Vincent was grinning; apparently he liked this sort of thing. Lee's oar flailed and caught only air, but Miss Sundown neither screamed nor reproached him. Between lectures, at least, she was no chatterbox. He wondered if she could see his forearms tremble.

During their noon halt on the sixth day, Joe stood up suddenly, squinting downstream. Along a stock trail on the Oregon shore, a pair of horsemen rode.

"Company coming. Get him out of here."

Grace pulled a startled Lee into a willow thicket while Joe dug through packs in the bow and seized a round miner's pan, a small pick, a battered slouch hat. He wadded up his vest and thrust it under his shirt, gouged a fistful of dirt from the riverbank, waded out.

Ten feet from the willows, the strangers reined in. Two showy chestnuts, one with a forehead blaze. Two slouching riders, edgy and armed. Grace looked for Joe but found only a stooped, slow-footed man wandering the shallows, not Joe as more years would wash over him but an elderly stranger, grubby, potbellied, harmless. A little lonely. Even the shape of his face was different.

"Afternoon, boys. Didn't hear you comin' in on me."

The voice was a codger's whisper, cracked by whiskey and sun. One horseman nodded, the other stared about. Grace thought both had been drinking. Good. The less observant, the better. A week of silver stubble plus a handful of mud, hastily applied, were not much insurance.

"You alone, Pop?"

"Yes sir, but I ain't your Pop. Least no gal ever told me so."

An old joke from an old man. The young rider grinned. He was a short, black-haired boy, barely above school age. The other looked disapproving. Lanky; a long-jawed, sunburned face; a country accent that stirred her memory. Not Missouri, she thought. Kentucky, maybe.

"Any luck with the pan?"

"Just seeing if the sand runs black here. Water's too low for sluice work. I started out in May, then had to set high up quick during that flood."

Grace saw the Southerner register Joe's Yankee vowels, not favorably. The riders checked the boat, now a convincing mess of tarp and rope.

"You hear of any trouble in this stretch?"

"Trouble? What sort?"

The horsemen glanced at each other.

"Well, rustling, for one."

"Lord, no! Not heard that at all. Are you boys lawmen?"

"No, but we want to help catch them," the younger one said quickly.

"Catch who, son?" Joe shuffled upstream, clutching the pan, breathing hard.

"Some China boys got killed, back around Deep Creek," said the Kentucky man.

"Probably their own people did it," the boy offered.

In the thicket, Grace read Lee's lips: *Son of a bitch.*

"Stands to reason, young man. But I ain't seen a thing. Sorry, can't oblige."

"He hath delivered me out of all trouble," said the tall rider suddenly.

"Lord's will be done," the prospector told him. His vague mild eyes slid to the river again. The other nodded, satisfied, and told their new acquaintance to come visit the cabin at Dug Bar; they had food and liquor and could always do with some company. The old man thought it over, then brightened.

"Maybe I will. That's mighty white of you fellows, mighty white indeed." He touched his hat, then creaked about the shallows with a great show of industry till both rode out of sight.

Lee emerged from the willows and stared downriver. "Those bastards. Blaming the Chinese. But they bought every word, sir."

"Too good a chance to miss," Joe told him. "I thought to go in as a miner anyway." He looked over at Grace, eyebrows raised.

"If we start now," she said.

"Your call," said Joe, heaving rucksacks into the boat.

She told a bewildered Lee just enough to keep him calm. The advantage of the long summer evening plus a late moon, the problem of running a river as night came on, especially this river. In some places the Snake nearly flowed on edge, deeper than it was wide. In other stretches, boulders the size of locomotives stood midstream, and more could fall at any second from the steep-raked slopes above. The hazard of floating driftwood was constant. And three rapids still lay ahead — less daunting than usual, with the river so low. Otherwise the twilight passage would be quite insane, but that she did not explain to Lee Loi.

The boat slipped quietly along the Idaho-side cliffs, somber in the dying day. Lee looked up, then up some more. He whistled at the sight of shattered rock towers and mile-long talus slides.

"Pull!" Grace snapped, straining to read the river. When they slid into a calmer stretch, only the scoop and splash of her bailing bucket broke the silence. Lee drew a shaky breath and started to speak, but Joe shook his head: sound carried. They lined another riffle, then rowed on, watching the Oregon ridges all the way, dark against the titanic sunset.

At Dug Bar, a river bend away from the rustlers' cabin, Joe checked the depth across the bedded gravel. He measured a scant foot on his oar and motioned for the others to step out. The cold water pulled at their legs.

"We'll drag here," he whispered. "Any scraping, ease off."

Grace held up a forefinger — *Wait* — then pulled a twist of rags from her pocket and muffled both oarlocks, winding, tying. Joe nodded to Lee and began to edge the boat through the shallows. Afterglow shivered and dissolved in the eddies as the Snake caught the last of the day and gave it back redoubled, just enough to let them press on.

Ten years back, Chief Joseph and his Nez Perce crossed near Dug Bar during high water, improvising rafts, swimming livestock. A thirty-day evacuation order from the Army encouraged ingenuity. Joe glanced at Grace, but she seemed as serene as her midsummer moon.

And now came the old Douglas cabin at last, in a clearing on the Oregon side. Lamplight shone behind greased-paper windows, and a dozen horses stirred in the corral. Men's voices sounded inside; a dog barked twice, but no one came out.

Half past nine, and at the bottom of the canyon even the river light was a strange, dim purple. Where Deep Creek rushed into the Snake, Grace threw her weight against the tiller. The oars dug once, twice. The boat made a tight swing and grated on the gravel beach, holding until the men clambered out and dragged it ashore.

Grace Sundown lay awake, gazing at Orion. Joe and Lee Loi had again set their bedrolls on either side of her. She did not protest their chivalry, although Lee, unconscious, looked about six. He'd done well, everything considered. She shut her eyes, but then she saw far too many rocks, rapids, and close calls.

Oh, how she'd lied, back at the Lewiston docks. This was her first trip to Deep Creek in over twenty years. Only a merciless cram session with a Lewiston boatman — a grateful Henry Stanton patient — had brought them here intact.

Six days on the river, and still sleep would not come. She turned her head. Joe was watching her. Grace went back to admiring the Idaho stars. The Snake allowed no reprieves, nor did she.

33

FINDINGS

A T FIRST LIGHT Joe set a can of water to heat for their break-fast of mush and tea, then opened a roll of graph paper and began to sketch the site of the Chinese camp. Deep Creek split the beach in two, and the Snake scooped shallow coves north and south. He could see a game trail on the far bank and a shore path leading north out of camp. A big stoved-in skiff lay near the water, just as Lee She said. This site was a perfect trap.

As the rough grid map took shape, Lee Loi looked over Joe's shoulder.

"You want us to search in those squares?"

Joe nodded. "Working slowly, please. It's been a month. A lot may be buried."

"Like what?"

"You tell me. How was it organized? Where did they sleep and eat?"

"I'd start over there." Lee pointed at two crumbling stone walls near a hackberry tree. "That big trash pile and those foundations."

"The walls aren't Chinese. They were here before," Miss Sun-down told him, tying on her big-brimmed hat.

"Let's check the graves first," said Joe, then saw Lee Loi's frown.

"What's wrong?"

"If these men were mutilated, like the ones at Lewiston . . . well, the common belief is, if you're not buried whole with your face toward heaven, you may arrive in pieces. Did the underboss say?"

"He did, and they were. If you can't get to the afterlife, what happens?"

Lee gazed at the line of mounds along the hillside, each with its cairn of river pebbles.

"You stay a ghost. Lost." *And hungry,* he thought, but did not say.

"Try some excavating," Joe said after a moment, leading them back toward the blackened debris. The May flood had left the mining camp in worse shape than he'd guessed. Above the high-water line, Joe stood looking at dozens of low depressions pitting the rocky ground. Manmade. Pick-and-shovel trial holes. Why reopen old diggings in such wild country? Even along the sheltered canyon, creeks could freeze; upriver miners normally wintered over at Lewiston. And why so many men to work a played-out site? For every ounce of dust they'd glean a pile of rock and sand the size of a house. Two houses.

Joe joined the others on hands and knees, prodding, troweling. When he showed them a sample tally—*watermelon seeds (8); abacus, smashed; rags & cotton batting, scorched*—they nodded but kept working. Good enough. He went to rummage in his packs, then moved behind a boulder.

Half an hour later, Miss Sundown sat back on her heels.

"What do we have?"

Lee shrugged. "Wood and canvas, mostly. Bedding, clothes? Somebody tore down everything and torched the wreckage."

Vincent said, behind them, "Take a look, will you?"

Lee Loi stared, rapt; he loved theatricals. Worn denim pants, cracked boots: suddenly the judge looked both old and poor. Ash mixed with grease turned Vincent's hair lank, though since he was not balding, the battered slouch hat would stay on day and night.

To Lee the disguise seemed perfect. Miss Sundown conceded it was a start. She began to scour a pair of leather galluses with sand while Vincent rubbed dirt into face and forearms. Lee wished his employees would use full sentences.

"Where's —?"

"Here."

"Too much?"

"More. No, give me that."

Vincent's palms were not work-callused, but Lee realized with a shock that the judge had blistered them on purpose, by gripping his oars just a little wrong all the way up the Snake. The backs of his hands showed ropy veins yet did not look truly aged. After a painful pass through a blackberry tangle it was harder to tell. Miss Sundown pressed him like a prosecuting attorney.

"When they ask your name, what will you say?"

"Joe Salem."

"Where do you winter?"

"Lewiston. Ma Nickerson's boarding house."

"You don't mean it."

"Sure. Ma would back me." He turned to Lee. "It's a . . ."

At the hesitation, Miss Sundown's chin went up. "Brothel," she said. "Your biggest strike this year?"

"Four nuggets up by Cochran's."

"What does a troy ounce go for these days? Quickly."

"Fine weather we're having."

"Fifteen-sixty. As any miner would know."

Miss Sundown double-checked Vincent's pockets, then decided fingernails should be more ragged, ears even grimier.

"Dirty feet?" said Lee. He knew he should not help, but Miss Sundown took his part and Vincent acquiesced, grumbling, then slopped cold tea down the collarless gray shirt, a garment of amazing antiquity and ripeness. Miss Sundown gave him one of her looks.

"Where in the world —"

"Bought it off the town drunk before we left. Be glad it's not his union suit."

36

He dug out a flat tin box of dark wax, tamped some on his incisors with a toothpick, and sent Lee a hideous gap-toothed grin. Lee smiled back, but it was an effort. He had never before sent another person into danger. Every minute Vincent seemed to fade a little more, replaced by a shabby stranger.

"You've done this before, I take it," Grace said, arms crossed.

"Now and then," Joe admitted. He refrained from any full-out turn as the senile prospector. It always disturbed Grace when he disappeared too far into a part. She was no actress; even in a game of parlor charades, he never did want her on his side. And that veiled hat of hers would not deceive an infant child.

Joe watched her fray the edges of his bedroll, hands quick and capable as any surgeon's. He could only guess at the toll of the years: this cool, self-contained woman displayed no trace of the funny, impulsive girl back at Lapwai, nor of the firebrand he glimpsed at Big Hole. Joe saw the Sam Yup man glance at her blue jeans yet again, then look quickly away. Well, plenty of Territory women wore trousers to manage a family farm or mine. People saw what they wanted to see. Take young Mr. Lee: conventional to the core. A week alone up the Snake with Grace Sundown was just what he needed. Poor bastard.

Joe ran a filthy finger around his ankle holster, trying in vain for comfort, then slid in the little derringer.

"Doesn't show at all," Lee said, peering. "If the boat stays, how do you get to Dug Cabin?"

"I know an upper path," Grace said. "Safer than along the shore. Ready?"

Coming back to Deep Creek was harder than she expected, even without the strain of constantly, covertly scanning every ridge and gully. Her stomach was still in revolt; before leaving Lewiston she had read the full coroner's file on the Chinese murders. And Joe was enjoying the play-acting far too much. His timing was consistently a fraction off. Next week, *East Lynne.*

• • •

Lee Loi watched Vincent shrug on a battered rucksack and blanket roll, hoist pick and pan, then follow Miss Sundown up along the ravine carved by Deep Creek. Once they turned a high slope and vanished, Lee crawled onto the nearest horizontal boulder and lay on the sun-warmed granite, flexing his aching hands. Both knees felt permanently wrenched. Already the day was hot as blazes, not that those two seemed to care. They ought to be in rocking chairs, not off scaling mountains on five hours' sleep. Lee knew he should get up. This might be his only chance to explore Deep Creek alone. Flat on his back beside a wild river among the graves of his countrymen, he never missed Company headquarters more: the other rising young men to rag, the important documents to deploy, the varnished pine desk where ink block and brush waited beside inkwell and steel pen. Three weeks ago he wore a bespoke shirt and sipped vintage *pu-erh* tea on a terrace overlooking San Francisco Bay. Another universe.

Lee shut his eyes and summoned all the breakneck vitality of Dai Fow, San Francisco's Big Chinatown: the street-corner fortunetellers, the elbowing bargain hunters, the calls of poultry men and barrel makers, the sellers of sour plum juice pushing through the crowd. He saw again the long baskets of salt fish and bitter melon, fresh bean sprouts heaped and tangled in the produce stalls, fat eels coiled in tanks. And everywhere the bolts of brocade, crimson and sky blue, carried over merchants' shoulders like banners of war.

Go away, esteemed dead. After a while, he slept.

In forty minutes Joe and Grace were on a ridge so high that they could see into Idaho and Oregon, east and west. After crossing the crest they waded a river of bluebells, and the meadows of golden lupine rose past her waist. A warm late-morning breeze stirred the grass as Grace pointed out the path down a winding ravine.

"You come out on the far side, then walk along Dug Bar to the cabin."

He made sure of the landmarks. "Thanks for the guiding."

"Be careful."

Not Joe, not Joseph. He said, "What do you think of our client?"

"Very Yale. Very green. They should have sent a more senior man, considering. He's keeping a fair amount back. I can't tell what."

"Yet."

"As you say."

"If I'm not back in a week, leave without me."

She nodded. This was a day for risks. He took another.

"I told you once, I won't leave you forever."

"Did you? I don't recall."

She snapped her fingers, then held her hand out, open and flat.

"No."

"Yes."

Damn that Henry. Joe turned his back, unhooked his partial lower plate, hesitated a second, then dropped it into her waiting palm. The denture was made of gold wire and ivory. Joe hated it. Every time he went to Portland, he had to get the blasted thing fixed. Grace wrapped it in a handful of long grasses, stowed it in a pocket, and turned south without a word, taking the highland trail at a steady pace.

VICTORY MEAT

JUNE 25, 1887

JOE APPROACHED Dug Cabin along a bend of rocky shore, feeling like a damn fool. He had not used the sourdough character in years, and now his early mimicry was bodily fact. How could he blend into cabin routine when he needed to get up twice in the night? His hearing was going downhill with the rest of him; he'd left that out of his catalog of infirmities for Lee Loi. What if he missed some vital exchange? The whole case could be wrecked. *My fault.*

Like every lawman in the West, Joe dreaded Chinese trouble. Public feeling against the newcomers was intractable, but so were the Imperial diplomats who raised hell in San Francisco and Washington after every killing, every riot, every Chinatown sacked and purged. Lewiston might prefer head-in-the-sand, but Joe knew that Chinese in California were suing for their rights now, fighting back in court, trying to get elected officials declared negligent in capital cases. And next time the Idaho dead might not be strangers and sojourners. To protect his town, a week of playing the simpleton was nothing. Nothing.

He found a rock ledge and sat down. As good a place as any to stow his tools. His hands were icy and he could not catch his breath. This was more than first-act nerves. He felt old and toothless. Hell, he *was* old and toothless. And alone.

He had to admit that by sacrificing the last of his vanity, Grace had

40

also upped his chances of surviving this venture. Why she bothered he could not say. Probably because if he died in the attempt, Lee Loi might balk at her fee.

But then he felt himself shift and split, the miracle of real pretending roused once more. *Oh, yes.* He shut his eyes. Salem was not very smart and far too trusting, an old retriever still eager to please. Joe let the front of his mind cloud over with age and ignorance — his other self off to one side as always, assessing, judging, the recording angel — and as he came up the low, sandy bank by Dug Cabin, he felt Vincent and Salem meld at last with a nearly audible click, like the closing of a well-made box.

Just in time. Chimney smoke drifted white against green aspen leaves. On the sagging porch, five men watched him wave.

"Afternoon, boys. Joe Salem."

They did not stir or answer. After a pause, he hobbled a little closer.

"Saw two fellas yesterday who said come around for a meal."

In the silence, he heard the river and the wind. Finally one spoke.

"Come on up, mister. Heard you might visit."

"Much obliged." Joe moved toward the porch, keeping his hands in view. When he got to the long, flat stone that served as its lowest step he paused, blinking in the strong sunlight, letting them look him over as long as they liked.

"You kind of old to be working this country, Pop."

This time he made no joke about the name. "I been telling myself that, these past few weeks."

He mounted the cabin steps, letting his bad foot drag for once, saying, "Joe Salem, howdy," and offering to shake until he got all the names: Frank Vaughan, Hiram Maynard, Carl Hughes, Bobby McMillan. He had met Maynard and McMillan, the horsemen beside the Snake. McMillan was maybe sixteen, a little pudgy still; Vaughan not much older. The others were hard cases. Restless, cold-eyed. Joe had jailed hundreds like them.

The tallest of the crew, lounging in the cabin doorway, was a little

41

more kempt than the rest, and more civil. He looked to be in his early forties, towheaded and smiling, with eyes the pale, flat blue of faded denim.

"Bruce Evans. My pleasure. Where you from, Salem?"

"Back East, a long time ago. Massachusetts."

"Shee-yet. A Union man."

Tennessee? Or maybe Virginia.

"No, left in '49. Been out West ever since. I fought Indians in '56, but my foot got frostbit."

"Me and Tee, we fought with the Rebs."

"Is that a fact? I met plenty of Southern boys in the gold camps, before the War and after."

Joe wondered who Tee was; apparently someone absent.

"Yeah, and old LaRue was Union. So we got a little happy family here."

"Well, that's good. It was all a long time ago. I ain't too political."

Evans was looking beyond him, toward the river.

"Where's your boat? Bobby said you had one."

"Oh, it's a ways back. I like to walk the shore and look for good sand."

"Sure—you miners. Always hunting that next strike. Well, come on in, have a drink."

Evans led everyone into the dim, hot one-room cabin. Canned goods sat jumbled on the dirt floor beside a long plank table. From a rafter over the dry sink hung a smoked ham crusted with flies. In the far corner lay a good-sized mongrel dog, eyes on the newcomer.

"Zeke, you black rascal. C'mere," said Evans.

The other men looked at Zeke without an ounce of affection.

"Seems like a fighter," Joe said. He could see the scarred ears. A match dog, then, conditioned by whip and boot to attack anyone except his owner.

Evans grinned. "He's a killer. I had him in many a fight, and he won them all. Right, Zeke?" He rubbed the dog's nape. "And he likes victory meat too, huh, boy?"

Joe heard boots on the porch. Two men joined them. The same

age as Evans, or thereabouts. J. T. Canfield, nicknamed Tee, had yellow teeth, sparse brown hair, and a wrestler's shoulders. Homer LaRue, stout and ruddy, glanced at the cold stove and made a face. Evans patted his head.

"Old fatty here, he'd rather eat than fuck, ain't that right, Homer?"

"Lay off that shit, Evans," said LaRue.

"Who does the cooking?" Joe asked.

The blond man laughed.

"Bobby, sometimes. When he ain't crying for his maw."

McMillan slouched in adolescent misery. Joe nodded to him.

"I used to cook in hotels. Got some flour, some saleratus? Bobby can get me started, can't you, son?"

Tinned beef stew over hot biscuits for early supper, and he was their new best friend. The cabin was stifling, but cowboy fare took no notice of seasons. When Canfield brought out two bottles of rye whiskey, Joe took his tin mug back to the stove, let it sit, then cut the rye with water. At the table, Evans began to talk of Shiloh.

"Why hell, Grant brought up more troops and we was still beating him, till we ran low on ammunition. So we pulled back. I was with Bragg on the west. Could have skipped out right then, been on my way to Arkansas."

"But you had to wait for Vicksburg, right, Blue?"

LaRue was goading Evans, but carefully.

"I told a squirt lieutenant I had to go to the hospital tent, told him twice, and he called me a coward. I shot the fucker right in his nuts. He went down like a tree, with a little bounce. Then I borrowed a horse and was off to Texas. No more war for me. Say now, I believe that's mine." He flipped the last biscuit out of LaRue's reach and tossed it to the dog.

When it was almost full dark, Joe told LaRue he needed to stay at his upstream camp to protect his tools but would return tomorrow or the next day and cook another dinner, maybe help with breakfast too. The fat man waved a hand, then turned back to the card game.

• • •

The next day was so hot that Joe stayed on his bedroll under a rock ledge, enduring. In such weather the rustlers would sleep the day out. Another morning came, cooler, with mist rising from the Snake until nearly ten. Young McMillan and Vaughan, glad for diversion, joined him by the creek for a lesson in salting a pan of slurry with pounded buckshot; gold followed the lead. The boys were fifteen and seventeen, raised on neighboring Wallowa County ranches and out for adventure. Neither seemed overly criminal. Frank was all hands and feet, a skinny, inquisitive kid. He favored one leg a little, and said he'd fallen on some rocks. Bobby was dark-haired too, but four inches shorter, touchy and morose.

Joe talked with them about dogs and shotguns, and agreed that laying fence and chopping wood on the family spread was no match for the free life. After a while he trotted out his worst prospector jokes, the ones that made his own children run from the room — "Where can you buy the best mining tools? Pan Francisco!" — until at last he heard young McMillan's odd cracked laugh, which started as a croak, ended in a giggle. Bobby's voice had picked this summer to change.

Neither minded talking about their new trade, and by late afternoon Joe had a fair idea of the rustling operation: seven or eight men stealing horses in both Oregon and Idaho, crossing the Snake at Dug Bar, using Dug Cabin to rest the stock and alter brands, then selling to immigrant families and mining-camp packers on both sides of the river. Seven saddles sat on the corral's top rail. The cabin slept three plus two in each streamside tent. Why had the *Teller* reported twenty-five to thirty rustlers? Much too high.

Joe got the boys to find stove wood, dished up fried canned meat with cornbread and syrup, then went for a breath of air, so tired it was hard to think. He hadn't cooked this much in years. He was barely settled when Evans came up the porch steps and jerked his head.

The others scattered, even LaRue. Evans saw them off with a sardonic little bow, one elbow cocked, free hand circling twice, the urban dandy to the life, then claimed Canfield's rump-sprung rocker. Joe braced for interrogation, but Evans merely began to reminisce about a youth of driving hogs and cattle through the Cumberland Gap.

"Just loaf along. Make a few miles, let the stock forage, hunt a while, move on."

Joe nodded. "Not many women, I'll bet?"

Evans yawned. "Always something to fuck. Had a widow for a while, she had a farm and a kid, and I gave her a good time. After that I got down to Memphis. Went to gamble on the cockfights. They had good whores there, gals that could suck your bone dry, Salem."

"I notice you get called Blue. What kind of handle is that?"

"Blue is for Bleddyn, a good Welsh name. Pa was Welsh. Sang when he got drunk, and that was often. Ma was a looker. Irish. Smart too, taught me reading and sums, told me all the old stories about fays and banshees and whatnot. Died when I was in short pants."

"So after the War you come out West?"

Evans scowled. "Regular biographer, ain't you?"

"Just passing time. I like to visit. Everyone's got a different story about coming West. Want to hear mine?"

"Hell, no," Evans said. "Mine's better." In Memphis he killed a gambler and fled to Arkansas, then on into north Louisiana. Everyone back there knew he was someone of account. Reputation meant everything, he told Joe. And frolics. He liked frolics.

"I stayed for the fun at Colfax," Evans confided, "but some didn't care for my methods."

Joe hoped to hell Blue was lying. The siege of Negro refugees inside the Colfax courthouse had ended in mass shooting and mutilated dead. To be thrown out by the Klan as overzealous took some doing.

After '73, as far as Joe could tell, Evans drove cattle in Texas, Kansas, Montana, then Kansas again. He did time in Abilene for a killing, but the jury acquitted him for lack of evidence.

"I know my law, friend. I could plead before the bar in Oregon or Idaho."

Joe didn't doubt it. "For sure. About any white man is allowed to plead out here."

Evans agreed, at length. Ever since Little Bighorn in '76, any fool could see white folks had better wake up. The Nez Perce War in

'77 was just more of the same. And look at those Germans last year, blowing up Chicago.

"Now we got the hordes of Asia on our hands, monkeys by the thousands taking work away from decent citizens." He gestured at a pile of newsprint. Joe recognized *The Wasp*, out of San Francisco.

"What's that, missionary papers?"

"That's the Bible on keeping this country strong."

Joe thumbed a few issues, trying to read at arm's length in the waning light. In cartoon after cartoon, the Chinese were grotesques who bred with white women to make fish babies, smacked their lips over rats and dogs, hung a pigtail on the new Statue of Liberty. Editorials howled against the Six Companies and the murderous tongs. The layout was handsome, the engravings intricate, the copy a torrent of middle-class venom. Joe whistled.

"Pretty rough stuff. I don't know too many Chinese. They stick to themselves in the camps."

"I find some China boys alone, they better watch out, is all I can say."

"Your fellows told me some got killed up the river last month."

Evans swiveled and looked hard at Joe. "So I heard. It was probably a fight among them, you know, over who got to eat the birdshit that night." He laughed. "They ain't worth a fuck, Salem. They ain't even human. Yellow niggers. Like sheep or pigs. Only they're damn clever about taking jobs and salting away the money. Send it all home to China. Don't even want to be buried here. I say we got to get rid of every one, before they wreck this country."

Evans rose and took a long piss over the porch rail. Zeke came silently to his side. Evans looked up at the evening star.

"So I told you a lot tonight, Salem. How much you think was true?"

Joe knew the answer to that one. "As much as you want it to be, I guess."

Evans snapped his fingers at the dog. It lay down to let Joe pass.

"Come back tomorrow, old man. Or else I'll maybe come find you."

ELEMENTS

O N THE LOW SLOPE beside Deep Creek, six big tents hung from driftwood poles. In the boss tent, Chea Po and Lee She slept at the rear and used the front for camp business. Hong Lee ruled the cookhouse, a rough-built rock shelter. Sacks and barrels packed its lean-to: rice and oil, dried oysters and mushrooms, dried apples and seaweed. Yap and Dow stared until Lee She sent them off to bury the gut pile.

The butchering stand at creekside held the carcasses of two mule deer, shot that morning at the edge of camp. These days, Chinese in Gam Saan could not legally own firearms, but the party still had two pistols for protection and two Spencer carbines for killing fresh meat. Lee She acquired all four before leaving Lewiston, by means he would not discuss, even with Elder Boss. Their only other weapons were tools: picks and shovels, a half-dozen hatchets for chopping wood, and two heavy Collins machetes.

Without the guns, they would all starve. Once the weather turned, every man needed three pounds of meat every day. The pace of a secondary-extraction dig made even the strongest miners stagger as they left a shift. To make a profit, the sluices ran seven days a week. As winter set in and the light failed, the crews would work from can-see to can't-see.

• • •

47

When the young geomancer declared the cookhouse door could not face north, Hong Lee protested. His work was lonely. He wanted a river view. Mole held firm.

"The rock is too close, sir," he said patiently, amazed that Hong Lee did not care. An Duk did not like to contradict an elder, and annoying the cook was bad policy in any mining camp, but this was too important not to insist. "It blocks the best *qi*. Southeast, for abundance."

Grumbling, Hong Lee yielded. Metaphysics made him nervous. Yet when the camp was done, he produced another barrel – late watermelons packed in straw, hauled all the way from Lewiston – and told young Dow to hand Mole the first slice.

The two boys were a rarity: America-born Chinese, fathers long gone, mothers dead of fever. Dow was too thin but strong for his age and a born worrier. He and Chea Po got along very well. Yap, two years younger, was illiterate in both Chinese and English but could calculate long sums in his head and made friends with anyone, though the cook was his hero.

On mild fall afternoons, Elder Boss sometimes gave them leave to explore the alpine meadows above camp. Souvenirs rode home in Dow's hat. A double handful of hazelnuts. An obsidian arrowhead. A horned toad, inedible but lucky. A magpie feather, luckier still. Lim Ah added their reports to his map, which every week grew denser with detail.

Fong Low, the camp assayer, showed the cousins how to use an abacus. Hoy Sek, the herbalist, made them carry his collecting sacks as he ranged the slopes above Deep Creek, searching out plants to quicken and plants to soothe. Dow showed a flicker of promise in that art, Hoy Sek said. Yap, he hoped, had other skills, like ditch-digging.

The mining crews taught them too. Why washing hair on holidays rinsed out luck. When to clench the teeth while pissing, in order to hold *qi* inside the body when the male orifice is open and vulnerable. How to poke a nugget up your ass fast, if fortune smiled and the crew boss turned away. For just that reason, Chea Po rarely left the work-sites. Lee She, newly promoted to underboss, was even more watch-ful. Besides, gold in the Snake mostly floated, tiny glittering flakes, impossible to capture. By their second week at Deep Creek the boys stopped trying; a fortune ran through their fingers every time. No sieve, no net, could hold it.

Fall hardened into winter. Clouds hung low for days, hiding the cliff tops, weeping fine mist. Chea Po yearned to work the tantalizing bands of black sand in Robinson Gulch, but Company orders stood. *Work first along Dug Creek, then Robinson Gulch and Dug Bar.* He sent crews to sample from the old Douglas cabin back into the hills. Near the house they found a coin or two, a pair of pearl earrings, a rusted tin packed with rotted dollar bills, then nothing more. Chea Po took it all to the assayer, a thoughtful, steady man who still kept the farm-country accent of his Toisan boyhood. Fong Low put down his magnifying glass.

"All small value. Too bad. Are we after treasure, then?"

Chea Po did not answer. He disliked evading an old friend, but Company instructions were explicit. On this coveted contract trip, the Sam Yup paid all expenses plus a bonus to Chea Po as leader. Come June, he would return a rich man to the grown daughters he remembered only as toddlers. And to Mei, eighteen when he left, twice that now. An arranged marriage, but sound. With the money he sent home she had paid off their acres, invested in more, settled the doctor bills for his father's lung trouble, and managed a good bride price for both girls. A Sam Yup windfall excused any last de-lay. How his youngest howled when he left, despite Mei's attempts to hush her. Chea Po heard the wails all down the harbor road, though he did not once look back. *Shebude.*

Snow flurries swirled on the day the miners found the old Douglas cabin surrounded by a vocal flock of sheep. Two *da bidze* sat on the front porch, partners who leased the place from a local rancher. Lee

She, translating, learned that Louis Kapper and Robert James would stay the winter, their animals grazing the sheltered riverbanks and steep grassy slopes.

Chea Po bowed to both. Harmless until proven otherwise, he decided. The shepherds made no objection to mining, but some things foreigners must not see, so Dug Creek was out of bounds till spring. The crews would mine Dug Bar and the Gulch instead. A maze of sectioned wooden sluices went up, and then rocker boxes for washing soil. As two miners shoveled in gravel and sand, two more pulled the big handles back and forth, waiting only for gold particles to settle, stopping only when grit jammed the lines.

Beside the Snake, cairns of promising granite rose and fell as the river detail washed and checked each chunk by hand to find any shining vein. Some Chinese miners filtered sand through blankets, then burned each one to smelt the gold on the spot, but Elder Boss said no. Too conspicuous. Anyone working near the water knew to drop and stay down if a strange boat came near. One chilly morning Lee She spent twenty minutes behind a boulder, waiting out a pair of bearded white men in slouch hats, arguing as they rowed. *Drunk*, Lee She thought, then saw the shorter one cupping his ear and realized the other man was pointing at a pair of elk crossing the nearest ridge. Not drunk, deaf. And stupid. Even with a supremely lucky shot, retrieving the meat and packing it down to the river would be two days' work. The sourdoughs never noticed the sluices, the rock piles, the tied-down boats. *Da bidze* were like that.

An Duk worked daily with assayer and mapper to examine settlings from the rockers. Fong Low calculated values and quality, Lim Ah plotted soil yields, but only An Duk and his big circular compass could divine the living flows of energy and so tell the crews where to dig.

This stretch of the Snake was almost beyond his skills. Robinson Gulch, Dug Bar, Deep Creek: half the time, the cycles of generation and destruction felt distorted, or else they came in on him too fast, like a river in flood. These grim mountains were the very bones of the world. In the canyon of the Snake, nothing softened the Five Elements. The miners wrestled every moment with primal matter. Water, metal, earth, wood, fire.

Whenever the geomancer walked onto a prospective site with luopan and tripod and set to feeling out the local *qi,* his boyhood friends Lim Ah and Lee She stayed with him, one at each elbow. The crews watched from a respectful distance. Ground-reading took fortitude. Sitting in the boss tent to inspect the latest settlings was not so bad; a little sweating, a lot of dizziness. If only their takings were not so meager. The geomancer watched as Fong Low slid the counterweight up the rod of his rule scale, then used a carved bone to scrape gold dust into small glass flasks. A single vial might bring a thousand dollars, with a third going to the Sam Yup Company and the rest to the miners, in shares reflecting seniority. But with this slow yield rate, none of them would see a profit.

At one morning meeting in the boss tent, Lee She asked, "Should we look for caches?" The question was about as spontaneous as a rock to the head. Assayer, geomancer, herbalist, and cook waited in silence. They all liked Second Boss, but dissembling was not among his talents. Of course the Company wanted them to find something other than gold. Nobody glanced at Elder Boss. The silence deepened. Then Chea Po leaned forward, drew a careful breath, and began to talk freely for the first time since leaving Lewiston.

WHITE GHOSTS

NOVEMBER–DECEMBER 1886

KAPPER AND JAMES explained Thanksgiving to Lee She, who told Elder Boss, who liked the idea. The men needed a holiday. Their neighbors arrived in camp at midmorning, James carrying eight new-shot geese, Kapper his fiddle. Shepherds and miners sat against an old rock wall or beside the lone bare hackberry and played dominoes, then fan-tan, dealing long white cards with yells of laughter and shaking pebbles instead of coins from a cup.

In the cookhouse, kettles of rice steamed and puckered. Hong Lee, peering into three big woks, told his helpers to keep alert. Oil in the dark depths had begun to shimmer; the moment of *wok hei,* perfect flavor, would soon be passing.

As tin bowls of roast fowl and stir-fried salmon went around, James stood to sing the Old Hundredth. An Duk kept his gaze averted. Even well-meaning *da bidze* smelled bad, like milk, and their poor, pale eyes repelled him. For this formal occasion, Kapper had somehow produced a wrinkled white shirt. Such ignorance. In China, white is for mourning. Black is the color boy children wear, to make them strong; the color of winter, of water, of secrets.

The first true snow arrived, a dusting along the Snake, far deeper on the heights. Despite the growing cold, the miners persevered, hungry for bonanza. At least twice a week, crews of searchers moved along every upslope trail, hunting telltale mounds of earth or rock that might mark a cache.

One clear afternoon An Duk climbed the ridge above camp and looked toward an infinity of peaks, lilac in the fading light, range on range split by the lead-gray waters of the Snake. Duk was a low-lander, by birth and inclination; proper country to him meant the rainy green coast of southeast China and its red-roofed villages of blue brick, where markets sold pineapple and sugar cane. These barren backlands distressed him, personally and professionally. They only looked empty. Warding the camp and worksites against the murdered Tom Douglas was an endless chore.

If only the expedition had another geomancer! But Hoy Sek knew only herb lore. Fong Low, the assayer, was Christian now and could no longer help. Chea Po's taste for numerology would always keep him from real power. Lee She had the eye but not the will.

An Duk turned toward camp, a damp west wind at his back as he walked downslope. For months he had not seen one new face, civilized or *da bidze*. Almost no one came across Dug Bar any more, except stockmen hunting strays, or the rare chartered Wells Fargo coach carrying mail and payrolls to some distant diggings. At times a lone rider on a buckskin pony did ascend a game path toward the ridgeline, but he never stayed long or came near.

Dow and Yap called to An Duk from behind the cook shack. Two snowballs hit his neck. An Duk tackled Dow and returned the favor. Most of the miners were a little afraid of Duk, but at nineteen he was not quite beyond a good snow fight.

One morning near the turn of the year, the Deep Creek camp witnessed the passage of a massive white sturgeon.

"Come look!" the boys yelled, running from tent to tent, and the miners got to the shoreline in time to see the colossal fish move by, almost at the river's surface, its shining back and sides covered in five wide rows of bony pale gray plates, like armor for a god.

Yap stood entranced. Dow said, "It looks like a *dragon*."

Fong Low told him that was truer than he knew. Even in Gam Saan, dragons ruled all the free-running waters, but rivers especially. This great beast might be a colleague of Wang-Lung, the yellow dragon who taught an emperor how to write, or Pan-Lung, the coiling dragon of the deep, or even Futs-Lung, who guards all treasure, natural and manmade — the dragon who erupts from the underworld when you least expect him, so eager is he to report to heaven.

Chea Po guessed this particular Snake River sturgeon must weigh nearly twenty-five thousand taels, or eighteen hundred American pounds. A fish so large might be a century old, he told Dow and Yap. The boys watched a half-hour more as the great beast explored an eddy at the mouth of Deep Creek, swimming along the bank with a foot or two of sharklike dorsal fin showing above the dark water, then drifting sideways and dropping back, over and over.

"What an omen!" said Mole. Chea Po felt happier than he had in weeks.

MISSION BOY

JUNE 25, 1887

MISS SUNDOWN LOOKED from Lee's penciled list to the soot-streaked rubbish pile. "You've left out quite a lot. He wants a precise record. I'm afraid this won't do."

Even at riverside, the canyon temperature was close to a hundred. Lee put down the tablet and went to dip his hat in the pear-brown Snake, letting the water soak his hair and shirt. He watched her trowel, examine, write, move on. When she knelt or stood up it was all one movement, supple as an otter. Did the woman never tire? Or think to compliment a fellow? Maybe she was the kind of river guide who tickled fat trout in the shallows, then fried them in cornmeal. But as canyon shadows lengthened, she handed him soda crackers and tinned meat. He ate it all, then realized she had set no second plate.

As a budget item, she was a patent failure. Vincent believed in good hot meals, and he foiled vicious criminals to boot. Miss Sundown dealt with luggage, found water, pointed out rattlesnakes, and criticized people. No wonder she was a spinster. Except for knowing the back way to Dug Bar, she hadn't demonstrated much woodcraft. Lee wondered yet again if she was Vincent's popsy, and yet again dismissed the notion. The chill between them was clear, and Vincent, at least, was too old for carnal relations.

"Ma'am — Miss Grace — if you don't mind, who *are* you?"

At her polite inquiring glance, he lost his head.

"I think I have a right to ask. I never heard of a lady guide before. And I'm sick of being jollied along, okay? I *am* —" Courage and breath ran out together.

"Paying the bills," she said, nodding. "I'm delighted. Teachers don't earn that much."

"Wait. You're not a tracker?"

"Sometimes, yes. And Mr. Vincent and I are only trying to keep you safe."

"I favor that," said Lee, but he shook his head like a dog coming out of water. She knotted the canvas food bag and stepped over a dry wash to sit beside him.

"It's no great mystery. In summer I work for my cousin, Georges Sundown. He's a horse breeder over in Oregon. We take city people on riding trips into the Cascades. Wilderness is fashionable these days, and a female guide means wives and daughters may come along. Sadly, they've all read that wretched *Ramona*."

"You dress this way there too?" Lee burst out.

Miss Sundown said gravely, "No, I have a divided riding skirt, nice and long. The Oregon tours aren't so strenuous. In winter I teach at the Sacred Heart girls' academy back in Portland. Geography, French, deportment."

"Killing bears," said Lee, greatly daring.

"On occasion. My father was French, you understand, my mother Nimipu. Nez Perce."

He swallowed hard. She passed him a tin cup of raisins.

"Dessert. At any rate — Lee, are you listening? — Georges and I first learned to track here at Deep Creek. His father, my mother's brother, kept the old ways. Right to the end. Georges sent me on this job, even though it left us short-handed in high season. We thought it was important. Here I am."

"That leaves out a lot," Lee Loi muttered.

"Yes. But you noticed. Not many would."

She stood up. Lee did not move.

56

"And the judge?"

"Another noticer. We don't get along, but it's nothing to do with these killings. You'll have your answers. More than you want."

Lee's eyes dropped first.

Next day they rowed to Robinson Gulch and searched there too, wandering through the wreckage of a sluice system at riverside and recovering dozens of spent bullet casings, plus a half-fractured stick like a ruler with colored emblems etched along the sides.

"What do you think?"

He studied it. "The little shapes are plants, I'd say. Maybe an herbal guide?" He slid it into their burlap-sack evidence bag.

As they waited out noontime heat, he asked with vast casualness what tracking really entailed. Mostly common sense, she said lightly. Don't step on the evidence; learn stillness. One broken cracker remained from lunch and she spread its crumbs atop Lee's hat, then coached him in a curious hissing call—*pissh, pissssh*. When he glanced around for further instruction, she was gone, without trace or word.

Trapped under the laden hat, he waited, called, waited, then felt a thump as some tiny creature landed to feast. He could only track his guest's progress by its taps and flutters.

"Junco," said Miss Sundown in his ear, making him jump.

After supper they dug again beside the rock wall and found four dented tin bowls. Lee, excited, declared the site some kind of kitchen.

"A cook keeps up fires all day, and this gully would hide the smoke. They really did know what 'a Chinaman's chance' means out here. Anyone could sneak in and just . . . I never thought—I mean, everyone knows . . ."

Grace finished his sentence in her head, or close to it: *That the lower classes don't feel as we do.* To American eyes the dead miners were all Chinese alike, but to a Lee Loi the lost were business pawns, ciphers on a balance sheet. And peasants. Granting them feelings and faces seemed to be new terrain. The men who worked the mines and railroads of the West were not coolie slaves, no matter what politicians claimed, but some were so deep in debt to the Six Companies that they might as well be indentured. *Rented like shovels,* Joe said bitterly, out of Lee Loi's hearing. But then Joe's family had been for abolition, decades before the War.

"Tell me about your college life," she said. "How did you get to Connecticut, of all places?"

His back was still to her. "I was a Mission kid. It's a long story."

"Good," said Grace. Behind them a canyon wren sang a descant and left. Evening light was turning the gray cliff across the river to plum and Prussian blue. She set a mug of tea beside him, and the last of the raisins.

When Lee Loi was eight, his parents let him join the Chinese Educational Mission. A progressive scholar named Yung Wing was gathering boys to study in America, all the way through college, to become the engineers, doctors, and lawyers of modern China. Lee's parents saw the honor, his grandfather the danger.

"He said I'd cut off my queue, fold my silk coat, and never return. He was right, I guess."

"What do you remember about your parents?"

"They eloped. Bad form. My mother was an innkeeper's daughter, up in the hills. My father was a Canton banker's son who came for a holiday and stayed for the pretty tea-maid. My grandfather disowned him, then changed his mind when he heard there was to be a . . . a happy event. But he also gave away my father's seat in the bank to a younger brother who had ambition to spare. Still does. My uncle's not exactly one for wine and calligraphy under the pines."

"What did your mother think of all this?"

"I don't know." He had never considered it. "I remember her red bean soup. And every morning she let me drop pebbles down our well because I liked the sound. Not much else. I used to go with her to buy rice and vinegar. She always praised me for helping. Probably I just got in the way."

"So you obeyed your parents, and left your world."

"They put us on a Pacific Mail steamer," said Lee, "first to Yokohama, then America. Six weeks at sea. We played tag on the deck. In San Francisco old men came up to us in the streets, weeping because they hadn't seen Chinese boys for decades. *Shebude,* they kept saying."

Miss Sundown laid another piece of driftwood on the fire. "*Seh-boo-deh.* And that is . . . ?"

"Canton people, Toisan people—you think it to yourself, leaving behind some place you love. Or someone. *Shebude.* Can't bear to let go. So best not look back."

Lee studied his tin mug. "We stayed with foster families all over New England. For seven years, I lived with Dr. and Mrs. Bartlett. I owe them a lot. The white boys called me China Girl—because of my queue, you know. But I gave more black eyes than I got. One spring Master Yung let us buy coats and trousers, and by then I was pretty far gone. Eating with a knife and fork, helping the Bartletts with their chickens. Playing third base."

"Did the other boys change too?"

"So fast that one inspector reported the Mission as a failure, and a new director arrived, sent to shut us down if he could. Some boys were in debt and others turned Christian. Master Wang said we were all a disgrace."

By then Lee Loi was sixteen. At the news that his father had died, he thought of quitting, but Master Yung, a Yale graduate, helped Lee enter with the Class of '83, as proof that the Asian scholars' program could succeed.

"I held my own in recitations. Played baseball. Sang in *Pinafore.* Cut off my queue, started going to New York a lot, even pledged DKE. Another China student—Mun Yew Chung, my year, great man—he ended up coxing for the crew. Y. C. was a real Bible thumper, never swore, but in the last minute of the Harvard race he finally yelled 'Damn it, boys, pull!' and they won."

The spring of '82 was hardest. "Sixty of us were at work on degrees, but Peking called everyone home because the Chinese Exclusion Act was about to pass here."

Lee left valise and book box on the westbound train, swung off the rear platform at the Springfield stop, and walked twelve miles to the Bartlett home, desperate to stay.

"I wrote my mother to ask forgiveness, and months later she replied: *Do what you must, my son and lord, though we may never meet in this life again.*"

"Oh my," said Miss Sundown.

Lee began jabbing a twig at the sandy ground.

"I studied hard to bring my parents honor," he told her finally. "Soon I need to give them descendants. I still send her all the money I can. But long before that letter came, I went back to New Haven. I found a waiter's job, and a room, and finished my classes. Then the Sam Yup needed a bilingual finance man and hired me straight off."

Miss Sundown said nothing, only began to bank the fire. Without being asked, Lee went to collect the bedding. *Progress,* she thought, and slept. Lee Loi lay with his hands under his chin, watching the moon rise twice over—in the river, in the sky.

When the racket of birdsong woke Lee at dawn, his blanket was heavy with dew and the fancy Lewiston jacket under his head smelled of wood smoke. Miss Sundown was gone. Then he spotted her halfway along the slope south of Deep Creek, wading toward him through knee-high grass. Above her was the dark mouth of a little cave. He'd never noticed it. And she had never pointed it out. He splashed across the stream to meet her.

"What are you *doing?*"

"Posting a letter."

"You mean leaving it up there? Why? Who's it for?"

"Mind your own business, Lee," she said, heading for the excavation site. It was six in the morning, but he knew by now that she did not believe in breakfast. Or rest, or small talk. After a moment he went to the riverbank, found his trowel, and started digging.

IMBALANCE

JANUARY–FEBRUARY 1887

L EE SHE HAD THE GIFT of sleep. Chea Po envied the way the younger man could pull his coat over his head and be dreaming in seconds, not staring at the dark and bargaining with heaven. As days of sleet sent frost up the inside face of every tent, the crews had almost stopped gambling in the warming tent at night. Another worry. A Canton man will bet on the hour a wind shifts from east to west. Joking was rare now at the sluices, and enough arguments broke out that Hoy Sek said the camp was sliding toward the five imbalances that shorten life: too little good food and contented sex, too much emotion and desire for fortune, too much thinking.

Early in First Month the Snake River winds turned so bitter that crews could not feel their fingers inside leather work gloves and flumes began freezing up. Struggling back toward camp one evening, Lee She was astonished to see snowflakes the size of his hand. They had six hours of daylight and used every second, but the work was slowing. Lee She thought he might never be warm again, yet as Second Boss he could show no weakness, no fear. He went up and down the lines, tongue-lashing every team into redoubled labor. When one crewman slipped on snow-covered tailings and sent a half-day of gleanings spilling off the riffle bars, Lee She let rage take him, grabbing the man's collar and grinding his face into the wet silt. The worker fought free and screamed back; under the grit and mud

61

he saw Lim Ah. Mole had to separate them, though he was half Lim Ah's size. The three friends did not speak for days.

The rough humor and ritual insult of any long dig now had a vicious edge, and Lee She knew how fast mouth fights turned to fist fights. Men quarreled like scholars over Canton news a decade old: the year of a big fire, the name of a dumpling vendor. Late on one shift two of Lee She's best miners swung at each other with shovels. One hit a shoulder, the other clipped a chin, and their blows dislodged a section of sluice. The blast of water swept both into the icy Snake.

Since the men died in rage and terror, their ghosts might turn on the living; herbalist and geomancer worked for hours to pacify the sundered spirits. Ordinarily, if one miner attacked another, Chea Po would publicly whip the offender, then order him to kneel and beg forgiveness. But he could not command obedience of a ghost, much less two.

In the boss tent, Chea Po and Lee She sat in silence. The deaths were on both their heads: they had not moved fast enough to defuse bad feeling. With the New Year ten days off, they set everyone to purging the camp: mud wrung from bedding and work clothes, earth thrown down latrines. Miners went in relays to the hot springs downstream, to soak in steaming water as snowflakes drifted down.

Hong Lee managed a semblance of a feast, serving steamed whole fish for abundance and noodles in broth for prosperity. No savory turnip cake, no extra servings to signify good fortune. These days he slept across the threshold of his supply tent with a cleaver in his hand. But he did send around a bowl of fried watermelon seeds, saved since fall to make a New Year's tidbit.

Near midnight Dow and Yap burst into the mess tent with a blanket over their heads, roaring and stamping. The miners cheered; every New Year needed a lion dance. Elder Boss handed each boy a ten-cent piece wrapped in a scrap of red flannel, the traditional *lai see* money from elders to juniors. The crew's best hunter carried a rifle outside and fired six shots, the number of fast progress toward wealth. Half an hour later, two worried shepherds appeared, fearing trouble, then joined the party. When Chea Po gave his New Year's toast—"To say farewell to the land of the Flowery Flag"—the approving yells went on so long that a puzzled Kapper and James turned to Lee She.

"Good health, long life, and money," said Younger Boss blandly, and clinked his tin cup against theirs.

An Duk tried to join the merriment, but his smile was strained. They were moving from a dog year to a pig year, normally a lucky change; pig years were good for prosperity and home life. But this was a rarity, a fire pig year, water over flame, two elements eternally at odds. Even worse, it was a yin fire year. Conflict was coming, and it centered on gold. If violence and grief were inevitable, An Duk hoped they would strike somewhere far away. It seemed likely. Even the gods must have forgotten this hellhole of a Gam Saan canyon.

Five weeks on, the snows grew deeper, the prospecting worse. The shepherds invited Chea Po to work Dug Creek as well as Dug Bar and Robinson Gulch, but soon half the mining camp was down with cough and fever. Hoy Sek tried everything—licorice tea to cool the blood, *pu* foods to strengthen it—but no vinegar broth or coin water could save the pair of brothers from south Canton who died of pneumonia on the same night.

The loss of four men was the essence of ill luck, and some miners now openly said that Tom Douglas's ghost had cursed the whole dig. Chea Po sent the geomancer back to Dug Creek, and at his neutral report the men subsided, morose and anxious.

In morning conference, Hoy Sek proposed a weekly pipe of opium. Chea Po was opposed. In this brutal, exacting work, dulled men could soon be dead. But beside him, the cook spoke up. "Let them, old friend. Otherwise we could have trouble."

Chea Po pushed open the tent flap and walked toward the riverbank, his scarred hands thrust inside the muddy sleeves of his padded jacket. Since fall, the tin jar of opium and the long bamboo pipes had stayed in Hong Lee's spice locker, insurance against a dark night of the spirit. In other winter camps, Elder Boss had seen Chinese miners plot for treasure even as frostbite festered their hands and feet; had watched a big-nose down a quart of bright-eye — bourbon, laced with cocaine — then strip a dying comrade for his gold dust.

Fear and despair killed too. That evening Hoy Sek used a loop of wire to capture a dozen small sticky chunks from the opium jar, heating them over the tiny spirit lamp until each cloudy black crystal glowed amber. The warming tent filled with sweet tarry smoke. Outside, snow beat down on the passing river.

Not everyone wanted escape. An Duk, the geomancer, reveled in the dream worlds the pipe showed him. Fong Low, the assayer, stayed away. Hong Lee refused every time, saying opium did not mix with the fire and steel of his trade. When the men partook, he kept the two boys with him in the cookhouse.

But in the privacy of their tent Lee She urged Chea Po to use this door into summer, and Elder Boss began looking forward to the miraculous glow that eased the ache in his bones and his back. Sometimes Mei came to him, young and glad, with golden lotus blossoms in her hand and red ribbons in her long black hair.

MR. SALEM

FOR THREE DAYS old Mr. Salem shambled about cabin and creek, turning elk into steak and steak into stew, always ready to sit and visit. He was a good storyteller, though now and again he would lose the thread, sit humming and staring, and need to be prompted. But he took a real interest in everyone. Hiram Maynard traded Bible verses with the old man, and interpretations too. No one else (except Evans, sometimes) would indulge Maynard's passion for exegesis. After Carl Hughes found that the wandering miner knew horses, they sat on the porch most mornings and talked of trotters and pacers and the best drench for colic: a little aloe, a lot of cascara.

Slowly Joe pieced out the early story of the rustling operation. Evans and Canfield did their recruiting last winter, pulling a gang from the region around Imnaha, Oregon; got serious about stock-lifting in April; began squatting at the Douglas cabin by early May. They made no secret of their thievery. Evans called it dry mining.

Yet these months of profitable crime made the killings more peculiar, not less. Most rustlers would seize any gold and merely run the aliens off. Sections of a competent sluice system were still in place near the river, but Joe could spot no distinctive evidence of Chinese use. The floodwaters had erased too much.

Opportunity they had, with the miners working so near. The means for slaughter were clear as well, for Joe could now testify that much of the ammunition at Dug Cabin was .44 caliber, able to kill at one hundred yards, and shared among six revolvers — five Colts, one Smith & Wesson — and four lever-action rifles, two Kennedys and two Winchesters, one with a chipped bore and another with barrel rust. Evans carried a Remington pistol, an Army model from just before the War.

Evans liked to be different. Joe figured he did it to get an edge on people: *I know something you don't.* But Joe was also confident that many of the bullets entered at the Lewiston inquest would match the weapons he saw at the cabin.

Motive still escaped him, poke and eavesdrop though he might. Gold lust alone did not explain the scale of the murderous rampage, or the extremes of its cruelty.

Only three of the rustlers felt like professional criminals. The boys were runaways, in over their heads; Maynard a God-struck bad man — the Northwest still had a surprising number — and Hughes a good horseman but indifferent rancher, along for the money. Probably Hughes was the rebranding specialist. All it took was a piece of heavy wire heated gray-hot, the color of fire ashes, and a good eye for the slash or curve that made an *F* an *E*, an *R* a *B*. No one used the running iron when Joe was there to see, but each morning more horses had new-scarred flanks.

Tee Canfield was a thug, a bone-breaker. Joe knew the name. Wanted for robbery and rustling. LaRue felt like a moneyman, maybe counterfeiting, maybe bank swindles. He might shoot you in the back, but only if he couldn't run. And LaRue and Evans circled each other like wary dogs.

Watching Evans dominate the rest, Joe found himself thinking *Nice touch* and *That shut him up* and even, once, *Well, I'd do it another way.* He'd seen this natural magnetism, this mix of menace and humor, only in certain preachers and lecturers, some ambitious businessmen (John Vollmer back in Lewiston, for one), and quite a few fellow politicians. Blue was reasonably good-looking, preternaturally quick, and not quite human; his eyes had the chill of deep water. Joe

66

suspected that Evans, alone of the rustlers, did not find Mr. Salem endearing.

But Evans spent time with him nonetheless, even wading in to help pan. Blue knew enough to shake and tilt the dish beneath the surface to let grit and debris float away, and he swirled the leavings like an expert. Dug Bar and the nearby creeks shared the dark, gleaming placer sands coveted by pick-and-pan miners; over time, dense metals like copper and silver sank through the earth, moving down and out, usually toward water, and gold was heaviest and most elusive of all.

Blue wanted to know Mr. Salem's views on everything. Food, changes in the Territory, the mining life, politics. Joe Salem was flattered by all the interest. So was Joe Vincent, just a touch. One afternoon Evans seemed melancholy. He sat on the stream bank, shredding a clump of moss strand by strand. Joe waited him out.

"I worry about those boys," Blue said finally. He looked up, eyes sober and direct, quite without mockery. "They worked for Carl, you know, over in Imnaha. After school. Tagged along here. Too far, I thought, to send them back alone."

Joe nodded. Evans gave him a smile of rare sweetness. Although dirty and unshaven, when he smiled like that, few citizens would hesitate to hand him a baby for minding. For an instant Joe could imagine the eager, active boy in the hardened man, and thought of the mother who tried to teach him all she could in the little time granted her.

Blue dropped the bits of moss. The current bore them away.

"The rest of us are pretty much beyond redemption, but if it ever comes to shooting and such—I'd like them both far off, and safe."

He pushed himself up and walked back toward Dug Cabin, the fair head bent.

On the fourth day, doing his best to turn a chaotic larder into meals for eight, Joe made potato soup. A bad move. Soup was pap for the sick, as the eel and cutthroat trout in the Snake were strictly food for bears. He studied his clientele. Canfield in particular looked both hungry and mean. As Joe retreated up the shore path, he improved the time by rehearsing Mr. Salem's halting gait, which of late had turned a little too free. He refined the voice too, conjuring up companions, playing all the parts. *Talk and walk, Vincent. Concentrate.*

Enacting the dimwit for days on end was harder than he'd guessed. In previous outings Salem was a cracker-barrel sage; people told him too much out of sheer boredom. This time instinct made Joe show his throat from the first, but it wasn't working. What if the kindly old-timer got a little sharper? Less the codger, more the—

An arm closed around Joe's neck, yanking his head back. A gun barrel dug painfully into his right ear. Pick and pan clattered onto the stony shore. He smelled sweat and ginseng. *Evans.* Joe had no trouble producing an old man's wail.

"Don't like to discomfit you, *Mister* Salem. Maybe you'd care to show me your boat."

Jesus in the wilderness. This was how you died. Too lazy to make the lie airtight. Of course Evans would check where the nosy stranger went each night. Joe saw the miner's pan start to float downstream, wailed again, and struggled, but only as much as Salem might. Blue let him go, laughing.

Joe floundered into the shallows to grab the pan. How long had Evans watched him? He could not remember falling entirely out of character on the walk up the Snake, but at best Salem would look subject to fits, at worst like a goddamn overconfident lawman working up a part. The voices were mostly Salem; the vocabulary, not quite. Joe had been in tighter situations, but not many. *Head up, play it out, you never know.*

Blue waited on the shore, practicing fast-draw with his pistol, twirling it by the guard, tossing and catching. Joe came toward him, staggering, hangdog.

"Son, two nights ago they took my boat. Every last thing I had in this world. And I just thought, since you boys been so white to me, that maybe I—"

"Who's *they?*"

"Damn Indians—who else is out here?"

68

"And you thought—"

"Th-that I could maybe earn the price of a horse. By cooking and such."

"And such."

Evans studied him, head cocked. Then, like forgiveness, the smile came again.

"I watch you every day, working so hard. Don't mind that Tee. He's a hard-ass. We'll get you on your way. Least we can do."

Relief made Joe stagger a little more, and he found he yearned to tell Evans the whole truth, even as he recognized his own best interrogation techniques. The gentle voice, the rueful twinkle. Usually they brought results. Now he knew why. He also knew he was a breath away from floating face-down to Portland. People disappeared all the time, especially up Hells Canyon, even in this civilized age.

Blue collected Mr. Salem's bedroll and knapsack from under the rock ledge, then nodded him back toward Dug Cabin. As they followed the shore path north, twilight stole color from the river, turning the jade current to violet, then gray.

"Sorry to scare you, Pop," murmured Evans after a while. "I thought for a bit you were a stock detective. I got to be careful. But like I said, we'll see you right."

"Blessed are the merciful," said Mr. Salem, trying to keep pace, not doing too well.

"Don't I know it," said Blue Evans.

Next morning the rustlers rode across Dug Bar and into Idaho, disappearing up the narrow side canyon that led to the rim country, far above the Snake. Joe took full advantage.

A faint depression in the riverbank near the cabin yielded three decomposing bodies, still in the baggy denims and rough linen shirts that Chinese miners favored. The faces had fallen prey to carcass beetles and maggots, but corpse wax was forming on the cheek fat, which seemed right for a month to six weeks after death. All three decaying throats looked slit.

Joe wondered if the bodies had washed up here, or if the rustlers brought these miners back to the cabin for more torture, then knifed them all. He collected a jacket button and some black hair from each victim as evidence, then searched every pocket he could reach, but the only distinctive find was a brass Chinese coin with a square hole in the center. Someone's lucky piece.

He remade the grave with a jeweler's care, then brushed out his boot tracks and returned to set up a kettle of ham and beans, watched by a surly Zeke. Joe offered the black dog a sliver of meat and nearly lost a finger.

He knew what happened to match dogs that quit or faltered. For that betrayal they might be shot, or burned, or drowned, or hanged, or beaten to death with an ax handle. Oregon and Idaho had a lot of Southerners now, many still defiant. They loved dog-fighting and states' rights as much as they hated race-mixing. Sometimes it seemed the War had taken a breather, then sent all its unfinished business west and north. The region was short on Negro residents, but Chinese laborers made a fine target for leftover rage. Evans was more sentimental about his dog than some, but Joe wondered what would happen the day Zeke lost a big-money fight.

A search of the cabin yielded a bundle of cash in someone's spare boots and two small vials of gold in the depths of a musty straw mattress. No markings. Could be anyone's. He crawled under the rotting porch, ducked behind the cabin to inspect a former garden, now an overgrown weed patch, and even felt all around the bottom of a rain barrel. Nothing and nothing. He used the privy's shard of looking glass to renew the black wax on his upper teeth, checked his neck for fleas, then went glumly back to stir the beans.

All week Joe had told himself these men were innocent of anything but the capital crime of rustling until he could show otherwise. All week his intuition had shouted *Guilty*. Three bodies in the cabin's front yard only made it official.

More than any killer he'd ever known, Joe wanted Evans to hang. Thinking clearly around Blue was like fighting ether at the dentist.

Now and then Joe still caught himself hoping to find the man honest work, or else offer pointers on running for office. Talent deserved rescue. *Why not just adopt him and be done with it? He's probably good with old people.* But self-mockery helped only a little.

The alien dead at Joe's feet broke him free. He sat by the Snake, head down, gasping like a man snatched from an undertow, more afraid than ever, and started thinking his way back into the slaughters of May.

He knew too much; he knew almost nothing. How do you kill thirty-one Chinese?

No, he thought. *No. Thirty-one men.* It must take days: days for the impaled to die, inch by inch. Days for the gut-shot to expire of sepsis, each miner twitching in a pool of clotted blood and shit. Days for bound men raped with their own shovel handles to crawl to the Snake, desperate for water; for the handless flayed to surrender to shock, their living lidless eyes already a feast for black fly and raven.

Did Maynard pray as he tortured? Did Bobby McMillan laugh? After a life in law-keeping and politics, Joe figured he had few illusions, but the thought of schoolboys cutting a neck artery and watching blood spurt high unnerved him. Yet it happened every fall at hog-killing time, on every farm in Idaho. What a pile of crap from Evans, about the innocents in his care.

In warm weather Dug Cabin was not that isolated, by Snake River standards. The risk of chance witnesses to the carnage was real. During the hours of slaughter, did they post lookouts at Deep Creek and the Gulch? LaRue might think ahead that coldly. Evans? No question.

But how to keep the others at such ghastly labors, their silence ensured? Why both torture and kill? Surely the aim was to get the miners' gold, not risk prison and hanging. Except for Maynard's clumsy interrogation by the Snake and Blue's calculated rant on the porch, Joe had not intercepted one reference to the Chinese killings. What they said at night when real drinking began, he did not know. And time was short.

71

If ever he took this case to a jury, the mechanics of mass murder would be a key. Did the gang row from site to site, ambushing at will, and did the Chinese try to flee or fight? How exactly do you resist seven men with high-powered weapons? At Robinson Gulch as at Deep Creek, the hunters of men had plenty of cover, plenty of high ground. Both were important. Joe had sent friends and neighbors to fight and die in wilderness very like this once, but in wartime a surprise attack was different. Permitted. Whatever Deep Creek had been, it wasn't war.

When the riders returned that evening with a new string of five workhorses, they found the old prospector curled up at the cabin's threshold, mumbling. A depleted bottle lay under the nearest chair. The porch smelled like a distillery and so did he. LaRue kicked him awake.

Mr. Salem beamed up at the circle of hostile faces and staggered off to fetch supper, shuffling gamely to and fro with laden plates. He ate last, hunched at the far end of the table and gumming the beans, but his eyes would not focus and often the spoon missed his mouth entirely. It confused him every time. He tried to lick the plate and missed that too. Even the dour Tee Canfield was laughing.

The old man put both hands between his knees and began to rock, ashamed, nearly crying. Joe was about to slide artistically under the table when a hand took his elbow.

"Come on, Grandpa."

Frank Vaughan was pulling him up, thrusting a shoulder under his arm, guiding him to a blanket in the corner. Bobby McMillan came to help, sliding a rolled-up shirt under Joe's head with a worried glance at the other men. To get Mr. Salem more comfortable the boys tried to take his hat, but he clutched the brim with such zeal that they let him keep it.

Ten feet away, Evans was making Zeke jump for his dinner of skinned jackrabbit, encouraging the dog to snap and tear. Bobby flinched as Evans strolled over, but the blond man only bent to pull off Salem's boots. The ankle holster stayed put; the left stocking came off to reveal alarmingly dirt-encrusted toes. Joe — drooling, whimpering — silently blessed Lee Loi.

"Check his stash," Evans said. Hands fumbled under the neck of the greasy shirt.

"Five dollars, one nugget," young Vaughan reported, his voice shaking only a little. Four gold nuggets lay in the leather pouch.

"Keep an eye on him, so he don't choke on his own puke. Later we'll have some fun. Zeke's more 'n ready."

Joe remembered the Chinese faces in the autopsy reports, gnawed to bone; recalled the bound hands and feet. *Jesus.* He lay sprawled on the blanket, mouth half open, and felt sweat trickle down his backbone. Something touched his right eyelid, soft as thistledown, caressed the eyeball, followed along the curve of the brow bone, paused, went away. It felt like a fingertip.

"Look, Bobby. I said, look."

Get the fuck away from me, Evans, Joe thought, but lay still.

"Here," said Blue's voice, gentle in the darkness. "See? And here."

Joe thought he was ready, but Blue's fingernails dug hard in the left eye socket instead, prying, lifting. Joe saw a flash of red, then white, before pain seamed the upper eyelid. Joe rolled his head away, moaning in drunken protest. He knew what had happened. Like the old-time eye gougers, Evans kept one thumbnail honed, sharp as any knife. Joe was betting that Blue would not kill an unconscious white man outright in front of six witnesses, but he knew a warning when he felt one. Bruce Blue Evans, his mark.

"Hey," said a young voice to his left. Frank Vaughan. "Come on. Hey."

Evans chuckled. "Pay the forfeit, then."

Joe heard the kiss, and the drunken raspberries and cheers from the table.

Two hours. Three. Joe dared not turn over, though his back was an agony of cramp. Blood from his cut eyelid had run all down the side of his face, judging by the flies now paying a call. Candlelight from tin reflectors danced on the log walls as talk at the table grew contentious. Good. Anything to keep Zeke on the chain.

"—didn't risk my neck for no three hundred—"

"—cut out while we can—"

"—not riding so high without your fancy friend—"

"—who's to say it ain't no sin—"

"—just a couple of sacks, could've gone to Lewiston and be done with it—"

"—can't hold out on us much longer, Blue—"

The Dixie in Evans's voice suddenly got stronger. "And you cain't do much without me, damn low-down lazy ass-draggers."

Morning dawned hazy and hot, with a vast red sun. Seven days? Eight? If Grace didn't wait, he'd have a long walk back, but any boatman on the Snake would trade a nugget for a ride to Lewiston.

Joe slid out to the privy at first light, then ducked into the lean-to. He'd run out of time the day before, giving its rubbish heap only a cursory search. *Just a couple of sacks.* Under rotting potatoes and rusted cans, he discovered two stained, crumpled burlap bags with stenciled Chinese markings, eased one open, felt the inside seams, and found a few rice grains. Joe folded that bag small and thrust it down his pants leg. Reconnaissance was done.

Mr. Salem lifted a hand to the early risers—Hughes and Maynard—and drifted off, hauling pick and pan. They were drinking his fresh coffee and eating the last of the canned peaches. He'd set those out specially. Sweet tooth mostly beat blood lust, but Joe knew how bored they all got by noon, Zeke more than any, and he wanted to be long gone.

From the corner of his eye he saw LaRue come onto the porch too, looking hung over. *Never mind me, boys. Part of the landscape.* He wandered the stony shore, weaving this way and that, ending up a few yards more to the north each time, making always for the river bend and the Deep Creek trail beyond.

INNER BOX

APRIL–MAY 1887

C HEA PO HAD NEVER been so glad to see spring. A pair of canyon wrens nested near the main camp, too small to shoot and eat, too cheeky to ignore. Rain swelled Deep Creek, sped the river current and made the work easier, but the take was still scant. Gulch, bar, and cove were pockmarked with trial holes. Since his admission to the camp that the Company wanted a hidden box found, the miners swung picks and shovels at every likely site, galvanized by thoughts of treasure.

Past time to follow the last Company directive: *If no success by spring, send men to try at Salt Creek.* The order contradicted his strongest instinct, to hold the camp together, and he was sorely tempted to defiance. Salt Creek was miles upriver, past a major run of rapids. Twelve men, no more. Lee She would head them. Orders were orders. Even now, Elder Boss had to believe that the Sam Yup looked after its own.

We need you for a special job up the Snake, the Company officer said, after a lavish dinner at Lewiston's Hip Sip lodge. *Frost Moon to Grain Rains — October to May. We want you as leader, no one else. Many influentials in Dai Fow know your reputation for honest dealing.*

Who? Who? I don't deserve your praise, Chea said, ducking the compliments as modesty demanded. He could hire anyone he liked,

75

so long as every man was a Sam Yup client. Chea Po would have done that anyway. He was a Sam Yup man himself, of course.

Ning Yung, Hop Wo, Kong Chow, Yung Wo, Yan Wo, Sam Yup: the Six Companies could help you locate compatriots, secure loans, find jobs. When Americans made trouble in the lives of civilized persons, a Company protected you, even if it meant hiring barbarian lawyers. The Six ran San Francisco's Chinatown, controlled the labor markets, and spoke for Chinese anywhere in Gam Saan, from New York to Los Angeles. Having them behind you was well worth that huge bite from earnings, or so Chea Po always believed.

Like every other experienced mining boss, he'd heard the Companies were under pressure from the rising West Coast tongs, a situation best met by knowing how to wait and why. Secret societies, criminal money, placeless outcasts without a clan; he wanted none of it. Personal loyalty came first, and his lay with family and Company.

He thought of Mei, his daughters, and his ancestors, and he bowed the Sam Yup man back onto the coast steamer. The Company's letter of credit lay safely in his pocket. At least one of his Snake River crew would probably have *guanxi,* connections to some Sam Yup official. Good. Then his responsibility was not so absolute. If the Company was desperate enough to mount an expedition this large, at odds this long, Chea Po intended to have a look at the prize, orders or no. But then, as ever, he would do his duty.

An Duk knelt beside the two vessels bound for Salt Creek and cast the Eight Diagrams, seeking journey omens. Water came up twice, in the configuration that meant *danger, rapid rivers, the abyss.* He thought hard of Beuk Aie, god of flood, lord of destiny, patron of profit, then tried again, but got the mountain. *Stillness, anger, sorrow.* Lee She was waiting, one hand on his amulet, so Mole looked up and made the good-fortune sign anyway, clasping his hands chest-high. His friend's relief made it easier to live with the lie.

Every week the Snake grew busier. Several boats a day now went by Dug Bar, and the rowers always stared, sometimes hostile, always curious. "Having any luck, boys?" "How long you been here?" The

Chinese only shook their heads. But the growing exposure made Chea Po uneasy.

Early in April, Kapper and James crossed to Idaho and drove their flock into high pastures. There the sheep could fatten until June, then go to slaughter or clipping before the long autumn drive back into the canyon. *Next year at home,* thought Chea Po, *I should invest in sheep.*

The following day brought the Feast of Pure Brightness, also called Tomb-Sweeping Day, to honor departed ancestors. Chea Po recalled the gilded festival boats on Canton's broad Pearl River: the holiday scent of night-fragrant flowers, the goat-horn lanterns outside each city teahouse, the willow branch clutched in his daughter's chubby hand. He would give a great deal for ten minutes with the street-corner cricket-sellers, whose glossy fighting insects rode like tiny emperors in woven rice-stem cages the size of teacups. In memory, all the starveling crooked alleys and narrow lanes of his boyhood quarter shone with fragrant mud and silver mist.

At least the Pure Brightness kites were the same. Elder Boss watched Dow and Yap row downstream and tie off on a rock. With a fresh breeze at their backs, they played out two wobbly creations of hoarded paper scraps. The little kites swung past the dark canyon walls, attracting a single golden eagle. At this favorable sign the miners drank their watery nettle soup with lighter hearts, every sip a blessing.

The next week seven strangers rode in to the Dug Bar cabin and stayed. They studied the Chinese workings, then lingered in the patchy shade of Robinson Gulch cedars, watching the crews sluice and rock. One newcomer, smiling and fair-haired, seemed friendlier than the rest and tried to ask questions, even wanted to borrow a boat. Chea Po told the cook to say *Sorry, not possible.* Dow and Yap, ordered to listen but not speak, found the tall man's soft slurring accent hard to follow, though his queries seemed ordinary enough: *How big is your crew, anyway? How's your luck been?*

The stockmen set to work, swimming horses when the water ran

77

high, herding the string across otherwise. Elder Boss decided to ignore the splashing and yelling. The boys could not. The animals were never the same twice.

One day the riders left their cabin unguarded, despite the wealth of canned goods inside. Yap hung on the windowsill, moaning. Dow gave him a shove.

"We're scouts, not thieves."

Over the winter, Dow had grown two inches. Bony wrists stuck out of his jacket sleeves, and his boots pinched. The cousins peered behind the cabin but found only a rain barrel, a hillock of rusted tin cans, and a wire-fenced weed patch that was once a garden.

"Was there a Mrs. Douglas?" Yap wondered aloud. Dow knew why; he too remembered their mothers hoeing bean hills and thinning carrots, laughing together as they worked. He felt the hot tears start, circled the ruined garden to kick at the rock pile, and paused.

"See that fern? It doesn't belong there. It only grows up in the hills."

The culprit was a small innocuous specimen, pale green and tristemmed. Dow did have a good eye for plants, honed by Hoy Sek's relentless tutelage, and ever since Chea Po's revelation, treasurehunting had obsessed both boys. In this barren land, any anomaly was worth investigating. They ran for the toolshed.

Two feet down in sandy loam, the shovel struck solid matter. Unearthed, the crate was the size of a small valise, a faded legend stenciled on one dirty slat: *Wells Fargo & Co.* They hauled it out; carefully patted back the last dirt clods. Back at Deep Creek, Yap waited among the riverside boulders, arms tight around the crate, while Dow ran for Elder Boss.

Chea Po knelt and studied the find, saying nothing. He looked in all directions, then pulled out a box of smooth cedar, metal-edged. The lock was smashed, the polished cover splintered. Chea Po glanced at the boys and raised the lid.

They saw a dozen packets of American currency, bound with tapes of almond-colored paper. Chea Po guessed the box once held at least two bundles more. In a tray beneath the stacks of fifty-dollar bills sat six small bags of pale canvas. He untied one and glimpsed coins stamped with the likeness of an eagle. The gold rang under his questing fingers. At the bottom of the strongbox lay pages of Western print, weighed down with red wax seals. Legal documents, then.

"What do these say?"

Dow thumbed the papers. He could read English, but not quickly.

"Lawyer words about property," he said, uncertain. "Some say 'Oregon and Transcontinental Company' and this says 'Northern Pacific,' but the rest are for The St. Paul, Minneapolis, and Manitoba Railway Company."

What did the Sam Yup want with railroad land claims? *Hundreds of us died on Gam Saan rail crews,* Chea Po thought. *Thousands.* The legal papers were as tainted as the money. He studied the crate again. It was entirely ordinary, no special labels or seals, but had the Company charged him with sending a Sam Yup treasure box half-way across the West, Chea Po too would choose a drab disguise. The chest had already cost the lives of four of his men. And old Douglas died as well for this box of secrets, shot in the head by . . . who?

Elder Boss felt cold and sick, thinking of the angry ghosts tied forever to such wealth, hovering, unholy, unappeasable. He rocked back on his heels, wondering what to do, and looked again at Dow and Yap.

NEWS

JUNE 30, 1887

IN TWENTY MINUTES Joe reached a deserted Deep Creek. Yes. Bedrolls under a rock ledge. They had not left him. Too tired to shave or change his shirt, he sat against a boulder and turned his face sunward. Every few minutes his head fell forward, jerking him awake. He dared not lie down, not with Blue Evans nearby.

His bad foot hurt and he kneaded it hard, listening to the river's hypnotic chuckle. His court docket, the Tammany Creek estate, Libby: after a week as Mr. Salem he could barely remember any of them. That happened sometimes.

The devil of it was, he could almost see how Blue's rustlers might conclude that butchering Chinese was not like killing white men. Scraps of recollection floated up, not all from the pages of *The Wasp*. Harry Akers, joking about drunks desperate enough to drink from a Chinaman's boot. A Tammany neighbor, pointing to a smoky fall bonfire: "What you burning in there, Joe — a Chinaman?" Libby, refusing to hire Chinese help because everyone knew they spit on the ironing; Libby telling an Irish maid, "Wash that fruit extra well, you don't know if a Chinaman's touched it."

Whispers in a long-ago gold camp: *Their women's cunts run crossways.* Chat over brandy at the Leland house: *The Jews of the East — they'll keep their gold in the mud walls of a hut and die before telling you.* Half of white Lewiston believed that Chinese buried their dead with money in the mouth, then stole it all back. *Don't lick coins,*

80

they might have been pissed on by a Chinaman. Pestilential Chinks. Crazy Chinamen, running amok. *Get a Chinese mad enough and he'll kill you with one blow.* Even Nell, hopscotching in the yard: *Step on a crack, break a Chinaman's back.*

And then a river of dead.

Death, water, journeys. Joe Vincent's father was a Massachusetts seaman who died young in a West Indies alley, an idealist to the end, trying to save a slave from a beating. In widowhood, Joe's mother turned their Salem home into a boarding house, and by thirteen her only son could clean, cook, and manage. He made them extra money by serving at the inns downtown, and at summer lodgings and private estates along the shore.

At seventeen, after his mother's death, Joe became a journeyman printer. In the shop's garret lending library he devoured essays, histories, and adventure tales: Darwin's *Voyage of the Beagle,* Dana's California dispatches. He yearned to sail the glamorous China-trade clippers that came and went at Pickering Wharf, but instead took ship from Nantucket for the Western gold fields, a six-month journey through the icebergs of Cape Horn.

He learned to work a mining claim and defend it too, but found steadier money in clean beds and hot food. At twenty-one, he was running tent hotels in the gold camps, hiring, firing, breaking up fights; at twenty-seven, he was living hand to mouth in the Sandwich Islands, working odd jobs and writing bad verse while sharing his bed with a succession of local girls. He made them laugh, but none would ever marry a penniless *ha'ole.*

After leaving Maui, Joe headed for the Pacific Northwest frontier, working as a printer when he could and a carpenter otherwise. He served in an Oregon militia during a brief, vicious Indian war; captured, he endured a forced winter march. The Army rescued Private Vincent, but his left foot was frostbitten. He trained himself to ignore the pain, to walk with a sailor's rolling gait, then decided to try the new Idaho Territory. A life of adventure was starting to wear thin. He had friends across half the globe but no lasting human ties, except maybe to his own dead. At thirty-four he was old to re-enlist, but up beyond the Missouri any volunteer was welcome. Sergeant J. K. Vincent was ordered to Fort Lapwai near the Camas Prairie, thirteen miles from Lewiston.

The first time he came over the low pass by Craig's Mountain, Joe thought he was riding toward an immense lake. But the shimmering, dancing blueness ahead was sixty miles of camas lily in fullest flower, lovely as the summer Atlantic off Ipswich and Cape Ann. He reined in and studied it a while. This vast, serene valley rimmed by mountains made him feel odd. Right. He searched for some other word, and found it: content.

Just after noon Joe heard a boat ground on the pebbled shore, then voices coming up the path, Lee Loi explaining foreign exchange markets, Grace asking all the right questions. Lee seemed to know a lot, but Joe did not want to learn about per capita interest. He turned his head away. The voices stopped abruptly.

Joe whispered, "They can hear you in Boise."

"Are you all right, sir?" Lee Loi crouched beside him, stricken. "Sir, what happened? Your mouth — and God, your eye —"

"Hush," said Grace. "Joe, can you sit up more? Loi, help him."

Joe wanted to explain. The words would not come. Mr. Salem's toothless mumble did not help. He peered at his hand. A leather flask had arrived there somehow. Brandy. *Good* brandy. *Vive la France.*

"Leave some for later, Joe." The flask went away. He lost track of time for a little while. A cold cloth dabbed the cuts and bruises around his aching eye socket.

A hand on his shoulder, rocking. "Did you see them, sir? What did you find?"

"Let him rest," said Grace sharply, very far off now, but Joe knew the question was important and forced a reply before darkness spun him away.

"I got some evidence. Some. But not enough to prosecute."

• • •

In Lewiston on June 29, Alonzo Leland handed a last item to his typesetter. No good waiting for Joe — and no point, either. Enterprise was the soul of journalism.

HUNT FOR MURDERERS

J. K. Vincent, James McCormick and a Chinese left on Saturday last on a tour up Snake River, to ascertain if possible the murderers of the 10 Chinese miners. They will proceed to the camp about 150 miles above here. We hope the guilty parties will be found and brought to justice.

The Chinese in San Francisco have sent up to parties here to take all steps necessary to ferret out the facts in regard to the killing of their countrymen in a mining camp on the Snake River, and have provided the means to pay for the investigation and to pay for bringing the guilty parties to justice if found.

It is alleged that their camp outfit has been found in a broken up condition, including tools, blankets, and cooking utensils, and their boat with holes cut in the bottom with axes, showing it to have been done with design to destroy every vestige of evidence of the existence of a camp.

The condition of the deserted camp, the chopping of the boat, the bullet holes and mangled condition of the bodies and their state of nudity all indicate that a foul murder has been committed but by whom and for what purpose is the question to be solved.

REWARD

MAY 22–27, 1887

WHEN CHEA PO told his mining crews their Deep Creek stay was done, the men crowded around him, listening hard. Seven days to strike the camp and worksites and load the boats before Lee She and the Salt Creek group returned, and back in Lewiston a letter would go express to the Sam Yup.

"I will say you worked with courage and honor. That everyone deserves reward." He put his hand on his heart and kept it there, so they would see he meant it. The miners milled about like a festival crowd. Some came to Elder Boss and bowed, then bowed once more.

My brave strong sons, thought Chea Po, permitting himself one flash of sentiment. The herbalist slipped off to soak his last bags of ginseng and wolfberry in Hong Lee's big galvanized tub. Once the mining crews reached town, the Lewiston whorehouses would do extra business. A good bowl of spring tonic roused the blood.

Lim Ah climbed the Deep Creek ridge to read the skies. Storm clouds to the south and west, he told Chea Po. Boss and mapper stood at the waterline, thinking of the tasks ahead: break down the Deep Creek camp, clear the last Robinson Gulch sluices. Lim Ah and Chea Po had both heard gunfire off toward the north, maybe from hunters. Lim Ah said he would row over to the Gulch come morning, with half a dozen workers, and help the crew there finish up.

"A fast ride back," said Elder Boss, watching logs, brush, and dead sheep turning in the main current. Somewhere south, a big rain was making the river rise. Deep Creek ran high, spilling over the gravel apron near the shore.

Lim Ah studied the crag across the river. On scrolls in the Hip Sip lodge back in Lewiston, he had seen sugar-loaf summits impossibly steep and abrupt, yet just such a height sheltered them here, a touch of China in the Idaho backlands. All winter he had found shapes and stories in these jagged hills. Camel mountain, lotus peak.

"I won't miss this place," the mapper said.

Their final day at Deep Creek dawned still and humid, promising heat by afternoon, thunder by night. Chea Po let the two boys go exploring one last time. As they ran up the game trail, Yap tore ahead. Dow hesitated. Hong Lee and Elder Boss, conferring beside the cook shack, saw him look back, but waved him toward the hills.

At Robinson Gulch the miners worked through a second overcast morning, then rested. One-third rations meant short hours, not by choice. Everyone was in low condition. Even the youngest men had joint pains or loose teeth, and small wounds took weeks to heal. An Duk volunteered to be on watch. He knew the crews tried to spare him the hardest work. So he sat with shovel laid by, guarding his friends, lulled to a half-drowse himself by the river's voice.

An Duk started awake. High in the rocks he saw two white men, sighting their long guns; heard the rifles crack. Across the clearing, sleepers stirred and sat up, confused. One miner jerked upward, a dark stain spreading on his chest. Another ran, shouted, fell backward. Another. Two miners — three — broke for the boats but died before they touched the oars. An Duk grabbed his shovel and scrambled sideways into the boulder field. Blood soaked his right sleeve, dyed his hand scarlet. Blind with pain, he hit a rock face and went to his knees. *They'll kill us all.*

He crawled along the base of the boulders, feeling his way until his vision cleared and he could see the broad-shouldered *da bidze* above him, firing down into the Gulch, whooping as he shot, the rifle hot and smoking, spent shells clinking on stone.

The geomancer crouched, gasping, as the shooters moved forward to start the close-in killing. The big man lagged behind. An Duk, five feet tall, hoisted the shovel in his good hand and swung it hard at the stranger's throat, praying to send one enemy into the Void, to howl forever in the eighteen hells.

PART II

HOMECOMINGS

·

HENRY STANTON, HALF AWAKE, put out a hand and felt the bed's left side. Cold and lonely. He hated baching. Mary was off in Seattle, helping a niece through a third confinement. Henry was trying to be big about it, with mixed results. Every day he met the mailman at the front gate, like a lovelorn schoolboy.

Downstairs the screen door thumped as Mrs. Reilly arrived to rouse the house. Excellent woman. A good plain cook, no fuss over bloodstained shirts. Ideal. Beyond the bedroom window he saw only grayness. Fog on the river, then. And now low female voices on the back porch.

Under the patchwork quilt, Henry tensed. Wagon smash-up? Broken arm? Lewiston had two younger physicians — or one doctor, one jumped-up vet — and neither liked emergency rides to mining camps or distant cabins. Henry still took every call. Instead of going horseback, he drove a hack across swollen streams and through blizzards, his one concession to sixty-four years. Mary's idea.

No summons came. Instead he heard the pump handle in the kitchen sink, bringing rainwater from the cellar cistern, and the scrape of a tin tub across the wooden floor. Only one person he knew could want a bath at this hour. They were back and safe. Henry sank gratefully into sleep.

At eight, in the dark little dining room, he discovered his favorite

89

raisin rolls, fresh enough to leave patches of steam on the china plate. Grace backed through the swinging kitchen door, holding a dish of applesauce. In dark skirt and demure white shirtwaist (raided from Mary, no doubt), she looked ready for a Ladies' Aid tea.

"Did you sleep well, Autre-papa?"

Her feet left the floor with the force of his bear hug. "How was the trip?"

"Joe drank all your best brandy."

"Melancholia?" said Henry, interested.

"Worn out. He walked into a nest of killers and lived with them for a week. At *his* age. He took Lee back to the hotel, or rather Lee took him. But you should look at his eye."

"I'll stop by. Nothing from Jackson, by the way."

"I left Georges's letter, but I didn't spot Jackson once. I hope he says yes – I don't want him hanged any more than you do. Certainly not by Joe."

"Sound policy," said her foster father. "My dear, where did you get these rolls?"

"Wildenthaler's." Only one who knew her well could hear the tiny hesitation.

"Did you go, or Mrs. Reilly?"

"I tried first, then sent her over. She said she didn't mind."

"They won't serve you?" Stanton pushed away his plate. "I don't like it."

Grace picked up the old tin coffeepot. "No surprise. Come sit out back. I'll tell you about the river, and you may tell *me* all the scrofulous humors you've cured."

He tried to smile. Scrofulous humors, indeed.

The back of the Stantons' two-story white frame house was Henry's office and surgery. Late that afternoon he sat at his desk, looking at a little brown photograph of his wife. The likeness was not good. Mary was meant for motion, not repose. The picture beside it showed Grace, bare-shouldered and smiling in a dark satin ball dress. Taken ten years ago? No, eleven. In New Orleans. They had no picture more recent.

Early on the Fourth, Grace and Henry drove east along the Clearwater toward the mission town of Lapwai, taking four camp chairs, a sheaf of Mary's crimson roses, and a crate of medical supplies. Dust rose behind the buggy as they wound through high, bare foothills. Above the miles of wheat field, meadowlarks caroled. The morning was flawless but turning hot.

By Territory standards Lapwai was an old town, spread along a valley. They passed the big boarding school for Indian children, then skirted the silent barracks and officers' quarters. Ten years ago Fort Lapwai garrisoned a thousand soldiers. In the spring of '77, told to leave the Wallowas forever, Chief Joseph and his Nez Perce bands crossed near Dug Bar but then made for Canada, not their assigned reservation at Lapwai. The Army went after them. An easy roundup became an epic five-month chase, a fighting retreat through some of the roughest country in the Northwest.

Surrender or die. The Sacred Heart headmistress assigned Grace no classes in history. Even in a Portland schoolroom she could not read aloud the British officer's cry on the village green at Lexington, a century past. *Disperse, ye villains, ye rebels, disperse! Why don't ye lay down your arms?* A decade after the '77 war, Lapwai was still an occupied town. When the soldiers left the bureaucrats arrived, and their message was no more heartening. *Conform or starve.*

"They've added on," said Grace, leaning around the buggy struts to see the school.

"Is that nostalgia I hear?"

"Not a bit."

She turned away from the playground where she cut her knee, the shabby little teacherage, the sutler's hut, the path to the creek. Another world, another self.

Beside a graveyard shaded by cottonwoods, she reined in and gave Henry a hand down. With no one to see, he did not protest, only took the roses and went toward a stone marked "Oliver Stanton." Grace led the horses to the water and talked to them as they drank. Henry preferred to mourn his son alone.

For their open-air clinic at the Lapwai Indian agency, Grace did double duty, relaying symptoms and measuring out cures — a dose of salts for bowel trouble, a paper of jalap for the ague. Swabbing throats, Henry reflected that the Nez Perce were great gossips. Worse than the Irish. When sounding out a problem or a place, he and Joe used the same rules. Find out who runs things, who most deserves help, who is buying what and why.

A horse breeder with a cut hand told them about shipping twenty-six animals to Connecticut, then confided he had a large cash offer for his land. As Henry dealt out lint and bandage, Grace's admiring questions slipped from English to Nimipu. *Well done,* Henry thought. In the horseman's long reply he could pick out only one proper noun: *Vollmer.* He'd been hearing it all day.

Business kept steady. A woman with a scalded face, a baby failing to thrive. One putrid fever (probably typhus), two infected toes, three girls with lingering coughs. Grace had to ask the crowd for word after word. She thought in English, still dreamed sometimes in French. She could follow Nimipu conversation but sounded childish when joining in, and knew it.

Here she would have connection always, full acceptance never, for she spent her city winters teaching little girls the leading products of Chile, the fourteen verbs that take *être,* and how to tell a fish fork from a bone dish. She was thirty-eight, civilized to the point of parody, and most days so bored she could scream. She never did. She was a model and a credit. She had perfect posture, made lists of her lists, and arrived ten minutes early for appointments. She could also skin a deer, navigate by the stars, and persuade a stranded tourist down a rock face in the rain, but after a lifetime of quickness her knees had begun to protest days in the saddle and nights on the ground. Wherever she turned, she saw only high walls and closed doors. She read a lot. In eleven years, she had not had one full night's sleep.

Across the assembly field, a bell began to ring. As the holiday crowd flowed past, a scrap of paper fell onto her aproned lap. She never saw who tossed it. In the shadow of the buggy, Grace scanned the penciled scrawl. *2 waiting for you at Temple. On the other no but thanks.*

Jackson's reply. Baffled by the first phrase — two what? What Temple? — she passed the note to Henry, who said, "He may mean the Beuk Aie, down near A Street. Built since your time, my dear. It was good of Georges to offer that job. But Jackson has always gone his own way."

Grace knew he was right. Even she could not really imagine Jackson Sundown, known Nez Perce fugitive, as J. Sundown, Oregon ranch hand, of fixed address and regular habits. Georges would be upset, but for all three of them it was the trying that mattered. She looked up. Henry was waiting. For an instant she wished for her veiled hat, but if showing her face was an effort, hiding it was ridiculous. With the long-sighted patience of any small community, most of Lapwai acted as if she had just stepped out to run an errand.

"How was the research?" Henry asked as they walked.

"Profitable, I think."

An enthusiastic young Indian affairs agent, George Norris, spoke from the porch of a low gray headquarters building. *Must be new,* Grace thought, watching the crowd. Over six hundred had turned out, nearly all Nimipu, though Grace noticed three Lewiston carriage parties arriving with parasols and picnic baskets, avid for savagery. She had not been back to Lapwai in a decade; the Stantons always came to Portland. The changes amazed her. American dress was the reservation norm now — drab farmer suits, cheap calico dresses — and silence the rule. No one talked of the missing except in whispers.

Norris was full of plans. Going in for cattle, adding better fencing; local farmers still encroached on treaty land to graze stock and cut tribal timber. Older men seemed doubtful. Younger families clearly meant to try. The People were moving on, she saw, making the best of a riven and diminished life, even as Eastern newcomers and their eighteen-mule combines turned more of the Camas Prairie to cropland every year. Grace could just remember digging lily bulbs there, then helping her tireless grandmother mash the roasted roots, sweet and solid as any pear.

As Norris finished, a mock war band galloped in, waving rifles, putting on a show, crowding past the town visitors to halt in a flourish of dust beside the cheering, whistling Nimipu. The beautiful horses circled and curvetted. The troop's leader bore an heirloom war bonnet that reached nearly to his bare waist. Thirty years ago Grace had seen its twin in a lodge near Dug Bar: the beaded headband, the magnificent double train of eagle feathers and ermine tips. The other riders wore only moccasins, loincloths, and breastplates of bone, with red and yellow paint slashed gorgeously across body and face: warriors dressed for glory one last time.

Red for blood and war, yellow for rebirth and victory, and nowhere the white of peace. Henry looked at Grace, looked again, and offered his arm. She squeezed his hand, then swept up the overskirt of her walking dress to show off its tiny bustle, ferociously modern. Henry gave the Lewiston carriages a courteous bow, Grace the coolest of nods. All the way across the dusty field, she felt the eyes.

> The Indians were fully armed, with rifles and pistols, causing one female member of our party to declare that we should go home right now. Taken together, they were a diabolical crowd. We were informed by several of the old members of the tribe that this was a very correct representation of the preparations of old for the war-path ... It is hoped that the government will provide that untaken Nez Perce lands can be soon thrown open to settlement by the whites, under some right from the government, for we have waited long and patiently for that end.
>
> — *Lewiston Teller*, July 6, 1887

Lee Loi began his Lewiston Fourth of July with a tour of the riverfront Chinese district, trying to look serious yet approachable. A new beginning for a new man. Before the trip to Deep Creek he had been a consummate ass. *My apologies, esteemed dead.* How many Congregational services had he sat through in boyhood with the Bartletts, counting the minutes till lunch, never considering what it really meant to hunger and thirst after justice?

The village intimacy of C Street cheered him. Elderly men sat on kitchen chairs, rolling cigars and stacking them in silk-lined boxes. Baskets tilted against storefronts showed off early melons, fresh peas, bunches of spring onions. Merchants flew red silk banners with golden names: *Everlasting Harmony. Ten Thousand Customers Constantly Arriving. Profit Like Rushing Waters.* Most C Street merchants ordered direct from Portland warehouses, which ordered direct from Canton, and the eternal smells of home rose from yard and alley—fermented bean curd, garlic and ginger hissing in hot oil, the eye-watering reek of chicken dung, the good strong odor of valuable night soil. From an open window came the click of mahjong tiles. *Even here the Middle Kingdom lives,* Lee Loi thought, feeling stern and proud.

Four hours later he sat in the Hip Sip lodge, looking without appetite at a bowl of noodles for which he had just paid double price. Another underappreciated word from the Christian scriptures occurred to him: pariah. When he stood at a store counter, the room emptied. If he tried a street-corner conversation, his targets hurried off, or walked by as if he were not there. He felt like a ghost, dreaded, disembodied, but at least ghosts got to be angry, and this second public failure was his fault too, barging in like a—

"Ha! Little Big-Nose."

"*Hai,*" said Lee, too dispirited to rise to the insult but coming to his feet for the necessary bow. "That's me. Very glad to meet you again, sir."

The Hip Sip manager was a middle-aged man with a substantial belly. From Canton's Yi De Road district, Lee recalled, and a stalwart of the Beuk Aie Temple.

"Having a rough time?"

"I deserve it," said Lee.

"You do," said the other. Lee searched for fellowship in the broad, pox-scarred face but found none. "I have a delivery for you out back. Normally I wouldn't give a Company man the price of shit, but I owe someone a favor. Come on."

In the dimness of the hallway the older man waited, hand on door-knob. He knocked twice, hurried Lee through, then followed him in. The lock turned.

INDEPENDENCE

JULY 4, 1887

WHEN JOE VINCENT treated his youngest child to holiday pancakes at the hotel, Nell took small bites, sat up straight, and let every conversational gambit die. Her usual wild enthusiasms were so quenched that Joe looked her over with special care, but she seemed healthy enough, only listless. He knew that in a year or three he might yearn to drop her in the Snake more days than not, but whether he owed this new polite edition to growing pains or to the aftereffects of finding dead Chinese, he could not tell.

"Seconds on the sausage?"

"No, thank you, Pa."

Silence.

Like him, Nell was spending the summer in town. She slept at her Leland grandparents' house, but Rachel was a vague, sweet shut-in and Alonzo nearly as busy as Joe, so the noisy, cheerful home of her school friend Becky Binnard soon absorbed her. When Joe apologized to Becky's parents for the extra trouble, Sarah Binnard, plump and forthright, told him that in her opinion it did the child good, and at a table as long as theirs, one more hardly mattered.

He left Nell in front of Grostein & Binnard with two dollars spending money, then started down Main Street. On lampposts and porches the Stars and Stripes hung limp in the morning heat. He could see almost no trace of the May flood. Hardly anyone talked of it any more. To live in boomer country meant looking forward, and

97

only forward. As Alonzo urged his *Teller* readers, "Wake up. Rustle. Hustle. Be go-aheadative. Toot your horn and toot it loud."

Beside the livery stable the Lewiston Boneshakers, eager to parade, were tying tricolor ribbons to their bicycle handlebars. Joe changed course. He had a weakness for mechanical wonders – a patent varnish, an improved tool sharpener – and he loved freewheeling as much as he disliked being chief aide to Alonzo Leland, the day's Grand Marshal. Next year Joe Junior could damn well do it. Good practice for the future *Teller* publisher.

Across the street Alonzo Leland and John Vollmer watched Joe work the crowd. Both knew he would surely run for Congress as a Republican; neither liked the prospect of trying to control him once in office. Joe had been funny of late. Funny as in peculiar, though his jokes were getting worse, too. Even now, a dozen citizens stood listening to some ridiculous story about a woman who petitioned him in court for a legal name change.

"What's your name right now, ma'am?"

"Ophelia Pucklewartz."

"Well, I can see how you'd want something else. What did you have in mind?"

"Why . . . Gertrude!"

Unlike Vollmer, Alonzo could not quite disguise his irritation. In *Teller* news columns, little digs at his lenient son-in-law now appeared almost weekly:

The application of J. K. Vincent to reduce the bond of pensioner Harry Graham was not granted.

Your reporter was in police judge Vincent's office on Monday morning when Marshal Akers brought in two victims – Of what? The bottle; charge drunk and disorderly, each fined $5 and costs, amounting to $14 each. This is much under the accepted penalties for such behavior.

J. K. Vincent is trying to raise money for a prisoners' library in the state penitentiary.

• • •

An hour later Alonzo and Joe stood waving at a cavalcade of ladies on horseback, then applauded the Lewiston Hook and Ladder Company. A bunting-draped hay cart bore a beaming Goddess of Liberty with a gilt-paper crown, and close behind came thirty-eight marching girls in white, carrying cardboard shields painted to represent each state.

"Next year, Nell as number thirty-nine, hey, J. K.?"

Joe smiled, shrugged, and pointed to the Boneshakers, rolling well in close formation. Alonzo was easy to distract. Four torch boys followed the cyclists, then the local dentist dressed as a soldier of 1776. Alonzo saluted every one. He loved being Grand Marshal.

By midafternoon half the town was out at Thatcher's Grove for a reading of the Declaration, followed by as many speeches as patriotic endurance allowed. Thirty years had passed since Lewiston was a riverbank full of elk, twenty-five since its days as a tent city squatting on Nez Perce land, illegal as hell. Lewiston had dignity now, tall trees, traditions. The public exhibition on the Fourth was as fixed as the pole star, down to a schoolboy orator and an original verse offering from Miss Sadie Poe.

Derby in hand, Joe joined the line of dark-suited dignitaries along the rear of the platform. As an ex-mayor, Henry Stanton was entitled to a seat; too bad he was off at Lapwai. Joe missed his company, but did not forgive that telegram to Grace. When she turned up at the docks, he'd nearly had an apoplexy.

Alonzo spoke first. Leland was famous in the Territory as the man who once held the Assembly floor for seventeen hours. Other legislators tiptoed off, leaving the chamber in darkness; when they returned after breakfast, Leland was still there, still talking. Alonzo was a pioneer settler, though, as well as Lewiston's most irrepressible cheerleader, and the *Teller* rarely failed to entertain. The indulgent crowd applauded him safely back to his chair.

John Vollmer rose, and real quiet fell. The banker was respected if not liked, a hard man beneath the urbane tailoring and big blond mustache. Half the region owed Vollmer money and the other half wanted him to invest in their schemes. He was the biggest taxpayer

99

in the Territory. At a guess, he owned fifty thousand acres in north Idaho alone. He spoke of his German immigrant father, a refugee from revolution, then recounted his own climb to wealth. A battle-hardened Union soldier at eighteen. A go-getting Northwest new-comer by twenty-two, learning the wine and spirits business. Al-though he first came to Lewiston in wholesale liquor sales, he left that profitable calling at the dictates of his conscience. ("Bravo, sir!" called the Woman's Christian Temperance Union vice president. Vollmer bowed.)

But his love for the Territory drew him back. Seeking wholesome advancement after the conflict with our Indian so-called neighbors (hisses), he bought up the land and livestock they were unfit to man-age and, yes, sold both at profit (applause). He built stores and more stores, formed the region's first bank, branched into steamships, be-lieved in the future of the telephone. He would stop at nothing to bring Lewiston's citizens the same chance for prosperity. And, God willing, he would even bring a railway line to this soon-to-be capital of that worthiest of states, beautiful North Idaho (tumult).

Touching, tidy, and almost true, thought Joe. No mention of ser-vice in the Nez Perce War. Vollmer ceded center stage with a gen-teel bow and a circling hand, delightfully European, just this side of irony.

Only twenty years in public office kept Joe's smile in place. Blue Evans, ushering his troupe of killers off the cabin porch with that very gesture. Homer LaRue, late at night, ready as ever to provoke. *Your fancy friend.* LaRue saw too clearly, talked too much. Victory meat for Zeke, and soon.

A gentleman's bow and a turn of phrase were a long way from ad-missible evidence. Yet where else could Evans learn that mocking sa-lute? Over twenty years ago, Joe first saw Vollmer bow that way. A spruce young liquor salesman, commending the birth of Joe Vincent, Jr. Mockery? Joe couldn't tell then. Ten years ago—no, eleven—he ceased to care.

Alonzo Leland rose again to pace the platform, testifying like a

revival preacher to his long dream of statehood. Eight hundred up-
turned faces followed him, rapt.

"What we want is simple and right. The four northern coun-
ties geographically belong to Washington Territory. The taxation of
Idaho is extortionate and prohibitory. Unless we are granted the dignity of a state, we are vassals to the caprice of any administration, pre-
vented from making our own laws, appointing our own officials, even
conveying our own mails!"

Committees, ardent editorials, trips to Boise, a hundred political
junkets with Libby as hostess; Joe knew how hard Alonzo worked to
sustain his optimism. Lobbying would be hot and heavy all summer,
with Lewiston boosted at every turn. The former territorial capital.
Friendly, growing, eager to hustle. Scandal-free. *Dead Chinese? What
dead Chinese?* With Vollmer pushing statehood too, North Idaho's
chances had just doubled. Tripled.

"In the south we have prisons and the capitol building; in north
Idaho we have churches, colleges and schools, and we are as balmy
at Thanksgiving as Iowa or Missouri on the Fourth of July!"

The Lewiston silver band and glee club crashed into "The Star-
Spangled Banner." Leland and Vollmer raised arms in joint salute.
Alonzo tugged the banker forward, but Vollmer only smiled and let
Alonzo bask in the cheering until the publisher produced a handker-
chief to dab away his tears. Judge Vincent applauded with the rest.

At twilight Joe stood alone under the picnic-grove trees, sipping
one of Christ Weisgerber's free beers. Despite pointed glances from
WCTU members, the crowd at the town brewer's stand lined up
three deep all day. Joe thought he just might have a second pilsner.
Possibly a third. At least the fireworks would be good — direct from
San Francisco and sponsored by Vollmer and Company. John went
there a lot. Lee Loi might know of him. In business anything was
possible, even a tie between the baron of North Idaho and the killer
at Dug Bar.

Seeing his once and future constituents go at the twenty-five-cent dinner, from chicken pie to orange layer cake, Joe did not look forward to the Congress run, with its endless public feeds. But he liked the idea of Washington. Libby had made clear that if elected, he would bach it. She had too much to do here. Joe thought he could translate that one: Lib could queen it far more successfully in the Territory. She disliked Mary Stanton for many reasons, not least that Mary was from Old Georgetown and had danced with President Polk at her long-ago coming-out. Joe had not been East since '49. When the Snake River bluffs cracked with drought or the chinook came late, he missed the billowing greenery of the Commonwealth. He'd like to show Nell places like Salem and Concord and Faneuil Hall.

From the shadow of the pines, he watched Lonny strut and Letty giggle as they circled the pond with some noisy friends from the High School. Both had their mother's strawberry-blond fairness, Lon stocky as a footballer, Letty fetchingly rounded. He hated to say it, but any trip East would be wasted on his two middle children. Pure Leland, both of them: joiners, enthusiasts, never missed a party or a jaunt, never felt the need to look beyond North Idaho. The long summer stay at Lake Waha, broken by one trip back for the excitements of the Fourth, was another ironclad Lewiston ritual, at least for the well-to-do, and Lib loved the lake season as much as Letty and Lonny.

Joe glanced across Thatcher's Pond and saw his wife and her father climbing into the Vollmer carriage. Heading back to John's for a nightcap, no doubt. Decent of them, as well as strategic. Selina Vollmer found big gatherings difficult, but Lib had befriended her and kept at it, though Lina was ditchwater-dull. Lib still looked awfully good, for nearly forty. Her blue dress with all the lace was nice. It stuck out in back, but then they all did these days.

He and Libby had not exchanged a word all week. Once, from the platform, he caught her eye, but her gaze moved past him like a chilly stranger's. With exaggerated slowness, she lowered her parasol down to her shoulder and turned away, so all he saw was a pale silk orb.

• • •

At ten-thirty, a note from Marshal Akers found Joe at Raymond House. He'd quit on the second beer and gone back to his rooms to read, a habit when he felt low. He shut the book and walked down the street. Lamplight showed in the back hallway of Luna House. Akers was upstairs, guarding his prisoners in the former hotel bedrooms that served as town jail. Lewiston had a sheriff, but Akers was taking more and more of the criminal work.

Joe put his head around the door and saw three Chinese ranged along a wooden bench: Lee Loi, with a bruised, swollen chin, and two shabby boys who kept their eyes on the floor.

"Friends of yours, Judge? Brought in for disturbing the peace. I put 'em on bread and water as a precaution."

"You're right, Harry. Desperate characters. I can take it from here."

Akers holstered his Colt and left, grinning. Joe gestured everyone into the upstairs hallway, taking hold of both boys' collars as they passed.

"Look what I found at the Hip Sip," said Lee, searching for a clean corner of the roller towel to press against his jaw. "Great employees you have, by the way. Eight hours we've been here. That one told us to move along, I said what for, it's a public street, and he hit me. He *knows* who I am."

Akers was getting bolder. "Sorry, that was a message to me as much as you. You're lucky he stopped at a fat lip."

Joe held the boys at arm's length. "Gentlemen, we spoke last fall, remember? Now I need your help, so don't even think of running off."

The younger one stayed quiet in Joe's grip, avoiding his gaze, but the taller boy twisted free and said something urgent to Lee. "He's not sick, but he wants Dr. Stanton," Lee told Joe.

"Fine. Mr. Lee and I will take you right now. The people there are kind and you'll be safe."

They hurried up the hill through quiet streets. At dirt-floor taverns along the river flats, firecrackers were still going off, sounding like distant gunfire.

The Stantons' parlor was lamplit, despite the hour, and through the open window Joe heard Henry's voice, then Grace's laugh. That was a new one. Three weeks on the river and hardly a smile, except to calm Lee Loi. Henry answered the door in his old red dressing gown and Joe started to explain, but the boys pushed by him to stare at Grace, standing at the parlor door in skirt and shirtwaist.

"Are you the lady teacher?" the older boy demanded. His English was as good as Joe recalled. "*His* cousin?"

Grace nodded. Georges aside, she had only one cousin. They ran to her, kicking up the rag rug as they went. The smaller boy began to cry, the noisy snorting sobs of a child who has been brave too long. Looking up astonished at Joe and Lee, Grace went to her knees on the front-hall floor, Chu Yap and Lim Dow enfolded in her embrace.

A flash of memory came to Joe, of a windy field near Lapwai long ago. Grace and Georges as adolescents, standing on either side of a chestnut pony, arms raised to steady the three-year-old who refused to hold the mane but instead sat straight and laughed with delight. Georges's small brother. Jackson Sundown.

FIT COMPANY

JULY 6, 1887

A GAIN DOW SAID, "I don't know."
He barely glanced at the medicine stick from Robinson Gulch. Joe was losing patience. The evidence retrieved from upriver lay spread on the floor of his barn, a hundred burned and battered fragments of mining-camp life, but explaining any of it seemed beyond Dow's powers. Joe took back the painted rod and held up a list of names.

"Then listen to these. We want an accurate set to use in court. Tell me if you hear one you don't recognize. Chea Po? Chea Sun? Chea Yow?"

Lee said something encouraging. Dow ignored him.

"Chea Shun, Chea Cheong?" Joe tried not to look much at either boy. "Chea Ling. Chea Chow. Chea Lin Chung?"

Grace murmured, "Won't you tell us?" She sat between Dow and Yap, dark skirts pooled on the barn's plank floor. Yap leaned against her for a moment, yawning.

"Kong Mun Kow," said Joe. "Kong Ngan?"

At their one meeting, Younger Boss had dictated the names of Deep Creek crew members, but Joe's phonetic spelling was hit-and-miss. Lee Loi said the Sam Yup had no official roster. Field bosses handled hiring and payment; workers were workers. Caught either way, Joe thought. The Company took its percentage, regardless. And

Alonzo's latest editorial could not be clearer: *A Chinaman is no more a citizen than a coyote.*

"We'll call it a day," Joe said, defeated. George Craig, the rancher who owned Dug Cabin, had sent back word that he would obey Judge Vincent's request to leave the squatters undisturbed. Tomorrow Joe would put Grace and Lee in the courthouse records room and hope for the best. In a library Grace was a terrier after weasels, and surely Lee had learned to read ledgers by now. Joe had hopes for Lee. The young banker was better company these days, no question; Grace always was good with balky colts. If Lee wanted to wear himself out by bringing her lemonade and leaping up to offer the best chair, that was his lookout. The Sam Yup check had cleared. Joe was earning every penny.

By late afternoon his troops had nothing to show. Lee said his Beuk Aie contacts were still mum, the census records were vague about Chinese, and no, he didn't know a Mr. Vollmer. Grace was tracking Vollmer's Camas Prairie land buys, mostly because Joe and Henry thought them odd, but it was slow work. She could find no connection between Vollmer and Evans, and if any of the rustlers appeared in census records, they weren't in Nez Perce County. Joe began to pace. Juries needed a paper trail.

The records room at Luna House was hot and gloomy. Lee was collarless and in shirtsleeves. Grace worked in silence, a lock of dark hair fallen out of her Psyche knot. Joe leafed through a pile of deeds. He was starting to know both boys, but it wasn't easy. The younger one, Yap, seemed the more resilient, a natural little go-getter. Dow was tense, controlled, watchful. No wonder, considering their last eighteen months. Both were bunking at the Stanton house. A word with Abe Binnard let Joe outfit them well enough, but according to Grace, Dow slept little, said less, and was hoarding bread under the mattress.

Even discounting shock, the boys' lack of emotion about the deaths upriver seemed unnatural. They'd spent over half a year with

Chea Po and his men. Did Dow and Yap not want the investigation to proceed?

"Your idea of justice isn't ours," Lee said. His jaw still showed a stain of purple, thanks to Akers. "There's no Chinese God in heaven to balance the scales, no laws for protecting all men the same. Revenge is surer. Fast, slow, it doesn't matter. All our troubles stay private, all our fights are to the finish."

"Anything else shows weakness," said Grace, from behind a Pike's Peak of tax ledgers.

"Try New England some time," Joe told her. "But they're young to be so . . ."

"Inscrutable?" she said politely.

"I was going to say, scarred." He looked at Lee. "Those two can forget any ideas about private vengeance. Tell Dow I said so."

The afternoon passed in silence, except for the scratch of steel nibs and the thump of bound volumes and document boxes. Date of sale, seller and buyer, location by survey numbers, taxes charged. Joe came across names he hadn't seen in years. His mind drifted to a Chinese houseboy who once worked at Raymond House. Chan, yes. Each morning, silent as a shadow, Chan went from bedroom to bedroom with hot towels, lather, and straight razor, deftly shaving the male guests as they lay in bed. A marvel of luxury, in winter especially. Now Joe wondered, *What kept that man from cutting all our throats? In his place, I might have.*

On Monday, Joe found under his hotel-office door a fourteen-page summary of Camas Prairie land transactions, succinctly analyzed. No note, no signature, but he recognized the neat level hand.

At ten-thirty, on his way to C Street, Lee Loi stopped at Raymond House with a message: Dow was pretty sure that vials of gold dust from the Chinese mining expedition lay under the big stone step at the Douglas cabin. He wanted Mr. Vincent to know. Joe remembered it well; he'd stood right on it his first day as old Salem, sweating out the killers' scrutiny. Christ almighty. Four inches away.

"*Pretty* sure?"

"That's what he said. Right after Jackson Sundown found them at Deep Creek they had to wait out a hard rain, almost in the rustlers' backyard. Dow and Jackson both saw Evans—or someone just like him—hiding the evidence in plain sight, so to speak. I can't get anything more. Dow clammed up again."

"Well, go back and try again. On the evidence we have now, I can't arrest a dog."

By noon Joe arrived at Henry's office and lured him out for a drive.

"I've got ham sandwiches and beer. We'll go on the bluffs, get some fresh air."

Fresh air was their long-standing code for a private discussion. When they reached the open land above town, Joe pulled up. Only grazing beef cattle were in earshot.

"There's talk about you," Henry said. "As in, why can't you hand this off to Oregon and be done with it? As in, doesn't he see that chopped-up Chinese are bad for business?"

The more he tried to guard his town, Joe thought, the less it seemed to listen. When Henry was mayor and Joe sheriff, they owned adjacent houses near the corner of Fourth and Main. In years of bluff-top drives the two hashed out change after change: gold booms and slumps, the spread of Camas Prairie farms, the growing power of John Vollmer. Everyone in Lewiston knew that Stanton's bark had no bite, that Joe would rather talk than shoot. But the Chinese investigation was inching Joe away from Lewiston's inner circle. Already he could feel the chill.

Henry said, "As to your friend upriver, the answer is no. Evans isn't insane. He doesn't have a disease, like a mad dog has hydrophobia."

"For Christ's sake, Henry, he calls dead bodies victory meat."

"But he's no cannibal. To him the Chinese are subhuman. He might let his dog do the honors, though, after he skinned the bodies. And he did persuade the gang to join in."

"He must have forced them at gunpoint."

"One or two might have enjoyed it. The rest went along. From what you say, the man is a natural predator. When his private wolf pack took a liking to the old miner, I doubt Evans was pleased. You got out just in time."

Joe thought, watching a west wind stir the acres of shortgrass.

"This skinning business. Does he want the victims' power?"

"He enjoys their fear. Inside, Evans is cold, dark, and hollow. He sees the whole world as a threat and strikes first. Doctors call it moral alienation. In layman's language, born bad."

Joe looked over. "In property law, alienation is the transfer of title from seller to buyer. Nothing evil about it."

"Property follows the law of supply and demand. My patients need healing. I need their fees. We make an exchange. They feel better, and so do I. But for Evans, the transfer is all one-way. He can charm, even mesmerize, but he feels nothing. So he feeds on others' strong emotions. Terror, greed, the sexual relation."

Joe said, "Henry."

"You may recognize the pattern."

"Doctor, enough."

Of all Joe's voices, Henry liked that one least. He pressed on.

"Lesser forms of the condition are everywhere. Take John Vollmer. Land and wealth for a hundred lifetimes, more people under his control every year. Fear and obedience nourish him, and he never gives any thanks."

Henry waited. Sometimes a clean cut through scar tissue worked.

Finally Joe said, "Where do you rank Alonzo in all this?"

And sometimes not. "Vollmer ally. But he won't take bribes, you know. Likes to run his own show."

Joe thought. "And be fair, Vollmer has feelings. You remember when his little girl got sick?"

"Evangeline. Sweet child. He doted on her. Evie contracted fever — typhoid malarial fever I called it on the death certificate. Bad water, probably. John was beside himself."

Joe shook the reins, turning the rig for home. For half a mile they rode in silence. Above the bluffs a red-tailed hawk glided, plunged earthward, then climbed again with something limp in its claws.

"I still don't understand how Evans got the gang to kill so many."

"Were you attracted to him?"

"What?" Joe said, startled.

"Did you find him familiar somehow? Entertaining, even? Worthy of aid?"

"Yes."

"That's mirroring. Showing you back to you. Very flattering, to those uncertain of their worth. And in Evans's case, instinctive. You posed as a man of limited mind and means, and still he smelled out your deepest weakness. He asked for help."

"You thought I shouldn't take this on, didn't you?"

"Single-handed crime-solving has its seductions too. *I'll show this town, go out with a splash,* all that. I know the last six months have been hard on you."

"I'm trying to do my duty."

"As police judge? You're meant to be fixing bails and kissing babies, not risking your neck for the Sam Yup."

"As in upholding civil order. I got the evidence, Henry. Some, at least."

"And you have a new scar to prove it. You don't need to prove anything. You gave twenty years to this town."

Joe drove awhile in silence, studying the brown tent-shaped hills of Washington, cut into river drainage by wind and time.

"All right. I did enjoy seeing Blue work the others, at least in the early going. Then I wanted to better his condition. I'll find him a good job in town, I thought. Maybe with the bank. So he seduces, as you say, and the others come to trust him?"

"The fat one—LaRue?—sounds like he's fighting constantly not to succumb. But Evans had months to break the others to his will. He becomes the perfect friend, even a kind of lover. I'm just like you, the mirror says. Your secrets are safe with me."

Joe said, "And so they choose – and are doomed?" His voice was pleasant, even, detached.

Ah, Joe. "He chose them. Handpicked. He could never kill that many by himself. So he made more copies of Evans."

"In the camps, one sick whore could pass the clap to dozens of men."

"Yes. An infection, spreading. From boredom to cruelty to frenzy."

"Not guilty by reason of insanity, then?"

"Oh, they knew what they were doing. The terrible part? It felt like fun."

"He called it a frolic. Some outing. Getting confessions will be even tougher than I thought."

Henry nodded. "He has them trapped. They have to back each other. Possibly he made them vow to kill any one who tries to sell out the rest."

The buggy found the winding road that led down off the rimrock. The grade was steep and the drop-off sheer, but Joe was used to driving it; he hardly noticed. Henry held the brim of his hat as they made the last hairpin turn.

"This won't be solved by putting a set of Dickens in every jail cell, or whatever your latest scheme may be. Missionary impulses won't serve here."

"I know," said Joe.

"You can't reform Evans. Nor will he stop of his own accord."

Joe pulled up to the Raymond House stables in silence. Henry waited.

"When I shut my eyes at night, all I see are the men we pulled from the river," Joe said at last. "I don't know who will stand with me. But I want Evans taken, and I want him tried."

"Fit company though few," Stanton told him.

HELL MONEY

JOE SAT DOWN at the records room table, eyed the last chicken sandwich, and made a face.

"The sheriff up at White Bird wrote me. He thinks someone's passing stolen bank notes."

"How far is White Bird?" Lee asked.

"About eighty miles. Four, five days' ride. If we go, it won't be direct. We'd need to make a little tour, see and be seen, then head downstream to Deep Creek."

He leaned sideways to study their roughed-in map. Across the Camas Prairie, Vollmer-owned lands ran in a half-mile-wide corridor, east and south. The bloc was nearly solid; no checkerboard acquisitions here.

"How long has he been buying?"

"Since 1882 or so," Grace said.

"A long time to hold speculated options. He needs to wrap it up." Joe was thinking out loud. "I doubt he wants to deal with the Union Pacific. They don't build so much as buy up other lines, and they're nowhere near reaching here. Oregon Railroad and Navigation has made it to Moscow, but that's forty miles off. The Northern Pacific is already at Seattle. But the SPM and M—"

"St. Paul, Minneapolis, and Manitoba," Grace told Lee.

"—is laying track all the way to Helena this year, and scouting a

Montana pass to get them over the Divide. Once into Idaho they'll build feeder lines, not along the Snake, but through big valleys like the Camas. Vollmer and any investors could make a mint. He hinted as much on the Fourth."

"I wired a fraternity brother in banking," said Lee. "Five years ago the Sam Yup put $250,000 into a San Francisco escrow account under Vollmer's name. If he's spending Sam Yup cash, they'll sell to the rail company, give Vollmer a cut, make an inside profit, and nail down a labor contract for the whole project way ahead of the other five Companies."

"If your group has such a big investment in this area, why didn't they tell you?"

Lee took a deep breath. "They did, in a way. I was supposed to file the complaints and hire you. They also said the miners were sent to find a Company chest. I was to see if that happened."

Silence. Finally Joe said, "If you'd spoken up when we were there, we all could have looked for the damn chest, Lee. What kind of game are you playing?"

Lee glanced at Grace. No comfort there. "They gave me two incentives. Promotion and raise if recovered. If not, deportation. My status in the States is, um, irregular."

Joe's poker face was back. So was Judge Vincent.

"Sir," Lee said, pleading now, "truth is different in China. It's not a right. There's no obligation to disclose. The disorder at the mining camp—"

"*Disorder?*"

"—it endangers all Chinese in this country. The Company would rather wall off any damage, isolate, cover up. The Consulate wants the murderers exposed. Reparations paid now mean leverage against the American government down the line."

Grace said, "And how do they feel about solving the killings for real?"

Lee tried to explain. Vollmer had bided his time with nerve and foresight, but no *da bidze* would wait a generation for the best moment to deal, as a Chinese businessman might. The pressure to recover the chest would be much less if the Six Companies were not battling the newer crime syndicates. The war for Gam Saan profit was sapping the Six, and the Sam Yup needed any major labor contract it could get.

"I'm sorry," he said to Joe. "I didn't know you then."

"That argument won't hold. Why does the Sam Yup need Vollmer so badly? As the American buyer of record?"

Lee nodded.

Joe turned to Grace. "You remember Rob Grostein? He got back from Portland yesterday with a rumor about Vollmer and big railroad deals. Rob's never steered me wrong yet." He began to backcast. "All right, the miners went up the Snake with two missions, a cover—mining gold—and a real mission, to find a Sam Yup chest. What's in it, by the way?"

"Cash and documents. Maybe land deeds for the railroad right-of-way. You can get a lot into a standard Wells Fargo lockbox—" Lee stopped when he saw Joe's face.

"You never said Wells Fargo."

"Oh. Sorry. They said a Wells Fargo express box."

"What is it?" Grace said, watching Joe.

"Tom Douglas. Shot in the head in '83. I never knew who, I never knew why."

"Does this help?" Lee asked. "How does it help?"

"Vollmer went to San Francisco a lot that summer," said Joe. "Alonzo kept putting it in the *Teller* as social news, and for once Vollmer didn't like it. A Wells Fargo run got robbed that August, crossing Dug Bar—old Tom, as usual—but I could never get the stage people to file a claim or even a complaint. They kept putting me off. Eventually I left it. Two months later, someone shot Tom Douglas. I think we're seeing Blue at work in everything, from the murder of Douglas to the torture of your miners. It all starts when Evans gets to the area. It hasn't stopped yet. The two lines of crime—the dealings of Vollmer and the Sam Yup, Evans and his bloody work—they intersect at Deep Creek."

"Pity that Younger Boss took off," said Grace. "If only we had—"

"Another witness. Lee She didn't know the boys survived."

"Could they testify? They're underage Chinese."

"Technically, no," said Lee. "Underage, but born in the States."

"Then maybe—"

"Depends on the judge, the venue, and most of all the jury," said Joe heavily. "But yes, maybe they could tell what they know in open court. If in fact they know something we don't." He took a turn around the table, hands behind his back.

"Say Vollmer and Evans do go back a ways. Say Evans was once a Vollmer enforcer. When he gave me his life story, he went very light on the '70s and early '80s, when Vollmer wasn't shy about hired muscle. Try this. In '83 the Sam Yup sends Vollmer their deeds and seed money by special stage. To Vollmer's Grangeville office, for double security, since he owns the town." Joe was pacing still, intent on stair-step logic. "But Tom Douglas, business as usual, shoots the guard—who lived, by the way—and robs the stage. The guard and driver identified him. All the Wells Fargo men knew Douglas."

Lee said, "The Sam Yup's hands were tied. No white agent could be trusted to recover the box. No Chinese could plausibly get in and out."

Joe nodded. "Vollmer says to Evans, *Get my box back.* Evans turns too wild, kills Douglas, keeps the box as his personal insurance, says to Vollmer, *What box?* Blue's in no hurry. Vollmer's power can only grow. But then he gets bored and hungry. Starts reading *The Wasp,* boning up on social theory. Decides to kill thirty-odd Chinese miners in the name of patriotism. And easy gold, of course. Why not? He's got Vollmer by the—got a protector now who will hush up mass murder. That Vollmer likely hates it just adds savor for Blue."

When Henry learned they would return to Deep Creek, he sat a long while in the parlor with Joe and Grace. Lee stayed on the back porch, perusing the *Teller*'s better headlines: "Coal Deposit Discovered Near Omaha That Makes Pittsburgh Look Sick!" "Eight-Acre Diamond Field Found Near Paducah, Kentucky!" "Huge Flaming

Geyser Found 100 Miles West of Bismarck, North Dakota!" "Blizzard Stops All Trains Near London, England!"

He looked up. Dow and Yap were beside him, waiting in silence. Dow held out a handful of change. Lee took it. Nearly three dollars.

Before he could ask, Dow said, in English, "We earned it. Neighborhood jobs. The doctor said it was all right."

"Good for you," said Lee, baffled. Grace and Joe came onto the porch and stood listening.

"Please, we want you to take something back to . . . you know. This is to buy hell money for them."

"And lanterns," Yap said firmly.

Lee looked up at his fellow investigators. "It's a custom. Spirit money, heaven money, hell money. Looks like bank notes, or little tickets. You buy and burn it, or leave it on graves, or else float it downstream in paper lanterns with candles inside. August is best, when the gates of hell supposedly open, but any time works. It's money for the afterlife. Guidance for the lost."

"Does it free them?" Grace asked.

Lee wanted to say "In folklore," but the boys were too intent. "Ghosts are lost and hungry. If they can take revenge, they do. Any living person is fair game. The Chinese hells are pretty awful, and ghosts aren't particular. Hell money's also a bribe to keep them away from us."

"If they do get relief, what then?"

Lee shifted uneasily. "The Dark Lady, Meng Po, guards the door between worlds. She offers the dead a cup, the Drink of Forgetfulness. Some say it's tea, or a broth of herbs; some say wine. Once you drink she sends you back, reborn, purged of all sin and all memory."

Yap tugged his sleeve. "You'll go buy everything? You'll burn it when you're there, and say the words?"

Lee said, "Sure, kid."

Grace and Lee spent one more day in the records room. Tales heard at Lapwai of high prices offered for ordinary grazing land worried

116

her still. The man with the twenty-six horses lived ten miles in the wrong direction; why would Vollmer want his acres? She started plotting the holdings on every side of the horseman's place, moving between tax records and plat maps. North and south, she found five parcels under the same name: Selina Brown Vollmer.

John Vollmer's timid Kentucky wife seemed an unlikely land speculator, but there she was, deed after deed. All but one had been filed under B; Vollmer evidently had friends in the courthouse. Had Grace not been taking a rest and idly looking for Binnard, she would never have noticed. But together the holdings suggested a second potential rail route, slightly less direct but also less controversial, because most of the farming and rangeland disturbed would be tribal, not white. The President had just reauthorized rights-of-way through Indian land. Vollmer's belt-and-suspenders strategy was wise.

A few miles on, the owner names shifted. Vincent. Vincent. Vincent. Vincent. Vincent. She started a new roster, a new set of maps. Lee bent over the results and whistled. For forty miles, east and west, the same group of landowners recurred: E. Vincent, J. S. Vincent, A. Vincent, L. Vincent. Libby, Joe Junior, Lon, and Letty. No Nell. All purchased within a year, the properties blocked both Vollmer corridors plus every chance of access in between. Joe's own name appeared nowhere in the Camas tax rolls, but even a friendly observer would never believe he knew nothing about it.

"Joe needs to hear this," Grace said. "Do you want to go over?"

Lee did not; the morning was dark and windy, and at the moment Joe was not talking to him much.

Grace headed for E Street. No need for discretion. The whole town knew she was back.

RAPTOR GLANCE

JULY 12, 1887

WHEN GRACE SLIPPED into the Vincent & Co. auction rooms, John Vollmer, Alonzo Leland, and two men she did not recognize were competing for a walnut table with gilded feet. Joe, from his podium, spotted her at once.

"And the lovely lady offers double? No? But a customer of rare discernment, just the same, you don't see tiger maple every day — ten, now five, now five, who'll bid a dime? Fifteen, that's right, who'll bid a quarter? Thank you sir, I've got thirty-five, thirty-five, will Madam bid forty?"

Do shut up, Joe. Annoyed, she stepped behind a pillar, which did no good at all; it was cast iron and four inches wide. At forty-five dollars, Joe's hammer came down. Vollmer had won. Vollmer kept watching Joe, Grace saw; Joe Junior watched only Alonzo, and Alonzo was staring at her. Did he recall their last encounter? No doubt. He looked like he had just bitten a lemon.

Joseph Vincent, Jr., burly and blond, stood at Alonzo's elbow. Joe and his namesake were not a bit alike, and in personality the son was clearly all Leland, as ebullient and opinionated as his idolized grandfather. But young Joseph and Vollmer, seen in profile, could be —

Home was ten minutes' walk. Grace made it in five.

"Joe's oldest boy. And Vollmer. Everyone knows?"

"Just about, I should think," said Henry. "Except possibly Joe."

"How can he not?"

Henry thought a moment.

"You recall how his father died? Fatally generous — the Lelands smelled it right away. The more outrageous Libby got in their early years, the more Joe believed he had to save her. Typical Leland. Can't wear them down, can't shut them up. Young Nell is the only salvageable one."

Grace studied the threadbare office carpet. "I owe him far too much."

"My dear, he helped you when we couldn't, a favor you can't forgive."

Beyond the window a cloudbank swallowed the sun, taking with it the best of the day.

"You may remember that Joe was always a good mimic. On your river trip you saw him act a part, for cause. He was rusty and reckless and nearly came to grief. But once Joe takes hold, he's hard to dissuade. I never told you of his other dramas. The last was three years ago, when he and the federals stopped a ring of insurance crooks over at Helena, and again at Denver. Joe went in as a rich Boston dude, easily rooked. Five months, no curtain calls. Saved a great many people their war pensions."

"What other celebrated imitations does he do? I've seen the American hero, remember."

Henry Stanton sighed. "My dear, such bitterness is unbecoming."

"Why are you telling me all this? You never interfere."

"As is sarcasm. Would you make me tea?" said Henry. "I might rest a bit."

As Joe gathered up the auction sheets, a finger caressed his wrist.

"So good with the crowd, so clever with the bids. Father is right, you should be in Congress."

Christ almighty. She was supposed to be up at the lake. Grace had vanished. Just as well. He followed his wife out to the carryall.

"What do you want, Lib?"

119

She slid the lap robe over his knees as well as hers and kept stroking his wrist. Dinner would be late, then. He hoped she'd told the cook. Under the draped canvas he felt an assessing hand slide over his leg, press, and cup, and press again.

"Christ almighty," he said again, this time out loud. "We're in the middle of town."

Her sidelong smile widened.

After four children, Libby Leland Vincent's measurements were almost unchanged, even at the waist. With a discipline most women could not muster, she wore her steels day and night. She was striking rather than pretty, with a sharp nose and thick red-gold hair, and her rosebud mouth was hardly ever still. It ran in the family. Some listeners escaped exhausted, others enchanted, but in the end she almost always got her way.

Winning excited Libby, combat even more. But oh, the moods. Ever since the first weeks of their marriage, when Joe tried to amuse or distract his young wife, she would toss her fine head and give him the sidewise raptor glance that meant trouble. Placating, soothing—he'd tried it all. He could find no pattern to her inner weather.

When Lib put her mind to it, she was terrific fun. But if she could not dominate a room, she went off to survey the books and pictures with a knowing, crooked smile; when bored or vexed, she walked out with no excuse or farewell; if Joe was having too good a time at a pig roast or basket social, she insisted that he take her away and then sat in the carriage, miserably silent or else railing, just long enough to keep him from returning alone. She wept beautifully, and often.

And she needed him so. When he was out of reach, she grew sulky, then frantic. For years little demands deluged him, at home and in town: *Bring me stamps. Drive me to the milliner's. I don't feel strong today.* At eleven she might send him a note to say how grateful she was that he was hers, urging him to skip some dull meeting to come home and play; by two he might read that she felt herself so useless that she swore she could do herself harm. *I am ugly,* she told him, *I am insane, I want to die,* and Joe would rush to reassure her that she was lovely and precious. He never knew which threats were real, but he dared ignore none.

After one of her flights of talk, she would ask him, *How much of that do you think was true?* and he soon learned the only answer. *As much as you want it to be.*

After she learned how Joe spent his marriage portion, Libby decided to pay their main expenses from Leland funds. She would manage the family accounts; he could run his affairs as he pleased. So many married women had to be careful about ardor. The lemon half in the silk stocking and the vinegar sponge were not surefire, so relations were best kept to the last week of the month, to sweeten a husband at bill-paying time. But Lib craved the marital act. They both did. At supper she might consent only to celery or blancmange, yet behind doors she rained bites and kisses on his belly, swallowing him with a bawd's offhand skill, then riding him on the big walnut four-poster, on the bedroom floor, in the claw-footed tub. At first he tried to keep the windows closed. He lost that battle too.

After the fall of '76, Joe refurbished his downtown barn and took a permanent set of rooms at Raymond House. On public occasions he and Libby were always together. Family business matters they handled with all the dispatch and warmth of a salvage firm. Their beddings were infrequent but still edged with ferocity and, lately, performed in silence. What the children thought, he had no idea. No one in town said anything. But then Mr. and Mrs. Vincent were very good at public faces.

Libby was an only daughter. Thanks to the Leland money, they were still married, and still rich. Not Portland rich, or even Spokane rich, and a long, long way from Vollmer rich. But substantial enough for Libby to chair the Presbyterian Ladies' Circle and for Joe to buy any gadget or horse that pleased him; to allow Letty carte blanche at the dressmaker's and Lonny his custom buggy; rich enough for Joe Junior at twenty to commence married life in a house larger than any that Joe Vincent, Sr., had occupied before his thirty-fifth year.

For the children's sake, Joe was always present on holidays, al-

121

ways rode up to Lake Waha in August. He came to dinner Wednesdays and Sundays, first to the Main Street house, then to the grand new country place out at Tammany. Though he often spent such occasions staring at the chandelier, he saw that Joe Junior needed him not at all, and that Lonny and Letty in adolescence might wheedle Libby but listened only to their friends.

When the rains and floods of late May kept five Vincents inside and together for a solid week, no one came off well, except maybe Nell. His youngest got her rearing from the help and in other people's homes, try though Joe might to include her in his crowded life. He recalled her at the age of seven, disheveled and stubborn, lugging food, water, and even an umbrella out to a stray cat in the rain.

Strange that he knew the names of half the dogs and cats in town but so little about his three oldest children. It would help if they didn't refer to him as The Wallet. Perhaps if they ever asked him anything about his work, his thoughts, his past, he might feel less shoved aside in his own house. Twelve rooms of rosewood chairs and wax bouquets but no place for him, not even a corner. So he walked the streets of his town, ran for election, tried not to be bored, tried not to think. Unless he went on to Washington, he might never have to.

UPCOUNTRY

JULY 15, 1887

G RACE VETOED A PACKHORSE. She did consent to Joe's beloved miner's pan, and also a patent collapsible shovel that gave him and Lee immense satisfaction. She couldn't think why. They left at sunrise, riding southeast toward the great bowl of the Camas.

Small settlements went by, offering little except corrals and water, as the country alternated between long vistas of open grass and patches of conifer that grew thicker with every slow ascent. Grangeville lay on a high plateau. Grace said its other name was Sike-Sike, or Foot of the Mountain. They passed a flour mill, a scattered business district of white frame buildings, a fair-sized hotel.

"Ten years ago the Indian troubles began along here," Joe told Lee. Cottonwood, Grangeville, Mount Idaho, White Bird. "Merchants drove out from every town to trade with the refugees. The Nez Perce were ideal customers. People in a hurry, paying in gold."

Grace sat looking at the somnolent main street and the hazy blue wall of the Bitterroot range beyond. "I'll meet you on the other side of town," she said. "Don't rush on my account."

Joe called in at the sheriff's office and wandered through Grangeville stores to howdy and chat, but no one had any news about strangers with money. He expected none, only wanted word to spread that he was asking. The postmaster did have a letter forwarded by stage, its return address "Consulate of the Imperial Chinese Government,

San Francisco." After they located Grace in the shade of a lodgepole pine, Joe found his spectacles and broke the heavy red seals.

"Greetings, et cetera, and boiled down the message is, in accord with the Sam Yup Company, the Consulate has offered rewards for apprehension of the killers and now seeks details on the investigation, signed Liung Ting-tsan, Consul General, and F. A. Bee, Consul, both of San Francisco. How do we keep them happy?"

Grace mounted her chestnut and turned back toward town. "What you need is the impression of industry without intelligence. I'll do it."

She waited in a corner of the hotel porch, eyes on the floorboards, until Joe brought out paper and pen. Her final copy was a masterpiece of blots and scrawl.

July 19, 1887

Dear Sir,

I have been and am still in the employ of the Chinese company, ferreting out the matter. From what I have so far found, things seem to show that white men were the murderers, as some of the provisions "flour" I have traced directly to them. I have been in Lee Loi's employ, have been up Snake River above where the murder was committed. Water so high, impossible to find out what was done but will soon make a trip to the Salmon River. I have been following up, for six days, a white man who was at their camp and one who is the last one known to have been there. He has told some very curious stories about the matter, and some circumstances look very suspicious.

But there is in that vicinity some twenty or thirty bad men and I was watched very closely for nine days. I expect to start again up Snake river on the east side and will get into their camp again by some means and know what has been done with their property, if the agent here thinks best. It was the most Cold Blooded Cowardly trechery I have ever heard tell of on this Coast, and I am a '49er. Every one was shot, cut up, and stripped and thrown in the River. The Chinese here have paid me for what I have done so far, but Government ought to take it in hand, for with actions like this none are safe.

J. K. Vincent
United States Commissioner

"Commissioner of what? A lunatic asylum?" said Joe, incensed, but Lee's relief was clear.

"I like the white man with suspicious stories. Stolen provisions — that's good too. And nine days among the suspects with more to come sounds like you're adding up a bill. Now I'll have some breathing room. We'll have. Thanks."

Grace and Joe were already in the saddle, studying the mountains. Lee took the hint and swung his roan in behind. What more could these two want of him? He was paying top dollar. When the southward trail split, high on a sunny ridge, Lee reined in and watched his employees confer. The midsummer wind bore the scent of mountain country after rain — wet dust and grama grass, wild rose and sagebrush.

Vincent was unremittingly cordial — before the Exclusion Act, Lee had stayed in enough Eastern hotels to recognize the manner — yet shared nothing of substance any more. From the first "Breakfast coming up" to the last "Have everything you need?" it was all small talk.

The genteel doctor's daughter, smiling over sherry and seed cake, was only a memory, or else a mirage. On this second errand into wilderness, Grace was either silent or snappish, and she would not keep her sleeves long or wear her hat. Lee realized how careful of her complexion she had been all that first trip up the Snake. He had heard the American idiom "brown as an Indian," but watching her now, he could not imagine why she courted trouble so, or why Joe allowed it.

The Sam Yup miners' lonely fate was starting to haunt Lee's dreams. He fought sleep, and woke up gasping. He also knew the dead of Deep Creek had plenty of company across the Northwest. Twenty-seven Chinese miners killed in a Wyoming labor riot, three years back. Five merchants lynched in Pierce City, just over these foothills. Hundreds more driven out to starve as mobs wrecked Tacoma's Chinese section while the mayor watched. At crossroads and country stores, their little party was drawing enough hostile stares to make Lee's heart race, though he tried to seem calm.

But other American men bared their heads and stood at quiet attention as the three of them rode by, and sometimes women curtsied.

Politeness to the politician, Lee supposed; the farther they got from Lewiston, the more Joe rode point, lifting a hand to everyone they met.

White Bird was only a post office and a dirt-floor saloon. Joe mailed the Consulate letter and ambled from table to table, asking about horse thieves and new money. He carried bowls of dubious stew out to Grace and Lee as they waited in the street. The proprietor would not seat them, no matter how many Lewiston judges did the asking.

As they rode back up the steep valley beyond town, the land fell into darkness, but the sky flamed turtle-shell orange. Even as the sun set the moon rose, a miner's pan washed in pale lemon-gold. Bats began to skim low. Once they made camp, Grace tended the horses, turned her head away from a proffered plate of beans, and spread her bedroll. In the twilight she lay with her back to them both.

To stretch their legs, Joe and Lee walked along the rutted road, then stood watching the sun set over the dark mountain masses to the west. Lee had been saddle-sore their first day out but fine thereafter. Pretty good, he decided, for a city man.

"Is it the vapors?" He knew nothing about ladies' afflictions, and Grace defied category. "What's going on? I told *you* everything."

"Did you? I knew this part of the trip might be trouble, but not how much. We may have to send her back. Henry thought so too."

Mount Idaho was another nondescript upcountry village, but with a glorious view of valley and range. For a wonder, the hitching post was in shade. Nearby stood a lone log bench and a public pump: the city park. Grace would not dismount, only sat with feet out of the stirrups, head down. Joe filled a trough for the horses, topped off the canteens, and led a wary Lee Loi toward the one hotel.

"I like this place," said Joe as they walked.

"What for?" Lee had almost stopped trying to be civil.

"I could rest here, that's all. Good sun, fine trees."

Wonderful, thought Lee. *Two of them.* The midafternoon dining room was empty but also modern; it had a window. Lee tackled a noble beef sandwich with mashed potato and brown gravy. Rural Idaho might be looking up. A sturdy woman in her forties brought more rolls.

"How's life treating you, Joe?"

"Could be better." He nodded across the street.

Peg Koerner took a long look, marched out, helped Grace down, came back, and handed Joe a mug of coffee.

"Go on. Just you."

The screen door closed behind him. Peg lifted the wire fly cage off a raisin pie and gave Lee Loi another slice.

"So that's Grace Sundown. Darker than I expected."

Lee dug in. This country busybody was alarmingly frank, but she served him without hesitation and was perhaps the fifth person in Idaho to address him like a human being.

"I was gone that week, you know. Never saw her come through. He's paid for the upkeep of the graves these ten years. Does she know that?"

Joe was on the bench now, legs outstretched. He seemed to have all the time in the world.

"I don't know," Lee said. "I guess I don't know anything."

"Which way are you going?"

"Back to the river."

"She'll be better then. Look."

Joe said something to the summer air. Grace shook her head. She had the mug in both hands now and was starting to drink.

"Go visit the burying ground if you like. Lee can walk you over. Do him good."

"Joe, I *failed* them."

"Some lived."

"More didn't. Georges almost died too. Oh, I should have gone straight to Lapwai."

127

"Not with half the Army between you and home."

"Do you know, they hardly ever cried? Even the little ones. No. I should have found a way."

Peg said to Lee, "You have how much experience in the Territory?"

"Five weeks."

"Those two taught you anything?"

"Not to step off sandbars downstream. Not to put my hands up on rock ledges." He thought. "I can get a bird to sit on my hat."

"Can you now," said Peg, whisking away his plate.

Twenty minutes later, still watching from his window-side table, Lee saw Joe exit the sheriff's office, then stop next door to collect Grace. A fair, stocky man of thirty escorted her to the street, where all three stood talking. Lee assumed the unpainted frame building was the local newspaper; the stranger wore an editor's green eyeshade. Grace hugged him. Was she crying? Was he? Lee couldn't quite see. Mount Idaho was a very odd town. But when Joe and Grace returned to the dining room, both sounded wholly carefree.

"Come on, Lee!"

"Let's go, my man. Miles to cover yet."

He had yearned to be included, but not like this. Peg gave him a little push. She stood at the window as they rode out. More sorrow ahead, that was clear. She went behind the counter and began slicing carrots for the dinner stew.

The switchback trail was so rough and narrow that Grace told Lee to leave all decisions to the horse. He clung to the saddle horn and kept his eyes on the swaying brown rump of her mount, not the treetops beyond the drop-off or the thread of moving water far below. A last crooked canyon led to a hidden ranch beneath granite cliffs, its river landing a rare access point on the Idaho shore. Joe had not seen the place since before the Nez Perce War. The new owner was a young Dutchman who wore his hat cocked on the back of his head and stood in the lighted doorway with both hands on the lintel, rocking as he spoke. In the distance, starlight rippled on the Snake.

Joe and the rancher began to talk rates for feed and board, both enjoying the ritual dickering. All three horses would stay here until someone rode them back to Lewiston in a month or two. The boat Joe bought outright; this far upstream, all rides were one-way. Lee listened awhile, then wandered inside, aware his presence was driving up the price.

Grace stayed in the double darkness of the covered porch.

No one came out to press her to join them. She sat listening to the river. *Say, what was your name in the States?* Grace could not tell if their host had any family inside, but she hoped so; this secret green valley was the kind of mountain-country refuge where children flourished.

GOING IN

LEE DRANK SOME WATER, warm from the canteen, then lay watching the pale morning sky. He thought of swimming, but the current looked daunting. Instead he waded to a rock and sat, feet in the river. All along the draw, wildflowers rioted crimson and blue.

Joe looked up from his notebook. "Hot, hotter, damn hot! Say there, leeches on your knee."

Lee swung his legs out of the water, too late.

"Leave them be," Joe said. "They'll gorge and fall off."

Ten yards downstream, Grace stood up in the moss-green shallows, a ball of soap in her hand. Both straps of her white cotton combinations had fallen off her shoulders, and the wet translucent fabric clung to the strong hollow of her back. Lee took a sudden interest in the canyon walls. Joe studied Grace. Turning for the river had steadied her. She seemed all right again—blithe, even. He waved her in, and spread their penciled map for Lee.

"We're coming up on Deep Creek from the south. The river's still low, no matter what we told your Sam Yup friends. Two rapids, Grace says, maybe one portage. Evans's trail is lukewarm at best. They may be finding buyers for stolen stock, but they're not passing much money, if any. August Petersen in White Bird says he must have been mistaken on that score. Which I translate as bought off."

"Who's doing the buying?" Lee asked.

"Vollmer owns the town," Grace said behind him, tucking in her shirt. "*And* the sheriff. Just like Grangeville and White Bird."

"I'm surprised Gus even wrote me. He lied to my face well enough. Of course, that fleapit tavern was full of witnesses. The only free agent is Pete Baxter in Mount Idaho, who's got bad rustling on the north and west but also a few horses returned, which no one can figure."

Joe glanced at Grace, who looked perfectly blank. Jackson was still in the business, then, by his own eccentric lights. Jesus, what a family.

"No one's lifting a finger except Pete, and he's got so much ground to cover that once he rides by, he's not back around for a month, and everyone knows it. They've all read the calls in the *Teller* for a volunteer posse and they've all had a good laugh." Joe turned to Lee. "From this point on, you hear an order from either one of us, act first, talk later. Clear? You're sure? God forbid Evans catches us, but if it happens, then her chances are best. Yours? Not so good. Mine — Grace, you know what to do."

She nodded.

"Say it."

"I know what to do."

"Make sure he understands." Joe got up and headed for the water.

Grace knelt beside Lee, saying gently, "Ask your questions. Anything."

"Has Joe ever killed people?"

He never wondered before, but somewhere on that harrowing switchback the smiling public figure had become a hunter. Lee missed the Joe who always made sure he had enough blankets, who remembered to bring the Oolong tea.

Grace said, "More than he'd like, I'm sure. Listen. Evans might keep me alive to . . . amuse . . . his men. Anyone recognizes Mr. Salem, and Joe's dead. But you'd be last. Worst. If there's no way out, I've promised Joe to dispatch him any way I can. Slit the carotid artery, drive a sharp stick up the nose into the brain. I can try to do the same for you. Believe me when I say it's better to go at the hand of a friend."

She did not add that if she killed one of them, Evans or Canfield would almost certainly shoot her on the spot. In the head, if she was lucky. If not, Evans would hog-tie her, ram a gun up her, and pull the trigger. She never heard of such a thing until Joe and Henry sat her down in the Stanton parlor and explained what they might face. One of the Chinese miners had a similar fate. Henry's best-guess forensic reconstruction: a small, round-bodied man, age around twenty. Dow said he was the camp geomancer, someone named An Duk.

Lee absorbed her offer and tried not to bolt. Probably he could walk out of the canyon in three or four days if he started soon. As in *now*.

"I don't advise it." He had said nothing aloud. "Last time I told you Joe and I were only trying to keep you safe. That's still so. We are discussing the worst outcome."

"The worst . . . there's no other way? And how could *you* get past seven men?"

She did not answer, only ran her tongue slowly across her lower lip. Her mouth stayed half open, her eyes half closed. She gave a tiny moan, scarcely more than a whisper, then slowly arched her back. Her breasts rose beneath the loose cotton shirt; her breath came faster. She moaned again and rolled her head. One hand rose to the base of her throat and fluttered there.

Lee's mouth fell open. God, look at her. But even as he marveled, he understood: the fact of his nearness was too much for her at last. Perhaps mortal peril at his side had brought her to her senses. She did not sound like a woman coming to her senses; anything but. Did she—? Could he—?

Then he was flat on his back, a hunting knife just under his ear. He had the sense to lie still. The point described a small businesslike circle, pressed the skin, then withdrew.

"Like that," she said. "Better embarrassed than dead, Loi. When you're in the field, trust *no one*, do you understand?"

• • •

Grace climbed off his chest and went to help with the loading. Joe gave her a small smile, but she could tell his thoughts were elsewhere. She looked back at Lee. He was almost ready to meet her eye. Something new surfacing there; high time. Interesting, the way he sensed the cavalryman within the genial politician. And better that she puncture his self-conceit than Joe. On this trip they could afford no passengers. Grace let down her long braid, then put on her hat at last.

"Food bag?"

She passed it over.

"And the tarp."

Joe swung the last canvas rucksacks into the bow. To return to the killers' cabin on no more than a boy's word was madness. But without the gold there was no case. And he couldn't back out, not with Grace watching. Time had touched her so lightly. Unfair. He knew he had not aged well. He had lost an election that should have been a stroll, he lived at the office, he saw his wife as little as possible, and every time he stepped into the hotel or called an auction he wanted to head for the docks. Some men kept a bottle in their desk drawer. Joe had steamer schedules.

When they hauled out at Deep Creek, almost too tired to talk, Grace took her time but found no new human tracks, no sign of searches for cache or crate.

"Probably moved on," Joe said, rubbing his sore elbows. "It's almost two months."

He sat on a rock to empty his boots of river water and study the weather-battered mounds of burned canvas. Weeds grew in the scraped earth of the search area. Seeing its expanse, Joe realized how hard Lee and Grace had worked to collect and log the debris of so many lives during his absence. He thought about thanking them but could not muster the energy.

Lee wandered the cove. "I piled up driftwood against that rock, making the character for *mountain,* and nothing's moved. I know that doesn't prove much."

"We'll be safer sleeping across the way," Joe said. An hour later they had a sheltered camp among boulders at the end of a shallow Idaho-side cove. A trail back to the Dug Bar crossing led north, but south was only a drop-off overlooking fast current. Joe stared at the upstream rapids.

"If we've lost them—"

"Would Evans give up rustling so easily? He's in pretty deep."

"Up to his fucking neck. Sorry, sorry."

Grace thought of Jackson. "Could they be back in the Wallowas? I know one other valley, maybe two, that might suit."

He was heading for the shore, face tight and hard.

"The sooner I make a try for that cache, the happier I'll be. If anyone's there, they sit inside about now, even on hot nights. I come around from the river side, in and out, they'll never know."

"Joe, you can't just turn up, even once it's full dark. If you're trying to spare Lee and me, think again. At least let me come."

"I'm going in. Get some rest. I won't be long."

"Wait!"

She ran to scrabble in the packs. When she got back, the boat was already in the water.

"What?"

She handed him two strips of jerky. "For the dog."

Without looking at her, he shoved them in his pocket and rowed away.

CROSSRIVER

A N HOUR, THEN AN HOUR MORE. In the late twilight, Grace went up the game trail to watch the new moon rise, telling Lee that she would only be ten minutes. He nodded but did not look up. He hated being alone in camp.

At the river lookout the path ran between two smooth boulders, shoulder-high. The rock faces kept a hint of daytime heat and she laid a hand on each one, pressing her palms flat, liking the warmth. Above her head the canyon night was under way—a pair of owls, a shooting star—but to the north, toward Dug Bar, all was silent.

Then, across the river, gunshots. The *pop-poppop* of sidearms, not the crack and boom of rifles. Lanterns moved along the far shore, a line of bobbing lights. Ahead of them, a man was running. Joe. His bad foot would not let him go full out, but he could manage a lope and he was loping now, covering more ground than she thought possible. A hundred yards behind she could make out five pursuers, firing at every sound and shadow. Three on foot, two on horseback.

"Holy Mary Mother of God," said Grace, and ran. She got down to the river just as Joe turned to look back along the shore path, then spun half around and fell.

"He's hit!" Lee said at her side. They saw Joe struggle to his feet and disappear behind the boulders where Deep Creek joined the Snake. Then Lee was back, holding a flat stone tied to the end of their one coil of rope. He waited for her lead. She pointed.

"That open space, under the big pale rock. There."

Lee hefted the weighted rope, once, twice, judging the distance in the dimness. About as far as right field to second base. The high, arcing toss came down an instant before Joe stumbled again and went to his knees, nearly sprawling. Left-handed, he clutched the lifeline and wrapped it around his waist, turning, turning, then waded out chest-high and let the others reel him across until the main current bore him away, tugging Grace along the shore, the rope burning through her hands until she slammed into a shoreline rock and got herself braced.

The line swung through the dark water and then went taut. Joe's arm and head rose, then sank. Lee was already floundering waist-deep through the shallows. He threw himself into the Snake, unroped, swam hard a few yards, and brought Joe back to a quieter reach. Grace met them at the water's edge and got both as far as the sheltering rocks, yanking the rope along, the tied stone clattering behind. On the Oregon shore, men with guns and lanterns spilled into the Deep Creek cove and began to spread out, searching, shouting.

Lee held a gasping Joe upright as Grace pulled free the last of the rope, then helped lower him onto a blanket. She began to cut away the ruined shirt. The river plunge had cleaned the bullet hole in his shoulder, but blood still welled. She could see no exit wound, only livid flesh and swelling. The real damage would be internal. If the big artery in the shoulder was hit, he would be dead in minutes.

Voices sounded over the water, but the shooting had stopped. Pray God they would not try to ford. The light was going fast. Lee dug in the packs for the match safe. Grace gestured to him to take over the compress and upended the medical kit to find the muslin packet of spiderweb. It helped to clot blood, and she wished she had brought six times as much. But first she uncapped the little tin bottle of iodine in alcohol. Henry could extract a bullet later. Infection killed.

"Get your hand over his mouth. This is going to hurt."

Lee held Joe down as the antiseptic seared.

"Jesus, Grace."

"Keep him quiet. Don't get bitten. And — *now.*"

Lee swore at her in Chinese. In the near-dark, she crawled a few feet to look through a gap in the rocks and saw the last of the searchers riding off. When she got back to the blanket, Joe was silent again, but to her horror she saw his eyes were open and aware.

"I'm sorry, sweetheart. Hang on. Loi, another."

She laid in the precious clump of spiderweb, padded the wound with her spare camisole, and tied the bandage strip by feel as the next match flared and died. Both of her charges were shivering, Joe less than Lee. Not good. Getting off his sodden boots and work pants was a struggle and he fainted early on, which made redressing him far easier. The minute they were done, Grace slowly, slowly lay down beside him on the bloodstained blanket, covering as much of his icy body as she could without jarring the wounded shoulder.

"That was a wonderful thing you did, but you *must* get dry," she said to Lee, not turning her head. "We can't risk a fire. Put the other blanket over me, then get on every bit of clothing we have left." She felt Joe's terrible chill leaching her own warmth and pressed her palms along his ribs, willing him to heal. But when she laid an ear to his chest, she could barely find his heartbeat, and all night long, each time she lifted her head from a fitful sleep to see if he still breathed, she wiped Joe's blood from her cheek.

In the gray dawn she felt him wake.

"*This* is nice," Joe said, sleepy still.

"Don't move!" Half his shirt was dark.

After a moment he whispered, "How bad?"

"Bad. We need to get you home. Joe, where's the boat? Joe, no, stay with me."

"Tied up," he said, after a while. She could get no more out of him.

Lee was sitting up, listening. She shoved bread and cheese into his hand, gave him a canteen, and led him back along the shore path toward the rustlers' cabin.

137

"Cross there," she said, "looking like you have every right to, hat on, face down. It's never more than knee-deep. Joe likes brush piles and coves, that's all I can tell you. Stay out of eyeshot, whatever you do. As soon as they wake up, they'll ride back along and search both sides. Get flat and stay flat. No exposed skin, no open eyes."

He nodded and stepped into the Snake.

Late afternoon, earliest twilight, and Lee still not back.

"What . . . time?" said Joe suddenly, eyes closed. He could not raise his head. She gave him the wetted corner of her bandana to suck.

"About seven. Sssh." Even that small effort started a trickle of blood at the corner of his mouth. His shoulder looked dreadful, and on a hot evening his good hand was cold as clay. She held it in both of hers. When she thought he had drifted off, she whispered, "Joe, you idiot. Why did you do it?"

He tried to speak but no sound came. She bent to hear.

"I wanted to be thirty again. Hell, I wanted to be fifty."

Lee Loi found the boat at last, in a backwater searched twice before. He dropped behind a rock when the hunt went by and went to ground again when he saw horses on the opposite bank. Five riders, going toward the Idaho-side camp. Minutes later he heard distant shouting. Smoke rose near the boulder where he knew Joe lay. On the still air the report of two shots reached him clearly, about ten seconds apart.

As the rustlers rode back toward Dug Bar, Lee saw in their midst the tall blond man that Joe had said to fear above any other. When at last Lee rowed for the cove opposite Deep Creek, he came ashore to chaos. The rustlers had wrecked the camp with cruel abandon, packs slashed and set on fire, food ruined and scattered, rifle and shovel gone. Beside the rocks where Joe had lain was an open empty grave, fresh-dug. No sign of Grace.

Had Evans thrown them into the river, like the miners? Lee called their names anyway, first low, then louder. "Don't do this," he said to the darkening air. *Shebude.* He had not seen much death and could not think what to do next. He dreaded finding their broken bodies. He could not bear knowing they were ghosts, raving and starving in some alien hell.

Did Christian ghosts do that? Would the Lady of Forgetfulness come for them too? He never wondered before. He never heard Joe say a word about religion. Grace was a Catholic. He once knew a soft warm Irish girl, but she and he did not speak of faith.

Lee ran from boulder to boulder, searching, plunging on. No Joe, no Grace. He could not catch his breath, nor could he cry. There was no point. Night was coming on. What would they tell him? *Conserve your warmth, save your strength.*

He saw a patch of shortgrass near the strange untenanted grave, crawled onto it, and began to lie down. It seemed as sensible a course as any, alone and hunted, stranded up the Snake with no food and no friends.

"Loi, get *off*," the grass said. He rolled and was up in one fast movement, aware in the back of his mind that a month before he could never have done that. He stared about. Grace's voice, muffled, but no Grace. The ground at his feet rippled and heaved. Knees appeared, hands, eyes. Five or six strips of turf fell away in a cascade of dirt as she pushed herself up from the shallow trench. If you knew where to look you could see the disturbance, but he had been utterly fooled. He pulled her to her feet. The patent shovel came with her.

"I think they got the rifle. Help me with Joe."

She felt at one end of the long dirt mound beside the grave, then uncovered a round of metal about two inches down. It took Lee a moment to recognize the base of the miner's pan, inverted over Joe's face like a small iron tent. Grace felt under his jaw and said he was still with them, just. Shoveling earth away from Joe's legs, Lee remembered the shots. She pointed.

"Someone got mad."

He could see the blast marks in the opened earth.

"How did you dig this so fast?"

"I had all day." It was not a reproach. "I thought it might scare them. And I made a brush pile. Another way to hide if anyone came. The grass trick takes five minutes, just knife and hands, if you're in practice. Which I'm not."

They left Joe wrapped in the last blanket amid the piles of sand and dirt; he would be warmer so. Grace wet his lips with river water and bathed his face, then tried to salvage something, anything, from the wrecked camp. She rescued only a lone crushed sack of common crackers. They shared the crumbs in silence. Lee was cold, but his jacket was rag and ashes now, and so was hers. The moon hung in a cloudless sky, brightening the whaleback ridge above Deep Creek.

"To Lewiston it's what, three days' rowing? Tomorrow, do we try to hail a boat? It might be faster."

"Hail a boat. Loi, *look at us.* A half-breed and a Chinaman, filthy, no money, up Hells Canyon, and who's that white man with them? Why, North Idaho's leading candidate for Congress, seven eighths dead of a bullet in the lung. They'd hang us right here, if they could find a tree."

For a change, she sounded quite human.

"What do we *do?*"

"I don't know. Stop asking. Let me think."

But then she was up again, running across the clearing to peer around the edge of the tallest boulder. Lee came too. At the moment he hated her guts, but he hated being alone in the dark more. He looked and swore. A single light was moving their way from Dug Bar, along the shore path. A lantern.

Grace piled brush around and over Joe as fast as Lee could drag it. Evans would find him in any serious search, but at least in the darkness Joe was out of easy view. The two of them were well and truly trapped. Lee found himself hunched beside a granite boulder, scrabbling at the ground with his bare hands and not getting far, when along his nape he felt a slow warm breath, and then another. He stopped digging and pressed his forehead against the rock. Grace had clearly lost her mind, but he found he could only crouch in the starry darkness, sunk in the accepting calm of the rabbit that sees the hawk turn before stooping.

"Loi, breathe with me. In. And out. That's it."

One arm was around his shoulder and a hand stroked his neck, gently, gently. He fought not to weep.

"Loi, don't, please don't. I'm so sorry, truly I am. None of this is your fault. Now listen. He feeds on fear. He smells it out. So let's fool him and be something that isn't afraid. That doesn't even know how. Can you do that for me?"

Lee shrugged.

"We need to hide for a while, *p'tit*. Disappear, like I did with the grass. Like Joe when he's acting. But this is another kind of disappearing, all right? Going into, going through. Step aside from yourself awhile; think about rock. Rock under water. Your mother's well, the stones you dropped down it. Be those. I know it's dark. I know it's strange. Let go all over. More."

He saw it now. These patient hills, these boulders, they lived as well, only slower, stronger. Humans to them were like fireflies in the night. But if you were rock too, the monster might pass by and never know. Never know. The feather-touches down his neck kept on. So right, and now too late. His head kept falling forward. He wanted to thank her but could not find the sound that made her name. She tugged him into the shadows and lay beside him, holding his hand.

She said, very low, "If he finds us, don't be too brave, my dear. Just go. Wait for me if you can or look for Joe."

He knew then. He turned his face away. Her fingers trembled in his, tiny bone-deep shivers, but her voice was steady and loving.

"Rock under water. Yes, exactly. That heavy. That still." She freed his hand. "Go ahead. I'm right here."

Lee Loi shut his eyes and sought the darkness.

"What will you be?"

Her voice was almost a thought. "Leaves. Rain."

141

ELSEWHERE

JULY 23, 1887

AW YOU RUN. Oh, yes."
The easy Cracker cadence was near and clear. "Roam all you want, grunt all you like. Got you in a hog pen now. Cliff above, water behind, only one way out, savvy? Sure you do. Thinking to the end, that's what I like to see."

Steel whined on a pocket whetstone, once, twice.

"I always show the knife, you know that." A touch of pique, but patient still. "Truss you up, show the knife, peel a little rind. Maybe take just one eye. Maybe some tongue. You say what, now? Look at me. Now look away. Now down. All the way. Show your betters some respect. Savvy? No, won't even learn a word of English, stinking pigtail heathen, Gadarene fucking swine."

Lantern light swung and flared on the river rocks. Blue's voice came and went as he quartered the wrecked campsite.

"Killed my Zeke, I'll show you . . . Take your balls and make you watch. Fuck you up the shithole good and slow, cut you a crossways cunt, fuck that too . . ."

He paused, casting about for any movement, any breath, then circled the granite boulders, studied the scuffled earth near an aspen, walked to the river's edge, waited, returned.

Another silence, then: "So back for breakfast, all. Sleep tight."

The footfalls retreated, with the lantern light. The fraction of Lee

Loi that still registered such matters saw that Joe was right: Evans only looked human. Grace was right too. Only the elements could withstand such evil. *Quiet,* said the leaves, not in words. *Dark.*

Lee Loi sank back into the well of stones.

Grace put her hands to her eyes, shuddering. She forced herself to breathe, to move, to reason. How had Joe stood it so long? At this rate, the whole Northwest would be a killing ground. Thirty-one dead in seven weeks, and eager for more.

Saw you run. Her shirt and pants, her one dark braid: from across the river Evans likely glimpsed the two of them carrying Joe to cover and in the low light took both for Chinese.

At least she had saved Loi. Rather, he had saved himself, grasping in minutes what she once took days to master. And in a tradition not his own. A true natural. She had only shown him a door into otherness. Need did the rest; it happened sometimes. With luck, the Beuk Aie would know what to do for him. Lee was all the way back now, whispering question after question when she craved only wind and wordless sleep. They felt their way out of the boulder field, then down to the river, holding each other up, moving as if fifty years had passed, not fifty minutes. No sign of Evans.

"Do you think we have till morning?"

Grace shook her head. "Half an hour. Less. You bring the boat. I'll get Joe ready."

Lee hesitated, scanning the dark shoreline.

"No. Wait. There's something —"

He had caught the wrongness faster than she, though not so strongly. Grace felt herself falling sideways. It seemed to take a long time. Lee turned and caught her, but she could barely hear, barely see. The tangle of presence edged nearer.

"*No.* Oh, no, Loi, please, talk to them, hold them off. Tell them who we are, what we want. I can't — they don't know me —"

He gave her one wild look and spoke to the night in Cantonese, self-consciously at first, and then with great force. A few of the minds were almost awake but not persuaded. The rest knew nothing but grinding appetite. Grace, on hands and knees at the water's edge, could tell that nearly all the dead had shed memory and personality like a snake its skin, but could not go forward as they ought. Of course they roamed the canyon, angry and lost. Rage, fear, and gold lust held them trapped between worlds, starved for revenge, not particular about targets. No mercy there.

Lee was still arguing, still appealing, when the world tore and Grace was thrown into some low bare sloping space, like an airless cellar with no horizon and no exit, crammed with human souls (she thought they were human) that crawled endlessly over and under one another, pushing and howling. Everything in that awful elsewhere was reversed, white on black like a photographic negative, and knowing she was trapped made her howl too.

A snap, a slam, and she was back beside the Snake, prone now, and gasping. Grace raised her head and saw from Lee's drained, despairing face that he had been somewhere worse. *Help the others,* she thought, knowing no one and nothing would hear. So the miners must have prayed in their last moment. *Joe, Lee. Oh please, leave me, save them.*

The faint cold moonlight on the Snake coalesced, rose, and became a robed Chinese woman, dignified and smiling, older than rain, stronger than stone. She moved toward them, not quite treading the current. *Meng Po,* thought Lee, astounded, just as the roiling cloud of ghosts enveloped her. Another being of moon and night arced from the dark river, then settled its long silver bulk at the mouth of the cove like a living wall, cutting off the way to free-running water. Grace thought it might be a gigantic sturgeon, the largest she had ever witnessed. Lee Loi saw a dragon. In the living cloud above their heads, there and not there, Grace had the impression of a parley, a negotiation. What price would the ghosts require? She could only lie at the river's rim and wait. The verdict filled her.

A task. And a sacrifice.

Joe's price would be hardest and highest. It always was, for the hostage, and he was a strong man very close to death. The ghosts would not be pleased to lose such a meal. Grace could not think what to give up. It seemed that life had already stripped her of everything she ever loved or wanted. She had said her final Hail Mary among the boulders — *now and at the hour of our death, amen* — but had not been able to finish the Our Father. Now she knew why. *Oh, not that. It's all I have.* But nothing else would satisfy the bond.

Forgive us our trespasses as we forgive those who trespass against us. All her life she had fought that one sentence. But to free these companions she would do it, and she would mean it. Grace Sundown laid her forehead on the stones of the riverbank, closed her eyes, and let vengeance go. It was not quite enough, so she sent away self-pity too. Her unseen judges seemed satisfied.

What was asked of Lee Loi she might never know, but Grace thought he was as shaken as she. Meng Po was near again. Grace smelled the draught of forgetfulness, like a wind from the shores of heaven, and her head swam with longing, but she knew it was not for her. Loi looked at the Lady's face and understood that he need not fear when his time came to take the cup from her hand. Beside Joe the Lady paused a long while and then moved on. The ghosts of Deep Creek and Robinson Gulch swarmed to her side.

Leave these poor morsels. The ghosts hesitated. *I will show you a true feast. Come, that you shall know him again. First meat, then drink.*

Go, she said to Grace and Lee Loi as she went by, hungry ghosts streaming above, around, behind, below. Grace felt her grandmother's remembered touch then, a loving fingertip along the cheek. *Go, M'a Min.* The darkness parted and let them through. Grace snatched up their last canteen from the stony shore as she and Lee ran the boat out with a half-conscious Joe propped in the thwarts. The great sturgeon was nowhere in sight. The ghosts had left them a little water and all their human wits; it was more than enough.

Thank you, esteemed dead. As the current took them north, Grace looked to the Idaho side and saw the single lantern again, moving back along the path toward their ruined campsite.

145

SUMMER FAMILY

JULY 27, 1887

NELL VINCENT DESPISED snivelers. But she did seize Dr. Stanton's hand as Dow and Mr. Lee carried her father along the dock, wrapped to the chin in a bloody blanket. He looked dead. She heard herself sob, a hideous gulping noise. Yet he opened his eyes, found her, and sent her a smile and wink. She ran to help with the stretcher, desperate to be near.

"How did you know?" she heard Mr. Lee ask the doctor.

"The boys insisted. First real animation I'd seen in them. I thought it couldn't hurt to drive down, even at six in the morning. Damned if you didn't show."

From the wagon box, Nell studied the travelers. Dow had told her that no one who went upriver to Deep Creek came back the same, if they came back at all, and clearly he was right. Mr. Lee and Miss Sundown looked like the wreck of the *Hesperus*. When Mr. Lee came to Lewiston, he reminded her of Lon's and Letty's friends, the popular stuck-up ones. But the Lee Loi who knelt beside her father was fully adult, focused and grim.

And Miss Perfect looked a fright. Nell and Becky had followed her downtown once, hoping for excitement, but saw only a slender, unsmiling grownup, swift and purposeful. You could tell right away that her sums always checked, that her thank-you notes were copperplate.

She also drew the eye, and held it, in some way that Nell could not identify. *Élan,* said Becky's mother. Because of her French blood. At the moment the paragon crouched in a wagon bed, wet and muddy, keeping a grimy shoulder bandage in place. Dr. Stanton looked over once; she shook her head.

As they pulled into the Stantons' corner lot, Nell checked her father. Even this brief wagon trip had jolted him half off the stretcher, and under the summer tan his face was an ugly gray-white. She swung her legs over the seat and slid down beside Mr. Lee.

"If you take his arms, I'll move his feet," she told them both. "Don't hurt him, now."

Miss Sundown said she wouldn't.

Reassuring Nell took everything Joe had, his best acting ever. Henry was afraid to use more than a touch of the ether cone, breaking his lifetime rule never to operate on a friend. In the riverside darkness Grace had missed the exit wound, hidden in the armpit. The blood loss was considerable, the collarbone fractured, but Stanton found no infection.

Joe was a terrible patient, mulish and defiant. He tried to get up too soon, and the crash brought Henry running. He told Joe to behave or expect valerian in his milk. Not even the most robust male could take a bullet so near the axillary artery and recover in a week.

Soon an open secret spread through town: Joe Vincent was shot and his Chinese investigation was going forward, headquartered at the Stantons'. By great good fortune, most citizens of influence were at the lake, on and off, for July and August, except the Grosteins and Binnards, who had no invitation to buy a camp there and never would. Every morning some workman or housewife dropped a bucket of berries or a dozen rolls on the Stanton porch. Joe and Henry were popular, and more in Lewiston admired Grace than she knew.

Mrs. Reilly confirmed to everyone that Libby sent her husband no note of concern. Nor did the three older children ride in to see him. Alonzo sent a bill for auction-house ads, pinned to an anti-Chinese tract. The Leland-Vincent ménage was not exactly summering in Denver, or even on the Oregon coast. Stagecoach ads ran in the *Teller* each week: *Ho! For Lake Waha. Parties desiring to go out to the lake from town will be taken out by good coaches, on good roads, at 6 am to arrive after breakfast. Convenient returns. Round-trip fare $3.*

Only Henry dared ask. Joe said, "Reminds me of the hands who sent a get-well card to the rancher. 'By a vote of five to four, we wish you a speedy recovery.' I'd settle for that. Don't wait around." He turned over slowly on his good side to face the wall. When Henry spoke again, Joe did not respond.

Nell made soup. She, Dow, and Yap took over much of the catering, no mean task the way the house population was growing. All their menus featured pie. The need for clean laundry was prodigious; by week's end, the backyard mangle expired under the strain and thereafter Joe sent all linen to Raymond House, earning the undying gratitude of Mrs. Reilly. He also directed the bank to give Grace extra money for the housekeeping. She did not demur. Lee and the boys ate like a threshing crew. Besides, domestic command suited Nell; most mornings she sat at the kitchen table checking her many lists, waving away all offers of help.

Early on, she whispered to her father, "Are they *very* poor?" The Tammany Creek house required a staff of six — farm manager, stableman, cook-housekeeper, and three hired girls. The Binnards lived in solid mercantile comfort. The Stantons' little white four-square fascinated Nell, but also alarmed her: so clean, so worn. The beds were only painted iron, the towels thin and elderly, and all the quilts discreetly mended, like the doctor's suits. No conversation pieces improved the parlor, no bottles of sand from the Holy Land, no beaded door curtain. Only books, and watercolors of Dartmoor and the Devon coast. But the garden was wonderful.

As Grace changed the dressing on his shoulder, Joe said, "Libby lost interest early. Nell didn't stay pretty or biddable. Smart, though. I always thought that if you and I — that she would be —"

"I know. Rest."

He lay looking out the window at the summer sky. She waited.

"Are you still bored, Gracie? Mary says you were so bored these last few years, you wanted to yell and throw things."

"No, Joe. Not bored."

"A disaster from start to finish," said Grace six days later. The Stanton backyard was narrow and secret, guarded on every side by Lewiston's famous poplar trees, grown tall and graceful after twenty years. They all felt safe there, and since the weather kept fine they made steady use of the battered wicker furniture and old red table. The thermometer stood at ninety; the house was airless, the copper drip pan in the icebox brimming.

"I was sadly unprofessional going upcountry, full of self-indulgent sulks. No, Joe, extenuating et cetera isn't enough. And I should have seen the Idaho-side camp was a trap with no back door. Joe's mistake was going off to the cabin alone. Loi, you did best of any of us, and you only started pulling your weight after Mount Idaho."

Lee nodded a thanks, knowing they were no closer to closing the case. Henry and Joe had the porch armchairs, Grace and Lee the back steps. The young people sat on the grass, riveted by the novelty of hearing grownups admit to error.

Lee watched Dow and Yap whisper together. Only their promise to Jackson Sundown kept them in Lewiston. That, and the fact they had nowhere to go. He wondered if he would ever know their real names. Long ago he resigned himself to being *Loi* in the States, not *Low* or *Lou*, but Lim Dow and Chu Yap were obviously paper names, picked to confuse adults and officials. No Chinese would press them. No American would know the difference. Telling the boys he never burned the hell money had been surprisingly hard.

"Lee."

He looked up.

"We wouldn't have made it back without you," Joe said.

"But what happened at the cabin?"

Joe sighed. "I left the boat where you found it and walked in.

They were back and eating supper, so I thought I'd chance getting closer."

"All the same bunch still?"

"I think the two runaways were gone. Vaughan and McMillan. I didn't eavesdrop to speak of, just went after evidence. I pried up the stone, like you said." He nodded to Dow. "I saw at least four vials, was reaching for them, when I got a cold wet nose in the ear. Blue's dog, Zeke. He knew me from last time, but when I tried to keep reaching he growled, and when I tried standing up he snarled. He meant business. I knew they would hear him any minute."

Joe hesitated. Grace was watching him soberly. He couldn't tell her how happy Zeke had been to see Joe Salem at first, or how he fed the beast her jerky and felt it lick his hand before he snapped its neck.

"What did you do?" Nell demanded. "Did you kill him?"

Joe nodded.

"Good," said Grace and Nell in the same breath.

"Like two pumas," said Henry. "You had no choice, Joe. What next?"

"Evans came out for a smoke and saw the dog there. Back home it's called looking for his familiar. I swear he knew. And once he yelled he'd kill the bastardly son of a bitch who did it, I moved right along. They saw me take off. You know the rest. I'll have to ask Oregon to arrest and hold them before they split up. The dog aside, they could see someone made a try for the gold cache."

"You need an indictment, right?" said Lee.

"On some lesser charge. I'll telegraph the sheriff at Joseph to arrest the gang for rustling. Or as the law reads, altering and defacing the brand of a horse that is the property of another."

"What the hell happened to mass murder?"

"Not enough evidence yet. Make too large an initial claim, juries won't convict. We can adjust the charge after some arrests. As an officer of the court, I can testify to seeing the bodies, plus the presence of gold-dust vials. Four at least under the stone step."

"Not enough for a small-town jury, and you know it," said Henry, abandoning tact.

"Sir?" Dow stood by Joe's armchair. "Sir, did you see them?"

Puzzled, Joe looked at Lee and Grace.

"Yes," she said.

"Are they angry?" Yap whispered. Lee dropped into Cantonese, and soon the boys nodded. They murmured together, but Grace saw no tears. Lee listened to a last question, then answered in English, so she could hear. "There was one who liked me a little. One that didn't. And one, no, two who tried to hold the others back."

"Hong Lee!" Yap said eagerly.

"Elder Boss," said Dow. The knowledge did not seem to ease him.

"Can you tell us more?" said Joe, bewildered but game. "Tell us what you saw that day?"

"I tried to make him not look." Dow frowned at his cousin.

Yap said, "But I did anyway. To remember."

Thanks to Chea Po's indulgence, the boys had a fine May outing. Yap collected so many rocks that his pockets sagged. Dow lay on his stomach, pulling up grass with an assayer's care, trying to keep every stem perfect. The blades he set between his thumbs and whistled, not very well; the pale juicy stems he ate. Fresh grass sap was nectar after months of cabbage and fish. The tender greens and grays of a spring day softened the Seven Devils range on the Idaho side, but overhead they saw line after line of long, swift clouds racing by, cream above, blue-gray below. The sky to the west was nearly violet.

As they crested the last ridge, they saw smoke. For the second time in an hour the boys lay together in tall grass. From the hilltop they saw their winter family die, one by one. The cries and gunshots went on so long that Dow began praying to all the gods for surcease, or maybe a miracle. Yap curled up for a while and pretended none of it was real, but then crept to the edge of the heights just in time to see an ax sink into Hong Lee's head. It took three raiders to hold the cook down. Both boys recognized the killer: the tall, fair leader from Dug Cabin.

Dow stared at the assayer's gutted body beside a burning tent. *That was stupid,* he thought wildly, *killing the two in camp who spoke the most English.* The rustlers kept Chea Po for last. The boys could see him over by the boss tent, tied hand and foot, one eye socket empty, his round cheeks crusted with dirt and blood. When the tall man smiled and walked toward Elder Boss, Dow buried his face in the grass.

All night they huddled on the chilly starlit ridge, staring this way and that for ghosts; all next morning they waited for someone, any-one, to return from Robinson Gulch. By noon Dow knew that no one ever would. Lee She and the Salt Creek crew were due in soon, but he had no idea when. Maybe they were all dead too.

Dizzy with hunger and fear, the boys crept through the burned-over camp. Animals had already torn at the bodies. Yap ran about, trying to roust the vultures, but more kept landing all the time. The humid air seemed full of dark wings. Dow tried to think what to do, but the boats were stoved in and rain starting. He put his head back and opened his mouth, tasting sweet water and salt tears.

Dow was digging in the cook-shack ruins when a voice behind him said, "Kid. Speak any English?"

Dow nodded.

"Then let's go."

Beside a buckskin pony stood the horseman they had seen from time to time in the hills. The boys had never talked to him, only waved. Rain dripped from his hat brim. Dow could not see much of his face in the twilight, but he sounded kind and his skin was copper-brown. Dow let out his breath in relief.

"Where's the other one?"

Dow pointed to a half-burned tent. The rain was pelting down now, and the Deep Creek camp smelled of ash and blood. The new-comer linked his hands to give Dow a leg up, then reached under the tattered canvas and lifted a kicking, protesting Yap into the saddle. In two languages, Dow told his cousin to shut up.

OUR DISASTERS

AT BREAKFAST JOE SAID to Dow, "Any more thoughts on Mr. Lee's missing chest?"

Lee Loi added quickly, in Cantonese, "Keep in mind that the Judge nearly died to help your friends. If you can't trust me, little brother, at least help him."

"Him, maybe, but not you," Dow said back coldly. "Younger Boss told me last winter that the Sam Yup sold us out from the start."

A double rebuke. Dow was using Toisanese, and his country dialect was a hammer: an honest worker repelling the con man. But Dow had never before hinted of anything to find.

"All right, would you tell a judge over in Oregon what you told us last night?"

"If you find one who believes me."

"You're America-born," said Lee Loi.

Not really an answer, but Dow thought a minute, then nodded.

"He says he'll testify," Lee told Joe, who leaned forward in turn.

"Did the assayer's vials have any kind of markings on them?"

"No, sir. Just regular. Plain glass."

Joe glanced at Yap, but the younger boy was intent on bread and jelly.

"Son, can you think of anything that would help to hang the killers? Anything at all?"

Dow looked him in the eye. "No, sir."

Grace told them to take a baseball outdoors; the day was too nice for sitting.

Once out of earshot, Yap whispered, "Why not tell Judge about the box? Jackson said we could trust him. Sort of."

Dow snapped, "You heard. Everyone's still there, not really dead. We promised Elder Boss. We broke a plate and said the words: *May our souls shatter if we break this oath.*"

We used a piece of pine bark, thought Yap. Maybe that didn't count.

"I said it too. *Until seas run dry and rocks crumble.* But now is it better never to tell?"

Dow threw his cousin the ball. "We swore," he said again.

Nell hurried across the new-cut lawn to join them, untying her apron as she ran.

When Grace and Lee tried to explain about the ghosts, Joe lay down on the day bed. "I refuse to credit this cockeyed tale. There are limits, and I've reached them."

"I'm off, then," said Lee, saluting Henry as he went. "To see a man about a dog."

Grace knew he was going to the Beuk Aie, yet again. She was not invited. She was only a woman, and from their viewpoint an interfering *da bidze* one at that.

"Would you like some of Nell's soup?"

"I would not. Grace — are you sure of what you saw?"

She knew how much it cost Joe even to ask.

"Saw? I mostly had my eyes shut. But my strong impression is that . . . they . . . were interested in you most, Lee next. I was incidental." The judgment on the shore had been bitterly clear. Her job was only to open the door, so that others might walk through.

She added, "But your questions about motive have one kind of answer now. The Chinese murders were so cruel because Evans likes his victims alive. Aware."

"I still don't understand how he missed you."

"You've been in battle," she said, gathering up glasses, spoons, towels, all the small clutter of a sickroom. "The smell of human fear is real."

She looked to Henry for confirmation, and he nodded.

"Even without a Zeke, I think, Evans picks it up. Loi was upset when he came for us —"

"Pissing in terror," Henry translated, for Joe's benefit.

"Yes, so I kept him calm, all right?"

Henry leaned forward. "How, *chérie?*"

"I'll get that soup," she said, and fled downstairs.

Henry turned to Joe, who had fallen asleep again like a candle going out. He was still very weak. Of the two of them, Grace worried Henry more. On their return, he assumed she would assist while he operated, tired though she was, yet once he readied his instruments, she had her head on her arms at the kitchen table and could not be roused. Dow volunteered, proved quick and steady, and even suggested Chinese herbs to hurry healing and cool the blood. Henry put the boy at fourteen or so; Grace at that age had also been helping.

The day they returned, Lee Loi spent eight hours bundled in a quilt on the parlor floor, then bounced up, briefed Henry on the trip, holding nothing back, and took himself off to a public bathhouse on C Street with Dow's list in his pocket. But Grace, on awakening, was as wild as Henry had ever seen her, all her English gone. He was not sure she recognized him. He coaxed her onto her old bed upstairs, using his rusty French, but she would neither sleep nor undress, only lie tense as a drawn bow until the patter of rain on the roof released a storm of tears. Henry could not comfort her, in any language. Her father, Louis Prindiville, often took days to settle after a long hunt, but never anything like this.

Lee returned that evening and told Henry to go to bed; yet at three in the morning, they both sat in Grace's moonlit room. Her eyes were closed, her hands clenched. Lee finally spoke.

"Doctor?"

"Henry."

"Henry. Neither of them should go upriver again. Ever. Don't let them."

Stanton did not pretend. "All right, we won't." He stroked Grace's hair and pulled the blanket higher. "Joe got your best evidence the first time around. Going back was folly. As for Grace—well, the grandmother did give her some training, early on. The talent runs in the family. But then her courses started, and the grandmother died, so her uncle Philip had two excuses to shut her out entirely, and he did. I wasn't sorry. The danger is appalling. She's told me she's no good at it."

"She's too good. I think she didn't want to . . . come back. I'm not sure either of them did, really."

"What about you?"

"My turn for lessons, I guess. The Beuk Aie gave me a name and address in San Francisco. They said not to wait around. I'll go pay a call."

He did not look happy.

On the third morning after their return, Henry found Grace downstairs in skirt and shirtwaist, helping Mrs. Reilly set the table for breakfast. She seemed tired and subdued, but nothing worse. That first dreadful night he plucked from her hair a handful of damp aspen leaves. He put them under the lining of his desk drawer, to show Mary.

Lee returned from the Beuk Aie with the name of a dry-goods merchant willing to say in open court that Chea Po had bought ninety sacks of rice early in October 1886, all delivered to the Lewiston docks, all matching the bag recovered at Dug Cabin. Joe asked for a meeting, but Lee said better not. The man would turn up at the time and place appointed.

"C Street is doing this for you, not me. When you were marshal, you took their arson cases seriously, you turned back their standard bribe but were polite about it, and you're paying for the keep of two stray boys. They don't expect impartial justice, but they know you do, in your strange American way. Being under obligation to a foreign devil judge disturbs them. You have no idea how much. This evens the score."

"I thought you were the Company man," Joe said.

"They also know that if this case goes forward, I won't have a position. Someone's greasing the skids right now. I'll be out at the branch office in Elko. I've seen it done, just never thought I'd be the nail."

At Joe's puzzled look, Lee explained, "A saying. Nails that stick up get pounded down. It's all right. I was good at hammering, once."

"What's your next move?"

Lee shrugged. But to Henry that evening he said, "Could the boys and I borrow your rig for an hour? We have an appointment down at the river." He held up a large paper bag. "Come along if you like."

Henry beamed. He loved ritual as much as Joe loathed it. Dow and Yap raced ahead to the carriage house.

Grace was in a porch rocker, rummaging through the mending basket. Lee could see only the top of her dark head, but he heard her anyway. *Take Nell.* The thread of connection set at Deep Creek still lay between them, the bond of two people who expected to die together. He did not think she had it with the others. Her affection for Henry did not require it, and whatever was between her and Joe was so rooted in this dry Idaho soil that Lee could only guess its depth.

"And Nell, if she would be so kind," he said aloud.

Grace was glad to stay sitting down. She had hours of mending yet and the beginning of a headache. If Henry were not going along, she would have to; Judge Vincent's daughter could not ride unescorted through town with three Chinese. This riotous temporary family was nothing she had anticipated. Every moment of the day, she felt pulled in a dozen directions. She was never alone. She wanted it to be over. She wanted it never to end.

Joe was working in the parlor; she could see the lamp. But soon he backed out the screen door, carrying two glasses of ginger beer.

157

They sat listening to the Mormon crickets drone, and the shouts of children playing in the vacant lot.

Grace put down the darning egg. The light was going anyway. She leaned her head on the rocker back and thought of the glowing paper lanterns moving downstream in the summer dusk, scarlet and yellow, green and peacock blue, carrying comfort for the dead.

"Grace."

"Mmm-hmm?" Her mind was half on the river still.

"Why did you come on this job? For real, now."

Her face was serene, but the shirt-folds that lay across her lap shifted an instant; he saw the needle glint.

"Georges heard that Jackson was up at Deep Creek all last winter and spring. We wanted to get him out of your jurisdiction, before Lewiston accused him of the Chinese murders. A rebel, a rustler, and Nimipu to boot — the perfect scapegoat."

"We?"

"Georges, Henry, Mary, me."

"You think I'd do that to Jackson?"

"We couldn't be sure. Considering your situation."

At last. Joe tipped back his chair. "All right. But why did *you* come, and not Georges?"

"To make some fast money. Lee doesn't know yet, but I'm charging double. And Georges has better things to do. *C'est tout.*"

Joe believed her first excuse more than the rest, but all cut deep, none more than the verdict about his jurisdiction. Except for the climb up the ridge at Deep Creek, the two of them had not been alone together since she came to Lewiston, nor tried to be. In town and upcountry she made sure of another's presence, day and night. The hours beside the Snake waiting for Lee and the boat did not count; west of the Mississippi, "delirious by reason of gunshot" still covered a lot. Since their second trip upriver Joe watched his back less, but the look in her eye those first nights out in June had made Dug Cabin seem a seaside jaunt.

"I thought you gave up hating. Back there."

"I gave up wanting vengeance. Now I have a good deal of free time."

"Which of our disasters are we discussing?"

"Oh, '77, of course. We shan't talk of the other, it's not suitable."

Joe knew she was right. He was prominent, she was notorious, and Libby was twenty miles away, no doubt laying for him. Just because he hadn't heard from her didn't mean she was ignorant of how and where he was spending his time. He put his elbows on his knees and looked sideways at Grace.

"I thought maybe . . . you came back because of me."

She was silent so long that he sighed and rose to go inside. Grace waved one hand, pointing to his pocket. He passed his handkerchief and she blew her nose, a long indelicate honk.

"Is that what you teach your deportment students?"

"Oh, Joe. There's not many who remember the old days, is all. As I get on in years, that past turns more precious. Sometimes I think it's the only place I'm at home. And I don't have so many friends that I can afford to throw one away."

God would punish her for such lies. But he should not have asked. Etiquette was the least of it, and desire too. She could not be alone with Joe for long because all too soon she heard only the guns and saw only the blue coat, the faces in the mountain stream. She knew he knew. She had promised the Lady to forgive. But forgetting was denied her. *Why, this is hell, nor am I out of it.* And tomorrow was the ninth of August.

"Even me?"

"Even you."

CAMAS LILY

AUGUST 9, 1887

PAPERWORK COVERED THE BACKYARD TABLE, secured against the warm high-country breeze by dark smooth river rocks from Mary's garden. Grace, absorbed in evidence charts, seemed withdrawn but sweet-tempered enough. Joe lay on a wicker chaise longue, arm in a sling, reading lists one-handed.

Lee caught Henry's eye and saw a faint nod. *See if she'll talk of the war,* he had said. *If she does we'll all rest easier.*

"Would you explain about '77? The Chinese don't understand it. I've asked."

Grace obliged with a quick, lucid summary. First, the outside pressure for land and gold that reduced millions of Nimipu acres to a few reservation enclaves; second, Chief Joseph's good-faith retreat from the Wallowas, wrecked by young warriors avenging a private feud; third, the Army's lust for payback after Plains tribes erased a good part of the Seventh Cavalry.

He watched her tick off points on her fingers, making sure he understood cause and effect. He could have used her at college. Henry was right: she could not resist a chance to instruct. And she had not answered his question.

"Please, what about you and the war?"

"I don't talk about it, Lee," she said, but without heat. The three men waited. Above, wind in the poplars made the leaves flutter, a sound like river falls.

"June of '76 was Little Bighorn," she said at last, then craned her neck to look at Lee. "You do know about Little Bighorn?"

He stuck out his tongue; she laughed. The most popular touring picture in the nation was an overwrought twenty-foot oil titled *Custer's Last Rally*. In city after city, huge crowds lined up for hours to see it.

"Well, that was the end of New Orleans for me. And Paris too."

"You wanted to go to France?" he asked cautiously, trying not to break her mood.

Joe said, "She got pretty close."

"I can claim citizenship through my father, you see — *citoyenne par héritage*. It was always a dream, a kind of back door, one I nearly went through. Years ago I had a fiancé, Loi. A painter. Quite a good one. We met in New Orleans. He went back to Paris ahead of me, and I was a week from sailing to join him when his mother cabled. Jean was dead. We still write, she and I."

Lee looked over at Henry, who mouthed, *Cholera*. Lee felt his stomach twist in sympathy. Cholera can kill a strong young man in hours — first the explosive watery diarrhea, then the wracking cramps as internal organs shred. The victim stays conscious to the end, a terrified soul trapped in a dissolving body. Lee wanted to say *Sorry*, but Grace was looking at the sky again.

New Orleans in 1872 was a raw commercial port, with ten daily newspapers and streets churned to red mud. Grace lived in a pleasant boarding house on the Rue Toulouse and coaxed the daughters of the rich through a postwar semblance of Sacred Heart education: French grammar, deportment, penmanship, a touch of history, and sufficient mathematics to run a household or a wastrel husband's business. She spent her evenings in cafés and coffeehouses with other young tutors, secretaries, and governesses from the city's great houses. Yankees, Europeans. She learned to argue, learned to flirt. And then she met Jean de Laperouse.

All this she narrated to Joe Vincent in long letters that now crossed a continent, not the Camas Prairie, for Henry had finally admitted who paid her school fees. Gratitude to a benefactor was a virtue. She was never going back to canyon country. And they were only letters. Jean raised his handsome brows when she explained about Joe — goodness, how she seemed to collect lithe, dark, difficult men — then took the pins out of her hair, one by one, and kissed her in a way that made her forget Idaho for a week.

Her passion for Jean was so bound up with their Delta life that she sometimes wondered if they might be strangers to each other amid the cool greens and grays of the Île-de-France. Their private New Orleans was all tropical color and quick sensation: the rattle of palmetto leaves under warm rain, blazing flambeaux along the avenues after a theater party, crape myrtle and jasmine twining alley and balcony, and morning and night the piercing scents of chicory coffee and boiling sugar cane, bitter, sweet.

They could not keep apart. All her careful boundaries seemed as dreamlike as one of his ravishing bayou watercolors. And she knew, without undue vanity, that she had never looked better, a wild camas lily among gardenias. No, no regrets.

The Stantons, pleased but worried, sent their consent to marriage and emigration. Monsieur and Madame de Laperouse swallowed hard, then wrote to her warmly. Dear friends of theirs had known her Prindiville grandparents, in some eminently correct French context that Grace could not quite follow, and found them most congenial. *On va s'arranger.*

"Before the War, he wouldn't have offered marriage," Joe said to Henry softly.

"*Plaçage,* you mean? The parents would have preferred it, but they didn't quite dare, not for the granddaughter of a Paris jurist. That goddamn Louis was the complete black sheep. The first time I met him, I wondered about his fancy accent."

Grace looked up and saw six listeners, not three; Nell had joined them, and with her Dow and Yap. Was she talking too freely about the years away? Well, caution, distance, denial — *assez*. It must be the wonderful mildness of the west wind, come all the way from the summer Pacific like a breeze from the Gulf. How sweet they all looked, staring at her like that. And though at Sacred Heart she attended school-day Mass with every appearance of devotion, she had not been to confession in years. Enough of that too. Grace slid down in the wicker chair, turned her face to the sun, and fell again into the past.

In the spring of 1876 Jean left for Paris, to find them a flat and show his dealer the American portfolio. In June word arrived of his death. Three weeks later came the shock of Little Bighorn. All that fall and winter she sensed a coolness among her society clientele, shading to profoundest chill. *Les peaux-rouges* were no longer so chic. And with the fine Parisian marriage lost, the only cards that came round to the Rue Toulouse bore brittle notes: "Grace dear, we shall not be needing you this year." She was last year's fashion. *Jean's tame Indian. How everyone must be laughing.* She could not bear to go out. She could hardly bring herself to eat. Her savings were nearly gone, but she could not ask Henry and Mary for a penny more.

"Don't look so upset, Lee," she said. "I didn't know it then, but Jean had left me a competence, enough to buy my little house in Portland, enough to give me some independence. But yes, a sad, lean eighteen months."

That fall her long correspondence with Joe turned angry and brittle, then ended altogether. He saw no future for the free tribes in a modern America. She wanted the treaties honestly enforced for once, and suffrage for Indian males. *If Negroes can vote now, why can't we?* Free blacks and freed slaves had not wiped out half a cavalry regiment, he wrote back, and no sane administration would tolerate insurgents of any tribe. Not now.

The start of the Nez Perce War in June '77 riveted the country and terrified Grace. Her uncle Philip and her cousins, Georges and Jackson, were the only close relatives she had left. They were all treaty, of course, and even the adamantly traditional Philip was Christian now,

163

but who knew what the government would do? To raise the train fare west she sold all she owned, and from Portland she cabled Georges. He was a prosperous horseman near Mount Hood, married and with a second child on the way. His reply made her gasp: her elderly uncle and thirteen-year-old Jackson were riding north with the defiant nontreaty bands. Georges was going after them. Grace cabled back: *Meet me Lapwai Sunday bringing Henrys wagon.* She spent her last dollar on a Lewiston steamer ticket. All the way there, that missing apostrophe bothered her.

In the last light of a summer evening, Grace sat slumped at the kitchen table, too tired to light the lamps. *Au-pa, Au-ma, what a time to be away,* she thought. Using the savings of years, they had gone to England to visit relatives in Devon and friends in Oxford. *Everyone leaves me,* she thought, swept by self-pity — Grandmother, Maman, Papa, Jean. Joe. *Stop it. I'll be rational come morning,* she told herself, forking at canned peaches without appetite. The Stanton family buggy and light wagon were both in the stable and so was Major, fat and bored; he was since her time, but she made friends first thing, taking him sugar and stroking his wide gray nose. Neighbors were looking after the house, and very well: rooms dusted, rose geraniums flourishing. Nine years away? It felt like nine minutes.

A pounding at the door. Grace shot to her feet. Five strange men stood in the yard. Lewiston business gentry, judging by the fancy vests, with Alonzo Leland in the lead. One held up a lantern as Leland mounted the front steps, and the wavering light cast dancing shadows along the green curtain of hop vines that veiled the porch. Grace felt herself start to tremble, a thin fine tremor from her lips all the way to the soles of her feet. In the woods she would have felt the danger from the first.

Henry glanced at Joe and saw the muscle along his jaw quilt with the effort of keeping still. So the Lelands hadn't told him. *Reaping the whirlwind,* thought Henry, *ten years late. Or twenty.*

• • •

"Good evening," Grace said cautiously to Alonzo Leland. "As you know, my foster parents are abroad. Did you wish to leave a message?"

"You're trespassing, m'dear," Alonzo told her. In the flaring lamplight, above the luxuriant beard, she saw the calm, happy eye of a fanatic.

"This is my home, sir," she said. "Now, if you'll excuse me—"

"Do you have title to this house?"

"No, but—"

"Are you the Stantons' legal ward?"

"Well, not precisely, but in every way that—"

"You are, in fine, an enemy alien, and we in this town and Territory are at war with you and yours. Our rifle pits are dug and ready. Be on your way."

Grace drew herself up. "I was born in the Idaho Territory, Mr. Leland. My mother's family were all treaty long before you came. And through my father I am a citizen of France, which last I heard was our best ally. Who are you all? And why are you being so rude?"

"Look in the mirror, lady," said one of her callers, from beside the big poplar. The town pharmacist, or was he the livery stable owner? "We represent the city's volunteer Committee for the Public Safety. And we say you need to move on."

Definitely the livery man. "I know you," said Grace, furious. "Henry saved your whole family from the morbid sore throat. *And* I recall you still owe on the bill. I'm not going anywhere, gentlemen. Now please leave, or I'll—"

"You have until noon," said Leland. "Then we get the marshal."

She could hear the silky enjoyment in his voice. Several of the men behind him took a tiny step nearer. Cougars did that, before they sprang. She would not ask, but Leland knew anyway.

"Mr. Vincent is no longer marshal. Like any American of conscience, he answered his country's need this summer. Our local boys in blue—"

"Then give me a horse," she said loudly, over the drone of his ora-

165

tory. "*Two* horses. Good ones, sound enough for wagon work, or I'm not going anywhere. Tie them to the fence tonight. You'll get them back. Now *out*."

She whirled, slammed the door, fumbled with the main lock, and sat with her back against the door, knees braced. Footsteps retreated, dwindled, ceased. She stood up slowly, lit a candle, and started packing. Her heart was pounding and every breath hurt. Shovel, hatchet, tinderbox. Blankets, an old sheet, the two small water barrels — she could not lift the big one — and the spare medical satchel. No hope of buying food in Lewiston, but she stripped the pantry of salt, olive oil, and tea. Georges would bring a rifle, surely.

In the attic sat a box of early keepsakes, sent home from Missouri. Under a Latin grammar Grace found her old knife and pinned its worn beaded sheath to her skirt band. Too late for subtlety. Money? The family cache under the floor boards yielded twenty dollars in gold. Thank God for Henry's old-fashioned dislike of banks; left to himself, she knew, he would convert it all to pieces of eight and bury it in the hydrangeas. Outside the bedroom window, a waxing moon silvered the roofs along Eugene Street. If someone brought horses soon, she could be on the Lapwai road by dawn.

BIG HOLE

AUGUST 9, 1887

G RACE SIGHED AND SAT UP. "So we went to find them, but it . . . wasn't to be," she said, pleating her apron, getting every edge just right. "I'm glad we tried, though. Well. Who wants sandwiches outside? I know I do."

Henry shook his head. "Daughter," he said. He almost never called her that.

Her chin rose. Damn him, for priming Lee about the war.

"Well, that's it, really," she said again.

"We don't want sandwiches." Dow's gaze was unrelenting. "Tell the rest."

Joe held his breath. No one else had the right to ask.

"*No.*"

"Yes."

Tracking the Army was no effort. Cavalry and infantry left a chaos of hoofprints and boot prints forty yards wide. The only constant was the double-rimmed trace of caisson wheels, heavy artillery pulled by mule team over trail, pass, and riverbank. The military progress overran and obscured almost every trace of eight hundred fleeing Nimipu, but from farmers along the way, Grace and Georges gleaned a fair idea of the exodus. Families and warriors, elders and babies. Hundreds of dogs, maybe two thousand horses. Rattling cross-country in the Stanton wagon, the cousins were amazed.

"How are they doing it?" asked Georges, rubbing down the tired team with a twist of dry grass. Grace checked the horses' legs, then handed him a dipper of water. Dear steady Georges, closer than a friend, kinder than a brother.

"Joseph and the rest must be working miracles," Georges said. "I guess they think if they make it into Montana they'll be safe."

Then the Army trail faded and split. End of their supply lines, Georges guessed, and maybe their authority as well. Perhaps it would be all right. The country was magnificent, snowcapped mountain ranges cloaked with conifers against a lapis sky. Every vista and valley, every pine-girdled meadow, eased her battered spirit. And the People seemed to be moving faster. Clearly they were cutting temporary lodgepoles now, not dragging every set from camp to camp.

Up the Lolo trail the travelers went, over the Continental Divide, then down along the Big Hole River's north fork. The going was rough and often swampy, the hogback ridges littered with granite boulders, the forest track full of blown-down logs and crippled horses, but they dared not abandon the wagon. Three weeks out and just at noon, they found the Nimipu camp.

Beside a little winding river, set between a steep hill on the north and a rolling flatland to the south, ninety lodges stood in a straggling V. Boys played the stick and bone game, men gossiped in small animated groups, and women of every age set about the endless make-and-mend of trail life. On the nearby hillside, hundreds of horses grazed. Georges and Grace were at first entranced — it could have been a moment from any Wallowas childhood summer — and then dismayed. No scouts found them, no guards offered challenge as they started walking, lodge to lodge.

In two hours they found Philip Sundown, beside the river with the other old men. Philip did not acknowledge Grace at all, and he told Georges that Christianity was cruel and false. Given such persecution, how could it be anything else? Georges reasoned with his father, pleaded, even ordered, but got only a turned back.

Among a crowd of half-grown boys they located Jackson, incandescent with defiance. He was Waaya-Tonah-Toesits-Kahn. Georges and Grace were cowards and traitors. He would follow his chief forever, and fight for the People to the end.

"He's as crazy as Pa," Georges said glumly, after a day and a night of circular argument. "What do you want to do?"

Grace shrugged. Caught between worlds, she had literally nowhere to go. Every night she searched for Jean in dreams dark and strange, ever running, calling, never finding. Every morning she woke with her sleeves wet.

"Come back to our place for a while," Georges said. "Ellen and I could both use you."

Her throat closed with gratitude and she could only nod. The high-country evenings were cold but clear, and as usual they slept under the wagon; anything was quieter than the airless streamside lodges, bursting with old people and toddlers. Next morning they would have to leave. It was the eighth of August.

"Grace."

She was on her feet, not knowing how she got there.

"Grace, please," said Joe again.

He wanted to speak, and she could not look at him. Were they alone upriver and not in a Lewiston backyard, her hand would have been at her knife hilt. *Oh, my People, my People.*

"All right," she said. He could talk all he wanted; it made no difference.

When Joe's old commanding officer dropped by Raymond House for a drink in June of '77, Joe wished for once that he had gone to the lake with Libby, the Lelands, and the Vollmers. He hadn't seen Lowry in years, and he wanted no part of the misbegotten Nez Perce campaign. Ed McConville was already at the head of Lewiston's twenty-man Company A for the First Regiment of Idaho Volunteers, but eighteen more citizens had put their names forward, enough for a Company B.

"The men will follow you, Joe," Lowry said. "You're known. Territorial rep, ex-cavalry, member of the GAR, all that."

"Pick on someone else," Joe told him.

"I'm asking. I can order if need be."

Duty then, duty always.

"I swore the oath," Joe said. "I'll serve. But I don't have to like it."

All through June and July, the retreating Nez Perce beat back the U.S. Army, first at White Bird, then along the Clearwater, outmaneuvering and escaping when they could, outfighting the professionals at every turn. By July, Lewiston volunteers had joined Colonel John Gibbon's forces, an uneasy mix of regular Army and local militias, moving in from the Montana side to stop the runaways and force them back to Lapwai.

Usually the night before battle meant singing and stories, tin plates piled with beef and biscuits, and then men passing around a stub of pencil to write messages for mothers and sweethearts. But this time a force of two hundred planned to ambush the Nez Perce village at dawn, creeping in on a clear night through marshy ground. *Trouble,* Joe thought. Gibbon loved publicity, and the epic flight of the Nez Perce was a national news story. Any minute Joe expected some eager reporter to tap him on the shoulder, like that poor devil Kellogg who died with Custer, pursuing a scoop.

Their attack orders made Joe's stomach hurt. Three fast volleys low into the lodges, then a charge. Joe and his troop were to cut through the village and secure the north end of the hillside, where the main horse herd grazed. Capturing the Nez Perce mounts could end the whole campaign. At least Company B did not have to fire on the sleeping. By two in the morning the American force lay in wait, so near the camp they could hear babies crying. Only an old oath and the trusting faces of the Lewiston men kept Joe from bolting.

If an order to open fire occurred, he missed it. Seconds after the first shot, whole families began tumbling from the tall lodges in the gray half-light, dragging children and dressing as they ran, desperate to find cover. There was no battlefield, only hand-to-hand fighting, a true melee. Sharpshooter fire lit up the tipis from within like Chinese lanterns. Bullets pinged and rattled on the lodgepoles. Men in blue began falling. The Nimipu warriors were fast to regroup, and their aim was excellent.

Joe had never seen a fight so intimate. He rolled and crawled with the flotsam of family life crunching beneath knees and hands – dolls, baskets, cooking spoons. He fended off a Nimipu matron swinging a skillet; glimpsed Colonel Gibbon, prone behind a dead horse, firing a hunting rifle; passed a little girl perched on a rock, peering at her shattered arm; saw an old man chanting a death song even as his pumping femoral artery dyed the grass scarlet.

As powder-burned soldiers waded waist-deep to shoot point-blank at children and old people trying to hide in streamside brush, a running trooper shouted, "Charge them to hell!" and from the willows a Nimipu warrior yelled back, in English, "Charge, hell, you goddamned sons of bitches, you ain't fighting Sioux!" The pretty winding river filled with floating bodies, Indian and white.

Above the camp Joe heard the howitzer start up at last. Two rounds, enough to startle horses on the hillside into motion. The Lewiston men had scrambled nearly to their assigned position when half a dozen mounted Nez Perce pounded past them and began dividing and scattering the great herd, urging the animals into the timber, where soldiers could never follow.

The Lewiston volunteers started cursing, enraged to have come this far only to lose out, and Joe was shouting too, pulling himself uphill by main force over shortgrass hillocks and rocky ledges. Two Nimipu circled perilously close to the angry troop. A woman and a boy, fine riders both. From the corner of his eye Joe saw a gun barrel rise: John Vollmer's.

"Hold your fire!" Joe called. And then, as Vollmer hesitated, "You can't shoot women and kids!"

Vollmer pulled the trigger just as Joe's shoulder hit his. The round went wild. Beside the surging, milling herd the woman looked up, startled, and Joe felt his heart stop. *Grace.* Astride a spotted pony, pale cotton skirts kilted up to her thighs, and grown so beautiful that he could only stare. The boy with her was likely Jackson, then. Their eyes met. Her face did not alter but her hands must have tightened, for her mount fought the bit and jumped sideways. She laid the reins hard across its sweating neck, turned, was gone.

When he raised his eyes to hers at last, Joe expected redoubled fury but met instead a thoughtful, level gaze. She was his oldest friend in the Territory, and his most resolute enemy. He had seen her body when she was seventeen, in the dappled shade of the Lapwai willows, but until this moment never her soul. A river had divided them always, and he'd paid a good deal, in every sense, to set her busy mind going; no good complaining when its judgments went against him. He had undervalued her; she had underestimated him. Twenty years on they might be ready to see each other whole: battered, human, flawed, forgiven.

"Let me," she said, and took up their story.

Georges and Grace wrapped Philip Sundown in Mary Stanton's muslin sheet and buried him among the pines. *Behold, I make all things new.* Then they hoisted a dozen silent children over the wagon tailboard, one by one: a little girl shot through the arm, a concussed boy with a broken leg, a husky toddler whose parents died together in the fighting by the stream. Georges used their last bag of oats to wedge in an unconscious ten-year-old with a fractured skull (a blow from a gun butt, most likely), but both of them knew the boy would not survive. Grace let her dusty skirts hang over the side of the wagon box, then groped for her sunbonnet. The less Indian they looked from a distance, the safer they would be from local vigilantes and Army sharpshooters.

They had not gone a quarter mile when Grace heard hooves behind them at the gallop and swung the rifle up and around. She was hoping for a clear shot at Colonel Gibbon, but Joe Vincent ran a close second. The rider in blue was very young. Grace was not sure he shaved.

"Captain Vincent's compliments, sir, ma'am, and I'm to escort you wherever you wish to go, and he hopes you are going to the nearest town with a doctor, because he asks a favor."

"Depends on the favor," said Georges.

"Please, would you take three of our worst wounded in the wagon? Captain says to tell you if they travois out with the rest they'll never make it."

Grace nodded. What did it matter? In the midst of life we are in death. Or maybe it was the other way around. She couldn't remember. By nightfall, two of the three enlisted men had expired: a farmboy private hit in the jaw, his face a ruin of blood and dirt, and a gut-shot Irish sergeant who whispered to her long and frantically (in Gaelic, she guessed), then fell into convulsions and took thirty strangling minutes to die. The children watched it all.

"I will not leave you," she told the grizzled stranger in her arms. She did not add "forever." Stranded on the wrong side of history, she could not afford sentiment ever again.

Joe was staring at the ground.

After a moment, Lee said, "Who won?"

"That time, the Nez Perce." Joe's voice was calm, but he looked exhausted. Grace got up, pulled back his shirt collar to check for bleeding, then sat beside him.

"They captured our artillery piece, seized the ammunition train, and escaped into the mountains," Joe said. "Went right through Yellowstone Park, scared the hell out of some tourists. But in the end, only a handful made it safe to Canada. The Army shot a lot of their horses, and stopped most of the Nez Perce just short of the border."

"Killed?" said Lee in horror.

"Shipped off to Oklahoma," Grace said. "Some are back at Lapwai, some on the Colville reservation over in Washington. Either way, it's permanent exile."

"And since that day you never saw each other?" Lee asked.

"Not until I got off the boat in Lewiston," said Grace.

"Or wrote?"

"No," said Joe.

Nell and the boys were in the kitchen, making lemonade. Henry had slipped out front for the mail.

Joe hesitated, then said, looking only at Lee, "In the fall of '76 Libby found Grace's letters to me, from Missouri and from New Orleans. She burned them. Then she punished me, in various ways. And through me, the children. We ended up with a standoff. I don't come around much, except when one of us needs some public show. She has her own money, thanks to Alonzo, and controls most of the rest. Your Sam Yup fee was pretty tempting. Also convenient."

"So when merchants in town won't serve Grace, it's not because she's—?"

"This part of the country sees more than a few mixed marriages. People will do it. No, it's because . . ." He glanced at Grace, who smiled but shook her head. "Well, let's just say she'd been living white for years, getting pretty high in the instep too, and then half of Lewiston saw her run off the Nez Perce herds."

"Henry lost custom because of me," Grace said. "I know it. They're pressed for money and getting old and it's my fault."

"Not entirely," said Joe. "Henry could charge more and sound off less. But some offenses in this town are never forgotten. You've already stayed too long."

Grace, also looking only at Lee Loi, slid her hand into Joe's.

"Please, Loi. Who recommended Joe for this job?"

He looked at them both for a long time.

"John Vollmer," he said at last.

FULL MOON

IN THE END they turned to crime. Vollmer was due back from San Francisco on the twelfth. Joe claimed cunning detection but in fact hung around the *Teller* office and read galleys. Vollmer's travels still turned up in the social news, leaked to Alonzo in advance. A trawl through back issues revealed five San Francisco trips in '86, four already in '87. They had no way of tallying unreported journeys, unless Lee could find out in the city.

As Vollmer came up Main Street, looking grouchy – the overnight boat was always an ordeal – Joe stepped off the Raymond House porch and made an offer: a hot bath, shave, and a sponging of his suit if John would consent to breakfast with Sir Thomas Entingham, about to leave town with a hunting party but anxious to meet the eminent Idaho financier.

"On the house," Joe said, waving him in. It always was. "I'll see your bags are safe."

Entingham was in fact a rich grocer from Manchester named Preston, staying the week. Lewiston got more tourists every year, foreign ones too. "A Wykehamist," said Stanton happily. No one knew what he meant, but after Henry had a word, in the mysterious way of the British abroad, Mr. Preston was glad to help a frontier lawman distract and delay. His North American visit had already included an opal mine, three bears, and a cattle drive. He said he could manage a Sir but not a Lord, and did, abetted shamelessly by Henry.

175

After hotcakes and eggs, Joe had the hotel cart brought around, told Vollmer he'd see him at the lake, then stuck his head into the private office. Grace looked up.

"I don't know what came over me."

Lee swung his feet off the desk.

"No, you're supposed to say, 'Evil companions led me astray.'"

"I'm telephoning the police," Joe told them. "Right after I read these."

He leaned over the copied documents. Their prize haul was a letter of intent from railroad giant James J. Hill of St. Paul. By 1890 Vollmer's Idaho Transit Company would build a new feeder road across the Camas for the St. Paul, Minneapolis, and Manitoba line. Joe knew Vollmer had been friendly with the rail magnate Henry Villard before the latter went bust five years back, defeated by the rugged terrain of eastern Oregon. Hill was not as visionary as Villard, but he had sounder financing and better luck. Joe also knew that Congress was forming an interstate commerce commission. To ensure survival for the Camas Railroad was no mean feat, at Washington prices. The bribes must be stretching even Vollmer. Grace passed Joe a second set of papers. Vollmer had cut a similar deal with the Northern Pacific.

"What else?"

Lee gave him a copied memorandum of understanding with the Sam Yup for a substantial labor contract: seven hundred men over two years to blast, grade, and lay track across the Camas, with an eight percent replacement margin.

Lee added, "They know that one in twelve client workers will die or get hurt. Some stretches up in Canada, you figure one mile of track laid, two dead Chinese."

Before the second trip to Deep Creek, Grace had written certain letters of her own. That she might want adult conversation not involving housework, blood, or bullets had not occurred to Henry until the expresses began arriving. He saw one handwriting he knew — Mary, in Seattle — and many he did not: Georges's wife, another Sacred Heart lay teacher, a widowed school friend in St. Louis, Kate someone; even, after a time, an envelope from France. He wondered what Grace had asked all these women and what their answers might be. They really were another species. Grace sent one more letter, without stamp or address. On the eleventh of August a young Nez Perce she had never met stopped her in the street with a reply: west end of the Lapwai meadows, at sunset, on the twelfth.

They took two buggies: Joe, Nell, and Lee in one, Grace and Henry, Dow and Yap in the other. When they stopped — in the middle of nowhere, Lee thought, where else? — he walked away from the flaring carriage lamps to scan the stars, looking for that best of all Chinese summer constellations, the Bridge of Birds, which reunites the separated. He thought he had just found it when a rider passed him in the twilight, two ponies on leading reins trotting behind.

As Jackson Sundown dismounted, Yap ran to hug his savior around the waist. Dow shook hands. *Almost a man,* thought Joe, *and careful of his dignity.* Jackson rumpled Yap's hair, nodded to the others, then spoke sharply to Grace in Nimipu. Her reply was mild. They neither approached each other nor embraced. Ten years, thought Joe.

Jackson asked her a second question and at the reply gave Joe a thoughtful look, but lost no time cinching on the boys' saddlebags, while Grace shortened stirrups. The young Chinese doctor over in John Day, deep into Oregon, would shelter both boys through the winter. Lee slipped Jackson a fat envelope for their keep.

Joe could follow almost none of the conversations around him. Welcome to the West. Lee spoke to Dow in Chinese; Grace talked with Jackson in Nimipu; Jackson dropped into English to hoist young Yap into the saddle and tell him he was doing fine, a real cowboy. Henry Stanton gestured for Jackson to roll up his pants leg, then brought over a lantern to examine the jagged wound in the lower calf.

"How are you feeling? Full use of the limb? Problems walking?"

"God damn it, Henry," said Joe.

"If a patient wants to get himself shot, it's his decision," said Stanton, applying ointment, snipping stitches. Joe could smell the goose grease. "I've been his doctor for . . . how long?"

"Twenty-four years," said Grace.

"Evans, I take it?" Joe nodded at the damage.

Jackson grinned. "They were beautiful horses, Judge. And happier back home. Well, some." He had the breathy pronunciation of many Nez Perce. Georges kept a touch of it, Grace none.

"Rustling from the rustlers," said Joe sourly. "You do know the penalty in Idaho? Thought so. Want to tell me what you saw at Dug Bar?"

Jackson hesitated, then jerked his head. Joe followed. He had hoped for an adult eyewitness, even an inadmissible one, but Jackson saw only the aftermath. He and the boys took the same ridge trail as Joe and Grace, but rain and darkness forced a halt above Dug Cabin. No, such proximity did not bother Jackson; the best place to hide is under the sheriff's bed. Yes, he and Dow saw one man come out of the cabin with a lantern, late and alone. Tall, fair, hatless. He might have been headed to the privy on a wet night, but working fast in a hard rain, the man instead pried up the stone step, buried a handful of small bottles—Jackson saw a glint of glass in the lantern light—and then was gone, back inside. Joe knew the rest.

"I'll keep an eye on your two," Jackson said.

"You do that. And—good to see you again."

They shook hands. Grace touched Jackson's cheek with one fingertip; Lee nodded thanks. Jackson turned to give Dow a leg up, but the boy instead went back to Joe and bowed, the deep formal bow owed to an Elder Boss. Joe bent his head in return.

Jackson got Dow mounted and then was up and away himself, vaulting into the saddle, barely a touch on the reins. Attractive young devil, and a sublime horseman, but born too late, Joe thought, watching the little group move off across the moonlit field. Twenty years back he would have been a fine war leader, perhaps a great one.

They got home at two in the morning and sat at the kitchen table for rhubarb pie and coffee, even Joe. He needed hardly any bismuth these days.

Lee said idly, "Why aren't you marshal any more?"

"Last fall I lost an election. By twenty-three votes."

"Stolen," Henry told Grace.

"Obviously. Why didn't you contest? Too proud?"

"Too old," said Joe. "Why stick around for another kicking? Harry Akers is Vollmer's man. I always knew this wasn't a clean town, but so long as I won and did some good, I got too used to living with it." He had never said this aloud before, even to Henry.

Lee pulled their charts over. "I don't think it's deeds that make the box important. Those you can get from the county recorder. But gold is gold, and they must have sent a lot, enough to justify Chea Po's expedition. Probably the Company had no idea of the bad conditions up-canyon, or didn't much care."

"Younger Boss was right when he told Dow they were all expendable," said Joe.

Lee nodded. "That attempt blows up in a big way, thanks to Evans, but the Sam Yup tries again. Cooperative to Vollmer's face but telling me, 'If you spot a Wells Fargo chest, get it back here.'" He drew a finger down the timeline. "Vollmer was in San Francisco when Joe's wire came. I bet he and the Company decided that Evans at large is less threat than Evans in jail and talking. So send some junior man to Lewiston — try Lee Loi, his uncle will thank us — and tell him to hire a local magistrate named Vincent."

"An honest fool if ever there was one," said Joe grimly.

Lee looked apologetic. "Vollmer seemed to think so. He doesn't like you. In Chinese business no one ever says anything right out, it's all implied. Discerned. But the results they hoped for are pretty clear: tell Lee Loi to offer the judge fifteen hundred to go upriver, assume Evans will shoot them both. With the good-faith gesture out of the way, pressure the Consulate to settle with the Americans for thirty dead miners at five hundred a head."

"Cynical, and probably accurate," Grace said, watching Henry yawn. "Vollmer must have cut Evans loose early in the '80s. Let's search the records again. We missed something. Deed, mortgage, court proceeding, *something*."

Joe sat looking at his witness list: two underage Chinese, one C Street merchant, one wanted Nez Perce, a pack of ghosts. Unless Dow and Yap had a change of heart, the box of secrets was forever lost. If they drew a friendly judge, Joe knew his own firsthand sightings might be admissible: the ammunition in the cabin that matched the Lewiston autopsies, the vials of gold dust, the bodies in the cabin grave. For physical evidence they had only the coroner's report, one Chinese coin, a handful of buttons and hair, and a single rice sack.

"I need state's evidence from Vaughan or McMillan, or both," Joe said. "I need it soon."

They got to Luna House on the stroke of nine, and at three-thirty Grace found a rescinded land deed for B. B. Evans, October 5, 1883, held in trust by the Vollmer Clearwater Company. A prime twenty-acre gold claim in the Clearwater diggings.

Lee said, "Yanked by Vollmer as punishment for botching the Tom Douglas job?"

"Maybe." Joe was searching the big book of plat maps. "Here we go. Not a year later, that whole basin came in big. Evans lost a fortune. Likely he knows it."

DEEP SUMMER

AUGUST 14, 1887

A FTER SUPPER the three investigators sat on the back porch and Grace presented her final bill to the Sam Yup: thirty dollars, payable to G. Sundown. The sum was ridiculously low. Joe had told Lee how much Sundown Mountain Tours charged per head; he'd been staggered.

"Be sure to keep it as Georges in your records," Joe cautioned. He leaned over. "What say we introduce you, madam?"

Grace was eating a peach from the orchards south of town, fruit so ripe that juice was welling everywhere; she waved assent. Joe turned back to Lee.

"The Nez Perce called her father Louis Sundown. Sounds more romantic than it was—the Hudson's Bay Company transferred him out here from Sundown, Manitoba. Some on her mother's side borrowed the name to use in the white world, hence Georges and Jackson. The whole region was easygoing like that, in the earlies. Not many people, no end of pretty land."

Lee waited.

"Around here she was Grace Sundown before she went East for school, but she's baptized Marie-Grace Prindiville. In French, *Prawn-duh-vee. Prin-duh-vill* in English. And by great coincidence a Miss Marie Prindiville has lived quietly in Portland since '77, giving vocabulary tests and wiping tourist noses."

"She's awfully dull," said Grace, licking sweet juice from her fingers. "Proper, you know. Alphabetizes her canned goods."

"But that first day, down at the docks, you called yourself Grace Sundown."

"Putting me on notice," said Joe. "Grace Sundown disappeared right after the Nez Perce War. Still known by sight in the Territory, but you're the first outsider to meet her in a decade."

Lee remembered the curtsies as they rode upcountry, and the stares of hatred. They hadn't been for him after all, or Joe either.

"Because of Big Hole?"

Grace smiled at Joe. "You're the storyteller."

Lee decided he approved of their truce. Strange, that down some other roads he might be a Canton banker with a pair of wives, Joe a Nantucket printer, and Grace the toast of Paris. *Joss,* Lee thought, trying to be Chinese about it, but looking again at her smile he thought, in English this time, *A pity.*

"Then hear the tale of Grace Sundown," said Joe, in his best oracular voice. "The first part you know. But what you do not is that after Big Hole her cousin fell ill and she had to find help for all in her care. If Georges had been able, he would have told her to save her breath, God-fearing taxpayers though they were. But Grace was raised white, mostly, and thought white, mostly, and she had a topnotch St. Louis convent education courtesy of one J. K. Vincent, proprietor of Vincent's Auction House on E Street between Third and Fourth, all business promptly and faithfully attended to—"

A peach pit sailed out of the dusk, aimed at his head. He caught it.

"Easy there. Where was I? Yes. And so she came out of the wilderness, with a wagon of living and dead, and a kinsman ill, and drove from town to town asking for aid, and there was none, and at last the young officer with her had to draw his sidearm to get the American soldiers buried. Then he was ordered back to his regiment, so she went on alone."

Joe stood with hands in pockets, looking at the evening star, then turned back to Lee.

"In Cottonwood, Grangeville, and White Bird the locals told her to leave or be shot, and each time she stood in the street and cursed them all, said they were hypocrites and whited sepulchers and no true Christians, and still the towns would not even give her water for the Nez Perce children. To the north, fighting was still on, you see. But up at Mount Idaho, the local people tended her cousin and buried her dead, and Grace Sundown lay by the graves for a day and a night, they say, then took her wagon and the last of the children and went into the west, a casualty of as nasty a little civil war as this nation has ever seen. She's only a story now, or maybe a song."

After a moment Lee asked, "How much of that is true?"

"As much as you want it to be, I guess," Grace told him. "We got up to Lapwai. Eventually. Five of the children survived. Georges still has a bad stomach from the dysentery."

"Plus a bullet hole in the ribs," said Joe. "Some overeager rancher near Grangeville."

Lee tried to match their calm.

"What happened to the young officer who helped you?"

"You saw him, I think," said Grace. "Steven runs the Mount Idaho newspaper."

"But where did you go?"

"To Portland, swearing never to set foot again in the Territory. Over in Oregon, public sympathy was with the People anyway. Georges went back to the horses, and to Ellen, and tried to forget what we'd seen. I couldn't forget, and the only places I felt halfway safe were the classroom and the mountains. The newspapers had got hold of it all, you see, and I didn't much care to play the tragic renegade."

"So you just—?"

"Disappeared. Mary and Henry helped, and the staff at Sacred Heart. Except this summer I did come back. To try to help Jackson, but really Joe too. I knew Lewiston would cover up the Chinese murders. Henry's wire said so. And neither Georges nor I want an Evans loose, on either side of the Snake. This time it was your people, Loi. Next time it might be ours. Or anyone's. If you can fight, you do."

"High time," Joe said.

Grace watched the last of the sunset wash the poplars gold, then red.

"Let's finish this first," she said, and with that he had to be content.

The next morning Grace was set to catch the Portland steamer, carpetbag in the hall, hat in hand. Lee was meeting her at the docks. She could not find Henry anywhere. Finally she pushed open the bedroom door and saw him perched on the tall old horsehair mattress, stocking feet dangling, holding a stethoscope to his chest. His bearded face was flushed and pensive. Their eyes met.

"Does Autre-maman know?"

"Of course."

"Is this why you called me home?"

"Not entirely," said Henry.

Joe sat at his desk in the barn downtown and reread the telegram from Oregon. The Wallowa County sheriff had raised a *posse comitatus* to arrest Evans, Canfield, LaRue, and any of their followers at or near Dug Cabin. They would go out in September and with any luck Judge Vincent could interrogate at the Joseph jail within the month.

"Wouldn't miss it," said Joe aloud. He was still getting used to the quiet. He sat through a staff meeting at the hotel — Lewiston was packed with visitors — then added his valise to the pile of luggage bound for Lake Waha. A visit to the auction house brought more good news: three large estates consigned, plus a big parcel of land south of town. Yes, '87 was going to be a profitable year, not that he would get to spend much of it.

Next morning a desultory town council meeting ended after twenty minutes, by reason of deep summer. Back at Raymond House, his Tuesday duty lunch with Joe Junior became a one-way lecture on statehood. A few men paused at their table to ask Joe how he was feeling, but only one inquired about progress on the Chinese case.

Amnesia by common consent. Joe had seen Lewiston's group mind in action before, but never so personally. He walked back to the barn and lay on the army cot, looking at dust motes rising in a shaft of sunlight. He hadn't swept in a while. Ten weeks, to be exact.

Lake Waha lay southeast of town, fifteen hundred feet above Lewiston and twenty degrees cooler. August 15 was the traditional day for men to join their families there, and as Joe rode the winding new road to the resort, he met a dozen business acquaintances and waved to more as the lake stage went past, its driver flourishing a braided whip.

Joe left a sulky Trim at Faunce's stable behind the hotel, agreed to pay town rates for two weeks of feed, and took the upper path to the private lakeside camps. Each big canvas tent, wood-framed and wood-floored, was made cozy with washstands and iron cots, carpets and oil lamps. Joe stood outside the Vincent camp for a moment, steeling himself to go in. He needn't have bothered. Libby had company.

"John," he said, nodding.

"Joe!" Vollmer put up a friendly hand. "Finally tore yourself away. Lina's off in Asotin for three weeks. Your good wife and I have joined our broods for a gay old time."

Libby smiled into her wineglass and said nothing. Too much explanation, Joe thought, keeping his own smile in place. Letty put her head through the partition, her bangs a mass of straggling spit curls. She was trying for a Titus coiffure but without success.

"Can I have five dollars?"

Joe handed it over.

"You'll win this time for sure, *liebchen*," Vollmer told her fondly. "Just watch out for that Scott boy—his feet are like rowboats." Letty dimpled at him and skipped down the path toward the milliner's wagon. "Costume dance tonight," Vollmer explained. "A grudge match. Last week she came in second."

"Oh," Joe said. He had not seen Lon or Letty for almost two months. The Fourth didn't count. He would barely see them now, he could tell; Lon was eighteen, Letty fifteen, and Waha summer romances were all-consuming. Joe knew they would dance at the shore pavilion until midnight, when moonlit paths around the lake beckoned. Joe Junior had done his courting with Teutonic precision, but Lon and Letty were both featherheads, in Joe's view, and if the drinking and flirting got out of hand he dreaded playing the stern paterfamilias. Maybe he could deputize Vollmer.

Nell was again staying at the Binnards', and Joe had arranged for her to come up to the lake with the Weisgerber girls on Saturday. He knew she had not gone fishing since their disastrous expedition to the Snake.

"How's the shoulder?" said Libby. She was in a feline, luxuriant mood; if Letty had not been on hand, Joe would have said Lib was fresh from bed.

"Fine," he said.

"Any luck?" asked Vollmer, accepting another glass of wine.

"Lost 'em," said Joe. "I guess we'll never know the full story. Nice young fellow from the Sam Yup — sorry to disappoint him. The Chinese consul won't be too happy either."

"Well, Joe, my thinking is very close to yours," said Vollmer.

"*Don't* be a bore, Joseph," said Libby, rising to change for dinner. "I won't let any morbid police business spoil my holiday."

Sunny days, cool nights. Every day Joe went lake bathing for an hour, and waited the other twenty-three for the mail wagon from Lewiston. Neither Grace nor Lee had written. He wondered if they ever thought of him. Alonzo's social notes in the *Teller* were all light and cheer.

> August 15, 1887. J. K. Vincent and family are camped on a slope leading down to a creek where the speckled trout frisk their tails and the grouse drink before breakfast. Many huckleberries to gather. We hunt and fish during the day and dance at night. 45 people showed up at Scott's hotel the other night. Sightings of cougar, grouse, bear, and coyote.

186

Sightings of other Vincents remained sporadic. Amazing how five people in the same tent could keep out of each other's way if they tried. The first night he discovered that Libby slept at the Leland camp, first saying it was so the children could have friends to stay, then pleading headache; the air in the pine grove was cooler, she declared, than down by the water's glare. The Vollmer tent was in the next clearing. Also amazing. Joe would have laughed, but his shoulder was still giving him hell.

Nell was glad to see him. She told him the plot of *Treasure Island* at some length but never talked of absent friends. Joe didn't want to, either. He cut her a nosegay of wild grasses instead, to put in her enamel camp mug. When they went out in the canoe, the morning air was chilly and bright. As they walked up to the dining tent for breakfast, he saw robins gathering, and the first touch of color on the aspens overhead.

VOWS

BEHIND JOE'S BARN grew a black cottonwood, the oldest in Lewiston. Its small, hard seeds supplied peashooters all over town. In spring the cottonwood smelled like balsam; Henry said that boiling its buds, then breathing the steam, would cure any cold. In fall its tower of foliage turned a strong, clear gold, and for a week or two soft caracoles of cotton down drifted like snow along streets and fences. In good weather Joe carried his office chair outside and conducted business beneath the fluttering leaves.

After a week in town he sat under the cottonwood, brooding. Lee had sent a short note to say he would trace Vollmer's San Francisco travels. Nothing from Grace. Deciding that the mails ran both ways, Joe bent over his lap board to pen a short letter, asking her to keep an eye on the Oregon papers. Obvious, but better than nothing. He covered Nell's progress at school (spotty marks in conduct), then the latest cases in police court. He tapped his teeth with the pen, folded the letter and slid it into an envelope, then suddenly pulled it out and turned the page over.

> I want you to know that I miss you, now more than ever. If you were here I would be a good deal more sure about many things, not least this Chinese case. You were always wiser than I about knowing what to do and whom to trust. All the mistakes I have made were with others, you most of all.

188

He looked at that awhile. Well, it was the truth from his side, and he'd better say it. If the result was another ten-year silence, at least he'd tried. He added a penny stamp to the envelope. Miss M. G. Prindiville, 1340 State Street, Portland. He would walk it down to the mail boat himself. Lewiston's postman was nearly as nosy as the Western Union manager.

In Lee Loi's second week back at work, the Sam Yup directors invited him to discuss Idaho. To review, if he would, a few trifling points. Next morning, no one in the finance office met his eye and at Lee's desk sat his worst rival, reading every file, looking amused. Lee walked stiffly over to the maze of chairs they called the bullpen and thereafter sat dealing with clients off the street like any new hire.

The summons from the Chinese consul was almost a relief. Decent of him to present the deportation order in person, but that was Fred Bee's style. Bee was a Forty-Niner, a Pony Express founder, and a first-rate American lawyer. By stage and by steamboat, he traveled across the West to upbraid mayors who allowed riot and killing. He battled in court to frame anti-Chinese violence as civil-rights outrage or international incident, sometimes both. A vigorous man with white muttonchop whiskers, he was hard to upset, hard to fool.

Beyond the French windows in Bee's upstairs office, Lee Loi saw only a swoop of telegraph wire against San Francisco's overcast autumn sky. Behind the desk hung an ink-on-silk of wind-tossed bamboo. Pretty cultured for a *da bidze*. The winter trip across the Pacific was going to be bad. Four weeks seasick in a bunk bed. The Sam Yup did not ship home disgraced employees in cabin class. Lee Loi knew almost no one in Canton any more except the mother who sent him away. He tried to recall her face; gave up.

The consul leaned back and studied Lee. Brains and English fluency were always assets in the Zongli Yamen, China's Foreign Office. San Francisco's Consulate had never been busier; the worldwide diaspora of Chinese was surging, the modernizers back home faltering. American laws against Asian labor grew harsher by the month.

Until this summer Bee had written off Lee Loi as a born banker. Not a lightweight, exactly, but happiest in a pack, smoking expensive cigars at receptions because it looked swell. Back in June, when Lee Loi came to the Consulate for a briefing, Bee figured the Snake River killings for a lost cause. Now he barely recognized the fit, somber man across the desk. His composure seemed real, if you ignored the twitching foot.

"I understand you took ten weeks to foul up a job that should have taken three."

"We got the evidence, sir."

Bee slid over a sheet of paper. With a pang, Lee saw Grace's hand-writing.

"What's this ridiculous document? Did Vincent write it?"

"No, sir."

"Did you?"

"No, sir."

"Who, then?"

"Our river guide. Georges Sundown."

"I happen to know your guide was a woman."

Might as well hang for a sheep as for a lamb. "Is the Legation working with Mr. Vollmer, sir? If so, I'm sorry to hear it. As to our guide, it's not my confidence to break. Sir."

"Young man, in this work you may well have to lie for your country. You needn't start yet. Now. Let me have your views on improving conditions in the States. In two sentences."

"I used to believe in *shun* — change by increments, like water on stone," Lee said, surprised into honesty. *What work?* "Now I'm not sure."

"Would you consider a job with us?"

"Sir, the Company said—"

"We know what they said. But a lot of you Mission men found ways to stay. Your own immigration is not at issue, never was. Students, merchants, diplomats, all still immune."

So the Company was closed to him. And if the Consulate had informants that good within the Sam Yup, the split was deepening.

"It's not all desk work and dinners," Bee told him. "You know Shi En?"

Lee nodded. Shi En was a casual friend, another Mission product.

Bee said, "A mob caught him in Los Angeles. He's alive, but in bad shape."

Lee jolted to full attention. It was real. They did need him. Poor old En.

Bee explained the salary, then the hazard pay.

The ghosts of Deep Creek were right, Lee thought. He would never be rich.

"I'll do it," he said. "Thank you."

"We're in a war, young man. I intend to force this government to obey its own laws by acting as if the laws in fact apply to all. A few successes thus far. Plenty of failures. Your Snake River case could go either way. Vincent's sensible, you say?"

"Well, hard to deter," Lee Loi told him.

That Saturday, Joe found under his office door one of Libby's pale blue notes. He used to get six a day, not one a year. *We must discuss an urgent matter. Meet me at Papa's house.* Now what? He hurried up Main Street.

In the parlor's subdued light, Libby turned from the tea table and considered him, head cocked. Beside her stood young Lon, miserable in a high starched collar.

"Lonny has wonderful news. Go ahead, dear."

Lon looked at the ceiling. "Well. I'm going to marry Emma Curtis."

"You're what? Marry? Lon, you're eighteen — you have no living!"

Libby said smoothly, "John has hired him for the Spokane store, as assistant manager. Lon will have his coming-of-age money from Father, of course. And Emma's dowry is very satisfactory."

"Who the hell is Emma — what, Curtis? I don't know any Curtis."

191

"They arrived in June and took a camp at Waha. Lon met Emma there. You weren't around."

"No, I was getting *shot* upriver. In August I was at the lake. I don't recall any introductions."

Lon reddened. "She's a very nice girl, governor."

"I don't care if she's Jenny Lind. And don't call me governor. She's eighteen too?"

"Um. A bit younger. Fifteen. Sir."

Letty's age. "Jesus in the wilderness."

His wife tossed her head. "Really, Joseph. I was no older, you recall—"

"Yes, well, we were in circumstances—"

"And so are they."

Joe turned to Lon. "Emma is with child? How far gone?"

Libby leaned forward. "We think about three months."

"On four months' acquaintance. I never knew you to move so fast, Lon."

"Joseph, enough. Reverend Elliot's, Monday at three. We expect you there."

"We?"

Once Joe sat with Alonzo in this parlor, drawing up terms for another marriage. *Three months,* she whispered, eyes brimming. Well over five, in fact. And not fifteen but eighteen.

"I mean Alice Curtis, Emma's mother. We've been in discussion since August."

"God *damn* it, Libby. I was at the lake in August."

"Yes, but my inclination was to wait and see."

By holding off this long, Joe thought, she'd probably doubled the dowry. She released Lon with a glance; he fled.

"We'll offer the reception. I've sent out some suitable—"

"It's a shotgun wedding, for Christ's sake. Best parade it as little as possible."

"No, you're quite wrong. Emma is not yet showing, and a reception can launch them nicely. They'll move next week, and of course delay announcing the birth. It's all planned."

He reached for his hat. "Then why in hell did you call me over?"

"Monday," she said.

On Monday morning Joe walked to the *Teller* office. The only man on duty was Walter Phillips, who took up a composing stick and talked baseball as he picked type. Detroit played St. Louis on Wednesday, and he was worried about getting box scores for the Thursday edition.

"So my notice will run on Thursday?" Joe asked.

"Sure. I'll proof it now."

Walter slapped type in a chase, inked the form, and ran a print on a piece of foolscap. Joe held it up to the window for light.

Notice to the Public:

As my son Alonzo K. Vincent has left his house without cause or provocation, I take this opportunity of giving notice that I will not be responsible for any debts that he may incur or contract for after this date.

J. K. Vincent
Tammany Hollow
October 3, 1887

Walter was reading his own copy. "October third is today, sir. We could change that to October sixth, the date of publication."

"No, today."

By the time Joe stood beside the Tammany staircase, holding a glass of Moët and looking passably cordial, he knew John Vollmer had provided the couple with an income *and* a house. Lon was headed for commercial eminence, debt-free. Joe could scarcely object. He drank off the champagne and turned to find a worried Nell hanging over the banister.

"Pa, Letty's crying. She won't talk to me. She got sick in the basin."

He hurried upstairs to sit on Letty's messy bed, bemused. "What is it, sugar?"

She huddled against a brass headboard. A year ago her dolls sat

193

propped there, even the armless ones, dismembered by a bored Lonny. Now she clutched a pillow to her belly and wept.

"Letitia," he said. And to Nell: "Find your mother."

Libby sent Nell for cologne and a damp cloth, dabbed Letty's wrists, then questioned her, low-voiced. At every halting reply, Libby's mouth compressed more. Under the violet silk Joe saw her shoulder come back, then drop. He suddenly wondered if she ever struck the children when in a passion. Nell might say. His wife stood up, shaking out her skirts.

"Three months, maybe four," she told Joe, all business.

"But who?"

Nell knelt on the rosebud carpet, holding a water glass. Should she be hearing this? Too late for propriety. Joe stroked Letty's heaving back and got her to sit up.

"Look at me," Lib told her. "I said, look at me. Now. All the way. I won't abide insolence. Who is it?"

Letty whispered, "Frank Scott."

Of Scott's Lake Hotel. The parents were downstairs, in the thick of the dancing.

Joe said, "Get them in here."

He so rarely gave a direct order that Libby left without a word.

Joe spent that week fuming, and the next. He could imagine the Nez Perce County talk. *Must be fine to be rich.* He began dragging the Chinese murders into every conversation he could, like a battering ram. In their usual booth at the Delmonico Lunch Parlor, over roast oysters and bean soup, Alonzo told him to ease off.

"They worked in Oregon and they died there. Leave it go. Be reasonable."

"My reason says this town lost thirty-one souls last May, and their killers are free. Who's next? Rachel? Nell?"

"Mongolians mostly kill their own. I know it, you know it. You call them souls, but I know a few preachers who'd argue that case."

"With one man in five baptized by American missionaries?"

194

"Oh, hell. Rice Christians. What do you care? You're out of your jurisdiction. You got paid. And excuse me for reminding, but you're not marshal any more."

Back at Raymond House, Joe peered in his mail slot. Finally. He tore open the envelope, elated, but found only what any friend might. A rueful account of her neglected garden, her plans to ice-skate on a local pond if the coastal winter ever allowed. Ice-skate? Joe blinked. Georges was trying to rebuild the Appaloosa strain, with some success. Lee's new Consulate job sounded promising.

At least Joe still had a tracker on his side.

> I went to the state library. Blue's men are all legal residents of Wallowa County, apparently law-abiding, most already in that country by '80. Fast work, considering. If you can't find them in Joseph, try Pine Creek. The papers here say that if the Northern Pacific joins the Union Pacific, they will split their territory and have a license to rob both north and south of the Snake.

Helpful, but Joe still felt like a boy missing his rightful birthday present. He turned the page.

> I liked what you wrote, Joe. Thank you. But whatever we were to each other is long ago now. And the marriage vow is to me a serious matter.

There it was. No better off than Lonny.

He slit open a letter from Tom Humphreys, sheriff of Wallowa County.

> On Sep 30, I arrested Bruce Evans and J T Canfield on charges of livestock theft. They have implicated a few others in their gang who appear to live here in W County. I would appreciate your help interviewing Evans and Canfield. No sign of Homer LaRue, who is said to have left this region in July. As my jail is not the most secure, I urge you to come soon if you want to make the other charges.

Joe knew Humphreys only by name, and he had never visited Joseph. His maps of Oregon showed a village below mountains, at the head of a large lake. Joe traced a course that led him across the Snake and along the flank of the Wallowas. Just over ninety miles, five days of rough trails. He wired Humphreys that he was leaving next morning and then, for form's sake, sent a note to Libby. *I shall be away on court business for some weeks. In emergency, Dr. Stanton can find me.*

He walked up the hill to tell the Stantons about the double marriage debacle and ask if they had heard from Grace.

"Busy as ever," Mary told him. "Once you get back, I'll go out to Portland."

"That's fine," said Joe, hearing what she did not say. Mary did not want him troubling Grace's hard-won peace, but she would not travel unless he kept an eye on Henry. Joe could look in twice a day. Mrs. Reilly did the rest. He passed over the name and address of Tom Humphreys.

"Wire me there, but as J. Salem. No one here can know I'm across the river."

Mary Stanton nodded. She did not like to think of Joe riding that lonely country on his own. She was still astonished by his long masquerade among the killers and his stubborn campaign to see the Chinese miners right. Henry said Joe would lose the nod for Congress if he kept it up. Better than anyone in Lewiston, Mary Stanton could imagine Joe Vincent in Washington. He would not have an easy time here or there, in his present maverick humor. Neither Grace nor Henry would talk much about the second trip upriver or its aftermath. No matter — eventually she would get it out of them.

Joe stood up. Mary, his old adversary, was looking at him with pity, which scared him, and the little house was too full of memory: Grace and Dow studying Henry's medical atlas under the parlor lamp; Grace at the piano, persuading Lee to carol the Lord Chancellor's songs from *Iolanthe;* Grace catching his gaze over some passing absurdity.

His eyes burned. *Oh, hell. Maudlin on one sherry.* He told Mary again that he was glad to see her back, apologized, and fled.

PART III

BEADED SHEATH

A T MIDMORNING Joe crossed the Snake with the first ferry, and by noon he was well south, riding cavalry style: walk, trot, lead. Trim kept her ears pricked forward, eager for each treeless turn and rise. She loved to work. Joe let her water at every creek. *A fine, wise, and handsome beast,* he told her, stroking the strong brown neck. Pleased by praise, she blew into his hair.

Wheat, barley, wheat. Hardly any game. This country used to be a hunter's paradise. And now open range at last, the road a dusty track through pale, dry grass. The mild day and steady creak of saddle leather let him doze a little, trusting the horse to keep the trail. He might have been riding the Camas again, tricked out in slouch hat, saber, and mustache. Sergeant J. K. Vincent, first-class pain in the ass. One of his more embarrassing younger selves, as lost as the wild Northwest that formed him.

If you want to smell Hell, join the cavalry, they sang, patrolling the Union's richest mountains. He threw off gold fever once, back in California. A fool's game, and unseemly. But sometimes the infection returned.

The soldiers at Fort Lapwai had no Rebels to chase, only an illicit army of gold-seekers pouring onto treaty land. Joe Vincent was a good rider, but Lieutenant Lowry needed a commissary clerk, so between sorties Joe ran the tiny outpost store, selling paregoric and mosquito bar to military families, the local Nez Perce, and the Indian Training School.

The sutler hut was gloomy and crowded. Against long odds, Joe kept it tidy and swept. One cloudy fall day the youngest teacher came by. Her dark wavy hair was bundled into a net—a losing battle there, too—and her tip-tilted hazel eyes, intelligent and direct, met his straightaway. Joe was reading Indian-agent reports on Lapwai. She asked his opinion.

"One-sided," he said, and she laughed.

Her name was Grace Sundown, and soon he could think of no one else. She was almost seventeen, and her late father had run a trading post near Lapwai. Joe assumed this Louis Sundown was French Canadian, like so many of the Hudson's Bay men, but no, he was a real Frenchman. A charming rover, Joe guessed. He knew the type.

A week after the Stantons came to Lapwai, Mary opened the cabin door to find an eager seven-year-old in calico and moccasins, her dark hair smoothed with bear grease. She handed over a wildflower bouquet, then launched into a long stream of questions. Mary Stanton stifled a gasp; the child sounded Parisian.

Small Marie-Grace learned English from the Stantons so fast that her proud parents sent her to the new Fort Lapwai school. Its staircase baffled her. She had never seen one. When a matron buttoned on the rough linen pinafore, then bobbed her hair, Grace began to argue. The uniform was surpassingly ugly, and to the Nimipu, short hair means mourning. At twelve she mourned for real. In one terrible week, diphtheria took her devout gentle mother, Tayam, then Louis Prindiville, and last of all the Stantons' son, a handsome, thoughtful boy named Oliver. Her parents' friends became a foster family born of shared sorrow—Autre-maman, Autre-papa.

At fifteen she returned to them from a last Wallowas summer, sullen and angry. The Stantons' worry redoubled. She could teach; she could marry. But Lapwai lay too far south for Grace to meet other country-born, the French-Indian and Scots-Indian children of the fur trade, and Georges's mother could produce no Nimipu suitors among the Christian treaty families. The girl was devoid of dowry, full of opinions, half white, and a sorry cook. Henry and Mary delayed their Lewiston move until Lapwai's Presbyterian superintendent agreed to hire a Catholic *métisse*.

"*Such* an honor," Grace told Joe. "I couldn't promise to convert, but I did say I wouldn't revert. Or not without a month's notice."

Joe smiled, but her alien faith troubled him as much as her mixed parentage. The sharp tongue he rather enjoyed. Lieutenant Lowry soon took him aside for a talk on the wiles of the French, the aborigines, and indeed all females. Joe persisted, and in a week he was Private Vincent once more, for Conduct Unbecoming.

Well, come fall he was done with the Army, and beyond the dusty parade ground shone a fine June day. Down by the creek he saw Grace, waiting; she leaned forward in the sidesaddle, then looked up, smiling, and laid her reins against the pony's neck. All that summer they rode together across the blooming Camas, or read poetry aloud beneath the willows of Lapwai Creek, or lay side by side in high grass, laughing, entwined, watching wind and meadowlarks. You could not grow up on the frontier without knowing what came next, after the searching kisses, the shed petticoats. Grace was more than willing, but always Joe held them back. He had no position, no fortune, no plans. They had only their ceaseless talk. Yet he made a promise.

"When my tour of duty is up, I'll go to Lewiston and find work. I'll write you every week."

She burst into tears, surprising them both.

"I will not leave you forever," he said, and held her a long while in the lamplit store.

That first month the Stantons rented him a bed, and he sent Grace his new life in hints and fragments. *Mary feeds me doughnuts. Henry tends my wounds from putting up their new shed. I am learning the auction trade; you would laugh to hear me fumble at the patter.* Grace replied in her small clear hand, turning each sheet to add more lines crossways. Notepaper was precious. Every Wednesday she waited by the Lewiston road for the mail carrier, handing him an envelope as he handed her one. Pleasures deferred, Joe Vincent assured her, are pleasures doubled.

The trail south was turning steep, twisting through an evergreen world cut by narrow streams, diamond quick, diamond clear. On his third evening out, Joe put the blanket around his shoulders and sat looking across the evening valleys. A picketed Trim grazed nearby. Joe folded the wax paper from his last town sandwich and put it in his pocket. All this fall his stomach had soured; to lie down now brought bile searing into his throat, so he sat against a rock, listening to the night.

Back in September (without telling even Henry) Joe had put in for the public contract to move soldiers' bones from the common graves at Big Hole and White Bird to the military cemetery at Fort Walla Walla. For ten years souvenir hunters had torn up Nez Perce War battlefields. Enough. He'd had a bellyful of ceremony lately, but that duty he would welcome. *Lord, let me know mine end, and the number of my days.* At the two hasty weddings this month, he'd given Letty away with a kiss, Lon with a handshake. *Love, comfort, honor, and keep.*

The gaudy river settlement made him feel nineteen again, back on shipboard and running before a gale. Lewiston was still half tents. Miners called it Ragtown, and beside it the California gold fields looked sedate. Henry's medical practice ran heavily to gunshot wounds. Only a fourth of the cemetery occupants died from natural causes. On Saturdays Joe held auctions, mostly of mining gear. If the bloodstains were too obvious, he gave a forty percent discount. The other six days he patrolled the mud streets. In a town this new, every able man took a turn in government. For a while Stanton was mayor; thanks to his military service, Joe got voted sheriff.

He found more work at the newspaper office, setting type. The publisher, a jovial Rhode Islander, invited Joe home. Little Miss Leland, shy and strawberry blond, kept her eyes down and murmured pieties. Once Joe saw a tear slide down her perfect cheek, and then another. After a decorous week of family meals, Alonzo took him aside. A heartless Army officer had left dear Elisabeth with child, then abandoned her. If Joe lent his name to mother and infant, a substantial cash gift would come his way. And his pick of jobs. And a house, of course.

Joe nearly told Leland what to do with his offer, until Alonzo tripled the money.

No sane man would hesitate. His standing in Lewiston would rocket. New Englanders both, Alonzo assured him, guiding the commonweal. A mixed-race wife would keep him an outsider forever. In Lewiston Grace was still legal, but across the river Oregon was passing miscegenation laws at a great clip: already a white man could not wed a woman more than half Indian, or a quarter Chinese.

And she was so damn smart. Unfair to keep her from a real education, the kind he never had. His Leland marriage portion could cover that. Seventeen years lay between them, after all. This way was better. For everyone.

The two girls were almost of an age, Grace slender and quick, healthy as a pony, Elisabeth fair, yielding, and buxom. With Grace every moment was a surprise, sometimes a battle, and her perfect trust was both honor and burden. With Libby he mainly felt ten feet tall and covered in hair. And she needed him so. He touched her pale plump hand in its crocheted mitt and won a sidelong smile. Their parlor wedding was quiet and quick. She hitched up her hoop skirt to cover the bulge and four months later bore a hefty blond boy, Joseph Vincent, Jr. To Alonzo's irritation, Dr. Stanton begged off the confinement.

When Joe brought the money for Grace's schooling, he thought Henry Stanton would hit him across the room. Mary took the draft and thanked him. She had seen Grace and Joe together only twice, and even seated well apart their amorous heat could have started a forest fire. Joe Vincent always said he was a Yankee, yet his father's Huguenot clan emigrated from the Channel Islands, practically in France. No wonder the pair of them were attracted. To save Grace from the short, hard life of a half-caste drudge, Mary Stanton would have cashed a check from Satan.

In the Nez Perce War, Joe walked with the Idaho men till Colonel McConville ordered him to ride. *Get up there and pretend you like it,* Ed told him. *They need to see someone in charge.* Here on the high, bare ridges of Oregon, the dead kept him company again. Like the Chinese crews at Deep Creek, the volunteers of '77 were often landless wanderers, hired hands. *Safe home soon,* he told them. Kiley, Landsgraf, Bichl, Johnson. Pease, of course. He was starting to lose names. Tired, that was all. And too much time with Lee and Grace. Any minute he'd go in for mesmerism, or table-rapping.

But he did say privately to Elder Boss, who understood both long odds and Evans, *My apologies, friend.* And then, to all the Chinese miners, *My regrets.* Of which he had many, not least that he was their last best chance and yet he lay in darkness, as voiceless as they.

Young Libby owed her ample breasts to pregnancy, Joe Vincent discovered, and her wide, bright eyes to belladonna, taken on a sugar lump. Her fragile, helpless air evaporated. Some of her tastes in bed would startle the madam of a cathouse. But after a lightly tethered life, Joe liked the inner circle, even in a town of two thousand. He liked it too much. In a passion of gratitude, he threw himself into public service, never dodging a meeting, a committee, a crisis. He even read law in the evenings with a local judge, for once not yielding to Libby's mockery or her demands that he stop. Henry Stanton's dislike began to thaw, just a touch. He was not so stiff-necked that he could snub a man growing late into his better self.

Years later, Henry did tell Joe the rest, how telegrams and letters had gone between Lewiston and the Academy of the Sacred Heart in St. Charles, Missouri. Sacred Heart boarding schools, elegant and demanding, adorned New York and Washington, St. Paul and Chicago, St. Louis and New Orleans. The French nuns who ran them also had a special New World mission: to train promising young women of Indian stock in every point of scholarship and social finesse. At nearly eighteen, Grace was a touch old for Academy life, but her parentage was ideal — perfect, in fact — and if she helped with lower-school teaching, then Joe's money would just cover four years, though not as a parlor boarder.

Grace paced and brooded. At least the nuns wanted her. Perhaps she had a vocation? She opened her cedar sewing box, found her mother's rosary of horn and silver, and tried to pray. The rosary was the first beautiful thing from the white world that Grace could remember. As a child, she loved to spill it from palm to palm, watching the chained beads pool and slither. Maybe the Virgin would send some sign. Joe sent neither explanation nor farewell.

The Lapwai teacherage had only one small hand mirror. In it Grace studied her high strong cheekbones, her betraying eyes. Some *métis* could pass as white, but no quantity of rice powder and carmine salve would ever give her the rose-petal, skim-milk fairness of a Libby Leland. Grace laid her head on her arms. She had no true place among the People. Three years back, her uncle Philip made that blisteringly clear.

American law held otherwise, of course. *An Indian or a half-breed shall be considered a subject person, not a citizen.* Twice outcast, then. A sort of talking beast. No wonder Joe turned away. But the law of France did not agree, said Autre-papa. So French she would be, and never waste another tear on Joseph Vincent, never again be taken for a fool.

St. Charles was fifteen hundred miles by trail, road, water, and rail, a desperately hard journey for an experienced man, let alone a slip of a girl. Mary and Henry wondered every day if they were right to send her. They would not see her again for years.

Grace climbed into the Fort Benton stage wearing Mary's winter coat and a blue crocheted fascinator against the mountain chill. In her reticule lay twenty dollars, a comb, a lace-edged handkerchief, the silver rosary, her grandmother's knife in its beaded sheath, and a letter of admission for one Marie-Grace Prindiville. She had no idea who that was but felt ready to find out. The stagecoach gathered speed and she was gone. Henry blew his nose. He had seen much raw courage in his time, but young Grace Sundown beat all.

On his last night of travel Joe stopped in Enterprise, six miles north of the Wallowa County jail. He needed a bath and shave, and a pressing for his dark suit after its week in the saddlebags. Enterprise was ten months old, a dozen frame houses surrounded by a hundred empty lots. But already it had a post office and dry-goods store, lumberyard and flour mill. The false fronts along Main Street were only half up. The hotel smelled of pine sap. Its manager was a bustling widow, who brought the big can of hot water up to his room herself, with a hopeful smile. Judge Vincent thanked her and shut the door.

FACING SOUTH

A S JOE RODE SOUTH at dawn, he watched first light turn the autumn sky pale sulphur, then brighten the peaks of the Wallowas. On the Idaho side of the Snake, he could see snowcaps on the Seven Devils range. Deep Creek and Dug Bar were forty miles northeast and five thousand feet down. Fine work by Tom Humphreys and his citizen posse.

And now he made out Joseph at last, low scattered buildings along a wide main street, a toy town amid the vastness. His older maps had it as Silver Lake. Odd to rename this place for the aging rebel chief who still called the Wallowas home. Joe wondered if locals thought a wartime association could mean tourist business. Joseph might be remote, but the scenery was top-notch. All the town lacked was a railroad.

At the Fine Hotel, he found the sheriff taking late breakfast. As Joe pulled up a chair, Humphreys hovered with a toothy, unctuous smile. This man brought in Evans and Canfield? Joe could smell whiskey in his coffee cup.

Beside Humphreys sat Frank McCully, slim, bearded, and self-possessed. Wallowa County was his domain, literally; in one year he'd persuaded voters and legislators to approve its formation, then made sure he ran general store, newspaper, and land office. McCully was twenty-nine. Like Jackson Sundown, another swashbuckler born too late.

The Fine Hotel was also the county jail. Evans and Canfield had separate upstairs quarters, guarded by a deputy. They slept and ate there, and the deputy walked them to an outhouse. McCully apologized.

"Joseph is the acting county seat. Voters decide next June if we or Enterprise get the permanent courthouse and jail. So this is the best we can do."

"My first jail was a log cabin," Joe told him. "If it got too crowded, I tied them all to a tree." A private joke. Except for the cottonwood behind his barn, early Lewiston was bare of anything but hackberry and sagebrush. Humphreys led him upstairs, nodding as if Joe had just quoted Cicero in the original.

The interrogation room looked right. Bare floor, bare walls. Two law books and a water pitcher stood on a long table, which Joe pulled closer to the window. He wanted the prisoners facing south, to have sun in their eyes.

At ten the deputy sent a clean-shaven Canfield through the door. He looked healthy enough and younger without a beard. Humphreys introduced Judge Vincent, from Idaho. The handcuffed man nodded, squinting in the strong morning light, then gave his name and residence as James T. Canfield of Pine Creek.

"You own a place there?"

Canfield looked Joe over, decided he was harmless.

"Yeah. I run about forty head."

"Mr. Canfield, let's talk about rustling, since that's the charge against you. What do you know about the subject? You know how rustlers work?"

"Shit, everyone does. Round up horses, change brands, sell them off."

"The charge is you were doing that, with others, for the past six, seven months." Canfield started to protest, but Joe went on. "That you drove them to Dug Cabin, changed the brands there, crossed the animals into Idaho, then turned around and did the same in Oregon."

"You got any proof of that?"

"I do. You know what the penalty is for horse theft, Canfield? On both sides of the river, it's death by hanging."

Canfield sat silent.

"As Mr. Humphreys will confirm, if you cooperate you may do prison time instead." True. The big penitentiary east of Boise held plenty of horse thieves.

"What do you mean, cooperate?"

"You worked with six others. I have their names and backgrounds." Joe unfolded his list and began to read: "Bruce B. Evans, age 41; Carl Hughes, 37; Hiram Maynard, 38. All neighbors of yours on Pine Creek—"

For the first time, Joe saw fear. "Judge, it was only horses."

"That's right. Grand theft, added up, but less if you cooperate."

Canfield didn't hesitate. "What do you want to know?"

"Do you admit that you rustled while living at Dug Bar from April to September?"

Tee had forgotten the time sequence. "Yep."

"And you did that with the following individuals?" Joe reeled off the six names.

Another nod.

"And that in late May of this year you and those six persons did also torture, mutilate, shoot, and kill some thirty Chinese miners?"

"Now wait. I'm here on a charge of horse theft, right, Sheriff?"

Humphreys said, "Answer the question, Tee."

"I don't have to answer nothing. This ain't a court."

Joe leaned forward. "Listen to me. You and the others killed those miners. You just admitted, before three witnesses, that you were at Dug Bar in late May. That puts you at the scene. You had means, and you had motive—to steal their gold."

Canfield stared back. "What's your evidence?"

"The bullets in the corpses were from your guns. You stole their rice, and I have the sacks. I have eyewitnesses to the crime. The only way you'll escape the hangman is to turn state's evidence and confess."

But Tee Canfield put his head down and kept it there. More afraid of Evans than any scaffold, Joe guessed. He nodded to the deputy.

McCully offered lunch downstairs. The hotel dining room was packed. Two local men held prisoner for weeks, and now an out-of-state judge, stern and formal in a black suit, Illinois watch and GAR pin: it was as good as a play. The minute he saw the eager faces, Joe knew that Humphreys was a talker.

McCully edged his way back to their table with a glass of rye for himself and a cider for Joe.

"You really got Tee going, Judge."

"You know him?"

"Everyone knows Tee Canfield. Friendly enough, pays most bills. Gone a lot. He and Blue raise horses, mostly."

"Tell me about Evans. He's always ranched?"

McCully looked surprised. "Blue came out here as a land agent back during the big rail push. He can be a charmer when he wants, and he got some real bargains. Foreclosures, mostly. Of course, he had John Vollmer's money behind him then. You must know Vollmer. Out of Lewiston, right? But pretty soon Blue went into ranching. Small operation, nice stock. I know, too nice. Until last summer he ran almost a thousand horses for a neighbor, Fred Nodine."

"On his own land?"

"And open range. They used about two thousand acres."

"Any chance Nodine was involved in the rustling?"

McCully stared into his drink. "I doubt it. Last July he said his herd was looking smaller. I asked Humphreys to check around for defaced brands. We showed drawings to Nodine, and he swore out a warrant. So when your request came in, we got a move on."

"Did our two ever talk about others working with them?"

"Not yet. But Nodine says he's missing one-fifty, and two men couldn't do that alone."

"Do you know the others?"

"Not LaRue, but the rest, sure."

"Surprise you?"

"No. It's hard to make a living out here, easy to steal. I lost twenty head myself."

"You have a personal interest in putting these men away?"

McCully started to rearrange the silverware. Joe waited.

"Mr. Vincent, if all we're prosecuting is theft, I wouldn't be so worried. These boys are local, and some from good families. I mean, their folks are ranchers, churchgoers, taxpayers—"

"And voters," Joe said. *Now we come to it.*

"They damn well vote. I've had a lot of inquiries on how all this will work out. A lot of concern about the effect on the area's reputation."

"Have you told anyone the charges might be mass murder?"

McCully finished his drink. "That would be obstruction of justice."

Carefully phrased. "It would," Joe said. He waited until McCully met his eye. "I still have the matter under investigation. I can easily prove rustling. The murder charges are tougher. Evans is at the heart of it, but he probably won't confess, and Canfield may not fold. So I've got to get to the others, and frankly, the only way is if some turn state's evidence."

McCully was a realist. "You might sleep out at our place tonight, then. Stay on as long as you need. I'll send word to the two closest families, McMillan and Vaughan, to come by for a talk."

Joe rose, and McCully followed. Neither had touched the plates of pork and fried potatoes. They headed back upstairs, boots loud on the bare pine risers.

RESPECT

OCTOBER 26, 1887

NAME: BRUCE BLEDDYN EVANS, from Pine Creek. Occupation: rancher. He laid his bound hands gently on the table and looked up at McCully.

"I'd offer to shake, Frank, but I'm a little tied up."

McCully started to smile back, then caught himself. "Let me make known Judge Vincent, from Lewiston."

Evans studied the newcomer, head cocked. "Judge Vincent, from Lewiston. Fine town. I've done business there, now and again."

Joe said nothing. Evans tried again.

"I see you are a GAR man, sir. My uncle, Indiana Fourth, fought at Shiloh."

"Is that a fact? I believe you were CSA yourself?"

"I had that honor. Sad times, best put behind us."

Joe let the silence spin out. "When did you come to Oregon, Mr. Evans?"

"Why, I reached these parts in '78."

Joe repeated his questions about rustling methods.

"Never a need to know such things, sir—fortunate in that regard."

"Why were you arrested at Dug Bar?"

"Out looking for my own strays, sir, like any conscientious rancher." Evans nodded at the rope around his wrists. "I'm a county taxpayer, Judge, held against my will on trumped-up charges. And now a stranger, begging your pardon, is making an inquisition. You'd be upset too."

"I would indeed, if the charges were false. But in your case—"

"I never stole any horses. I told you. Are you listening to me? Is that what McCully's writing down in his book? I'm getting damned tired of this treatment. I don't deserve it. I never been arrested or even accused in this county. Ask any of my friends. Folks who know I don't belong behind bars."

"Let's talk about your friends. What has happened to Homer LaRue?"

"Homer LaRue? Not had the pleasure."

"Union veteran. Heavyset."

Evans shrugged. His blue gaze looked entirely candid.

"What about Hiram Maynard? Or Carl Hughes? Do you deny knowing them?"

"Deny knowing them. No. They work for me sometimes."

"Bobby McMillan, Frank Vaughan?"

"Both youngsters. I believe I saw them at a dance once, over at Imnaha."

"You did. I understand Imnaha is where you formed up the gang."

"The gang? Now, I'm as fond of dime novels as the next man—"

"You recruited last spring and began to rustle horses, a good many from Fred Nodine. You took them to Dug Cabin, changed the brands, crossed at Dug Bar, then rustled animals in Idaho for sale back here."

Blue Evans glanced at McCully. "Frank, where'd you get this tinhorn? Can't afford a real judge? And Tom, you sit there and let him harass me? Next election, I just might run against you. Keep that in mind."

Joe laughed, and Blue's head whipped around.

"With your record, Mr. Evans? You've robbed and killed all the way across the map. Until last May, Oregon was about the only clean state on your list."

McCully and Humphreys traded glances. Blue leaned in.

"Judge, I don't know what you're playing at. We're speaking of horse theft, and now you're on to killing. That's a damn serious charge. You better have proof if you're going to fling around threats at regular citizens."

"You're no regular, Evans. You've done a string of killings in Idaho and Oregon since early '83. You even left proof marks. A tendency to skin your victims. Maybe a taste for their meat."

McCully said, "Good God!" but Evans only sighed.

"Now, that's crazy talk, Vincent. You put aside these harsh words. Maybe we should stop and reason together, say a little prayer."

Being near Blue Evans was still like swimming up through a dark current. Joe fought free.

"Did you pray over those miners when you slit their living eyes? Did you reason when you stuffed their balls down their throats?"

Evans whispered, "You don't know shit. No proof at all."

"Plenty of proof. You killed the Chinese at Deep Creek. You put your men up to it, recruited kids for your dirty work, made them all do every filthy thing you ordered."

"Chinese? You need to lie down, Judge. I don't have many dealings with Celestials, but I'd never harm one. Colorful people. Hard workers, they say."

A local jury would be back in fifteen minutes. Make that ten.

"You went to Dug Bar in April, watched the Chinese for a month, killed them in late May, and then stayed on another four months."

"Well, sure, I was there, but only this fall. Looking for lost stock. I *told* you."

Joe shook his head. "It's never enough, is it, Blue? You didn't need the miners' gold. You've got plenty already. You shot Tom Douglas in the head back in '83 and took that box. But still you wanted more. So you played your patron like you played your gang."

"That's not so."

"Yes. You were there. You had means and motive. You killed those men in every brutal way possible and you stole their gold. The

Lewiston coroner took bullets from their bodies that match the guns at Dug Cabin. I have three eyewitnesses."

Blue's face was entirely still except for the flaring nostrils. Joe could hear each rapid indrawn breath.

"Didn't know anyone was watching, did you? Everyone in this county will laugh when they hear. I've known fools and cowards, but you're the dumbest goddamn butcher I've ever met."

Evans slammed both hands down on the table. Books and pitcher jumped.

"You go to hell. You treat me with respect, or I'll—"

"You'll what? If I could get Zeke to testify against you, I would." Evans sat back in his chair. His eyes were almost all pupil.

"Who in the hell are you?"

Joe said, slow and soft, in another man's voice: "I guess . . . you'd call me . . . a regular biographer, mister."

Evans lunged. Joe threw himself hard to the left.

"Salem! You lying—"

Joe had the Colt Peacemaker out and cocked, pointing at Blue's face.

"Give me a reason, Evans."

Humphreys shouted. The deputy from the hallway ran in. McCully stood with his back pressed to the wall, hugging his notebook. As the Wallowa County lawmen held Evans down, Joe saw his true face at last: cunning and appetite, pale ire and envy. Blue stared at Joe, memorizing him. Joe heard himself say, chill as lakewater, "Shall we take this outbreak to be your confession to the Snake River massacre? That you were at the scene, had motive and means, and led the killings and torture?"

"My side of this conversation is done," Evans said. At the doorway, he looked back across his shoulder. "This ain't over, Vincent."

"Out," Joe said.

GOOD FAMILIES

OCTOBER 26–27, 1887

JOE RODE BESIDE McCully through a brilliant Indian summer afternoon. Humphreys promised to double-guard Canfield and Evans; Joe only hoped he meant it. Along the road to McCully's house, field on field, harvesting was under way. A killing frost might come any night. Gleaners tumbled pumpkins toward farm wagons, piled carrots onto tarpaulins, slashed cabbages from stalks. Conditions looked good, despite all the poor-mouthing from the father of Wallowa County. McCully turned in the saddle.

"Now what was that about, sir? One minute he's the Blue Evans I know, the next he's raving. And who's Zeke?"

"Evans's dog. I had to kill him. Kill it."

"But why call you Salem?"

"I was posing as a prospector by that name. To get the evidence. As you saw."

McCully opened his mouth, shut it again. *You'll go far,* Joe thought. To McCully he must seem older than Methuselah.

In the parlor next morning, Joe found six visitors, silent as a wax tableau. Martha McCully's coffee and spice cake sat untouched on the round mahogany table. Joe went around the circle, introducing himself. The Vaughans and McMillans looked like prosperous ranching couples, late thirties or early forties, ready for a fight. When he got to the two boys, they shook his hand with no sign of recognition. Frank looked a little older and heavier, Bobby a lot more sullen. His acne was worse.

"Folks, I want you to know that I sympathize with your situation. I know what it means to have a child in trouble, and I've been a lawman many years. I've seen all kinds of cases. Some are simple. This one's a tangle. Your sons are involved, but if they cooperate, it could go well for them."

Mrs. Vaughan waved a hand, like a girl in school.

"We didn't raise Frank to be a law-breaker, Mr. Vincent."

"I'm sure you didn't, ma'am."

Bobby's father said, "How serious is this, Judge? My son says he wasn't involved."

"The penalty for horse theft is hanging. And I'm sorry to tell you, but Bobby and Frank did steal horses."

"Got proof of that, do you?"

Joe nodded. "I do. Testimony from the buyers and an eyewitness to the thefts. But this case is far more serious. Unless they cooperate, your sons will face charges of mass murder."

Absolute silence. No outcry from the parents. Neither boy flinched.

They already know. That damned Humphreys.

"I have the coroner's report, if you'd like to read it. You may love your boys, but they engaged in unspeakable crimes."

"That's what you say. Everyone in this county knows they're of good character."

"But the facts are clear, Mr. Vaughan. Over thirty innocents are dead."

Mrs. McMillan's mouth was a grim little slot. "You won't find much sympathy here for that point of view, mister."

"What do you mean? That the miners are dead? It's undeniable."

Mrs. McMillan stood up. "How many were washed in the blood of the Lamb?"

217

Joe never got used to hearing theology trump reason. "Ma'am, the Book tells us, 'Thou Shall Not Kill,' plain as day. And Paul wrote in Galatians, 'There is neither Jew nor Greek, there is neither bond nor free, there is neither male nor female: for ye are all one in Christ Jesus.' It doesn't matter who the victim is — killing is a sin."

"That's for *people*. Not heathen. They ought never have come into this country."

"Ma, quit it!" Bobby stood up, looking scared. Frank pulled him into a corner for a hurried talk. The five adults waited.

Frank Vaughan turned to Joe. "Judge, what is it you want?"

"I want you to give state's evidence and testify about what happened."

"You mean about Evans?"

"About everyone. You were all involved. Remember Deep Creek, Bobby? The man by the cook tent. Remember him? You took a knife, and you —"

"They made me," said the boy, wide-eyed. "Old Blue, he *made* me. And that Chinaman, he was dead already."

"Dead men don't scream," said Joe. "His name was Fong Low. He was twenty-nine, with a son back in Canton. He was Christian. Like you. A man tied hand and foot, calling on Jesus, but oh, you were brave. You cut off all his fingers. You even chewed on a couple, right over the dying man's face, so he could see. Your chin got all red. Frank, you took your rifle butt and smashed that man in the mouth, broke all his teeth. Bobby, you took your Winchester and stuck it —"

Bobby's face wobbled. Terror, not remorse, Joe thought, but Mrs. McMillan held out her arms. Joe stepped between mother and son.

"Listen. It will go better if you both testify. Just tell the truth. All the truth. It may not set you free, but it will save your life."

Mr. McMillan stood. "All right. We understand you. I want to talk to McCully a bit and maybe a lawyer. We'll give you an answer by midmonth. I want your word you won't serve arrest warrants before that."

"You have it. You need to talk to Hughes and Maynard anyway, about state's evidence. If all four of you testify, the prosecutor might seek a lesser charge."

No one shook his hand in parting. No one thanked him for his efforts. No one recognized Mr. Salem. By noon Joe was riding toward Lewiston, head bent against a cold west wind.

EVERGREEN

NOVEMBER–DECEMBER 1887

JOE SAT AT HIS ROLLTOP DESK in coat and gloves, waiting for the wood stove to do its work. Lewiston winters were usually milder than this. Nothing in the barn office was out of place, but he got up and straightened anyway. Dusted off shelves. Might have missed something. He stared at two weeks' back correspondence, and at the long envelope balanced on top of the mail pile. Paced. Reviewed his calendar. Lunch with Alonzo and Joe Junior on Thursday. Court resumed on Friday. Finally he opened the telegram.

Regret prisoners escaped details in letter. F.D.M.

Cursing freely, Joe dug through the stack of mail.

Oct 28, 1887
Joseph, Oregon

Dear Judge Vincent,
    As you will know from my wire, Evans and Canfield escaped late last night. A deputy took Evans to the outhouse. He emerged with a six-shooter in hand. Made the deputy take him to the sheriff. Said to Mr. Humphreys, Let's take a walk, which he was obliged to do. They opened Canfield's room and released him. Handcuffed the lawmen, took their pistols, gun belts, and horses. They left, riding north and in no hurry.
    I shall investigate to determine who left that pistol for Evans. A

number of suspects come to mind. With C and E gone, we may get M and V to turn state's evidence. I await your instructions on this and any other matter.

Sincerely,

F. D. McCully

The families, Joe thought. The goddamned families. They planted a gun in the outhouse and got word to Evans. Maybe Bobby's father, maybe Frank's. And Tom Humphreys too lazy to keep the routine secure, or else too scared. The Snake River killings were now five months cold. With winter closing in, evidence and witnesses would vanish. Joe knew the rule of thumb for local justice as well as anyone. Prosecute in ninety days or kiss the case goodbye.

Mid-November passed. Nothing on depositions. Joe wrote to McCully, who replied that no one had come to see him. He would ask a deputy to make inquiries. Joe knew holidays and icy roads would stall everything. His own court business was ebbing; most days he had plenty of time to read by the stove. Nell was boarding in town with her grandparents — the new school was open at last — but each weekend he took her out to Tammany Hollow.

With Lonny off in Washington Territory and Letty a bride in Sacramento, the Tammany place felt enormous. Libby kept to her parlor upstairs, writing long editorials for Alonzo on the virtues of North Idaho. Nell read in her room, or tried to sound out tunes on the piano, false starts and wrong notes echoing through the house till Libby snapped at her to stop.

On Saturdays Joe and Nell rode fence lines with the farm manager, checking drainages and talking crops or watching red-tailed hawks wheel above the stubbled fields. He tried not to spoil Nell, for she had a stoic streak that spurned indulgence. His mother had been like that. To his eternal regret, he could not recall telling her that he loved her. He tried to make that up with Nell, a little; she was thirteen now, and Joe knew she worried about him, checking that he took his stomach pills, bringing him new magazines from the Lelands'. His weekend morning tea always had milk and honey set nearby, and always he assured her that he liked the toast a little burned. More flavor that way. At Presbyterian Sunday night service, back in town, she sometimes put her hand on his as they sang their favorite hymn, "Work, for the Night Is Coming." He didn't know what he would do without her.

Late in November the farm manager came looking for Mr. Vincent. Yates talked less than any man Joe knew, but he gathered that Libby and Yates had driven into town for shopping and returned to chaos. The two men rode back in icy wind over frozen ruts to find Libby and Mrs. Yates locked in the laundry room, armed with pokers.

Joe stifled a smile, but twenty minutes later he stood on the back porch with his hand on his Colt, feeling no urge to laugh. A half-dozen of the fancy new Rhode Island Reds lay around his feet, necks broken. Yates came from the stables to say that one of the farm horses had a cut hamstring and might need to be put down. Glass and china shards covered the dining room, table to floor; someone had kicked in the rosewood sideboard and smashed every wineglass and Minton plate. The kitchen was a swamp of flour, molasses, sugar, and crackers. In the carriage house Yates and Joe found buggy and wagon axles loosened, the best way to ensure accident on Lewiston's steep roads, and in the center of the parlor carpet lay a pile of fresh human shit.

The only place the Vincents could talk was Libby's bedroom.

"A good thing you weren't here. I think he would have killed anyone in the house."

"He? You know who did this? Oh, how can you stand there?"

Was she acting? Joe wasn't sure, but that afternoon Libby moved back to the Lelands'. Joe canceled his schedule for two days and worked with Yates to transport a mountain of hat boxes and brass-bound trunks. Yates had his own place just down the road and would stay on, but to prevent more raids he and Joe drained the water pump, removed all lamp oil, and boarded windows and doors.

Joe stood a minute on the barren veranda, recalling the house-warming gala of Christmas '86, when guests in wagons and sleighs had come from sixty miles around for dancing and a midnight supper of chicken and ham.

On the fall morning when he stopped Dow and Yap as they ran to the Sam Yup boats, Joe was out brooding over the costly, inconvenient move from town house to country mansion. One year ago. Now he cut a swag of evergreens and tied it on the doorknob. Pine boughs, for hope in adversity. A mourning wreath.

By December 1, light snow came to Lewiston. Joe kept up his daily walks. His old habit of patrol had never yielded, and he enjoyed the smiles and handshakes. People were friendlier, at least in public, since he'd laid off a little on the Chinese matter. Raymond House business slowed in winter, but he sat with the manager to check the books, then walked through the dining room, greeting the week's guests: a salesman from Seattle, a steamboat pilot, a minister bound with his pale, tense wife for a congregation near Juliaetta.

In Joe's hotel mail slot was an envelope posted in town that morning.

Mr. Salem, c/o Judge J. K. Vincent
Raymond House, Main Street
Lewiston, Idaho Territory

Inside was a single plaid hair ribbon slashed into pieces, the pieces half burned. Nell's. Joe knew it instantly; she lost about one a week. His chest hurt. Evans here in Lewiston, today. Had he paid a call on Vollmer? If so, John knew all about the Oregon confrontation, from the identity of Mr. Salem to the pointed questions on murder and gold. Libby would have told Vollmer about the attack on the Tammany house. The endless knot that bound them all was tightening.

The mutilated ribbon in the envelope *must* be Evans's work, and his alone. Surely even Vollmer drew the line at threatening a young girl. Nell was Joe's child; she was also Libby's. Joe had never been more grateful for his wife's choice of lover. She could bed the whole Idaho banking commission if it kept Nell safe.

But in memory he heard Vollmer on the hillside at Big Hole:

— *You can't shoot women and kids!*

— *The hell I can't. We're here to win. God damn you, Vincent. A perfect shot.*

All right. He could escort Nell to and from school — for a while. He could make the rounds of taverns and cathouses and informants, try to find and arrest Evans. And he could get his daughter out of town. With a bodyguard.

At six he headed for Main Street. Vollmer might control the telephone exchange and Leland the telegraph office, but Joe once saved the Western Union night clerk from house eviction with some pro bono maneuvering. Tonight was payback: one secure wire, no questions asked.

The next afternoon he tore open the Portland reply, cryptic, unsigned.

Arrive Dec 10 depart next day. One Presb one Epis.

Good. At the Sacred Heart Academy, Nell could room with two Protestants. That should appease the Lelands. Rachel, frail and hesitant, waited every afternoon for Nell's step on the stairs. Nell sat with her grandmother until twilight, threading embroidery needles, trading confidences.

With Libby back at the Main Street house, Rachel's footstool was Nell's sole refuge. Beside her sleek, vivacious mother, Nell wilted. Her lank brown locks resisted all improvement. So did her walk, her smile, her company conversation. Elbows *in,* to bring up the bosom, for those of us who have one; it brings the boys running. Can't you keep those shoes buttoned? Why are you reading *that?* Libby, martyred, took back the basket of curl papers and the painted-china hair receiver. *At least your sister was dressable.* Nell was a gawk, a born old maid. Not a particle of style. No one would ever want her, except maybe for her money. *You know I say this only for your own good.* At the upstairs dressing table, Nell slumped, enduring.

• • •

Joe walked Nell to and from school via the Chinese district. He felt safer there. She lingered, green wool tam starred with snowflakes, studying herbs and teas in a grocery window.

"I miss them."

"Me, too. I've not heard from Lee in a while."

As they neared the Leland house, Joe stopped her.

"Would you like to go to school in Portland? To Grace's school?"

Her look of passionate relief told all he needed to know.

Informing Libby was not the ordeal Joe expected. She barely seemed to care. Portland society sent its daughters to the Academy. Well enough. The North Idaho statehood drive was cresting; Lib and Alonzo had taken a Boise house till spring, for a barrage of fêtes and receptions. With her last adolescent off the premises, Libby could pass for thirty-odd, by gaslight. She sat at her mirrored dressing table, practicing faces: fascinated interest, thoughtful encouragement, coquettish indignation. Rehearsal could go on for hours. She used to stop when Joe came in; these days she did not bother. But she agreed to tell no one where Nell was.

"I'm tired of the subject. Arrange what you like. You always do."

"And for Christ's sake, don't tell John. Do you hear me? This is important."

"I'm her mother. Give me credit for some discretion."

On December tenth, Grace was not aboard the early steamer. Nor was she on the next run, nor the next. Joe and the Stantons did not know what to think; only earthquake or mortal illness came between Grace and any schedule. When next morning she walked down the gangplank of the overnight boat, they embraced her in near-silence. Henry was trembling; she held him close an extra moment. It was just after eight. She and Nell would have to leave at ten. Joe was glad of their reserved cabin, however noisy and airless; by the time they got back, Grace would have spent fifty hours in transit.

She peered at him in the half-darkness of the winter morning.

"Joe, you look terrible! Can't you get some tonic from Papa?"

"Hello to you, too. What happened?"

"Later," she said. "I feel like I've gone over Niagara Falls in a barrel. Backwards."

The winter passage was rough, but not that rough. Joe handed her into the buggy, passed up the carpetbag, told Henry he would drive.

"All *right*," she said, once they were at the Stanton kitchen table, drinking coffee. "I had one of my adventures, that's all. I went down to the state library in Salem to look up more land records. I knew if I went straight to the docks I could still make the boat. But they wouldn't let me on the return train. I showed the conductor my ticket and he said he couldn't be responsible. Too many complaints about Indians in the white cars."

"But surely—"

"Oh, *Maman*, you know what a gamble it all is. If I keep my veil down and my nose in the air, the steamers still take me, but trains are getting chancy. I have to insist I'm a foreigner and bribe the rail agent every time, and even then the last open seat is always the one by me. Two dollars used to do it. Now they want five. I got stubborn, that's all. And I *won't* ride in the baggage car. Sorry to worry you."

She turned to stare out the window, arms crossed. No one said anything. There was nothing to say.

Nell was in high spirits as they boarded. To Joe's amazement, she greeted Grace in French. "You've been practicing with Mary!" said Grace, impressed. Nell tugged her coat sleeve.

"What do I call you?"

"In class or at meals, I am Miss Prindiville and you are Miss Vincent. When it's just us, if you don't call me Grace, I'll be pretty mad."

"Wouldn't want *that*," Joe told his daughter. He gave her a long hug and asked the purser to show her on board. Grace and Joe stood together in the shadow of the dockmaster's shed.

"I don't have a Christmas present for you."

"I don't need one," she said. "Just keep at the case. If you get to trial, I'll come back to help."

Her gloved hand sought his for an instant. She went up the gang-way in falling snow. The steamer whistle sounded and the engine began to pound. Black smoke rose and flowed over the gray winter Snake.

I will not leave you forever. Grace and Nell waved from the stern until the river bent and they were lost to sight.

LONG NIGHT

MARCH 20, 1888

J—We had a scare yesterday. Evans was here, cool as you please, taking the registrar's tour like any parent. A smiling, fair-haired man, clean-shaven, maybe forty. The minute I heard him speak, I knew. I got Nell to the nurse's office & told them to treat her as a quarantine—no one in or out, no one except the headmistress or me . . .

Sister Genevieve was angular and Evans tall; Grace spotted them straightaway in the millrace of girls during class change. Two flights up, she flung open the door to the music studio, saw the Bechstein like a dark island above the Persian carpet's red and gold, saw Nell in gray school day dress and white starched hair bow, hands poised above the keyboard while Sister Louise set the metronome.

"Sister, excuse us. Nell—come with me, *now.*"

They ran through deserted halls, Grace pushing Nell flat against the wall before turning each corner. The library's green-shaded lamps flashed by. The corridor to the refectory, smelling of soup and carbolic. The junior cloakroom's umbrellas and galoshes. Nell's face was pale and set, but she kept up and asked no questions. They had practiced for an attack on the street or at Grace's house, but not here, never here.

Mother Antoinette, the headmistress, knew why the judge's daughter was in Portland. She opened a drawer, passed over ten dollars and change.

"You follow, Marie. I'll stay with Miss Vincent myself, and send for Mr. Angus." The Academy janitor was no General Grant, but he would do. "Are you armed?" said Mother Antoinette magnificently.

"I can manage, thank you," said Grace, half out the door.

The headmistress watched her second-best French teacher vanish down the side stairway. So that was the reserved, correct Miss Prindiville *en garde*. Or rather, Miss Sundown. The change was startling but satisfactory.

Grace commandeered the cook's gray coat and woolen head shawl and trailed Evans down the Academy steps, around the carriageway, through the grounds, and out the big wrought-iron gate. When he boarded a downtown horse-car, she was three rows behind, holding on to a swaying wicker seatback, head lowered. The clop of hooves on wet macadam slowed in traffic; beyond the rain-blurred window she glimpsed the first downtown office blocks. They passed the train station. Evans kept his seat. Was he going to a hotel? Or to the harbor? Let him try. Ten dollars bought plenty of deck passage. She risked another glance. A killer, neat and sober in dark broadcloth, paying his nickel, nodding to the conductor. Grace bent low to pull out her earrings — heirloom garnets from Mary, the color of Madeira wine.

> I thought this would all be safe enough — I was looking wonderfully washerwoman-like — but he spotted me. I swear I did everything right — but still he knew. At the ferry terminal he went into the men's necessary and I waited and waited, but nothing . . .

A luggage wagon full of steamer trunks rumbled by. On the dock outside, men pointed at the water and shouted. A hand gripped her shoulder.

"Are you following me, little lady?"

His face was inches away. She could smell ginseng on his breath. His skin was fair, with a few dark sun flecks. A fine straight nose, a sculptured, curling mouth. No one had said he was this handsome.

She shook her head. The voice was more citified but unmistakable. His hand tightened.

"Sure you are. Well, three dollars. Four if you're clean. What are you, anyway? Dago? High yaller?"

Her stomach twisted at the contact and she jerked away, but he flung up his other arm, like a man hailing a hansom cab, and Grace saw a policeman turn toward them. Of necessity, Portland kept its ferry terminal well patrolled.

"Is she bothering you, mister? Did she solicit?"

"Afraid so, Officer. Shameful and shameless. You'll enforce the law? I *am* grateful. You fellows do a fine job. Must be harder every day. Now, I have to catch my boat, but—"

"I'll see to it, sir."

Vest, watch chain, derby, pious expression: no one would stop this Evans or doubt him.

"Don't you need that man to swear out a complaint?"

"Don't you tell me the law. Turn out your pockets."

The patrolman rolled the earrings on his palm, admiring the dull wink of gold before they vanished inside his greatcoat, along with Mother Antoinette's money.

Evans was still within earshot, never taking his eyes from her face. Streetwalker or spy: he had her in check. Yes, he was good. She saw him take a step backward, then another, and the crowd swallowed him up, one more business traveler in a good dark suit. The policeman finished writing in his notebook, then reached for her.

"Wait!" Grace ran, dodged, scrambled onto a waiting-room bench, stood scanning on tiptoe, and found Evans at last, joining the tail end of the departure line for the Seattle packet. Seattle, Vancouver, points north. The big steamships carried a thousand passengers. How would Joe ever find him? Could Idaho extradite? And if he doubled back, they would never know. She glanced down. The policeman was still there.

The women's holding room at the Portland jail was cold and dim, and the racket was tremendous. Most in custody were white. Too many of the alcohol arrests were native. Losing the wars, losing the land, the shadow of the internment camps: in Portland, Lewis-ton, and across the West, it was all one word these days, *drunken-Indian.*

At eleven a young woman near the back went into labor. She said her name was Janey, and the cheerful tart who eased her onto the straw-covered floor went by Orna. Grace, hard up for yet another nom de guerre, told them she was Louisa May and went to ask the guard for a bucket of water and some soap. Another dozen women ar-rived, two of them obviously respectable, one limping from a twisted ankle, the other a spare, sensible person of fifty-five who saw Janey's ordeal and knelt to help. Her companion shrank back. Useless. Half the room crowded over to offer blankets, petticoat strips, and con-flicting advice. Janey was yelling, her bright hair in snake locks. Her three impromptu attendants worked by glances and nods. No mid-wives in jail that evening, and no medical officer in attendance, so at two-thirty in the morning Grace caught the slick bundle, cleared the mouth with a careful finger, and saw the child gulp its first air. A boy. Thanks to Henry, she had witnessed many first and last breaths, every one a sacrament. The delivery was straightforward and quick and Janey had obviously nursed before.

"A fine little man. You've got more, my dear?" said the older woman. Yes, two, both with her mother. In May she was turning twenty-one. No, she didn't want another factory job; she'd already lost a couple. Yes, she would get home somehow, to Spokane. Mrs. Matusak's, on the north mill road.

"Are you comfortable?" asked the newcomer. In the dimness, all four of them laughed quietly.

"I'll do," said Janey. She was falling asleep on the canvas pal-let even as they watched, the newborn rooting and gurgling at the breast. "But thank you . . ."

Grace suspected she wanted to get away from all the questions.

Orna sponged Janey's tired, pouchy face. With better nutrition and some false teeth, the younger woman might have a timid pretti-ness; her natural coloring was as pink, white, and gold as Libby Leland's. Grace sat back against the wall to wipe her arms on ruined skirts. To avoid passing childbed fever, she could not go near mother or infant again.

Was Orna really Janey's friend, or hoping to be her procuress? Cocooned in the Academy's polished-banister world, so defiantly European and genteel, Grace realized she had seen almost nothing of this other Portland, the most dangerous city in the West. Tending old grievances, she hadn't much cared.

"That was good work," said the gray-haired woman at her elbow. "How is it that you—?"

"Don't faint at blood? Use compound sentences? Come to be here? What?" Maybe she should be rude all the time, Grace thought. It felt wonderful.

"Any will do."

"It's all a mistake," said Grace. Orna snickered. Still, the older woman *had* helped. Grace chose lies of omission.

"I . . . learned from a doctor. Trail medicine. Enough to patch up tourists. I'm—a professional mountain guide, in season."

Now where had that come from? Even to herself, she always called it *helping Georges.*

"If the medical schools allowed it, might you have been a doctor yourself?"

"Yes," said Grace. She started to get up.

"What is it you do now? Off-season, so to speak?"

"Teach French in a Catholic school."

A patented conversation-killer. Over by the door, two old women began to hit each other, with dreamlike slowness.

"Do you like it?"

Grace sat. There was nowhere to go anyway. "I should, but I get . . . restless. I talk for a living and never, ever say what I think. For a while it was fine. Necessary. But now I'm awake again, and it's all too late. I can't do the mountain work much longer, you see, or re-train for a profession. Too old for both. So I stay quiet and mark papers, meek and mild."

In the fetid dark, listening to the baby mewl, she was telling a stranger things she had never said to Henry or Mary or Georges, and to Joe only a little.

"You're partly Salish, I would guess?"

"Nez Perce," said Grace. "Yes, I'm very articulate, considering. No, I don't think we need discuss it." If one more person started in on her breeding, she would do something drastic. "Your turn, by the way."

"Fair enough. My husband was in a bad accident. Overnight I was the breadwinner. Four children, all under fourteen. I tried millinery, then newspapering."

"A natural progression," said Grace, impressed despite herself. "And then?"

"Like you, I tired of silence. I began working for the vote."

"Really," said Grace, losing interest. Suffrage was fine if you were a middle-class white woman, but in very few states was she legally white.

"Are you not in favor?"

"Of suffrage? Only if it's universal. Women *and* Indians, imagine that."

A U.S. district court in Nebraska had ruled only nine years past that a male Indian was in fact a human being. No word on females.

"Schooling too," she said after a moment. "The chance for it, at least." On the reservation and off, ninety percent of the Territory signed with an *X*.

For once the older woman did not press. But then: "One last question. Are you by any chance acquainted with a Grace Sundown? She'd be about your age now."

"I know who you mean. I believe she's dead." *What the —*

"Pity."

Grace had no energy to ask why. Back taxes, probably. She leaned around to check on Janey once more; Orna waved her off. Grace put the gray overcoat under her head and lay on a bench with her back to them all, waiting for daylight. Her knees ached, and the noise was starting up again. Surely Mother Antoinette would think to storm the Portland jail with a cutlass between her teeth. Or at least post bail.

Later, in haste – Our prospective parent was a cattleman, originally from West Virginia, so charming, & praising all arrangements, which he studied with care. A Mr. Salem, he said.

Be sure I will keep alert, and the whole staff too. I shall also teach Nell certain useful moves, which she may employ on suitors if nothing else.

Last night aside, the bodyguard profession is most entertaining. If I wear black and scowl when we go exploring, I am taken for a foreign governess or an upper servant. I suspect you heard about the circus, and the archery lesson, and also Oregon's worst musicale. Nell covers for us if necessary, and very well. Can't imagine where she learned to do that. At first I cast it all as a great joke, but she would not be patronized. I can go among Catholics in town with no problem but otherwise the walls feel higher all the time.

Give my love to Mary and Henry. How is he, really? She won't say, which vexes me, but in her place I would do the same. I feel horrid about losing her garnets.

Loi is coming up April 2 on Consulate business. Risky duty, given the riots here. He says not to worry and promises a gala Chinatown dinner, which means I shall have to produce something in return, doubtless involving tinned meat. Nell says leave all to her, so perhaps I shall. I miss you too, if truth be told. Keep well – G

Joe looked out the window of his auction house. On the calendar it was spring, though five inches of fresh snow covered boardwalks and the office lamps glowed against the afternoon gloom. The town plow rumbled past, two patient Percherons dragging the big wooden blade toward Main Street. However, the river was open.

"Mike, I'll relieve you on those estimates if you take the sales all next week."

"Sure," said the junior auctioneer, sorting handbills. "You going somewhere?"

No need for secrecy. "Portland," Joe said.

REUNITED

APRIL 5, 1888

L EE LOI SAT at a borrowed desk in the Consulate's cramped Portland office, reading a circular from Washington. A California congressman thought all Chinese should carry a photo identification card, to prove legal residency. Lee hoped the so-called dog-tag plan would go away. He could end up assigned to it, as a known camera fiend. His latest was a sweet little box job from New York, so small that detectives used it, bought in case Joe required any more detecting. The last thing the West Coast consulates needed was an internal passport law. Over 110,000 Chinese lived in Gam Saan, 75,000 of them in California alone.

He looked up to see Joe Vincent at the front counter and bounded over, amazed.

"Joe, this is prime! What are you doing in Portland?"

"Pulling some strings. Checking on Nell."

"I heard most of it. Hard to imagine Grace in jail. No, wait, I take that back. But your Nell's a trouper. Tea, coffee, a drink? Fine to see you."

"Let's go for a walk," said Joe. He looked worried and tired, with new lines in his pleasant, mobile face. His hair was nearly all gray.

"How's the shoulder?"

"Fair. I feel it in cold weather."

They turned onto wet, leafless Burnside Street. In deference to an elder, Lee took the outside of the pavement. A passing bread van spattered him with mud.

"How are the boys?"

"I may have to put them in a Dai Fow school. Dr. Ing's about worn out. Dow learned some pulsology from him this winter. Yap's a stock boy in a dry-goods store. Keeps sending me questions about buyouts."

"How old is he now?"

"Thirteen, more or less. Nobody's sure."

Puddles reflected low rain clouds scudding overhead. Fir tree stumps filled empty lots. Joe gave a penny to the crossing sweeper, but Lee's spats were already a lost cause. They turned for the river, to admire the new bridge site. The Willamette was a half-mile wide, flowing north past marsh and island to merge with the Columbia, but the breeze smelled of coal smoke and bad drains. Misty rain beaded on their coats and faces like cloud breath.

"You may get help soon from the Imperial government."

"What? Can you say more?"

"We're demanding close to $350,000 in reparations for killing and property theft, probably including the Snake River massacre."

"Hot damn!" Joe threw up his hat. A passing dockhand laughed.

Late next day Joe walked along a block of small houses set back from the street, looking for 1340 State, which proved to be a two-story in the Queen Anne style, with gables and bow windows. No turret. Good, he hated turrets. Grace met him at the door, looking anxious. A smell of roast chicken filled the tiled entryway. Joe had an auctioneer's quick impression—pale-papered walls, golden oak furniture—before hearing Lee shout in the kitchen and then a string of frantic orders from Nell. "Come help," said Grace, seizing his hat.

Over apple slump and custard, Joe told about his afternoon with a retired U.S. senator.

"I went to see Jim Slater. He owns property out in La Grande. Interesting fellow, originally from Illinois. Also one of the few in eastern

Oregon who thinks the killers should hang. I said my greatest need was to arrest Evans, Canfield, and LaRue. He offered to petition the U.S. district attorney in Portland, even though it's an election year."

The great presidential campaign issue was Asian labor. With Chinese entry to the United States still frozen, battles over a new immigration ban consumed both governments. The timing was as bad as could be. If the measure passed, a Chinese citizen who left the States could not return for decades, if ever. Already the Six Companies offered cut-rate tickets home and free passage for emigrants over sixty.

Lee said, "Most of us, we're *here*. We can't go home. Talk about shortsighted. Who builds new railroads? Who picks the crops? Peking is angry. The Embassy in Washington plans to fight."

"They can try," said Joe. "You're using *Virginius*?" A tenuous precedent to force a big federal payback, but better than none. Twelve years ago, Spain's navy captured a gun-running ship, the *Virginius*, then executed dozens of crew men and passengers as pirates. To prevent future claims, Spain eventually paid $80,000 for every American and British life. Now China planned to apply that international indemnity rule to the Snake River deaths.

"Pray it works," said Lee. He passed Nell the custard jug, then looked at Joe. "You ever wish the Deep Creek bodies washed up in someone else's town?"

"All the time." It was only the truth. "But the murders came on my watch. Back in '86 I could have gone to the docks and stopped Chea Po's boats. I shrugged. And I let them go."

By eight, Joe lay in the reclining armchair by the fire, eyes closed, as content as he ever got. He liked this spare, unfashionable little house, nothing in it costly, everything well arranged. Out in the kitchen he heard laughter. Lee had brought Grace a novel about the Northwest uprising of '85 — *Annette, The Métis Spy* — and was reading bits out loud.

"'Before the songstress of the sunny Saskatchewan could gather her routed senses, the beastly rebel Riel was sent sprawling with a

237

sabre-blow' — wait, it gets better — 'and soon the Nez Perce lifted his torpid nostril. He could smell the ochre war-paint a mile off. But first, cold quail and fine wines awaited in the luncheon hamper.'"

Joe had read it, too. He thought it was a pretty good story, till now. Nell wrestled the book from Lee but an hour later was drowsing on the sofa, her head on Joe's lap. The others talked till nearly eleven, faster and faster.

Reunited, Lee thought fondly, *and every one of us the better for it.* He looked at Grace, then at Joe. He looked at Grace again. Then he took a steadying breath, leaned over, and told Nell, "Kiddo, the Consulate driver is coming any minute. Let me drop you back at school." And to Joe: "I'll take her to the door."

He decided he did it just right; lighthearted, oblivious. On the porch, saying goodbye, Grace took both his hands in hers and held them. *Thank you, Loi.*

Joe put on his reading glasses to study the big framed watercolor over the bookcase. Two snowy egrets, wading a Louisiana marsh at sunset. The fluent brushwork caught the wetland's life in ribbons and washes of pure color — spring green, cobalt, scarlet, oyster white. Joe leaned in, then back, trying to fix the moment of alchemy.

"He was a wonderful artist."

"Oh, he *was.*"

"It's a love letter," said Joe, staring at warm sea light across a sundown marsh.

She found his hand. "Come see the upstairs."

An hour later he murmured, "Why now?"

"I meant what I wrote. I won't interfere in a marriage. But you don't have one."

They lay watching the moonlight.

After a while Joe said, "Attacking the Tammany house was likely Evans on his own. But then Libby told Vollmer Nell's location, and Vollmer told Blue." He sighed. "No orders needed. John knew Evans would take it from there."

"Or else — I'm sorry, but —"

"Libby knows Evans. I see that. I don't care. I might have lost both you and Nell."

"We're not going anywhere."

"Because you jumped in. Christ, I want this over. I'm trying to do something right, for once, and it keeps blowing up in my face."

"I know. Old go-along, water-smooth Joe."

"It just seems like everything behind me, that I spent my life building, is ruined and broken. Libby takes fraud and murder in stride. The older kids are set, for better or worse. And people I spent years protecting cut me on the street, move their business elsewhere."

She rubbed her cheekbone along his good shoulder. Half a lifetime.

"So you'll stop?"

"I can't stop. I have to see it to the end. My fault, you know. In everything. I loved you from the start, Gracie, and I sent you away."

"Sleep," she said. Spring rain spattered on the roof.

"Ruined my life."

"Oh, save it for court, Joe."

They lay together, laughing. She wiped his eyes with the heel of her hand and kissed him. He didn't feel fifty-seven, or forty, or even thirty. He felt nineteen. *Thanks, Loi.*

Joe Vincent slept.

RED LEDGER

THE ONLY WAY he could know a case was to put it on paper. Fact pursued and captured, stacked in lists, circled and underlined. Meaning distilled to pattern, pattern locked into summary, every summary indexed. The smartest lawyers he knew could cite and quote with never a glance at the page. Joe needed a blueprint, root cellar to roof beam. He needed his notes. For the Snake River case, he needed a whole new ledger. In a Portland stationery shop, he ran a finger down the shelf, considering, and chose one in pale buff paper, lined, with fine black rules, left and right, and dark blue page numbers. Sturdy dark red covers, no label. A harvest book, the clerk said, for farmers and ranchers. Joe liked that kind of company. He was looking to plant and gather himself.

He returned to an ice-glazed Lewiston, cold and still after a late silver thaw. Few court cases came his way; Harry Akers avoided winter law enforcement. Auction work stayed scarce. Raymond House had a manager. Joe kept at his studies. Parties, theatricals, town meetings – he skipped them all. After a while the invitations tailed off, and also the handshakes.

The chinook swept in, the worst snows in memory melted, the river rose, but only a little, and again the wheat fields above the bluffs shimmered green. Yates wrote, asking if he wanted to ride the Tammany fence lines and plan improvements. Joe said maybe, meaning no. Libby and her father returned from Boise. The Vincents' glacial split frightened their well-off friends. Joe's invitations tailed off more.

In mid-April, McCully sent word that Frank Vaughan had turned state's evidence, naming the other six gang members in the Snake River killings. A circuit court grand jury indicted them all for murdering ten Chinese. *Whose real names to the grand jury are unknown,* the document said. Joe sat down hard, staring at the letter.

All through the spring came a barrage of blue notes. She would not stand for disrespect. She was going to the river to throw herself in. He was a —. Joe looked twice, amazed Libby knew that kind of language, or would write it down. She would publish his iniquities to the world. She wanted him to report to the Lelands' *immediately,* so she could tell a terrible secret, something no one else knew. She praised Nell's progress at boarding school. She wondered if he could look over her new editorials; he was so wise and good with words. She was dreadfully low and kept laudanum always by. She needed to know *at once* if he would try the Congress run. Joe ignored it all.

One warm, overcast morning, Alonzo Leland leaned on the barn's half-door.

"We don't see you much any more."

"You don't see me at all, Lon. The deal we made? It's over."

"God almighty, Joe. My poor Libby!"

"Not that poor. Better ask about her Camas land buys. And find a new Congressman. I won't run. Ever."

"Jesus. Have you gone mad? Is this about your damn Chinese obsession?"

"I'm through, Lon. Shut the door as you leave."

He could tell Alonzo stood outside a while before walking away.

Last fall, says the Wallowa *Signal,* a camp of thirty-four Chinese moved on one of the bars on Snake River to spend the winter mining for gold. It is known they had a large boat and a good supply of provisions, and, it is estimated, about $30,000 in gold dust. The bar on which they encamped is very isolated, and since spring has opened a party of men passing one day noticed no one around the camp, and on an investigation found the bodies of two Chinamen, who had undoubtedly been killed by shooting in the head, and the other Chinamen were nowhere to be found. Their tents were blown down, and everything looked as if it had been deserted for some time.

Is this a revival of the old story, that has been heretofore published, or is it some new account about missing Chinamen? Who knows that any thirty-four Chinamen went onto any such bar and went to mining last fall? We discredit the story and shall do so until further evidence be made manifest.

—Lewiston Teller, April 26, 1888

Every week Joe went to the Stantons' for supper, and he made sure they came to the hotel whenever the special was roast lamb, the doctor's favorite. The noisy main dining room was hard on Henry now — *too damn many strangers in this town* — so Joe served them in the private parlor, with candles and wine. The Stantons held hands under the table like a honeymoon couple, even with Joe there, an amazing concession. They always asked how the case was coming on. *I'm still learning,* he always said.

Time, land, water, violent death. And driving everything, the gold. He built a timeline, going back to the unexplained murders from '82 on, then Tom Douglas in '83, and so on down to the present. Then he wrote profiles of each person involved: name, place of origin, education, religion, lines of work, places lived, families, pastimes, failures, enemies, losses. The Chinese miners were hardest, in many cases impossible, even with Lee's expert aid.

From his first day as Lewiston marshal, Joe Vincent had kept ledgers, week by week: correspondence, news clippings, jotted observations on embezzlers and ether parties. Now he sat in the barn and scanned the volumes, intent on pattern. From 1874 to 1882 the logs stayed routine. Early in '83 he sensed something new, no more than a twitch on a thread, as inexplicables found their way into his private annals. The rancher who never came home from elk hunting. A young cowhand hamstrung and left to die in deep snow. An old reprobate shot in the head, near his mining cabin up the Snake.

After the November 1886 election, Joe Vincent wrote no more town ledgers. But reading back through his homemade chronicle of Nez Perce County life, he saw the trail of a human wolf.

Maps. He craved maps, and the upper Snake had almost none. He pasted together a half-dozen sheets of tracing paper and started drawing the Deep Creek region, peak and stream, range and valley, forest and town. Capturing the consecutive sweeps of action — miners, killers, trackers — sank the knowledge deep. Joe learned best by hand. Only if he set a passage in type, or wrote it out, did he have it by heart. He thought of Deep Creek, river, cove, and cliff, and longed for Lim Ah's map, eight months in the making. He even knew where it was: moldering in his barn's lean-to, a mass of scorched, decaying pulp down in the sacks of mining-camp debris. The boys pointed it out once. Of all the recovered evidence, Dow asked only to keep a scrap of dirty red flannel, Yap an obsidian arrowhead.

The stretch of river between Deep Creek and Dug Bar was such contested ground that Joe added the Nez Perce to his tale of place, asking first Grace, then Georges to send him memories from the years when tribal politics split the Nimipu, treaty families versus nontreaty, parent against child, husband against wife.

My grandparents rode out to meet the early wagon trains, replied Georges in his careful Training School hand, *and the first miners too, with food and offers of guiding. Kindness to strangers, that was our way.* A postscript, in Ellen's writing: *We all make mistakes.* Then Georges again: *Joe, that does not mean you.*

By May Joe knew that Frank Vaughan had recanted, telling a county judge that his earlier statements left a wrong impression. The six men were not acting together in the killings. Full blame, Frank now said, should go to Evans, Canfield, and LaRue. Bobby McMillan, Carl Hughes, and Hiram Maynard then gave nearly identical depositions to Frank McCully, the acting county clerk. McCully sent a copy to Joe.

Q. How far were you from the Chinese camp when this shooting took place?

A. About two or three hundred yards.

Q. How far was Robert McMillan?

A. Near me.

Q. Was anyone else near you?

A. Bruce Evans was near, but not so close as McMillan.

Q. Were Canfield and LaRue near you?

A. No, they were not.

Q. After the killing, did you and McMillan go down to the boat?

A. We went to the Chinese camp, but not to the boat.

Q. What did you see when you got down to this Chinese camp?

A. Four or five dead Chinamen.

Q. Were you a witness before the grand jury that indicted these persons?

A. Yes sir.

Q. Why did you implicate Maynard, Hughes, and McMillan then, and not now?

A. I didn't implicate them then any more than I have now.

Joe went back to McCully's letter. As soon as Vaughan gave his statement, thirty-four prominent local citizens (including the grand jury foreman) put up eight hundred dollars and petitioned for bail, on the grounds that the four were illegally held. Two judges agreed and let the men go.

Inventive. Joe wondered who their lawyer was. He then got a letter from Boise, offering the clerkship of Idaho's First Judicial District. He accepted. What the hell. Maybe a bribe, maybe a signal of support from the Democratic governor; maybe they actually wanted him.

Slater could not budge any district attorney in Portland, at any level, to hunt fugitives out of state. The Marshals' Service gave the same reply: no money, no power. Oregon's noisy populist governor said the Snake case was an Idaho matter because the bodies washed up on the river's eastern shore. Idaho replied that since the murders occurred in Oregon, the Territory had no jurisdiction. Joe resigned his shiny new clerkship. Another bridge, burning.

In June he added to the red ledger his pamphlets and newspaper clippings on anti-Chinese violence across the Northwest, listed and summarized. He also resigned from the Lewiston town council, the GAR post, the Board of Trade, and the North Idaho Cattle Fair committee.

After a bitter exchange on the church steps about heathen Chinese, he quit the Presbyterians too—the Leland choice, a sound political base—and next Sunday went cautiously across the street to the Unitarian meetinghouse, unsure of his welcome.

Halfway through the first Emerson reading, he saw in memory the print-shop attic of forty years past and the brown-haired apprentice sitting in a circle of light, sleeves turned up, copying passages from the *Essays* into his first commonplace ledger. The clink of a pen nib at a glass inkwell came back too, and the wild sea-smell of a whale-oil lamp. *Nature hates monopolies and exceptions. Treat men as pawns and ninepins, and you shall suffer as well as they.*

As July heat bleached the hills across the Snake and corn and tomatoes ripened in the market gardens along C Street, Joe went twice to Portland, once to meet with Senator Slater and the U.S. district attorney and once to argue for his own standing at the Oregon trial, now set for August 28.

Slater told him that people in power watched and waited. Over the fourteen months since Joe and Nell went fishing by the Snake, the Chinese question shadowed American affairs, foreign and domestic. The Supreme Court ruled twice in support of the Chinese-expulsion movement. In San Jose a Chinatown burned. Riots, round-ups, purges, strikes, boycotts. But the Chinese kept resisting, often with white support, defying job bans, forcing arrests in the criminal courts.

The Snake River massacre was likely the worst mass murder in the peacetime West. A guilty verdict plus federal reparations could sway world politics for years. If Chea Po and his miners had died near a city, the publicity would have been unrelenting. But even a front-page *New York Times* story out of Walla Walla — "Murdered for Their Gold Dust" — brought no rush of reporters to Enterprise or Lewiston. None, in fact. The Snake River country was just too far from everything and everyone. Evans knew that. Now Joe did too.

At the end of July he learned he could advise the Wallowa County prosecutor, a major concession. Consul Frederick Bee wrote to say that an official representative of the Imperial Chinese government would attend the Oregon trial: a Mr. Lee Loi.

Joe was living on savings. The auction business he sold off to a relieved junior partner, and Raymond House might have to follow. Weisgerber, the brewer, stopped his credit: *Sorry, Joe, wholesale orders are cash only.* Some he thought might back him did not. The Episcopal minister, yes, and the Catholic priest, but not the Methodist pastor or the Latter-Day Saints stake council. School principal and town greengrocer called him a renegade, the one behind his back, the other to his face, but the piano teacher shook his hand and the Grange president asked him to dinner. Ranchers and businessmen did not need the Chinese. Farmers might.

Joe kept his public face forbearing, like a five-dollar Good Shepherd chromo, until the livery stable owner told the Delmonico lunch crowd that Vincent was a disgrace to public office and a race traitor besides.

"I cut you a lot of favors, Walton!" Joe heard himself yell. "God damn it, I backed your first loan!"

Some of his constituents would not stand near. Others were too hearty. Quite a number still wanted to argue. *Bad for the town, Mr. Vincent, flat-out bad, can't you see?* His sole lunch companions now were Rob Grostein and Abe Binnard. Their matter-of-fact friendship kept him steady. Alonzo crossed the street to avoid him but sent statehood manifestos by the bushel. Every anguished cover note accused Joe of bringing down all they once built together. At least Alonzo had principles and stuck by them: *Never look back. Growth at any price.*

The Hip Sip manager let him know that Chea Po's grain merchant stood ready to testify. Joe deposed the man instead, to save a month of hard travel and lost profit. He had no idea what other Chinese of Lewiston thought about his private war. They never spoke to him, only bowed.

By August 1 the red ledger bulged and he tied it shut with twine. Harvest time was nearly on him. Last of all, he briefed the murder testimony. The early coroner reports, even ghastlier in retrospect. The interview with Lee She and his party of Salt Creek miners. The accounts by Dow, Yap, and Jackson. Sometimes — not always — the cousins recalled enough details about the Deep Creek slaughter for clear identification. The tall blond man who killed Elder Boss so slowly: Evans. The two boys who laughed as they tortured the assayer: McMillan and Vaughan. The man in dark hat and blue vest who shouted and wept as he chopped and slashed: Maynard, far gone in rapture, speaking in tongues.

Almost seven months since Joe last spoke to Libby. Not easy in a ten-street town. He supposed they would get an Indiana-style divorce, after separation for sixteen months. Multnomah County, over in Oregon, was a well-known divorce mill. Lee Loi's generation split up with no more sentiment than for a business deal gone bad, but his own peers invested heavily in false-front lives. Now if Lina Vollmer wanted to weigh in . . . but Joe knew she never would.

John Vollmer remained cordial, a well man checking an enemy's wasting disease. *Hello. Still here? Pity.* The Vollmer empire was growing so fast that local battles bored him, though some details he did not neglect. The replacement candidate for Congress was an ardent Vollmerite from Coeur d'Alene. Joe Junior was up in the silver-mine country too, thriving, like Lonny and Letty far away. Joe heard from none of them and figured he might never. The money was all Grandpa Leland's anyway. Cupboard love.

Once Joe did see the mask drop. One August afternoon he turned onto the Main Street boardwalk and came face to face with Vollmer and a delegation from Boise. Two of the legislators knew Joe from his stint as territorial representative. Trapped, he shook hands, endured introductions. A man from Eagle Rock, the newest boomtown on the Snake, said wisely, "Big plans for you all, we hear, thanks to John's colleagues back East."

"Cronies, don't you mean?" said Joe. The others looked at Vollmer.

He shoved his face near, color high, eyes narrowed. "I want an apology for that, Vincent."

"Judge Vincent to you, sir. Enjoy your stay, gentlemen." All the way down the boardwalk, he felt the eyes.

On his summer visits to Portland he saw neither Nell nor Grace. They were already in the Cascades, convincing Georges's tourists not to step off sandbars on the downstream side. Grace brushed off his thanks for keeping Nell safe, but both knew her St. Louis years were repaid. They now wrote to each other two and three times a week. When Lewiston society decamped for Lake Waha, no one invited Joe up. *Too bad about Vincent. Leave him alone with whatever the hell it is that he does.*

August 15. The red ledger was full. Lee Loi and Grace, Nell and the boys, were due any day. *And I'm still judge,* Joe told himself. *Until November the seventh. Ten weeks to track them, ten weeks to try them. Damn it, I'm still judge.*

"Will the killers talk? Can we find the others?"

"I nominate Nell for jury foreman," said Lee.

"Seconded. Maynard, Hughes, and young McMillan will speak in court. Frank Vaughan too, but as state's witness. I think LaRue is dead, killed by Evans or Canfield. Investigation is not really for a judge, so I'm outside the boundary of my duties a little."

A lot. What else should they know? He tried to think.

"The trial is in Enterprise, not Joseph. It's a raw little town, the new county seat. No courthouse yet. They'll probably use the hotel, which won't room anyone but Nell and me, so I rented a place for all of us."

To the boys he said, "We'll avoid the river, going over there. No one will see or hear you."

Lee saw Dow's relief and shared it. Those who waited at Deep Creek had been hungry a long while. After a baffling, painful year of study, Lee knew mostly that he would never make a geomancer, or even a village *wu*. However, he was no longer asleep, nor was he defenseless.

"Elder Boss and the rest got added to the big indemnity claim," he told Dow. "Forty lives."

Grace asked, "Does the money go to miners' families or a government pocket?"

"Direct to survivors. Win the trial, and another $100,000 goes on the claim. That's $2,500 per family. About eight years of lost income."

Yap said something anxious in Cantonese and put a hand to the amulet strung around his neck, a red clay fish.

"Until seas run dry and the rocks crumble," Lee told him.

Grace stood in the backyard, laundry snapping and belling around her in the burning midday wind. She unpegged another sheet. A noisy croquet match was under way, with Mary in the lead, thanks to Henry as umpire. If Oliver had lived, if she had married, what fine grandparents they would have made. All she'd brought them was trouble and disappointment. Maybe she should run away to sea. Or Europe, at long last. She said as much to Joe and Lee, when they called her in to tally documents.

"Europe? Feel free," Joe said. They were all hot and tired. Henry arrived, winded, and lowered himself into the armchair. Joe went to find the lemonade, Grace the gin. Henry put up both hands for the glass. His tremor was not so bad today. At the parlor window, Grace looked across the deserted late-summer street.

"You can visit Paris any time you want. The liners don't allow unaccompanied women, period. One of you would have to bring me, like a parcel. Like a pet."

Joe, still writing, held out a folder of legal papers. She took it.

"When conditions can't get any lower, someone digs out another cellar. How do you think Lee felt when the United States officially welcomed any immigrant except the insane, the syphilitic, and the Chinese?"

"Hear, hear," Lee said.

"Thank you. What if I say girls should go to Yale? Even you're shocked. Look at Georges. He's a good Episcopalian. He loves the Camas. But he and Ellen had to move two hundred miles away to qualify as civilized and claim their half-section. Do you think we *like* being picturesque every summer; yes sir, don't hit your horse like that, sir, isn't it remarkable, madam, we read *Harper's Weekly* too?"

"Georges reads the *Cattleman's Gazette*," Joe said. "And his bank balance. Otherwise, sounds like a pretty fair stump speech to me."

"Hear, hear," said Henry, raising his glass to Joe.

"Oh, stop," she said, counting pages. "School opens in a month."

Lee gave her a long look, then turned to Joe. "Is the trial open admission?"

"Yes, but they've timed it so farmers can't serve. Harvest hardship. The jury will all be ranchers, like the defendants. And my role is limited."

"Don't tell me you can't help prosecute."

"I can, but my boss is Jim Rand, the district attorney. He doesn't know that much about the case. I'll assist him." He patted the red ledger. "Use all my evidence. Write out questions and cross-examinations. Prepare him in every way. He's new at the job, and I'm used to juries."

Joe had not tried a case in a decade. Henry knew it; the others did not.

"What can we do?" asked Lee.

"Learn everything, both of you. In case you have to replace me."

He was serious, she saw, as serious as Lee when he showed them the leather belt of gold coins he wore beneath his coat. Diplomatic issue, for bribes and emergencies, replacing the gun he could not legally carry.

She browsed in the red ledger, amazed at the meticulous reconstruction, the lonely labor. The men who owned Idaho would never let Joe hold office again. He was too dangerous. She wondered if he understood that. Probably not. Even now he believed in reasoned justice. Lee too; the courts would be his battleground well into a new century. All her fights were lost.

At three-thirty in the morning, Henry went down to the back porch, a slow, shuffling journey. Grace could hear each rasping breath. In her girlhood he took the same stairs two at a time, buoyant, indestructible, always on call. His creased doctor's satchel and stovepipe hat still sat on the front-hall table. Au-ma must be more tired than she admitted, to sleep through one of his bad nights. Grace gave him time to settle, then brought a blanket for his legs and stroked his hand in silence. Above the poplars arced a lone shooting star, then a cascade of meteors, then darkness again.

"My dear, you're the warrior," he said finally. "Georges is too gentle. Jackson only cares about the horses."

"I can't, Papa."

"I think you must." And a moment later: "I'm sorry, you know. So very sorry."

She whispered, "I don't understand." Henry did not reply.

Curled on the glider, she kept watch until dawn, guarding their summer family, but against what dangers she could not say.

TACTICS

A T ENTERPRISE they moved into the rear of an empty store. The owner had gone to Montana, taking almost all the furniture but leaving the mice. Grace and Nell hung a calico curtain down the middle of the single stifling room, for decorum, even after so many days of wagon camping. The lot in back was hardpan and weeds. The neighbors kept pigs. And the trial was not at the hotel after all, but in a tent down the street.

"Tell me again why this place is a county seat?" Grace said. But she already knew. Enterprise offered a better railhead for the eastern Oregon wool clip. Ranches in this broad, sunny valley ran the best sheep she had ever seen.

Next morning Joe and Lee Loi rode over to Frank McCully's spread. Lee didn't care for McCully. He was like a Company elder: all smiles, no real help. Humphreys was even more deferential, but when the sheriff watched Joe, Lee saw a glint of venom.

"Evans and the rest came in too easy," Joe agreed as they trotted back to town. "But at this point—"

Lee twisted in the saddle to study forest and peak, fine as any stereoscope view of Switzerland. Only a big plate-glass camera would do these mountains justice. Lee had spent many childhood hours looking between his legs at a reverse world, choosing moments to save forever, imagining China's coastal skies leached to sepia or gray.

Dow and Yap, Oregon-born, were always asking about Canton Province. Lee surprised himself by remembering so much, from the whirl of fighting kites to wild games of tag with stall holders' sons at the Panyu greenmarket.

At least Joe and Grace seemed in good form, Lee thought, despite the coming ordeal. Most nights on the trail, Lee woke to hear them beside the dying campfire still, laughing softly, finishing each other's sentences. His parents used to talk together like that. Deep in her bedroll, Nell was listening too; she caught his eye and smiled.

On Tuesday, Joe woke to the sound of wheels. A line of wagons and buggies stretched through town. Hopping on one leg, wrestling a double handful of linen smallclothes, Lee nodded at the stove, where Nell had left tea and crackers. "Thanks," said Joe. Anything more he would not keep down.

"What's all that?"

"Chinese underwear," said Lee. Joe left him to it.

The tent was hot and packed. Dais and witness box looked built overnight, and seating was motley — kitchen chairs, barstools, rocking chairs, and pine logs arrayed on trampled grass. Prosecution and defense sat left and right at tables carried over from the hotel. The young district attorney, James Rand, thin and tense, was already going over notes.

As Joe pushed his way toward the prosecution table, he spotted Dow and Yap in the last row, with Nell and Grace between. Mrs. Vaughan and Mrs. McMillan were the only other female spectators. Town women loved murder trials, but this was rural Oregon, and word was out that the case was grisly. Twenty Chinese waited together in the rear; workmen, farm hands, a half-dozen merchants.

At ten Frank McCully ducked under the tent flap; he, not Humphreys, would serve as bailiff and clerk. Joe watched Peter O'Sullivan take the judge's chair. Frowning, dark-haired, well-tended belly, neat full beard. Blue suit. *Damn.*

Joe remembered Senator Slater's briefing all too well. Judge O'Sullivan was forty-three, Ireland-born, a Missouri grocery clerk turned farmer. Homesteaded near Enterprise eight years ago. Some experience back East as a small-town mayor. Dangerous when crossed. ("O'Sullivan has two suits," Slater warned. "Dark gray and dark blue. If he's trying to impress, he picks the gray. Blue is for politics.")

"All rise," McCully said.

Once the house settled, Rand stayed on his feet. "Your Honor, request permission to seat a distinguished visitor."

"Granted. Who is he? *Where* is he?"

"Right here, sir." Rand nodded toward the entrance.

A man in Chinese court dress strode down the center aisle. Over dark boots and breeches he wore a high-collared robe of dark blue silk, embroidered in gold and silver, the billowing hem split four ways, as for a warrior on horseback. A tall red cap trailed two broad black ribbons, and beneath the robe's nine-dragon folds shone the yellow jacket of a royal envoy. In this makeshift country courtroom suddenly stood the official representative of the Guangxu Emperor of the Glorious Succession, first in the House of Aisin-Gioro, His Imperial Majesty the Son of Heaven, ruler of the civilized world, earthly mirror of the August Personage of Jade, lord of ten thousand years.

Even Joe felt the power and strangeness like a punch in the stomach. Lee looked like a young god. Hauling that trunk halfway across Oregon was well worth it. Joe stood up.

"Judge O'Sullivan, allow me to introduce Mr. Lee Loi, senior attaché to the Chinese Imperial Consulate in San Francisco, sent here as diplomatic observer and representative by the Chinese consul, Mr. Frederick Bee."

O'Sullivan was half out of his chair.

"Jesus. Does he speak English?"

"Mr. Lee was graduated from an American college," said Joe, starting to enjoy himself for the first time in months. "A Congregationalist school of note in the New England states."

"Good morning, Judge," said the Chinese attaché, and bowed. "My credentials, sir."

He passed over the scroll of bona fides. O'Sullivan ran a cautious hand down its cascade of red seals and golden ribbons. *Bumpkin dazzlers,* the younger Consulate staff called them.

Lee turned toward the murmuring crowd and stood still for a moment, keeping his face stern, giving everyone a good look. Two of the older Chinese laborers knelt. He bowed again, just a touch, sat down behind the prosecutors, enameled fan case clicking against the wooden bench, and shook out the wide glimmering sleeves of his robe. The embroidered figures danced and shone: mountain, river, dragon, symbols of a just and balanced universe.

Joe passed over tablet and pencil, as planned. A Chinese envoy making careful notes might cow the judge a little, and they wanted an independent record. Lee started diagramming the right-hand table, with its imposing line of bearded attorneys.

"Who's over there?"

Joe whispered: "For the defense, Piper, McGorven, Ivanhoe, and Olmstead."

"They represent the four defendants?"

"Just the three accused."

"Who represents Vaughan?"

"Good question." Joe scanned the tent, then stared. "Son of a bitch."

"What?" If Lee moved his head too fast, the nobleman's cap slipped.

"Far right, second row, beside the Vaughans. Short and mean. He's a lawyer from Portland. Fancy firm. Can't think of his name. Grace may know."

Joe barely recognized the defendants filing toward the table. Sunday suits, scrubbed necks. Without the beards and backcountry grime, Hughes and Maynard looked years younger. Hughes winked at someone deep in the crowd. Maynard put his hand on Bobby's shoulder, and the boy shot him a grateful glance. All four looked for

Joe at once, then whispered together. Mr. Salem was no longer anonymous.

Rand listened to Joe's own whisper, then rose. "Your Honor, the defendants are sitting close to each other and talking. That will allow them to confer on testimony. We ask that they be moved apart and only allowed to speak with their defense counsels."

So ordered. Much pushing of chairs ensued. Lee added a hash mark in the margin. Score one for Joe.

McCully read the charges against the defendants, slowly and clearly, naming the six parties as Hiram Maynard, Carl Hughes, Robert McMillan, James T. Canfield, Bruce B. Evans, and Homer O. LaRue. Hughes raised a hand: his birth name was Hezekiah. The judge ordered a record change, then asked the three accused to rise and face the court.

"This procedure is an arraignment and you have heard the charges of murder. Normally we would now ask for your pleas, but three defendants are missing. We will therefore adjourn and continue tomorrow, when we will hear the pleas and empanel a jury."

To the audience he said, "All citizens volunteering for jury duty must appear at nine o'clock tomorrow and submit names, addresses, and ages to the court. Any objections?"

He looked around the tent. No one had expected such a brief session.

"Hearing none, we are adjourned until ten o'clock tomorrow morning."

In the hubbub, Joe conferred with Rand, then turned to Lee Loi, who said, "Sorry I got all dressed for a ten-minute dance. Why the holdup?"

"The jury delay? I wish I knew."

"Maybe he does," said Lee, looking toward Vaughan's urbane attorney.

"Got him," said Joe. "Jonas Herron, from Portland. His name is all over the Vollmer land deals. He must not like the odds. Tomorrow he'll have handpicked faces in line."

Lee watched the Chinese workmen at the back stand aside to let the crowd pass.

"Can you challenge?"

"Maybe. But the judge decides if challenges are valid. Out here, we'll be lucky to get men who can read. Our best hope is a hung jury. A Quaker or a Mennonite would help."

"They're scarce in this county," said Rand, studying Dow and Yap. "One more time, sir—what makes you think we can get those two on the stand?"

"O'Sullivan and I shook on it. Eyewitnesses, I said."

"Did you tell him they were Chinese?"

"Hardly."

"You know about O'Sullivan, then. And Pennoyer."

He did. Senator Slater's briefing was clear. Oregon's new governor was a showboating lumber baron from New York. During the big war he was openly pro-Confederate and all for slavery. Now he was all for unchecked, unrepentant profit. The citizens of Portland, he liked to announce, obviously spent more time in the outhouse than at their business affairs; just look at all the sewage in the Willamette River.

Governor Pennoyer hated bankers, colleges, and the federal government almost as much as he despised Chinese. Two summers back he had taken over a Portland civil rights convention and demanded the immediate expulsion of every Chinese in town, but the city's mayor, the former governor, hundreds of armed citizens, and two hundred special deputies faced down Pennoyer's mob—or his lawful militia of concerned citizens, depending on which newspaper reported.

To rural and labor voters, the governor was a hero; to moderates and reformers, a demagogue. But all agreed he was generous with political patronage. Pennoyer had even named Peter O'Sullivan to the lucrative post of Wallowa County road commissioner. Right after making him county judge.

"Pennoyer's a Harvard man," said Lee.

257

OBJECTIONS

O N WEDNESDAY MORNING both Joe and Lee were at the tent before nine. Lee still wore the tall hat and yellow envoy's jacket, but under a shorter, lighter robe. He'd made his point and didn't want heat stroke. The sky was like brass, the morning windless.

A line of volunteer jurors was already forming. Jonas Herron again stood with the Vaughan family, turning his back as Joe walked past. Joe went straight up the aisle to coach Jim Rand, showing papers, pointing out items, bucking up the prosecutor every few moments with a quick, encouraging smile.

The public filed in, a smaller crowd than yesterday. Grace, Nell, Dow, and Yap found seats in the back row. When O'Sullivan called the court to order and asked the defendants to rise and give their pleas, Lee thought they seemed far less nervous. Three responses of "Not guilty" brought a murmur of assent, and the judge gaveled for order. He began calling names from his jury list. Rand got nowhere.

"No sir, never heard of the killings. I do know Hiram a little. We ain't friends."

"I heard, but I forget the details. Bobby used to play with my son."

"I read something in the paper, a long time ago. Carl? Shoot, Carl is a neighbor."

Though Joe scribbled note after note, Rand won no challenges, except for the man with a grudge against the McMillan family, a fence dispute. Lee fanned his face with the tablet but kept writing. The line of hash marks, mostly against Joe, grew and grew.

Defense questioning stayed tepid. If a juror was illiterate, fine; if he had never employed a Chinese, even better. Often the lawyers turned to Herron, who would shake his head yes or no. Joe slid a note over to Rand.

"Your Honor, an objection."

"We're not at testimony yet, Mr. Rand. Raise a point of order instead."

"Sorry. Point of order. The defense lawyers are taking advice from an attorney for the state's chief witness, which is" — he squinted at Joe's handwriting — "irregular and illegal."

O'Sullivan told the lawyers to make their own decisions. Herron stared down the row at Joe.

Selection went so slowly that the audience began to drowse or talk, or slip over to the hotel for a drink. By twelve-thirty the trial had a dozen jurors, two alternates, and an adjournment until two o'clock. Grace warned Dow and Yap to stay together while she and Nell hurried the three blocks to their rented store and back; on a court day, only the desperate used public privies, and ladies not at all. Judge O'Sullivan, buttoned into his blue wool suit, was flushed and sweating. Herron and Joe seemed utterly composed.

When the judge asked for opening statements, Rand introduced his assisting counsel, then announced the prosecution would prove that Hughes, Maynard, and McMillan (he pointed out each one) committed multiple murder a year ago last May, at two places on the Snake River. He said nothing about the brutality of the killings, nor about witnesses.

Piper rose, introduced the other defense attorneys, and asked if he might speak on their behalf. O'Sullivan nodded. Piper put his hands in his pockets, strolled to the jury box, and talked about his ten fine years of hunting trips in the Wallowas and his admiration for decent people building a Christian civilization in an Indian wilderness. The audience sat up, gratified.

"— and for you to entrust me with protecting your neighbors from government inquisition gives me the same feeling of responsibility and dignity as was felt when the forefathers of our country arranged, in equally trying and primitive places, the acquisitions that gave our country birth and us a home of freedom. Verily, the spirit goes with the country, and the Pacific slope is as well favored with pioneers and patriots as was the Atlantic in years gone by."

Any way Grace turned, she was three hundred miles from a law library. A search on Piper and Herron would turn up something ripe; she just knew it. Back in March, Joe had asked McCully for the names of counsel. A local firm, over in Baker City. But this kind of legal talent defended rail barons and timber kings.

"Consider, friends, what the depositions say — and what they do not. The defendants killed no one, they made no plans to kill, and they could not prevent the killings. Those heinous acts were all the work of three men who long ago escaped these parts."

Looking pained, Piper told the jurors the charges were an insult to Wallowa County, and the trial a waste of public money. Grace winced; Nell's grip on her hand was fierce, the applause prolonged. O'Sullivan took his time about gaveling for order.

The district attorney called Frank Vaughan, but Piper rose once more to note that his esteemed colleague Mr. Herron of Portland would sit at the defense table to represent Mr. Vaughan's interests. Joe started scribbling again.

"Another point of order, Your Honor. Mr. Herron is not of this county and has not practiced in this region. Is he qualified to represent his client, especially if we get into matters requiring" — Rand peered at the note — "local knowledge?"

Herron smiled. "Well, sir, if you are inquiring about local knowledge, then I must ask why your associate prosecutor is not from this county at all, nor even from the great state of Oregon, but from the Territory of *I*-da-ho, many miles from here and far from the scene of the alleged crime. Is this gentleman qualified to assist you, in any way, at any time?'"

Rand stood his ground. "J. K. Vincent is an experienced investigator and has knowledge of this case highly relevant to our prosecution. He has served this region as a judge, a marshal, a sheriff, and a federal commissioner. If the United States has placed so much trust in him, then we can too."

Herron tipped his chair back. "I have no doubt that Mr. Vincent has served the public well in *I*-da-ho. He is also a hotelkeeper, and has served up many glasses of beer in his time, I warrant."

Laughter.

"You were always a good customer, Jonas," said Joe.

Again O'Sullivan pounded for order, and nodded to Rand, who again called Frank Vaughan, appearing for the prosecution but as a hostile witness. Frank kept his voice so low that Rand asked him each time to speak louder, but soon the young man sat mute, hands trapped between his knees. "You want a break, son?" O'Sullivan inquired. Frank shook his head.

Next Rand reviewed the legal grounding for the case, the rules of evidence, and the categories of murder, to be sure jurors understood the mechanics of this roundabout quest for justice. *Take it slow,* Joe had counseled. *Slow, firm, and simple.* But Rand was nervous and rushed through the key explanations; Joe wondered how much even a friendly jury might absorb. He stole another look at the defense team just as Herron crooked a finger; a junior attorney handed over the desired document in seconds. Nice to have staff. Rand had come to trial with a mere six pages of case notes.

"Can't you force a recess?" Lee whispered. Joe shook his head without turning around. Thinking for two was hard enough without facing Lee's distress, or Nell's trusting gaze.

The judge passed Frank Vaughan a tin cup of water. Some color came back and he sat straighter. Rand's questioning improved a little too. The jurors stayed awake as the district attorney explained the peculiar nature of Frank's testimony.

Back in March, facing the grand jury, Vaughan implicated Mc-
Millan, Maynard, and Hughes, leading to their arrest. Then in April
Frank gave a deposition that reversed his state's evidence: yes, kill-
ings occurred, but he had no involvement, nor had his three friends.
They were present but did not plan the crime. Nor did any partici-
pate, no sir. Maynard and Hughes stayed at the cabin. McMillan and
Vaughan went along, but "had no means of preventing the affair."

—What happened before leaving the cabin?

—I don't recall.

—What sort of planning did you hear?

—I'm not sure I remember.

—What happened at Deep Creek?

—I saw shootings. Four or five Chinese.

—At Robinson Gulch?

—The same.

—How did your leg get injured?

—My horse fell on me.

As the prosecution questioned, Jonas Herron kept up a drumbeat
of objections. *Irrelevant. Immaterial. Leading question. Calls for a
conclusion.* O'Sullivan overruled some, sustained others. Joe could
find no pattern, but kept passing notes to the floundering Rand as
Herron's list grew. *Calls for speculation. Ambiguous. Lack of founda-
tion. Argumentative. Inflammatory.*

Lee had never seen a criminal trial. He discovered that in law, one
cannot stand up and tell a story—"There we found cartridges and
hacked bodies; here are boys who saw the murders." This stop-start
maze of evidence and witnesses was confusing even him, and he had
walked both killing sites. Throughout the tent, men fidgeted on the
makeshift seats or tamped in a fresh chaw. Two jurymen nodded in
the heat, stunned by a hotel lunch of beans and chicken-fried steak.

"What happened next?" Rand kept saying.

"I don't remember," was Frank's only reply. Five times. Ten.

After a fruitless hour, Rand turned Frank over to Herron, at
O'Sullivan's direction. Joe thrust another note along the table.

"Your Honor, Mr. Vaughan is a witness, not a party. His attorney should not cross-examine."

"Overruled," O'Sullivan said serenely. "Special circumstance, capital case. As Mr. Vincent keeps telling me."

Jonas Herron, all gentle concern, lost no time outlining Frank's sterling character. A longtime member of the community with no prior criminal record. His folks were good people — *objection, his folks are not on trial* — and he was already an experienced ranch hand and decent Christian who would one day contribute to the prosperity of the region. Now the jury looked approving. Another lawyer who talked sense.

At four-thirty, adjournment.

On the way home Joe asked, "How do you think it went?"

"What?" said Lee. Division Street was so dusty that all of them walked with bandanas held over nose and mouth. Joe repeated the question.

"Herron is vile and Rand's an idiot," said Grace. "Can't you take over the prosecution?"

"It's touchy. O'Sullivan sees me as an outsider. I told him my county includes the land just across from Deep Creek. He said, and I quote, 'That don't matter.' And as Herron keeps reminding everyone, northeast Oregon has a bright future, unless big-time scandal interferes. I should introduce him to Alonzo."

Dow had been walking in front of them, listening. "What's your plan, sir?"

Joe saluted him. "This trial is the most irregular I've ever seen. So I may try to get called to the stand. Associate prosecutor turned expert witness. Why not? O'Sullivan said he'd accept you. Hell, maybe he'll take me too."

WITNESSES

O N THURSDAY THE JUDGE changed his mind and told the attorneys to call defense witnesses. Hearing that the prosecution had more evidence to present, O'Sullivan waved them off: later today, maybe tomorrow. Joe asked for a moment to explain the situation to the representative of the Imperial Chinese government. The judge nodded warily.

Lee whispered, "Does that help or hurt our side?"

"Help. Maybe. He's not giving us much choice."

The first defense witness was Robert McMillan, age sixteen. His attorney took him through the usual: good family, Sunday school, no prior arrests. Asked what he knew about "killing some Chinamen on Snake River," Bobby was vague to the point of vacancy. Hughes and Maynard had no hand in it; they were at the cabin, well downstream. Bobby and Frank went along with "the others" to the Chinese camp, to hire a boat. He didn't do much of anything there, and he had no way of preventing the others when the shooting started. He didn't tell about the killings earlier because he was afraid.

Rand asked Bobby if he was also at two shooting incidents in Robinson Gulch. Bobby didn't think so. Rand asked what kind of weapon he was carrying. A rifle. No, a Colt. Did anyone else have that kind of gun? Bobby couldn't remember. Why did investiga-

264

tors find over a hundred spent shells at Robinson Gulch and Deep Creek? Bobby couldn't explain.

Did he see Chinese tortured at both places? *Objection as irrelevant, sustained.* Did he recall the use of knives or axes in the killings? *Objection, sustained.* Rand went to the bench and argued, but the judge held firm. No further questions.

Lee wrote, *Denies all references to torture.*

The second witness was Hezekiah Hughes, also known as Carl, age thirty-seven, originally from Kentucky. The branding-iron man could have been a store clerk: round mild face, hair slicked down with macassar oil, blue shirt fastened high.

Hughes was so laconic that English did not seem to be his mother tongue. At first he denied knowing of any Chinese deaths, then clarified that he had "heard" of them. What was the distance from cabin to camp? Didn't know, never been there. Rand bore in: How far to Robinson Gulch? To Deep Creek? *Don't know.* What was his weapon? Was he in those places? Who killed the Chinese? How many died? *Wasn't there. Never saw any dead Chinese.* But he knew Maynard was innocent, because they were together at the cabin all that time.

When the Chinese died? *When you say they did.*

After the midday recess, Hiram Maynard took the stand. Lee stared at the thin sunburned face, last seen through the green haze of a willow thicket beside the Snake. *Some China boys got killed, back around Deep Creek.* And then Bobby: *Probably their own people did it.*

Maynard was at the Douglas cabin in late May, yes. He heard that Chinese were killed up by Deep Creek, yes. He was never that far south. He knew nothing about the killing, no sir. But he knew Hughes was innocent because they were together all the time.

Rand pushed him: Were you posted as lookouts? Is that why you were together? What weapon did you possess? Did you fire it at the Chinese? What do you think of Chinese? *Objection as irrelevant, sustained.* Maynard sat rock-still. No further questions.

Judge O'Sullivan checked his pocket watch. Three o'clock, an airless tent, a wilting jury. He beckoned to Joe and Rand: adjourned till the following morning.

As the crowd broke up, Grace felt two hands on her shoulders.

"*Manaa wees?*" said a voice in her ear. It sounded like Georges.

"*Ta'c wees,*" she said automatically, amazed, and turned to see a lean young man behind her, wearing plaid shirt, jeans, and moccasins. He so rarely smiled that any grin was like a sunburst.

"Oh, goodness! Is this safe? Oh, I'm so glad to see you!"

She gave Jackson a hug, and then everyone was on him, thumping him on the back, shaking his hand, even Joe.

"Last spring I started working for a sheep rancher north of here. I take supplies to herders and bring back their messages. One of them told me about the trial."

After dinner Joe asked him about serving as a witness.

"That's why I came. Will they let me?"

"All the accused are rustlers. That's the last charge on anyone's mind," said Joe, deliberately misunderstanding. "I told the judge we had more witnesses. He agreed to put them on. I'll run the testimony. Rand's just about worn out."

Day four brought thunder before dawn, and by ten a light steady rain. Barely thirty spectators sat in the dim, rank tent. O'Sullivan was not looking judicious. *Hangover,* thought Lee.

"Where's your district attorney, Mr. Vincent?"

Where's your county clerk? McCully's chair was vacant, but Joe saw that O'Sullivan had pencil and paper to hand.

"Mr. Rand is delayed, Your Honor. With your permission, I'll take over."

"Are you ready for summation? I hope you are."

"Sir, if you recall, we still have prosecution witnesses —"

"You should have put them on two days ago. Prosecution first, defense last."

"Yes, sir, but if you recall, you said to wait. The circumstances are unusual. Our main witness was hostile. We've challenged the defense testimony. Now we have three eyewitnesses to the crime, vital to our case."

"Eyewitnesses? You should have told me from the start."

Jonas Herron came up to join them. "Your Honor, I can present the defense summation."

Joe wheeled. "Mr. Herron, I'm consulting on a point of procedure."

"If the state is not ready —"

"More than ready, sir. We have witnesses to present."

"Witnesses? That's out of order." Herron looked wonderfully shocked.

"Mr. Rand had no objection," O'Sullivan declared.

Joe wheeled the other way. The young prosecutor had just arrived and came to his side.

"I thought it would show our willingness to cooperate," he whispered to Joe.

"You might have told me," Joe said, so angry he could not look at him. Goodbye to their best hope of reversible error.

"One second, Mr. Vincent. Who are these people, anyway?"

Joe hesitated and then nodded toward the rear. "The three young men sitting there, Your Honor. Last row, right side, on the aisle."

O'Sullivan peered over his glasses. "But I see two Chinese and — what is he, Indian?"

"Yes, sir. The boys are American, born in Oregon of Chinese parents. The man is Nez Perce, born here in Wallowa County, employed by a sheep rancher, Mr. Fred Turnbull."

Herron cleared his throat. "Your Honor, our law does not permit noncitizens to testify —"

Joe cut him off. "Judge, they're all American-born. And this is a capital murder case. I guarantee you, they saw exactly what happened at Deep Creek. The defendants are lying. They all took part in the killings. They chopped, gutted, and committed other gross indecencies —"

Herron looked alarmed, O'Sullivan angry. "Vincent, I told you before, I don't want to hear that kind of talk. And your so-called witnesses have no standing in an Oregon court."

"Sir, that's still debatable in Idaho. And the victims are from Lewiston."

"No, they ain't," said the judge, exasperated. "They're from China. Why don't you try working for your own people sometime?"

Joe unclamped his hands from the wooden chair back. If he got thrown out now for contempt of court, young Rand would be at Jonas Herron's mercy.

"Then I must ask you to allow the prosecution to swear me in, sir, as an expert witness. I have material evidence bearing on the issue of guilt."

O'Sullivan blew out his cheeks. He looked at Joe, and then at Herron.

"Jonas, what do you say? Those trout going to wait?"

"By all means, let's hear him out, Judge."

As they turned away, Herron leaned toward Joe. "Vincent, if you bring up atrocities, I will crucify you. Your jurisdiction is nil."

"Did I spoil your fishing trip, Jonas? I'll get you censured for bribing a judge."

O'Sullivan announced that the prosecution had an additional witness to examine. This procedure was unusual, but he would allow it, in view of the gravity of the charges.

"I call J. K. Vincent, Your Honor."

Rand asked Joe to summarize his background in law and then his work on this case. Joe gave a brief account of finding the bodies. Then he described infiltrating the rustlers' camp while in disguise, living with the suspects, finding the rice sack and the corpses at Dug Cabin, recovering evidence at two killing sites, returning to Deep Creek a month later, then confronting Canfield and Evans in custody. While he was dismayed at their escape, which doubtless had local support (*objection*), he was pleased with the efforts of Wallowa officials to bring their henchmen (*objection*) to justice.

"Take care, Mr. Vincent," O'Sullivan said.

Rand moved away from the witness chair. "Please tell the jury what happened on those days in late May a year ago."

Herron lifted a weary hand. *Speculative. Calls for conclusion. Immaterial.*

O'Sullivan checked the jury. The hour was late, the rain still rattling on the canvas overhead. "Go on, Mr. Vincent."

"Thank you, Your Honor."

Joe looked at the two dozen remaining listeners, then at the jury, waiting for full quiet. Grace and Lee hardly dared breathe.

"We go back to April of last year. The two shepherds leave Dug Cabin. Evans recruits the Pine Creek gang at a school dance in Imnaha. They plan to rustle Oregon horses and sell in Idaho. Dug Bar is the crossing point, and the cabin a good place to hole up. They see Chinese miners working Robinson Gulch and camped at Deep Creek. Ask what they're doing and why. Get no reply. Around May 20th, they see the miners celebrating. Only one reason miners jump around and yell. The rustlers figure the Chinese will take their gold and leave soon, so they plan a robbery.

"Then the plan turns to murder. Evans is the source. He hates Chinese. He doesn't know if the miners have weapons or will fight back. Surprise and firepower are his main tactics.

"They make a plan late on May 24th. Early on Wednesday, May 25th, they ride over the slopes to Robinson Gulch. Hughes and Maynard act as lookouts, up- and downriver. McMillan holds the horses, armed with a pistol. Three riflemen take position on the rocks, Canfield and LaRue upstream, Evans down. They start a crossfire."

Joe held up his hand-drawn maps of the scene and pointed out locations. Grace looked around; everyone was awake and listening. Joe was the best possible witness: a plainspoken man, in full command of the evidence, brave enough to face armed criminals to obtain it. How could they not be swayed?

"Evans and Canfield do most of the shooting. They kill some Chinese, wound others. When the miners are down, all six move in for what Evans calls a frolic. If they find a man alive, they torture him, asking, 'Where is the gold?' The miners don't know and can't say. Almost none speak English. And there *was* no big gold strike. They were all cheering that day because they'd learned they were going home.

"The rustlers shoot until ammunition runs out," Joe went on. "Then they start in with shovels and hatchets. Plenty of tools on hand, since the Chinese were there to break down sluices. That first day Evans and his gang carve up at least ten men, then throw the mutilated bodies in the river. By four o'clock they return to Dug Cabin with good appetites. Murder is hungry work. Vaughan stayed home to fix dinner. Worst cook in the bunch. He was afraid to go. Why Evans let him off, I'm not sure. Could be they were . . . special friends."

Frank started, along with Bobby.

"This first-day story is their whole defense. In the depositions, Vaughan stays home, McMillan holds horses, Hughes and Maynard are lookouts. Only the three fugitives are killers. But at the site I recovered shells that match all the guns I documented at Dug Cabin, still in their possession a month later. In *their* story, the accused omit the next two days."

Judge O'Sullivan interrupted to ask if anyone wished to leave. No one moved.

"On Thursday, May 26th, Evans, Canfield, and LaRue return to Robinson Gulch. They leave the other four behind, probably hoping to find the miners' gold and keep it for themselves, or hide it. A boat arrives with eight Chinese, searching for the comrades who never returned to Deep Creek. When they come ashore, another ambush begins. The three rustlers wound the miners, torture them, hack them apart. This time Evans's dog is along. The Lewiston coroner's report notes deep animal bites and extensive gnawing on several miners' faces. Evans calls that victory meat."

Joe paused. "The next part is very bad. Evans returns to Dug Cabin and orders the four others to come back with him. They do. At this point all seven men commit some of the worst acts on the dead bodies, and on the dying men."

He looked directly at the jury. "The legal terms for these acts are mutilation, torture, rape. They slit tongues and eyeballs. They rip open nostrils, hack off ears, slash windpipes." He mimed each action on his own body. Harder for a jury to reject horror demonstrated on a white man.

"So. A total of eighteen dead. About noon the third killing spree begins. The seven accused row to Deep Creek. In three hours they shoot, torture, skin, and chop twelve more men. Laughing, yelling, whooping. Bruce Evans calls this a frolic. My eyewitnesses saw it all.

"The killers are more organized now. They have a routine. They ask, 'Where is the gold?' All the English-speaking miners are gone. There never was any big gold strike. But the torture does not stop, nor the slaughter. They slice into bellies and pull the guts, big steaming handfuls. They cut away genitals, first the testicles and then—"

O'Sullivan cleared his throat.

"—then several bodies they violate by penetrating the rectums, either with axes or gun barrels, or with their own . . . organs. Next to Evans, Bobby McMillan is the best at skinning human flesh."

All eyes swung to McMillan, who sank a little in his chair. Joe looked again at Dow and Yap, who sat up straight and stared at Bobby, daring him to deny.

"In twenty-four hours, over thirty are dead. Hardworking, innocent men, half of them married with children, quite a few of them Christian. What does the Bible say, besides 'Thou Shall Not Kill'? The word of God tells us, 'You shall not wrong a stranger, or oppress him, for in the land of Egypt you were strangers too.'"

Beyond the tent flap, rain had softened to a drizzling mist. Joe kept his eyes on the jury.

"At Deep Creek, surrounded by the dead, the killers search. They find four vials of gold. Evans sneaks two more for himself. Six vials of gold dust. That's all. The killers rip apart the tents, wreck the cook shack, steal what little food is left, set fire to the whole camp. They throw the last bodies into the river and smash up the boats. Three of the dead wash up at Dug Cabin and are buried there, beside the river.

How do I know? I saw them. Other chopped-up bodies are found down at Lewiston, on June third, after the big Snake River flood. One fine day my daughter and I go fishing, and she catches a man."

Nell nodded at him. *Don't spare their feelings.*

"A month after the slaughter, on June 25th, I appear at the rustlers' cabin in the guise of Joe Salem, an elderly prospector. I interview all seven suspects. I collect material evidence. The gun details. The samples of hair and clothing from buried victims. The empty sack of Chinese rice. Here it is."

He pulled a shabby burlap bag from his coat pocket and walked over to the jury box. "Chinese writing," he told them, pointing to the stenciled characters.

"Says you," observed a voice from the audience.

"Try this," said Joe, and held up a small round jar. "Bullets taken from the victims' bodies by the Lewiston coroner."

He passed a sample to the jury foreman.

"Mostly they used repeating rifles and .45-60 Winchester cartridges. Fast action. First-rate killing power."

He poured the bullets out, then began dropping them back into the jar, ball by ball. It took a while. Ninety-three times metal rang against glass. Bobby McMillan started to stand. Carl Hughes reached over, grabbed the boy's collar, and forced him back into the chair.

Two jurymen traded glances. The rest sat motionless. Jonas Herron and Judge O'Sullivan offered neither comment nor protest. Rand asked Joe if he had anything more to say.

"Only this. First, the killings were brutal, in the extreme. Second, all seven in the gang killed, without a doubt. Third, this crime is the worst mass murder to date in the Northwest. Let me add a fourth: the Chinese were decent, law-abiding men, and none deserved this fate."

Rand turned to the judge. "Your Honor, the prosecution rests the people's case."

Herron rose. "A few last questions for the witness, if it please Your Honor."

O'Sullivan nodded. *Here it comes,* thought Lee.

"Is it not true, Mr. Vincent, that you were *paid* to look into the Chinese killings?"

"It is."

"And who hired you in the first place?"

"The miners' employer," said Joe. How the hell did Herron know? "Which is the Sam Yup Company, out in San Francisco. The Chinese consulate joined their request to investigate."

"How much did they slip you?"

"Objection," said Rand, a beat too late.

"Apologies. Let me rephrase. How much did the Chinese pay you?"

"Fifteen hundred dollars," said Joe.

Enough to buy a quarter section of pretty grazing land, build a house and barn, stock them to bursting, and pay ten years' taxes besides. Grace heard the murmurs and saw the shock run through the audience like wind over wheat. Herron waited a good sixty seconds, then bowed his head.

"We also rest, Your Honor. We are satisfied that we have made the best possible case for the defense, consistent with our state laws."

O'Sullivan's gavel came down. "Adjourned until ten o'clock tomorrow."

Back at the rented store, they ate a cold dinner in silence. Finally Joe said, "Thank you all. At least we told their story."

Grace said, for everyone, "Joe, you were wonderful."

Joe shook his head. Absolute failure brought with it the peace of the grave.

"O'Sullivan barely pretended to take notes. They never planned to record what our witnesses said, and even if they did, I figure any transcript gets burned or lost the minute we clear the county line. I knew that when I took the stand. Almost no objections, and I said every defamatory thing I could."

"Publish Lee's notes," said Yap. His voice shook. "That newspaper in Portland. Send it all there."

"These people, they really will bury it," said Nell. "For a hundred years."

"No chance of an Idaho trial?" Jackson asked.

"None. The governor won't allow it, the town doesn't want it, and the three worst killers are still at large. This was our last chance."

Lee said to Dow and Yap, "Come back to San Francisco with me. We can pick up the coast boat at Asotin, right?" Joe nodded.

Jackson looked at the boys. "Win or lose, what did you plan on doing?"

"Keep running," said Yap.

"Doesn't work," Jackson told him.

On the hot windy morning of September 1, the crowd had grown again. McCully was back at his clerk's stand. Humphreys and two deputies had ridden over from Joseph, the first sign all week of any sheriff.

Convenient, thought Joe, listening hard to the jury instructions in case O'Sullivan said anything to get the case reversed, but the summation was fair, with one peculiarity. While the three defendants were either Guilty or Not Guilty, Vaughan was a special case. Since he alone was indicted by a grand jury, Oregon law asked this petit jury to make a separate finding, declaring Frank's indictment either a True Bill or Not a True Bill.

Rand spread his hands. "We can't afford to call too many petit juries. This at least settles all the accusations."

Joe shrugged and watched the jurymen file toward the hotel. Not one looked at him. They were back within the hour.

"Members of the jury, have you reached a verdict upon which you are all agreed?"

"We have, Your Honor."

For Carl Hughes, Hiram Maynard, and Robert McMillan: Not Guilty.

Mrs. McMillan's scream could be heard in Lewiston. O'Sullivan pounded his gavel.

For Frank Vaughan: Not a True Bill.

For the three fugitives, Evans, Canfield, and LaRue: Case Continued.

Joe shook Rand's hand. The young prosecutor looked stricken. Shaken, too.

"I'm sorry, Judge."

"I hoped, but I'm not surprised."

"I guess if they killed thirty-one white men, it would have been different."

Joe clapped him on the back and walked out without a word or glance for any of the other authorities. He thought he saw Frank Vaughan trying to push toward him through the crowd, but he kept on going. His family fell in around him. Jackson carried Joe's gunbelt in one hand, the big Colt swinging gently above the rutted street. Grace kept her hand in her dress pocket, right on Joe's little derringer. But no one came after them, to confront or to commiserate. All the way to the rented store they could hear the jubilant roar of talk back in the tent. It sounded like quite a party.

Nell, jolting on the wagon seat as Grace drove north, turned to watch her father riding beside them. He had been silent nearly four hours, a record. Dow was watching him too.

"Do it," he said to her. Nell nodded.

SECRETS

SEPTEMBER 9, 1888

J OE WAS PUTTING his broom away when Nell called to him from the barn's half-door. On its ledge she laid a towel-shrouded bundle.

"Pa, you should look at this. I got it out of Mother's closet."

She unwrapped a small walnut lap desk, which Joe had never seen. He touched the polished brass lock, the corner fittings.

"Are you sure this is hers?"

"Oh, yes. She hides it. When I was little, I thought it was jewelry."

Nell held up the key, laid back the lid. Joe saw a pale blue leather diary and a collection of ribbon-tied letters. Then an account ledger. He paged through: investments and earnings, deposits and sales, going back to the early '70s. Some transactions he recognized, many not. A lot of the investing looked separate from the Leland money. His wife kept excellent double — no, triple — books.

Beneath the ledger sat a bundle of high-denomination bonds in the new Camas Prairie rail company, all in Libby's name. Joe studied a score of land deeds. Over the past year she had acquired a half-dozen properties, enough to block any Vollmer crossing along the Clearwater. At the bottom of the paper trove Joe found a stack of gold certificates, issued from '82 on, payable to the bearer.

"I read the diary," Nell said. "I sort of knew anyway. Are the papers important?"

"Yes. *Yes.* Sweetheart, thank you. But why?"

"I talked to Dow and Yap. They couldn't save Elder Boss — because they promised, you see, not that it mattered in the end — but we all thought . . . well, for you, this other box —"

"Let's go down to the river," said Joe. "The ticket office is still open."

Grace and Nell just made the three o'clock steamer. "I want you both out of town," Joe told them, and for a wonder they boarded without protest, though he had never seen Grace so worried, not even up the Snake. She kept a hand on his knee as they drove to the docks, then went straight on board. Too many eyes. Nell buried her face in his shoulder. She was going to be a tall girl. Joe walked back to the barn, pulled the lap desk from under the Deep Creek evidence sacks, and started reading the blue diary.

On Sunday morning Joe waited on the Leland front steps, aware that Libby never passed up a ride back from church in the Vollmer carriage.

"I'd like to speak to you two inside, please."

"Can't. I have to get back. We have guests," said Vollmer. No hello.

"This won't take long. It's in the nature of a business settlement."

"It's the Sabbath, Joe."

"Tomorrow I'm leaving town."

"Where are you off to now?"

"That's my affair. But anyone who would hire Jonas Herron should be willing to hear what I have to say."

As they filed in, Joe looked around the parlor. "I first met you here, Libby, do you recall?"

"Did you come to reminisce, Joseph? I'm not in the mood."

"And not a week later, your father offered me a large cash payment if I would marry you, because you were bearing another man's child."

"What of it? Did you have a better future planned?"

"At the time, I didn't think so. But you repeated the comedy twice more. Only Nell is mine."

"Nell was a miscalculation," said Libby coolly. "I take it you read my diary. Not so high-minded now, are we? And where's my desk?"

Vollmer turned on her. "You kept a fucking *diary?*"

"Twenty-five years' worth," said Joe. "I hereby turn all three of your children back to you, John, and I wish you luck. If President Cleveland can support a bastard, you can handle two extra."

"Where is it?"

"Sorry. That diary is my life insurance. I'm also keeping the gold certificates."

Libby began to curse. Ma Nickerson could take lessons.

"Shut up, Lib, and stay that way," said Vollmer, once she paused for breath.

"My original contract with Alonzo was $5,000. Then I have a property to exchange, the Tammany house and land. For once it's my name on the deed. A hundred sixty acres, all furnishings included—let's say an even $30,000. In gold."

"That's steep," said Vollmer.

"I'm adding compound interest for twenty years of lies. I'm not suing you for alienation of affections. We'll have no scandal. As I say, I'm leaving town."

Libby looked up at them both through her eyelashes, then slowly smoothed her brown velvet overskirt. The old-bone lace of her collar set off the delicacy of her face to perfection. Joe knew how much was careful paint, but she still could make young men turn in the street.

"Or we can all continue as we are," she told him. "I'll even look the other way when you go running to Miss Minnehaha out in Portland."

Vollmer had regrouped. "Libby gets title to the country property? What about the hotel?"

"I don't want his shitty hotel," Libby said. "I want the money."

Joe thought he had seen all her faces, heard all her voices, but this one was new to him, the flat growl of a mule-team driver.

Joe nodded at the documents from the lap desk, spread on Alonzo's parlor table.

"You'll have cash, property, and independence. But not as a grass widow. This is a petition for an Oregon divorce."

Vollmer was already turning pages, reading fast, showing no emotion. Libby studied the documents in turn. Joe had left the real bait on the last page, the grand total of all her assets should she agree. He was almost wiped out, except for the gold certificates and the fifteen hundred dollars from the Sam Yup. Libby would be a rich woman, not much past forty.

She picked up the pen. The spouses signed as parties, with Vollmer as witness. And again, transferring to Libby the Tammany estate. And again, to give Joe title to the nine certificates from '88; these alone were not payable to the bearer.

Joe nodded to Vollmer. "She's all yours. However" – he tapped the bound letter packets – "I'd read these first. She's working on land deals with quite a few of your opponents. Starting with the Union Pacific."

Libby began to weep, beautifully. Vollmer crammed the letters into his inside coat pocket and walked straight past her. He was almost out the door when Joe said, "About Evans."

Vollmer stopped.

"He was your Oregon land agent, your enforcer. You sent him after Tom Douglas, but he kept the Wells Fargo box, which proved your collusion with the Sam Yup. You told the Company the most likely hiding places, from Dug Bar to Salt Creek. The Chinese sent some forty men up the river and only twelve came back. You got the Sam Yup to hire me. Kill me, kill an honest investigation."

"Can you prove *any* of this, Vincent?"

"Libby's diary is thorough. And you and I, it turns out, are good at self-deceit. She doesn't much care who lives or dies, so long as she profits. She says a lot of hard things about me, but you should read her portrait of you. Like what you need to be called in bed."

Libby lost all color. Vollmer offered Joe his hand.

"In return for your silence, gold, divorce, support for her brats, and safe conduct. Do we have a deal?"

Vollmer just might become Idaho's first millionaire, Joe decided. In under ninety seconds he had read the odds, thrown over his lover of nearly three decades, and ensured his own safety. Joe nodded but declined to shake.

"I have the diary and a copy. If anything happens to me, the choicest parts will appear as serial installments in the *Oregonian*. Keep that in mind, all right?"

The front door slammed. Done, and done. Gold certificates and diary lay in Trim's saddlebag. Vollmer had the letters. Joe sat down on the loveseat and reached beneath to pull out the empty lap desk.

"Lots of room for new paper in here, Lib."

He looked up, then threw himself hard to the left. The heavy iron fireplace poker tore an eight-inch gash in the silk upholstery. Libby was stronger than she looked. He grabbed her wrists.

"Christ, just stop. *Enough.*"

He slapped her face, hard, and she dropped back onto the cushions, wordless, tearless. A year ago in Oregon, he saw blue eyes like that across an interrogation table. He picked up the gold certificates and his copies of the papers. She did not try to stop him.

In six months, she won't recall my name. Then he was out the door and riding up the hill to the Stantons', breathing like a man at altitude.

He told Henry everything, sparing no one.

"I'll write to you soon, from wherever I land."

"I should go too. But Mary likes it here. And I can't leave my patients."

And you have the dwindles, old friend, thought Joe. He stood up to go home, then remembered he didn't have one.

"Use the back bedroom," Henry said, not moving. "Breakfast at eight, Mary willing. But get your own hot water. I'm too damned old to get people hot water."

"Do I have to build you a shed?"

"Please don't. The last one was a disaster."

Joe put a hand on Henry's shoulder, then went upstairs and slept the night through for the first time in months.

He was up by six, got the stove going, saw the lunch packet Mary left for him. In return he propped an envelope against the chipped brown teapot: gold certificates for $8,000 and a note. *From the people of North Idaho — a pension, so very well earned.*

Then he mounted Trim and rode out. As they left Lewiston behind, a soft snow of cottonwood seed filled the air, drifting along the streets, settling on the mare's dark mane. Joe turned southeast, up the bluffs. At the top he did not look back.

COMPENSATION

SEPTEMBER 1888–NOVEMBER 1890

JOE RODE HARD toward the mountains with the Colt on his belt and his best hunting weapon in the saddle scabbard, ready to hand. Alone in rough country with a fortune in gold, he didn't trust Vollmer worth a damn. He camped well off the road by a creek, the .45-caliber Burgess repeating rifle always beside his bedroll.

Trust accounts at a coast bank would be best. In three years Nell might need college funds. Alonzo would underwrite a granddaughter's dowry, but never her tuition. Dow should have an apprenticeship with the best Chinese doctor Lee could locate. Yap — well, call it either bail money or seed money. He liked Yap; the kid was unsinkable. If Jackson would accept even a fraction, that miraculous talent with horses might not be wasted after all.

Grace was getting by, but a few more years as the decorous schoolteacher and her disguise would be truth. He'd staked her to a new life once before. His turn to hole up. He needed to disappear a while himself.

On the third day out, Joe made Cottonwood by midafternoon. He recalled passing through on the second trip to Deep Creek. Its Nimipu name was Kap-kap-peen, village in a hole. So it was: sleepy, flyblown, with one big log building that served as combination saloon, hotel, stable, and stage stop. He looked up the street. A blacksmith's shed, a Grostein & Binnard branch store, a dozen unpainted houses. Plain as could be. But the Camas was nearby, the town well was sound, he could see mountains but no rivers, and he was over the county line.

Good enough. Joe went looking for a meal. The front desk at Cottonwood House was deserted. So was the bar. He poked into several rooms, all discouraging: rope beds, butter-muslin windows, cracked bowl-and-pitcher sets. Out back were two empty corrals. One for sheep, he recalled, the other for wild-horse roundups. He banged on an iron kettle to draw some attention.

From the blacksmith shop, a head emerged. "What do you want?"

"A meal and a room," Joe called back.

The blacksmith came over, complaining. He was only looking after the place. The girl who kept it ran off with a stage driver. The owners were in Boise and staying there. Anyone wanting food, well, the store sold canned goods.

"Can you hire a new keeper?"

The man nodded.

"Mister, you're in luck," Joe said. "I'm the best hotel man in this Territory, and I need a job."

They shook on it: room and board for him, feed and a stall for Trim, plus thirty dollars a month. Private Vincent all over again: a dollar a day, beans and hay.

By Saturday, Joe never wanted to sweep another floor. He took Trim for a two-hour ride along the ridges, watching rain clouds blow in, dark as a bruise, then lay sleepless in his bare musty room, every muscle aching.

A week, and a life undone. At Raymond House he'd taken forty dollars from the till and left a note for the manager—*I may be gone awhile*—before filling his saddlebags with essentials only: socks, gloves, union suit, wool shirt, shaving case. Blanket roll behind the saddle. He first rode into Lewiston with not much more. Reading glasses. Bismuth pills. Forgot a winter coat. Damned if he'd go back for it. Remembered the good fishing rod, though.

He had a roof over his head and people to tend. Every third day a six-horse stage came through, if the roads stayed open and the driver's nerve held. Joe stood at the hotel door, counting passengers who staggered off the big Concord coach to fall on his chili soup and cornbread. Nine dinners, no overnights. Idaho had many beauty spots. Cottonwood was not on anyone's list.

"Tough trip?" Joe inquired. A rancher shuddered. "Like the agonies of the damned," said the clergyman across the table, downing his beer. Joe poured him another.

Cottonwood was sixty miles from Lewiston, but it felt like the Yukon. For the first time in twenty-five years, Joe had to kill chickens. As marshal he carried badge and gun; as judge he had the power to bind and loose. Now he was a hired man in a patched wool coat, hatchet in hand, chasing a thin red hen around a muddy yard. Kill, pluck, boil; haul, scrub, fold. *Like a goddamn Chinaman. Women's work.*

He was sorry for the thought, but the bitterness lingered. All that giving, poured out on sand. Why had he stayed so long, ignored so much? Jesus, what a wasteland of a life. Monarch of a little rat town on the edge of a silted river.

Joe's only Lewiston correspondent was Mary Stanton, who kept him informed on Henry's declining health. He had retired from practice, but Joe's money kept them secure. Libby was away on a grand tour of fashionable watering places: Calistoga, Mackinac Island, Mobile Bay. John Vollmer and his plain, stout wife seemed inseparable these days. Quite. Joe smiled. Mary Stanton was a good guesser.

By early November, stage traffic slowed to one coach a week. Joe could have closed up, except for the mailbags. The hotel was also the area post office. His bar had a few steady customers: ranchers, cowhands, and a circuit preacher fond of rye, who asked after the manager's faith.

"Buddhist," Joe said. He locked up the liquor and retreated. He found he had no desire to drink. Hitting someone, anyone, was a real possibility. If he did, he might not stop.

With Henry out of reach, Joe sought a companion in the empire of print. A hotel shelf yielded a few abandoned volumes – the Bible, a Shakespeare with the covers torn off, Emerson's *Essays,* Palgrave's *Golden Treasury.* Grace sent him Twain's story of life on the Mississippi, which Joe loved, and then General Grant's memoirs. He warmed to the old soldier's honesty about his years of exile between commissions, when he farmed, collected bills, and tanned hides.

Joe thought he might miss Lewiston's daily round, the local intrigues, the unfurling stories, but no. He missed the politics. Always he had been proud to be of Mr. Lincoln's party. Maybe he'd run the Deep Creek case all wrong. Maybe it was hubris and folly to go after the killers so hard. What did Lincoln say? *I have always found that mercy bears richer fruits than strict justice.* But Joe had tried both and got kicked in the teeth.

New England's mark was still on him, the deep-down sense of being unconditional elect, patched coat or no. When Alonzo tempted him, all those years ago, he'd felt as much gratified as grateful, his talents finally recognized. How brilliant Libby was at mirroring that self-conceit back to him, feeding on his vitality and goodwill like some goddamn vampire. How ready he was to believe every honeyed word.

He'd been a seducer himself, of course: auctions, hotel work, politics. What better dupe than the professional persuader? He could never trust himself to hold power again.

Only weeks after the trial, Bobby McMillan got a sore throat so bad that Maggie McMillan told her husband to ride for the doctor. Two days each way. By then Bobby was swollen at the neck and vomiting, his tongue like brown leather. The doctor took the parents outside. Diphtheria. Give Bobby laudanum; pray he goes easy.

When they told him, Bobby looked at his mother, then whispered, "Pa, I need to talk to you." About his summer with Evans and Canfield, mostly. At Robinson Gulch he went along to hold the horses. At Deep Creek he learned he liked to kill. Better than a hunting trip, better than a war. He felt sorry about what happened. He didn't want to get Frank and the others in trouble. But Evans was a bad man. Bobby didn't want to meet him in Hell.

"Let's do our country a favor and get rid of these Chinks," Evans had told them. "Then let's do us a favor and get their gold."

Hugh hushed Bobby, then called in his wife. "You listen and pray, son. Ask Jesus to forgive you. There's a better world coming."

Maggie wept and Hugh touched her on the shoulder. He looked out the window at the land he had worked for a dozen years. It was all to go to Bobby, and now he was dying.

Maggie McMillan followed her husband into the yard. "Promise you'll never tell. That judge over in Lewiston, he'd call a new trial." Hugh shook his head and went to feed the horses, and alone in the barn he wept as well.

The '88 election in which Joe did not run came and went. Popular votes stayed with Grover Cleveland, but Idaho Territory swung Republican, and was quick to claim its electoral power gave Harrison the White House. Joe did get letters of thanks and commiseration from Senator Slater and from Consul Fred Bee, both forwarded through Lee, as well as an unexpected plea from Rand. Judge O'Sullivan was making it hot for him in Wallowa County, but an assistant DA job was open in Pendleton, and would Judge Vincent recommend him?

Joe did, but he also told Rand it might not do much good. *You'd be surprised,* Rand replied.

Joe went to kill another chicken. The afternoon was dark and raw, starting to sleet. Soup weather. He sat by the big iron range, feeding in stove wood, gauging the coals. A dozen loaves of salt-rising bread sat in pans along the scrubbed worktable. In the shadows beneath, a calico alley cat purred and treaded in her bed of rags.

On the same December afternoon, Mary Stanton found an anxious Selina Vollmer on the doorstep. She asked for Henry; Mary said he could not be disturbed. In truth, he was sedated. But that she would not tell any Vollmer.

"What's wrong, Lina?"

Mrs. Vollmer put a hand on Mary's arm. "John's so ill."

"Henry has retired, Selina. He refers all his patients to Dr. Kelly."

"I know, and Kelly's too busy to come. But John wouldn't admit — and now —"

"Oh, my dear. I'll go see Mrs. Kelly."

In an hour Madison Kelly stood at Vollmer's bedside. "Hold the lamp closer," he told Selina. Red lesions fat with pus covered the banker's face, chest, and belly.

"Open your mouth," Kelly said. Yes, there too. Smallpox. Unmistakable. Vollmer was shivering under the bedclothes. The sumptuous room stank of sweat and vomit.

"How long has he been like this?"

"Two weeks now. He didn't want anyone to know."

Kelly snorted. "Worst way to behave. You're inoculated, ma'am? Well, burn all the bedding, at once. Anything he touches or wears, scald it. Understand?"

She nodded.

"All right. It's not the worst case I've seen. We're up to twenty in town, with more to come, and I fear we're going to lose half."

After she left, Kelly looked down at Vollmer. "John. These last few weeks, did you sleep elsewhere? Somewhere not . . . clean? I've traced the outbreak to a girl down at Ma's."

Vollmer lay still as any corpse, eyes closed, limbs flaccid.

Kelly shook his head. "If you were going to die of this, you'd be gone already. Maybe you should help me set up a board of health. Better sanitation in town, vaccinations in the school. For Evie's sake. Five years ago Vincent and Stanton wanted to do all that. No one offered funding."

Vollmer nodded. His voice was nearly gone.

"Set up anything you want. Just make sure I live."

From Lee, Joe learned that China had accepted U.S. reparations of over 276 million dollars. The paperwork was so complex that even the Embassy could not say for sure if the agreement covered the

Snake River deaths, but Lee was now certain that no one in China would receive indemnity payments for Chea Po's lost mining crew.

At the Consulate in San Francisco, staffers worked fifteen-hour days. The U.S. Supreme Court had just affirmed that "a race deemed difficult of assimilation" could be barred from entering the country, despite all prior treaties. Lee was on the road three weeks out of four. In their round-robin letters he was frank with Grace and Joe about his close calls; he was using every trick they ever taught him, and improvising more daily.

Joe searched Emerson's "Compensation" for encouragement. *Every secret is told, every crime is punished, every virtue rewarded, every wrong redressed, in silence and certainty.*

Lee's answer came by return mail. *Justice delayed is justice denied.*

Joe put down the letter and went to stir kettles of mutton stew. Roundup this week. The hotel was packed. His main news source was the *Oregonian,* which came six weeks late. He did study its reports on a series of London murders: harlot after harlot found dead in the slums, throats slit, bodies torn open, organs cut away. The death count might be eleven or more. Papers called the killer Jack the Ripper.

Grace sent a *Teller* clipping, an Oregon story Joe had missed. Over in Wallowa County, rancher Fred Nodine discovered two dozen of his prize horses shot to death. Close-in rifle fire. Mr. Humphreys, the county sheriff, had no suspects.

That was the last *Teller* story Joe ever saw. Soon after, the printing office at Second and Main burned down. Alonzo still retired rich, for a railroad was coming to the Camas at last, boosting Vollmer and Leland incomes, dooming the old Nimipu heartland. The Harvard ethnologist sent to redistribute land around Lapwai promised huge tracts to white farmers arriving from the Midwest. "We must be firm," she told Congress. An "unprogressive and comparatively degenerate people" could not be allowed to hold such valuable property.

Joe got a twenty-page rebuttal from 1340 State Street. He thought several pages carried tooth marks and one a tearstain, but could not be sure. Grace would not touch his money, would not leave her job, would not even write a letter to the newspapers protesting the land grab, under any name.

He might have been seriously annoyed, if he were not also living a lie. Two dozen Lewiston men had come through Cottonwood since the fall of '88; Joe served meals to most of them. He could not bear to use the codger's voice, but the new beard worked wonders, and the big hat. No one looks at the help.

Except Abe Binnard. In early November of 1890, Joe glanced up from the stove to find Abe holding out his plate for seconds.

"Good stew," he said. "Joe, you better get ready to go to Lapwai. Henry's dying. A family service only. And you. Grace is probably in Lewiston already. Mary sent for her. How can they find you fast? There's no telegraph in this godforsaken place."

"I'll start out now," Joe said. The blacksmith would have to cook.

Binnard persisted. "It might be two weeks yet, or two days. We can wire you via Grangeville, by express. What address? Manager, Cottonwood House, or Joe Vincent, Cottonwood?"

"Joe Vincent, Cottonwood. But not for much longer. It's time. Thanks, Abe."

Binnard clapped his shoulder, left a dollar on the kitchen counter for his dinner, and went out. Joe never got to thank him for managing the sale of Raymond House so discreetly. The most decent man in Lewiston. Along with Rob Grostein, and the Grange president, and the piano teacher, and the Beuk Aie elders – well, maybe a few of goodwill did live in the town he would never see again.

He was still angry. A month ago he wrote to Grace, *All those years, a kid on the roof, a holdup at the bank, a rancher's son fallen in with card sharps – call good old Joe, he'll be right over with a ladder and a deputy. Giving and giving, and giving some more.*

She let him vent, but only so much. *Yes, you helped your fancy friends. Also the Chinese, the People, the poor, the old, the swindled.*

Who saw you? The young. They'll remember, the good ones at least. Nell, the boys. I know, not the legacy you expected, girls and Chinese. Sorry. But don't you be.

Back in his Sergeant Vincent days, Joe got shot by a claim-jumper. The wound was bad. For weeks he refused to look under the bandage, for fear of gangrene. The Fort Lapwai doctor told him not to indulge in fool heroics; time cured almost everything, and fresh air did the rest. When he came back to be recertified for duty, a new medic looked him over. The other man, the Brit, had moved to Lewiston.

Joe wondered if Henry's advice still held. Here at the edge of nowhere, as another fall sank into winter and winter edged toward thaw, the nightmares kept on. Rage and shame swept over him so hard some days that he had to sit down and turn his head away. He was probably the most laconic hotelkeeper in North Idaho, not that his sheep-herding clientele minded. The lumberjack beard itched like fury. But once in a while, reeling in a rainbow trout or pausing with arms full of firewood to watch a high-country snowfall — once in a while, he thought he might heal.

FREE

JUST BEFORE THANKSGIVING, Henry Stanton died. Joe stood with Grace and Mary under the bare cemetery cottonwoods, rubbing a hand over his new-shaven chin. No hard frost had come to Lapwai's sheltered valley; the earth was still soft enough to dig. Only the priest from the Episcopal mission came with them to see Henry into the ground. Joe looked at the pair beside him, so alike: slender erect women, holding hands, black skirts whipping.

The old words went into the wind: *In the sure and certain hope of resurrection, we commend thy servant Henry . . . Grant that he may go from strength to strength in the life of perfect service in thy heavenly kingdom . . . We go down to the dust, yet even at the grave we make our song: alleluia.*

Mary knelt to set atop the coffin three locks of hair, tied with a blue ribbon: her own gray strand, a wavy tress from Grace, a bright curl cut from a child's head long ago.

Joe said only, "He was my best friend. And he loved this country."

Grace read a poem found in Henry's desk drawer. Joe was surprised to hear a modern verse; he'd pegged Henry for a Wordsworth man.

> *I bequeath myself to the dirt to grow from the grass I love,*
> *If you want me again look for me under your boot-soles.*
> *You will hardly know who I am or what I mean,*
> *But I shall be good health to you nevertheless.*

At the cemetery gate, a crowd waited for them. Henry once said the nine years here were some of their happiest. The Training School superintendent put out sandwiches, cake, and coffee, and a good thing too; over forty were at the gathering, white and Nimipu both. Joe never realized Grace knew so many in the area: veteran teachers, trading-post neighbors, Georges's in-laws, even a few old men who recalled Louis and Tayam. Joe kept looking around for Henry; it was just the kind of party he liked.

The next morning Joe sat for a few minutes in the Stanton buggy. Flurries already caught the mountain sunlight; delay was not wise. Mary was serene, Grace subdued.

"What?" Joe said to her finally.

"People at the reception kept saying, 'It's all right. It would have happened anyway. He made up for it a hundred times over.' So just tell me. *Please.*"

Joe and Mary looked at each other, appalled.

"Lewiston sits on treaty land," Joe said finally. "When Henry was mayor, he got federal permission to take it away from the Nez Perce. So the town could stay. Henry could have profited, but didn't. And he was sorry afterward. Sorrier than you can imagine."

Arms folded, looking at the hills, Grace said, "I can imagine quite a lot. Where was I?"

"Here, and then Missouri," said Joe. "Free of the trap, he thought. He hoped."

"Sweetheart, we assumed you knew," said Mary, taking her hand.

Grace remembered the years of free clinics on the reservation, the late-night rides to camps and cabins of the People, the dinners of scrambled egg or corn mush on Au-ma's good china.

"I suppose I must have."

Joe leaned forward and held them both. He wished he could cry as well. He looked over Grace's head at the burying ground. By morning, snow would cover the graves of both Henry and his son.

In January of 1891, Joe got two letters. One from Grace, stiff and dull. Weather, school fund drive, weather, Nell's ongoing war with geometry. An account of some long, improving novel about French coal mining. More weather. As a new sideline, Georges and Jackson were thinking about rodeo horses. She was not sure she approved. And kind of him to ask, but she attended few concerts or lectures any more. Nell could not always come, and so—.

Alarmed, he turned over the last page. Yes. A scribbled note. *Joe, I must do something, or I swear I will run mad. Using rapid-fire weapons on children, my God. Damn them all to Lee's eighteenth hell.*

He remembered hearing about the worst and hottest of the Chinese hells. A fine spot for old acquaintance, like Blue Evans or the Seventh Cavalry. Six weeks past in western South Dakota, the Seventh had opened fire on a winter encampment of Lakota traditionals. Old people, hotheaded young men, lots of families. Big Hole all over again. But this time ninety lay injured in the snow at Wounded Knee, and a hundred and fifty were dead, plus twenty-five troopers.

The other envelope was from Peg Koerner, up in Mount Idaho.

Tracked you with the help of Mrs Stanton. Thought you might like to buy our place. We could work out a deal. Pay us a little down and we'll take the rest in a mortgage. Jack hates the winters here and I'm tired of the business. Would rather live on the coast.

Joe made the trip and liked what he saw. The hotel was in good condition and the house full of light, with a rock fireplace, built-in shelves, and a wide back porch that looked toward the Camas. He ended up buying both. By spring he found a married couple to run Cottonwood House, bequeathed them his chili recipe and the calico cat, and rode south toward the high peaks.

Four o'clock on a rainy city afternoon. Grace put away the big atlas, sighing, and sat in her empty classroom, marking quizzes. *Sorry, Alice, Lima's not in Mexico. Yes, Corinne, Peru. But your spelling is frightful.*

"Miss Prindiville?" Mother Antoinette stood in the doorway, regal as ever. "Some people from town have asked to meet with you. All quite eminent, I believe."

Grace glanced at the fire escape beyond the classroom window. Mother Antoinette laughed.

"I don't think that will serve. Do you wish to speak with them?"

"Should I?"

"Hear them out, at least. Apparently they've been seeking you for quite some time. And remember, I can always find another teacher of French and geography. Deportment too, though I shall miss your excellent posture."

So this was how birds felt, startled, falling, not yet flying.

"But—"

"Marie, you came to us nearly broken. That's no longer so. If you refuse these people, I won't send you away. You're more than competent. The students like you. But a teacher who only endures, however discreetly, is not my first choice. And some duties only you can fulfill."

"What can they want?"

"My dear, go and see," said Mother Antoinette.

Downstairs, Grace put an ear to the frosted glass pane of the reception parlor door. Silence. When she stepped inside, five men and three women turned as one. Serious faces all, doubting, anxious, intent. Sober expensive dress. Mother Antoinette, not easily impressed, called them eminent. Grace was not the only *métis* teacher in the city, but almost. If Portland's powerful wanted her to step aside quietly, they could just think again.

On the parlor's brocade sofa sat the spare graying woman who helped birth Janey's child in the Portland jail. She sent Grace a small smile, with no apology or quarter. The strangers' thoughts beat in.

—can't afford a mistake, not on this—

—why, she looks quite white—

—she looks quite savage—

—That face! But can she talk?—

—still not sure about a Catholic . . .

Then, from a brown-bearded man of forty-five, sitting to one side:

—Bull's-eye.—

Outraged, she sought the woman from the jail again.

— Please, Marie. —

The bearded man stood and bowed. He had a lawyer's voice, trained and resonant.

"Miss Prindiville, forgive the intrusion. But should you care to answer one question, I — we — would be most grateful. Were you by any chance once known as Grace Sundown?"

They were all staring so. For an instant she clung to the old half-life. For an instant more she yearned to run to the mountains and vanish into leaf and air.

"That is my name."

What was the statute of limitations on disturbing the peace in wartime? How fast could Joe get here? But she could hear him now. *Head up. Play it out. You never know.*

Her callers rose, every one.

"We understand — we dare to hope — that certain reforms may interest you. Perhaps you would consent to work with us. For the good of all."

She could not fault his manner. The respect was plain, as plain as their need.

"What might you like changed?"

"Why, nearly everything," said Grace Sundown. *Starting with most of you.* But she sent the civic worthies a smile that had not surfaced since a spring ballroom in New Orleans long ago, for suddenly she felt light, strong, and wayward, ready to hammer on a dozen closed doors and kick in the rest.

— But can she talk? Christ almighty. *Try me.*

Summer, 1891. Joe knew others who might like his Mount Idaho view. Grace wrote back:

> Nell is deep in Greek & Latin with a special tutor. She wants to astonish Wellesley. At this rate she may be the wonder of all New England. Will I do instead? Love, G

On July 3, Joe waited at the Grangeville coach stop in his best suit. He owned one again. Grace stepped down, smiling, not a comb

295

out of place; she still had the mysterious French gift for staying neat, even after six hours on the worst stage in Idaho. Halfway up the grade road, she leaned over and kissed his cheek.

"Do you realize—" she said.

"That we've not been alone and free since you were seventeen?"

That evening they sat on the porch and looked down the slopes to see fireworks bloom across the valley. Idaho was a state at last, and North Idaho only an old dream. Joe wondered how Alonzo and Vollmer were taking defeat. Counting their money, probably; soon trains would run from Lewiston and Grangeville all the way to Portland and Seattle, Minneapolis and New York. Evidently John had met Lib's price on the parcels that blocked his feeder roads. Love was grand.

"It's getting so crowded," Grace said as Joe handed her a plate of strawberry pie. "When I was a girl—"

"You're saying that a lot."

"As befits my years. I rode here when the whole valley was open. Wolves. Elk."

"Would you bring it back, if you could?"

"Not likely. Though I miss that other West. The one that could have been."

Nell and the boys, like Lonny and Letty, belonged to the coming age. Joe kept an eye on this new world; it interested him. Motorcycles, elevators, moving-picture shows. At Lapwai he and Grace had known a man who spoke to Lewis and Clark.

He blew out the lamp and took her hand. "Want to see the upstairs?"

A week of delight slipped by. Drives, walks, talks. Through ferocious weeding, Grace reclaimed Peg Koerner's flower garden. Sometimes she napped in the porch hammock, looking even prettier than Joe remembered. They took to bed more often than he thought possible, at his age. Grace in the act of love was happy and frank, with no false modesty about how they fit together, curve on curve. His hands moved slowly over her, down a shoulder and arm and then retracing again, the fingers barely stroking skin, until she shuddered and clasped him. He put a hand on her hip, breathed deeply, forgot all his hurts, and slept.

"Tell me about the reform business," he said as they sat on a sun-warmed rock, watching distant thunderheads sail over the Camas Prairie.

"I never expected all the politics. They want beads and feathers and I won't go along."

"The audiences?"

"The organizers. Probably audiences too. Even with your coaching, I've had such disasters."

Joe read the coast papers. She was booed at the first public meeting, ignored at the second, drew an audience of nine at the third, got into a verbal brawl with a Pennoyer crony at the fourth, and at the fifth, brought four hundred cheering to their feet.

All the West Coast reform groups were swooning, Joe knew; she was booked every week this fall and winter, late trains and long hours bearing her away like a strong current to Seattle, Eugene, Laramie, Salt Lake, Denver, Oakland. Every rail ticket they bought her was for a first-class car, and she always had a lawyer along. When extra trouble seemed in the offing, she took a reporter too. Joe would never make it to Congress, but she might, in the witness chair, and Lee Loi as well.

"What do they say in Lapwai, I wonder?"

"That you always were a good little talker?"

At least he could still make her laugh. He hoped she would not forget him, out in the wide world, like Lee, like Nell. He was proud of them all.

At Grangeville they sat in the rig, unwilling to part. Joe was trying not to look desolate, but it took all his talents. She cradled his cheek in her hand.

"Stop that," she said. "I believe I'll spend next summer in the mountains. Working on speeches. And so forth."

"And so forth. Sounds promising. Come if you like."

"I do like."

WIDER VIEWS

O N NEW YEAR'S DAY the town publisher, Steven Dodge, stuck his head into Joe's hotel office.

"Got a minute?"

In Mount Idaho, everyone had plenty of time. "Sure," Joe said. Steven was always good company. His blond hair was receding, and his square, flushed face had a double chin. Fatherhood did that. Hard to believe the eager, green boy he'd sent to escort Grace and Georges back from Big Hole was now in his mid-thirties.

"Remember when you passed through here in '87? I later realized you were tracking the Deep Creek killers."

Joe felt his walls going up. Steven had never mentioned it before.

"So you know about that?"

"I planned to cover the trial, but Laura was due with our first, and it wasn't right to be away."

Joe was silent. Steven got to the point.

"I try to keep the *Idaho Free Messenger* true to its name. A mountain town gets wider views and all kinds of people. But our friends down the hill—"

"Grangeville's not friendly."

"—want to take over. All profit, all the time, and damn those who can't keep up."

"They're going to challenge for the county seat?"

"Next year. That's where you come in. We elect a new probate judge this spring. Some major land fights are coming up. Lots of pressure. We need a brave, honest man to run. A longtime Republican, if possible. And a veteran."

Joe won seventy percent of the vote, and in early March he opened his first session of court. The new black suit got extra wear; by mid-April he was again a justice of the peace.

On the first of May, Joe's door burst open, with Steven waving the *Walla Walla Statesman.*

"You've got to see this. One of the Deep Creek killers confessed."

"What? Who? Not Evans or Canfield?"

"No, one of those you tried." Steven ran his hand down the column. "Here. Robert McMillan, age sixteen. Jesus, that's young to be a mad killer."

"They were all sane. What made him confess?"

"Well, that's the news angle. He confessed back in '88, three, four weeks after the trial. He was dying of—let's see—diphtheria."

"Poor kid. Hard way to go. So who told?"

"The father. Hugh McMillan. He admits that Bobby was armed with rifle and revolver and fired down on the Chinese from high rocks."

"Does he admit to torture and mutilation?"

"No, he says Bobby killed only on the first day. As for the rest, he 'was acquainted with the facts as they were talked over by the participants in his presence.'"

"It's still a whitewash," said Joe. "But I can't see an Idaho retrial. No one wants one. We're a respectable State these days, not a wild Territory."

"So what happened to the rest of them?"

"LaRue, I'm certain, is dead, buried in Hells Canyon. Canfield was seen in Montana, but it's years now."

"You've heard the song?" Steven broke into a surprisingly good tenor.

It was late in the evening, when they brained the last man,
And in fear, bid farewell to their Snake River Land.

"What about the last one — Evans? Think he's dead too?"

"No," Joe said. If Blue were dead, he would know.

Grace did return for her summer visit. Most days Joe attended to
court business while she worked on the porch, looking up from her
tablet to gaze at prairie and mountains. She had never lived with a
great landscape spread before her, especially one so full of memories.
The two of them sat drinking wine and eating omelets as the evening
chill came on, bringing tendrils of fog along the valleys. Sometimes
they read to each other; sometimes they reminisced or set out the
chessboard. Henry and Joe had played for years, but Grace could
give him a game, just. Arguments mostly ended up in bed. Afterward, she liked to watch him drowse. He smelled the same as ever,
like salt and bay rum. Joe reached for her.

"Stay," he said.

"You treat me like a guest. Don't."

"Old habit. Hotel man."

"He's not so bad. I never liked the auctioneer."

"I know, selling to the highest bidder. Bad habit."

"Is that Henry talking, or you?"

Joe pulled her closer, spoon-fashion.

"Both. Do you miss safe, dull Marie?"

"She almost got me, that's true. Remember my old veiled hat? I
gave it to the kindergarten dress-up box. High time."

They made no secret of her presence, and to her amazement, the
village accepted her, mostly. Like Lapwai. She was known here too,
part of the town's story. She even made friends: the editor's wife, the
young female doctor.

"Winters up here must be awful," she said to Joe.

He passed her a pot to dry. "The real problem is ice. You can't get

300

wagons up and down these grades. I walk everywhere with a stick, so as not to slip."

"It mostly rains in Portland."

"Are you inviting me?"

"Of course. I have to be away so often now, and don't like leaving the house empty. Four blocks south, there's a college library. The electric trolley takes you right downtown. Theaters. Phonograph parlors. Hardware stores."

"What a romantic you are. Hardware stores? Sold. Your neighbors won't whisper?"

"They've given up expecting me to behave. I must say it's a relief. Oh, do come. Nell leaves us this year. I'm bound to be lonely."

In mid-August, Joe closed his docket, took a last walk-through of the hotel with the new young manager, and shut up his hillside house. Probate court would not reopen until March. Grangeville, four miles off, had a year-round JP. The migratory life appealed to Joe: he in Portland for winter, she in Mount Idaho for summer. Trim was already cadging sugar from Steven's children and carrying delivery bags like a true news horse. She still liked to work.

Joe too. In his valise lay a letter appointing Judge J. K. Vincent as Senator Slater's successor on the main Northwest railroad commission. First item on the September agenda was a knotty antitrust action against one John Vollmer, Esq., of Lewiston, Idaho. Joe linked his hands behind his head and smiled. Beyond the train window, a blue line of the Cascades range slipped by. Nearly there.

When Grace opened the State Street door, a crowd spilled out to greet him. Nell he expected, though not her pert new look: hair in a topknot with frizzled bangs, and a tailored skirt right down to the floor. Mary Stanton laughed at Joe's surprise, and he sent her a rueful grin, then saw who else stood in the entryway: Lee Loi, Dow, and Yap, come all the way from California for a gala hail-and-farewell. Tomorrow Nell would take a train to Chicago, then change for Albany and Boston. Just eight days, coast to coast. Mary was going as chaperone, then visiting her brother in Philadelphia once Nell was settled at college.

"I've not seen him since Centennial year. I'll stay awhile."

"But you will come back?"

"Of course. Out here is home."

She told him that Alonzo Leland had died, and Rachel too. Elisabeth remained a mystery. Rumor said she boarded trains and got off at random, staying in fancy railway hotels or big resorts, then boarding again and moving on. Rumor also said that a dapper blond man went with her now and again. Vollmer, Evans, some new friend—Joe didn't care. He knew one thing: she would never want for cash.

Lee was twenty-eight and still a natty dresser. Maybe a slight bulge at the waistcoat these days. The Chinese Foreign Office had told him to expect a new posting. Two years in London, then back to the West Coast. Dow was junior man in a Dai Fow medical practice, reading pulses, prescribing herbals; Yap, one of a dozen clerks in a big notions store. He seemed to know everyone in San Francisco. The store owner's daughter came up every other sentence.

"What about you?" Joe asked Lee.

"There's . . . well, someone I'd like you both to meet. A teacher at the new Chinatown school. Educated in Canada. Her great-uncle knew my father."

"And does she have advanced opinions?" Joe inquired, for Grace to hear.

"You have no idea," Lee said glumly.

After dinner, primed with two glasses of brandy, Joe showed everyone how he could wiggle his ears. Nell, applauding, could just recall him doing that back when she was small.

"Catnip to the ladies," he assured the boys. The young men.

"I'll stick to candy," said Yap. "But thanks." No one else could manage the feat except Dow, whose bravura performance earned him the last slice of apple cake.

He looked at the laughing faces around the table. His vow to Elder

Boss was secure. The Wells Fargo chest lay safe behind Dug Cabin, far up the Snake. While Yap kept watch, he'd helped Chea Po rebury the bundles of money, the documents, the bags of gold coin.

Let earth and water guard the box of secrets. Or maybe Futs-Lung, lord of treasure. All that canyon winter, someone—An Duk? Fong Low?—told wonderful stories of gods and dragons. Dow tried to summon the faces, the voices. This was the month of remembrance, after all.

Every time a patient improved under his care, Dow was grateful yet again to his first instructors in the healing art. Chea Po, for his steadfast kindness. Hoy Sek, for those merciless drills in botany. One last time he told them, *Shebude. And thank you.* But already they were leaving. Dow thought then of Dr. Stanton, who showed him so much, who told him of the *da bidze* physician's oath: *Whatever I see and hear, which ought not to be spoken of, I will never reveal. And he who teaches me shall be as my father, and his family as my own.*

They played forfeits by the fire until nearly eleven. Yap, still energetic, proposed poker.

"Unless it offends you, ma'am," he said to Mary. At seventeen, he was getting very courtly.

She patted his arm. "Let's try the kitchen table. You can teach me all about it."

"She doesn't take checks," Grace warned, and began to turn down the gas fixtures in parlor and front hall. Joe swept the last popcorn kernels from the hearth.

"I wish . . ." said Joe.

"I know. He always liked it here. But he did look in. Just for a minute."

"That was Henry?" said Lee, surprised. "He seemed so young."

"People often do," she said.

"Does Mary know?" Joe asked cautiously.

"Of course."

• • •

The house was asleep at last, every bed and sofa occupied. Joe stood at the door of Grace's backyard carriage house, watching the full moon. The August night was chilly, but quilts on sweet hay suited him fine. His back would have to learn to like it. The wild, clean smell of the firs made him think of Mount Idaho, and of Lapwai long ago. The view to the rear of the lot was toward Mount Hood, not the Willamette. That suited him too. Never again would he live beside a river, or go up one.

"Come back," said Grace from the tumble of bedding. She sounded sleepy.

"It's been an age," he said.

"Nineteen days. And I leave on Tuesday."

"How long this time?"

"A week."

He lay down beside her, slowly. "That's not so bad."

She found his hand in the darkness and laid it on her breast.

"It's not forever," she said.

DUG BAR

AUGUST 1892

THE CABIN BY THE WATER lay in shadow. Hackberry sap-
lings invaded the old corral. No shepherds or miners had
worked this stretch of the Snake in years. Tom Douglas, dead; all
those Chinese, dead; no flour gold was worth it. Sluice work was an-
tique. In the time a crew of forty once sifted a streamside placer by
hand, air-powered drills and cyanide could strip half a mountain of
its lead and zinc.

On the Idaho shore, a rider approached Dug Bar. Above the canyon walls a violet sky was cloudless, but far to the south rain fell,
for at the water's edge he heard the faint, steady hiss and chatter of
river rocks tumbling downstream. An easy crossing, though, so late
in summer; no need to swim the pinto mare.

The man who dismounted at the Douglas cabin was in his late forties, clean-shaven, with blond hair worn almost to the collar. Near the
wrecked porch steps he heaved up a long flat stone, pulled a Bowie
knife from his belt, and dug out the glass vials buried below. He held
all to the waning light, then moved behind the cabin, pried rusty iron
strips from an old rain barrel, and dug once more.

Two feet down he reached a wood-slat crate, lifted out the broken
chest inside, and filled both saddlebags, shaking sand from currency,
smiling at the chime of coinage. Legal documents he tore in two, then
dropped on the ground beside the smashed wood. The mare shied
at their pale flutter.

305

The traveler looked skyward. Last light still touched the Hells Canyon rim. He turned the horse back toward Dug Bar. Better to camp on the far shore. Tomorrow he would head to Grangeville, by way of Mount Idaho. A pleasure detour, long planned, long deferred.

Halfway across the old Nez Perce ford, just at the edge of his vision, rose a long flash of white, a gleaming arc in midriver. As the startled mare plunged sideways, mount and rider went into the Snake, shoulder-deep. He seized the cinch, found his knife, slashed at the saddlebag but struck too hard. Canvas and leather split as one.

He could not catch a single coin. He could not find the river bottom. An hour ago these shallows were barely shin-deep. Now his kicking feet found only cold current, pulling him under and away, but before the water swept over his face, he saw a door in the air swing wide and heard the howls of the hungry dead.

Eat, said a woman's voice, not to him. *Now eat your fill. For then you shall all drink deep.*

On the Idaho shore the mare waited a while, then trotted east, reins loose. A full moon rose over the canyon of the Snake. In the dark waters a great fish swam upstream, trolling as it went, drifting sideways and dropping back, over and over. A promising eddy waited near Deep Creek. Long as a river dory, splendid as a dragon, no one and nothing would disturb it there.

AFTERWORD

An actual event inspired *Deep Creek:* the May 1887 murders of more than thirty Chinese gold miners along the Snake River, in the remote stretch known today as Hells Canyon. The full story of this American tragedy may never be known. Modern interpreters differ on almost every point, agreeing only that news articles of the day are contradictory, local accounts biased, and court records incomplete.

Our book is historical fiction. We preserve the original timeline of events and incorporate many surviving documents. Several of our characters represent actual people of that time and place, such as Judge Joseph K. Vincent, John Vollmer, the miners Chea Po and Lee She, the Sam Yup agent Lee Loi, the pioneer publisher Alonzo Leland, and the Nez Perce horseman Jackson Sundown. We also alter many aspects of character and circumstance, invent motives, and imagine connections.

Did the real J. K. Vincent infiltrate the killers' upriver camp in search of evidence, disguised as an old miner? Some authorities say yes, others no. Did Vincent attend the Oregon trial? Unknown, but in fiction he may try to uphold a public trust and guard the integrity of his investigation. *Deep Creek* is our tale of what might have been.

In 2005 the U.S. Board on Geographic Names and the Oregon Geographic Names Board voted to recognize Deep Creek as a significant historic place. Now the rocky inlet where so many died has an additional name, Chinese Massacre Cove.

Deep Creek unfolds in a vanished Northwest: today Mount Idaho is a ghost town, and the Camas Prairie is no longer wild. The twenty-first-century Snake — dammed, controlled, satellite-mapped — is a far cry from the untamed flowage of 1887. Yet in its currents and eddies, white sturgeon still swim.

Our thanks to Cynthia Cannell, Becky Saletan, Andrea Schulz, Tom Bouman, and Lisa Glover for giving a first novel such safe guidance. David Howarth, Landon Jones, Jack Leckel, Richard Preston, and Robert Wilson provided insightful early readings.

For expert advice we thank Robert Mahony, Phillip Chen, Amy Gee, and Marilyn Jardin; Jerry Hughes of Hughes River Expeditions in Cambridge, Idaho; Master Sergeant Virgil Howarth USAF (Ret.); and Allen V. Pinkham, Sr., Historian, Nez Perce Tribe of Idaho.

For friendship and encouragement, we are grateful to Reid Beddow, Catherine Battersby, Lynette Bosch, Emery Castle, John Fleming, Sam Hynes, John McPhee, and Alan Williams.

For insight and inspiration, we owe much to William Gleason, Elyse Graham, Walt Litz, Charles McCarry, John Shearman, and Michael Wood.

We invite readers to visit our website, **www.dana-hand.com**, which offers character profiles, discussion questions, research sources, and maps and images of the *Deep Creek* country.